# AFTER THE CRASH

## How To Survive and Prosper During the Depression of the 1990s

- Why historians, economists, futurists, climatologists, physicists, and theologians agree there are dark days ahead

- How to make depression-proof investments in gold, silver, diamonds, real estate, and even the stock market

- Sample portfolios ranging from $10,000 to more than $1 million

- Ten key investment principles

- How to allocate resources among survival dollars, traditional investments, and depression-proof alternatives

- Thirty-five essential steps to take in preparing to survive and prosper during the depression of the 1990s

- And everything else you need to know and do to be prepared for the economic crisis that is upon us

# AFTER THE CRASH

## HOW TO SURVIVE AND PROSPER DURING THE DEPRESSION OF THE 1990s

**THIRD EDITION**

Geoffry F. Abert, Ph.D.

A SIGNET BOOK

NEW AMERICAN LIBRARY

## PUBLISHER'S NOTE

This publication is designed to provide accurate and authoritative information in regard to the subject matter covered. It is sold with the understanding that the publisher is not engaged in rendering legal, accounting or other professonal service. If legal advice or other expert assistance is required, the service of a competent professional person should be sought.

SIGNET, SIGNET CLASSIC, MENTOR, ONYX, PLUME, MERIDIAN
and NAL BOOKS are published by NAL PENGUIN INC.,
1633 Broadway, New York, New York 10019

First Printing (Third Edition), March, 1988
First Signet Printing, February, 1980

1  2  3  4  5  6  7  8  9

PRINTED IN THE UNITED STATES OF AMERICA

# CONTENTS

SECTION TWO
# HOW TO ACHIEVE PROSPERITY
# AMID POVERTY

SECTION THREE
# HOW TO SURVIVE ADVERSITY
# IN LUXURY

SECTION FOUR
# HOW TO FACE THE FUTURE
# WITHOUT FEAR

# PREFACE TO THE THIRD EDITION

In February of 1978, I decided to write a book describing my concerns about the direction of the U.S. economy. While collecting data for this project, I was amazed at the widespread recognition, among people on the street as well as some of the leading thinkers of our time, that we had mortgaged our future and that the debt was coming due. Establishment economists and right-wing ideologues, esoteric futurists and conservative historians, respectable scientists and far-out astrologers, conservative religious leaders and progressive humanists—all had been able to read some of the warning signs and, in their own specialized areas, were beginning to share their anxieties.

In the first edition of this book I attempted to bring together these diverse viewpoints. Then, adding my own analysis and recommendations, I offered some suggestions that could help an astute individual make preparations that would render the anticipated calamity tolerable, perhaps even pleasant. These recommendations included buying gold at a little over $200 per ounce, silver at $5.80 per ounce, and half-carat investment diamonds at $600. Two years later, gold was selling for $875 per ounce, silver reached a high of $37.75 per ounce, and half-carat investment diamonds were $1500–$2000. From the number of grateful letters received, it appears that *After the Crash* has helped many individuals to make preparations for a future that is frightening and dangerous.

In 1982, for the revised edition, I updated my recommendations and suggested that the depression I had foreseen was already beginning, pointing out that the peaks and valleys in our business cycles were becoming more frequent and more extreme. But that year proved to be just a preview of coming attractions. Unemployment was over 10 percent and inflation had "dropped" to slightly less. Business failures increased 45 percent and personal bankruptcies were up 11 percent. Farmers and airlines were almost bankrupt, and most of American industry was reeling from low productivity and increased foreign competition.

Had it not been for the controversial economic programs of the Reagan administration, the innovativeness of American industry and the commitment of U.S. workers, we would have continued to sink into financial chaos. But together we were able to gain five years of grace. By mid-1987 people were talking about the "American economic miracle," the greatest bull market of all time. Yet they overlooked the fact that the blush on the cheeks of our economy was more from fever than good health. True, the dollar was falling, personal debts were mushrooming, and the U.S. debt owed to other countries made Mexico and Brazil look like pikers. Somehow we were able to overlook these irritating warning signs until October 19, 1987. Even after the stock market had lost $1 trillion, or one-third of its value, many observers were trying to cover the cancer with cosmetics by saying the crash would only affect the greedy yuppies on Wall Street.

Don't you believe it! As a nation, we have sowed the seeds of our own decline. Now we will inherit the whirlwind of financial crisis.

But this story, at least your part of it, can have a positive ending. There is still time for you to survive and prosper in the turbulent era ahead.

I hope that the advice contained in this third edition will help you move quickly toward a game plan that will minimize the negative impact of the coming depression on you and your family. Best wishes for a happy depression!

## Section One

# WHAT'S HAPPENING HERE?

# CHAPTER 1

# WHAT'S HAPPENING
# TO THE GOOD LIFE?

The American dream never seemed closer than in the 1950s. Resounding victories against a major depression and a world war provided reassurance of the indomitable American ability to overcome difficulties. Unparalleled prosperity was emerging. Opportunities existed for all. A popular television program during the seventies called this era "Happy Days."

The fifties was a decade of progress, prosperity, and positive prospects. This, indeed, was the stuff of which dreams were made. Thirty years later a popular song summarized the mood by its title "The Class of '57 Had Its Dreams." We were a generation who didn't believe in limits. We could fine-tune the economy, make the world safe for democracy, eliminate poverty, and explore outer space while enjoying a drip-dry, perma-press, split-level life with instant cake mix, coffee, and affluence. All we had to add was water and dollars.

What was wrong with the formula? Why has our diet of instant gratification given us economic and physical malnutrition? Why have those bright, cheerful dreams of the class of '57 become nightmares of running in place? Where are the snake-oil salesmen who offered us gleaming promises with gilt-edged guarantees?

This book will give you some answers. It will explain how and why the American dream has gone sour. It will show how the mightiest nation in the world traded its natural birthright for a bowl of pottage and a quick fix. More important, it will show how to cope with the Frankensteinian monster that we have created.

I have no grand design to save the world. Frankly, I

13

believe that it is too late for us to avoid the economic crisis that looms just ahead. I know that the steps required to cope with our economic dilemmna are politically inexpedient. Our leaders lack the courage to lead because they know that their constituency wants simple, painless answers. Anyone with even a reasonable claim to leadership knows the two immutable laws of economics: there are no free lunches and no simple solutions.

### Is There Really a Problem?

Right now you may have some reservations about the whole thesis of this book. You have a vague feeling that things aren't exactly right. You may not be moving ahead as fast as you want to, but your income is higher than anyone in your family has ever made before. You have more cars, a bigger house, more gadgets, and bigger payments than you ever thought possible. It's true that you are not saving as large a percentage of your income as you once did and your debts are frightening whenever you happen to think about them, but that's the new American way.

For the next few minutes, take a tour with me to some of the major U.S. institutions: the government, American cities, and the family. We also will review the status of key subgroups such as workers, youths, and blacks. Our tour will conclude with a brief survey of a country that has traveled a little farther down the same road on which we seem to be headed. Let's explore the myth and the reality of American progress and prosperity.

## YOUR UNCLE IS BANKRUPT

Americans believe that big is better. By this measure we have a magnificent government. The federal government alone spends an amount equal to almost 25 percent of the nation's total production of goods and services. The government owns 760 billions acres—one third of the nation's total land. Uncle Sam also holds title to 405 buildings that cost $91 billion to construct. Additionally, the annual bill for rent on another 54,000 office buildings runs almost $700 million. In other words, the U.S. government occupies the space equivalent to 96 Sears Towers—the world's tallest building, with 110 floors. To handle the paperwork, generated by federal regulations and procedures, 211,000 clerks, typists, and secretaries are employed. A major portion of their work involves processing 4,504 different federal forms. The material generated by these forms each year would fill eleven Washington Monuments.

In 1950, government cost $1,600 per family. Now the cost is close to $12,000 per working family. This means that the average family spends between five and seven months per year working simply to pay all of its direct and hidden taxes. In the Dark Ages the serfs were required to spend only three months working for their masters. During the rest of the year they were free to work for themselves.

Specialists in the White House have estimated that the cost of useless and wasteful regulations by federal agents is over $130 billion per year, the equivalent of more than $2,000 annually for every U.S. family. A recent study by Dr. Murray L. Weidenbaum for the Joint Economic Committee of Congress showed that government regulations had added $666 to the price of a new automobile and between $1,500 and $2,500 to the cost of a new home. The Office of the Inspector General reported that the Department of Health, Education, and Welfare misspent between $6 billion and $7.4 billion in one year because of waste, fraud, and abuse. Four billion dollars was spent on health care programs, including Medicare and Medicaid payments, for unnecessary surgery, hospital studies, and X rays. Despite efforts to bring this problem under control, authorities estimate that the total theft and fraud against federal agencies could run as high as $25 billion per year. Some dramatic examples include:

- One firm was paid to paint 2.4 million square feet of space at GSA headquarters in Washington. The entire building has an area of only 1.9 million square feet. Some GSA building managers are accused of having received as much as $300,000 annually for their part in repair and maintenance shenanigans.

- The Cook County (Chicago) Welfare Queen is charged with using six aliases to draw more than $150,000 in allegedly illegal welfare payments. A graduate student in criminal justice, at the University of Illinois, she had applied to law school asking that application fees be waived because she was indigent. Indicted on 613 counts of theft of Medicaid, Food Stamp, and Aid to Dependent Children programs, she was arrested in the Criminal Court Building where she had gone to interview a judge as part of her graduate studies.
- In South Florida, a community council that received $1.3 million in job training funds diverted $22,000 to a privately run service station, paid money to a staff "psychologist" with no degree, and made loans to friends and family members.
- In Maryland's job training program, nine young women were paid $145 per week to attend a ballet school. The wife of a dentist received $11,000 a year in payments under the Comprehensive Education and Training Act.

You've heard about the ripoff artists in the welfare, food stamps and CETA programs. But I believe that many businessmen aren't much better. They should appreciate and defend the values of free enterprise and self-reliance. Yet all too often they seek bailouts, federal favors, or regulatory protection from competition.

The National Taxpayers Union estimates that there are over 900,000 totally ineligible welfare recipients receiving regular payments. They also point out that $250 billion has been spent for foreign aid, including money for the United States to provide financial assistance to both sides of a conflict in fourteen wars during the past twenty-five years. Excessive red tape, inept management, poorly trained frontline personnel, and careless investigative policies are costing taxpayers billions of dollars each year.

The U.S. economy is still productive. It generated goods and services at the rate of $4 trillion in 1987. But remember that the public debt in the United States is approaching $1 trillion and annual spending in Washington is approximately $1 trillion.

President Reagan's description of this $1 trillion budget for 1988 as "lean and tight" is hardly accurate. If you had started out at the birth of Christ spending $1,280,000 a day, you would have just now succeeded in getting rid of $1 trillion. Yet we will be spending that much in a single year, and many authorities feel that the figure will double in less than a decade. In order to get rid of $1 trillion this year, the government will have to spend an average of $1,900,000 a minute or $114 million an hour every day including holidays and Sundays.

You will notice that I am spelling out words like billion and trillion. They require so many zeros that they are distracting to the average reader. Let me provide a couple of additional reference points for these sums. If you were to spend $1,000 a day, a billion dollars would last for 2,738 years. Multiply that by a thousand to see how much money Washington will spend in 1988.

If you were to lay end on end one trillion dollar bills, they would stretch 4 million miles beyond the sun—which, for those of you who have forgotten junior high science, is 96,909,000 miles away.

We spend $285,388 per minute to pay interest on the national debt. At the present rate of real and inflationary growth in the cost of government, public spending at all levels will be $1.75 trillion by 1995, about 3½ times the 1975 level, and the average tax burden per family will be over $16,000. The total cost of government divided by the approximately 65 million families would average $29,000 per family. Does this convince you that governmental spending cannot possibly continue to grow as it has?

### What Do You Owe?

With reference to the chart on page 18, a national debt of over $1 trillion or even liabilities of approximately $1 trillion somehow don't concern me as much as the fact that my personal stake in all this is over $159,286. It bothers me even more when I realize the small percentage of people in this country who can be counted on to pay their liabilities. According to the North American Newspaper Alliance, over 125 million people are largely dependent on tax money. This includes government employees, the military, welfare recipients, public pensioners, and dependents of these groups. This is over 50 percent of the total population, and far more than the number who are productively employed in the private sector.

In the first edition of this book I predicted that President Carter, who campaigned on a promise to balance the budget by 1981, would go out of office with some record deficits. Well, in four years Carter rolled up deficits that totaled $181 billion. Unfortunately, his successor has exceeded that mark to become the all-time deficit-spending champ with a one-time annual deficit of $220 billion in 1986. Reagan has even exceeded the red-ink record previously held by the father of planned deficit financing, Franklin D. Roosevelt, who was so universally criticized by conservatives for his twelve-year deficit of $197 billion—a total exceeded in a single year by the Reagan administration.

Recently, I received the following invoice:

### TAXPAYER'S LIABILITY INDEX—JANUARY 15, 1987

| DEBT OR LIABILITY ITEM | FEDERAL OBLIGATIONS | YOUR SHARE* |
|---|---|---|
| Public Debt | $2,300,000,000,000 | $ 27,059 |
| Accounts Payable | 249,733,000,000 | 2,938 |
| Undelivered Orders | 550,816,000,000 | 6,480 |
| Long Term Contracts | 41,497,000,000 | 488 |
| Loan and Credit Guarantees | 756,863,000,000 | 8,904 |
| Insurance Commitments | 2,757,346,000,000 | 32,439 |
| Annuity Programs | 6,800,000,000,000 | 80,000 |
| Unadjudicated Claims: International Commitments & Other Contingencies | 83,104,000,0000 | 978 |
| TOTAL | *$13,539,359,000,000 | $159,286 |

*Based on 85 million real taxpayers (Prepared by National Taxpayers Union)

*Budget Bloat*

The federal budget for 1988—slightly more than $1 trillion—is nearly 35 times $30 billion deficit reduction accord reached by Congress and the administration.

You may be interested in a few of the items in the current budget. Combined with Social Security, entitlement programs (farm price supports, retirement, veterans, health, unemployment, and welfare) total more than $500 billion annually. Defense spending is nearly $300 billion. The interest paid on the federal deficit alone is $150 billion.

If you look at the official spending totals as a share of national output, you will find that in 1930 government at all levels was taking about 10 percent of gross national product. By 1987, it was taking nearly 50 percent of GNP. If we simply keep on doing what we have been doing, by the year 2000 government will be taking 67 percent of GNP.

The total government burden of our economy is a lot bigger than the officially acknowledged numbers. Add in so-called "off-budget" items (including federal loan guarantees and borrowing by government entities), regulatory costs imposed on private economy, and tens of billions of federally mandated outlays by state and local governments, and it is likely that federal activity, right now, is imposing a cost of over $1 trillion a year on our economy—out of a GNP of $4 trillion.

If the volume of dollars spent is depressing, the ineptitude with which it is spent is even more frightening. Everyone is concerned about the excessive profits earned by the giant oil companies. Yet the first year's budget for the Department of Energy was $10.6 billion. In order to protect you from the oil companies, the federal government is spending more than the total profits of the fourteen largest petroleum companies and about two-thirds of total industry's profits. Another way of looking at the same information is to say that the agency formed to protect you is going to cost the equivalent of four cents per gallon for all gasoline consumed in the United States.

If you want to be picky, you may want to know why

Congress has authorized $375,000 for a Pentagon study of the Frisbee, or $125,000 to find out why some people say "ain't," or $57,800 for a Federal Aviation Administration study of body measurements of airline stewardesses. (Compared to other projects, this one sounds like a real bargain.)

## CRISIS IN THE CITIES

After the turn of the century, Sam Lewis and Joe Young had America singing, "How're you gonna keep 'em down on the farm." After seeing the wonders of cities such as Paris, New York, and San Francisco, it seemed that people would be forsaking the farms in droves. For a while this was true. The good life could be found in cities, where there was easy access to good shopping, quality education, exciting entertainment, and lucrative employment.

Today, the exodus from the farm to the city has reversed. People, especially the well-to-do and middle class, are leaving the city because of its problems. Crime is out of control, taxes are exorbitant, and education is a farce. Many cities have become virtual jungles. As Dr. George Sternlieb of Rutgers University says, "You can't support the poor without the rich. Every time some taxpayer moves out of the city, the poor are left even poorer, and this is what is happening in every large city in America."

While the public rebels against taxes, cities throughout the country are literally wearing out. The evidence of this deterioration is easy to spot. We have become accustomed to streets and expressways pocked with potholes and cracks, signs above bridges warning us that they are unsafe, public buildings and schools in disrepair, sewers frequently backed-up and clogged, aged equipment and dangerous water systems.

According to the Congressional Joint Economic Committee, paying for maintenance and improvements in public works "may be the single greatest problem facing our nation's cities." As an illustration, New Orleans has a major sewage problem. According to the Director of the

Sewage and Water Board, "Our antiquated equipment just isn't doing the job. We are still using some equipment that we first installed in 1896—and we purchased it secondhand from Philadelphia." The sewer system in Pittsburgh still has brick sections that date back to 1877. Such antiques are not uncommon throughout the East. In some places, wood-lined mains are still in use. About 150 million gallons of water a day are lost in Boston through leaks.

The Environmental Protection Agency estimates that municipalities would have to spend $96 billion to build the facilities necessary to meet requirements of the 1972 Water Pollution Control Act. To prevent pollution from industrial waste waters would cost another $54 billion.

### A Rocky Road Ahead

Despite recent improvements in the overall condition of the nation's interstate highway system, major problems remain. According to a *Christian Science Monitor* article, 11 percent of the 43,593-mile system was considered in poor condition as of 1987. Leading the list of states was Kansas, where 67 percent of the interstate highways were deficient, followed by Rhode Island (37 percent), New Mexico (35 percent), Oregon (33 percent), and Missouri (32 percent).

Adding to the problem have been the consequences resulting from deregulation of the trucking industry. Higher pressure levels on truck tires, used to improve gas mileage, result in more weight on a smaller area. And higher allowable truck weights create more ruts, even in concrete roads. So serious is the problem that estimates are that the life expectancy of a twenty-year road may be reduced by up to five years.

Even if there were funds to rise above the highway problems, the air traffic situation would make that an unattractive alternative. In a 1987 *Washington Post* article Sally Quinn summarized her concerns about flying, which no doubt reflect the fears of many who fly the not-so-friendly skies: air traffic has increased by 26 percent over the past three years, while the number of experienced air traffic controllers has decreased by 27 percent since 1981; there were 512 near collisions in the first half of 1987, up from 390 during the same period in 1986; and the average number of hours of experience among pilots has dropped dramatically since 1983, from 2,300 to 1,400.

Transportation woes are not the only problems taxing the patience and resources of the American public. Many large cities are in desperate financial shape. At current funding levels, for example, New York City would complete replacement of its obsolete sewer system in three hundred years. Parks specialists recommend that major repairs on public parks be based on a twenty-five-year replacement rate: Manhattan was operating on a budget that allows for a nine-hundred-year replacement cycle. If the current level of city services is to be maintained, citizens are going to have to pay more than they are currently doing. There is no evidence that they are either willing or able to handle this burden.

American cities owe a total of $250 billion dollars in municipal debts. There is no historical precedent of any debt of this proportion having been paid off. Debts of this magnitude have always been repudiated—and no one is in a better position to do this than a government. Debts will continually be refinanced until no one is willing to accept the obviously empty pledges to pay and investors are left holding worthless paper.

### Moonlight Sonata

The number of individuals holding two or more jobs is currently approaching 5 million. During the 1970s the number of moonlighters increased almost 20 percent and the number of women holding multiple jobs doubled. Moreover, the average family today has 1.7 workers in it. About half of the families making the median income do so only because two members of the family work. Moonlighting, working wives, exhaustion, persistent worry, and fighting over money is the spotlight that shines through the picture window of middle-American homes. We dream of upward mobility, affluence, and getting ahead, but in reality we find ourselves quibbling with children about their allowances, skipping an annual physical checkup, and cashing in insurance policies. Epidemic advances in alcoholism, drug addiction, divorce, and early heart attacks are not unrelated to financial pressures created by this race for the good life.

"Middle-class earners feel rotten because a lot of them have not kept up with the median," says economist Rudolph G. Penner of the American Economic Institute. "The polls show that the general public is compassionate over the poor, but this is easier when your own share of the economic pie is growing. When your share is not growing and benefits are seen rising for the disadvantaged, there is bitterness."

Overall, the unemployment rate in the U.S. has improved in recent years. In October 1987 unemployment was officially at 6.0 percent, affecting almost 8 million people. The true picture of the underbelly of the economy, however, is not as rosy as this figure would indicate. Over the past few years many higher-paying jobs have been replaced by those at or close to minimum wage, often part-time and below the poverty level. In particular, nearly 2 million manufacturing jobs have been lost since 1980. Offsetting this loss has been a dramatic increase in the number of service sector jobs. But three-quarters of these are in low-paying retail trade and health and business services.

The near-term outlook for employment does not offer much hope of improvement. According to figures by the Commission of Labor Statistics, the labor force of the 1990s will be heavily black and female. And nine of every ten new jobs will be in the service sector—in occupations that traditionally are low paying.

Under continuing financial pressures Americans are finding it almost impossible to save. In the past decade the percentage of income allocated to savings has dropped by 33 percent. While some Americans do manage to put aside some money (3.1 percent), the rate is among the lowest in major industrialized countries. Canadians save almost 10 percent of their income. In Great Britain and

West Germany, the savings rate is almost 14 percent; in France it is over 16 percent; and the Japanese save 21.5 percent of their after-tax income. The American inability to save suggests the meager resources that we have to fall back on in case of personal or national financial problems. It also indicates that it will be very difficult for the country to secure the needed capital for new jobs throughout the future.

While Americans are finding it hard to save, we are experiencing absolutely no difficulty in borrowing. From 1983 to the present, household debt as a percentage of disposable income has risen from 25 percent to more than 30 percent. Consumer installment loans are being repaid at a slower rate than they were during the last recession. And the percentage of foreclosures on home loans has doubled in the last four years alone.

## PERIL IN THE PEPSI GENERATION

Children are learning the harsh realities of contemporary life at a very early age! There are almost 500,000 babies born each year out of wedlock (15 percent of all births). Most of these are to women in their teens and early twenties. Fifty percent are to teenagers. The Department of Health and Human Services believes, "There is definitely a high correlation between out-of-wedlock births, welfare costs, and many of our most pressing social problems."

One major impact is the $11.7 billion spent yearly in federal, state, and local aid to families with dependent children, the welfare program for poor families with no father at home. The Urban Institute in Washington has conducted research that suggests that women who begin the drift toward dependency as teenager mothers cost taxpayers about 6 billion dollars a year in welfare payments.

Depending on which state they live in, most teenage mothers with one illegitimate child can qualify for payments of $100 to $150 per month. To the average, mature middle-class citizen, this doesn't seem like much.

But to a fourteen-or fifteen-year-old ghetto teenager, it is a bigger allowance than she has ever received. She will probably continue living at home and qualify for food stamps, thus her food may cost only one fourth of the regular price. She and her child can receive free medical care and she may have regular homemaker service to help with domestic chores. In many cities, free day-care services are available. Despite this financial support, these mothers usually have no effective model for mothering. Consequently, they reinforce the behavior patterns which led them into dependency and repeat this destructive cycle with their own children.

University of Maryland sociologist Harriet B. Presser has studied the characteristics of unwed mothers and reports that half of them are in school when they become pregnant and half of these drop out. Nearly two-thirds have no high school diploma and only 44 percent have any work experience. As a result, only half are able to get even temporary employment during the first four years of motherhood. Almost 10 percent of all girls between fifteen and nineteen get pregnant each year. Within a year of giving birth, one-fourth of these teenage mothers are pregnant again.

While writing this book, I realized how serious the government was about the problem. The office of research at my university sent out a memorandum reporting that the agency was requesting research proposals "designed to explore the reasons for teenage pregnancy." Although I am not a sociologist, I think I have a sneaking suspicion how teeangers get pregnant. Unless some basic law of biology has been repealed, the process by which teenagers become pregnant is remarkably similar to the process by which other people achieve this condition. According to a recent study, 80 percent of all black, unmarried girls and half of their white counterparts have had intercourse. Moreover, less than half of the sexually active teenagers use contraceptives.

Teenage marriages are twice as likely to fail as marriages where both partners are in their twenties. Teenagers are more frequent crime victims than adults are now or were during their younger years. Murder is the second leading cause of death among Americans between the ages of 15 and 24, and suicide is the third. Forty percent of high school students have been the victims of violent crimes such as robbery, assault, or murder.

A report by the Ford Foundation notes that the number of juveniles arrested for violent crimes such as homicide, rape, robbery, and assault rose 293% during the past fifteen years and is increasing at more than double the rate of increase in adult arrests for violent crimes. In large cities the courts probably process less than 5 percent of the violent crimes committed by juveniles. While youth violence is more extensive in large cities, suburban and rural crime is increasing even more rapidly. Research in rural and small-town Oregon shows that one-fourth of all boys were caught committing crimes at least once during their adolescence.

Education was once used as the means of improving one's lot in life. Today, the quality of education and intellectual attainment seems to be declining. Prospects for jobs, even if an education is obtained, are discouraging. Until recently there was good evidence to support the claim that a college education paid off financially and helped a person become a better informed citizen. Today, the financial value of a college degree, especially in the arts or humanities, is in question.

Today, it's estimated that as many as one-third of the young men and two-thirds of the young women attending college are majoring in fields that are not their first choice because of the difficulty in getting jobs with degrees in the humanities. In the early 1970s the rate was 10 percent and 13 percent respectively. In a *New York Times* article Fred Hachinger asked, "Will we turn out useless and therefore disgruntled graduates? Will the United States repeat the dangerous example of Germany and Italy in the 1920s—create an unemployed, alienated and politically menacing proletariat?" This rhetorical question is based on the fact that one-third of the SS officers in Nazi Germany had Ph.D.s. There is clear evidence of disenchantment among men and women who face menial jobs or unemployment. For in addition to their frustration of lost income, they must also accept the loss of social status and their claim to the "good life." Thirty percent of all workers are "underemployed"—that is, their qualifications exceed the real requirements for the job they are currently holding.

The valedictorian at a Washington, D.C. high school was shocked to find that his SAT scores just weren't high enough to admit him to a local college. At Ohio State University, 1,700 of a recent freshman class of 7,100 had to take remedial English, and 2,000 had to take remedial math (and even Ohio State doesn't have that many varsity athletes). Federal funds are being expended to teach high school students how to read. Some states are passing competency requirements that suggest that high school seniors have to be able to read and write before they can receive their high school diploma.

Even if literacy requirements are tightened, what of those people who have already passed through the schools and out into adulthood? According to estimates, almost 30 million adult Americans—one in every six people over eighteen years old—cannot read sufficiently well to participate in contemporary society. The funding allocated to address this problem ($106 million in 1987) is woefully inadequate. Beefing up traditional programs would take fifty times as much. One alternative being considered is a Literacy Corps. College students would work as part-time tutors in schools and community agencies for credit. Estimates are that such a program could eventually result in up to 4 million hours of tutoring per year.

## THE FUTURE IS BLEAK FOR BLACKS

Although there have been significant gains in the number of middle-class black families, it is obvious that despite the best efforts of the war on poverty, the Great Society, civil rights legislation, and forced busing, black families are still experiencing economic problems of even greater magnitude than any other segment of American society. Recent progress in the war on poverty has not included many members of the black community. The number of blacks classified as poor is now higher than ever. The ratio of black family income to white family income has dropped to 57.1 percent. In other words, the average black family makes only a little more than half of the median family income for whites.

Among adult males, the unemployment rate for whites is less than half that for blacks. Among teenagers, unemployment for black teenagers is twice what it is for white teenagers. While 14 percent of people below eighteen are black, they account for 22 percent of all juvenile arrests and 52 percent of all juvenile arrests for violence.

Almost 41 percent of all black households are headed by women. In the past decade illegitimacy has risen from 25 to 50 percent of all black children born. Two of every five black children in the country are receiving financial assistance from welfare from the Aid to Dependent Children Program. In the past two decades black suicides have risen by 33 percent—almost three times as fast as the rate for the rest of the population. Homicide is the leading cause of death among black males under thirty.

The black section in any major city is a tinderbox. Poverty, prejudice, grandiose promises, and unreachable dreams are a highly flammable combination. For every successful black who has escaped the ghetto prison, there are ten who have seen the promised land but found that they can't pass the entrance exams. The real villain in this tragedy is the slick-talking politician who bought votes by making totally unrealistic promises. In some ways the obvious hypocrites were less dangerous than the well-meaning simpletons who tried to fulfill their promises when resources were not adequate. These ill-fated programs so clogged the financial machinery of the economy that real progress was impeded. Harvard psychiatrist Alvin Pouissant suggested only a few years ago that, "There is more decayed housing, more joblessness, more single parents raising children, more segregation in the North than in 1964 or 1967 [when riots swept the country]. It doesn't look good, and the anger is not going to disappear."

The statistics mentioned earlier in this section merely confirm the hypothesis that the "American dream" is more illusionary for blacks and other minorities than for the mainstream of U.S. society. This frustration, coupled with resentment that has built up for decades, has created a highly explosive situation in almost any city with a sizable minority population. We'll see in Chapter 4 how this could be ignited in our depression scenario.

## MEANWHILE, BACK IN THE WORLD . . .

Suppose, for the sake of amusement, that a drifting cloud of exotic interstellar gas were to descend on the United States in the near future and infect all our leaders with wisdom, intelligence, and a deep desire to serve their fellow citizens without regard to personal advancement. Our President would be blessed with foresight and ingenuity, our Congress would put aside petty politics for the greater good of society, and the rest of us would volunteer new taxes to fund their benevolent schemes. Would all our problems be solved?

Even fairy tales have limits. The limit to ours is that we are not isolated from the rest of the world; we are intimately bound up in its web of problems and dependencies. Brightening up our own skies would not chase away the clouds that hover elsewhere—clouds that no sun is going to penetrate anytime soon.

- Since the founding of UNICEF forty years ago, enormous advances have been made against the droughts and famines that plague so many of the world's children. Yet despite this progress, 280,000 children still die each *week* from infection and malnutrition. The worldwide economic recession is a large part of the cause. Many developing nations are burdened with huge balance-of-payment deficits. Because hard economic choices must be made in such situations, health conditions and educational standards are often the first areas affected.

- A report by the Worldwatch Institute on global environment problems warns that never before have so
  many vital systems—atmospheric chemistry, global
  temperature, reductions in living species—been out
  of equilibrium simultaneously. Restoring a balance
  will require urgent international planning and cooperation. And yet the largest international scientific
  collaboration in the world today is the Star Wars
  program.
- We proclaimed 1986 as the International Year of
  Peace. And yet global military expenditures rose to
  $900 billion, up nearly $100 billion from the year
  before. For more than a decade, military spending
  has increased faster than the rate of inflation. On a
  worldwide scale, the military establishment employs
  100 million people, representing about 6 percent of
  the world GNP.
- Despite the number and prominence of recent terrorist
  acts around the world, political violence is expected
  to escalate over the next decade. Advances in technology will make individual terrorists much more
  deadly than heretofore, and will make defending
  against them much more difficult. Such "advances"
  already include hand-launched armor-penetrating
  guided missiles and a briefcase-sized weapon that can
  fire twenty-five rounds a second and is equipped with
  a laser guide and a silencer.
- The shadow of the AIDS epidemic is growing longer
  and darker. Estimates of the number of virus carriers
  worldwide range between 5 and 10 million. Although
  the rate of spread is not known, even a 50 percent
  increase in infections per year—a conservative figure—
  would have catastrophic consequences. Already AIDS
  has overwhelmed the health-care system in Haiti and
  Central Africa, and further spread in countries not
  prepared to deal with such a crisis would cause debilitating political and social effects. The gloomy projections for the U.S., an economically and politically
  stable nation, underscore the grimness of the world-

wide problem. AIDS has the potential of leaving our
health-care system in a shambles, devastating the
Social Security system (by killing off large numbers
of young, productive workers), and severely decreas-
ing tax revenues.

# CHAPTER 2

# SIGNS OF
# THE TIMES

The decision to write the original edition of this book occurred on Monday, February 27, 1978, as I was reading the *Wall Street Journal.* On the first page, I noticed the following headlines: The U.S. Moves to Bolster the Faltering Dollar, Lack of Confidence Is Cited; Jimmy Carter Is Getting Worried about the Stock Market—First Democratic President Since World War II to See a Falling Stock Market in the First Year after the Election; Prolonged Market Declines Foreshadow Recession; Some Church Bonds Plunging into Default—Investor Losses Mount; Machine Orders Fell in January; Bankrupt W. T. Grant Trustee Agrees with Twenty-Six Lenders on a Settlement of $650 Million; Manufacturers Hanover Trust Is Focus of Union Hostility; Coal Pact Proposal Faces an Uphill Battle for Rank-and-File Ratification; The Swiss Government Moves to Curb Foreign Demand for Its Franc.

When a single issue of a traditionally conservative and positive publication such as the *Wall Street Journal* chronicles these kinds of problems, it is obvious that something is afoot. For several years as my horizons broadened, I had been concerned about economic trends. That single day's summary of financial news prompted me to do more intensive research. I was amazed to find that almost every segment of society was reporting equally discouraging indicators for the future. The more I looked into it, the more pervasive the pessimism appeared to be.

I had no desire to become a prophet of doom. I have chuckled, as I am sure you have, at the cartoons of bewhiskered guys in robes and sandals walking the city sidewalks with their placards announcing the impending end. That isn't my self-image, and yet, the more widely I read, the more fields I explored, the more consistent became the warning cries of the leading spokesmen in each field.

That was 1978. A decade later, we have seen the inflation rate reduced by more than half, we have seen the stock market climb to new and previously undreamed-of highs, and we have seen a steady rise in the standard of living of the average American citizen. Why, then, my continuing pessimism? Why this new edition of a gloomy book?

### All Roads Lead To . . . ?

My research leaves me with the inescapable conclusion that we still are racing toward catastrophe on several separate but related routes: Monetary and fiscal policy, government spending (especially welfare), pollution, food supplies, defense, crime, education, and morality. I don't see an approaching *end* of the world, but rather a time of dramatic reversal of things we take for granted. The upheavals will be so great and so unanticipated that they will alter the majority of the social structure we know today. However, it is quite likely that a few simple preparations and adjustments by those who anticipate the future will result in not only survival but prosperity in the brave new world that follows.

Success has always favored those who could read the signs of coming events and make appropriate adjustments even though everyone else was ignoring (or even laughing at) the warnings. Remember, it wasn't raining when Noah first started to build his ark. His neighbors ridiculed him for over a hundred years as he began to build that monstrous boat in his backyard. You too may be laughed at if you begin now to make preparations for a very difficult kind of life-style. My task in this chapter is to consider the evidence. The decision and the action, of course, have to be your own. I can only share with you the evidence here that has convinced me that special preparations are essential.

# THE HISTORIANS: STUDY THE PAST
## OR BE DOOMED TO REPEAT IT

Scholars who study the cycles and stages of history are not encouraging about the future of Western civilization. Historians can contribute a perspective that most of us lack because they are *by necessity* in the habit of looking at centuries and millennia rather than the short term to which we are most accustomed. Nevertheless, when a historian describes a likely result of a national trend and then it doesn't happen immediately, the warnings may be discounted.

There are several key examples of the general population's inability to think long-term. One is the well-known work of Professor Arnold Toynbee on the traits of ancient Rome in its declining days. Since Toynbee's ideas were first advanced in the 1930s, their impact has gradually reduced with each passing year. "I've heard that stuff about Rome and America all my life," responds a friend today, "and the country is still here and doing just as well as or better than it was when Toynbee first came out with it."

What that friend is overlooking—what so many of us overlook—is the insignificance of a mere forty or fifty years in the history of a nation. Americans have often pointed in derision at the changing governments of France, Italy, and "banana republics." Yet, we forget to compare our 200-year history with the 2,000-year history of most European countries. There is a most definite confirmation in history of the basic principles and national cycles suggested by Toynbee. What's more, those same principles were proposed by Plato and others from much earlier days and have been reinforced over and over again.

### Platonic Prophecy

Plato's description of the cycle said that the first national stage was the emergence and power of one person (either a dictator or a monarch). As time passes, this one person's power is spread among a few (either with the consent of the one or against his wishes). More rulers are included as the nation moves to a position of democracy (in which the majority are ruling). As the abuses of democracy proliferate, the minorities begin to seek their own through unlawful means (which leads to corruption or anarchy). As these conditions of lawlessness become more prevalent and more threatening to the majority, the stage is set for the reintroduction of a dictator or anyone who will take charge, short-circuit the troublesome individual rights, and restore order and security. With this dictator in power, the cycle begins again.

Over fifty years ago the German philosopher Otto Spengler predicted "The Decline of the West." Basically he agreed with the cycle described by Plato. He also added the idea that as the people gained a victory over the aristocracy, there would also be a victory of the city over the country, money over principle, and immediate gratification over tradition. These forces, he felt, would ultimately lead to primitive conditions which would replace civilized life. Of the advanced countries such as England, France, and the U.S., he concluded, "Race suicide set in long ago."

For our purposes in this book, we can begin by surrendering any hope that humans are solving the cyclical problems. The trappings and settings with which each new generation surrounds itself may look different, but the basic flaws of greed and selfishness and violence remain to maintain the historic cycles. Mankind seems to encounter the same basic problems whether he wears a toga to Rome or dacron polyester to Washington. Don't waste your own planning time hoping that humans will do better. Plan by the assumption that the cycles are set. If things *do* change for the better, you will be even better off than you planned. If not, you and your family will be as well prepared as possible to enter the next stage of evolution.

### The Roman Tradition and the U.S.

The similarities between the histories of Rome and the United States may already be obvious to you. Consider, for example, that Rome's time ran out when she:

1. Got most of her people off the farms and into the cities, where they more rapidly communicate counterproductive demands and disastrous panics;
2. Found herself importing more than she was exporting;
3. Became burdened with social welfare efforts to support the masses who were becoming harder to please and ever more antagonistic;
4. Allowed a single essential group to take control (in Rome, it was the army, for us it could be the military-industrial complex, the labor unions, or simply the poor);
5. Saw the emphasis on the "people to be pleased" move down from the aristocracy to the middle class and then to the lower class;
6. Had everybody adopting the values of the lower classes instead of modeling after and aspiring for the upper classes;
7. Suffered continuously escalating inflation and the resulting public assumption that such economic spiraling was normal and natural;
8. Was unable to provide general safety and protection for the citizens because of ever-increasing groups that took the law into their own hands;
9. Declared that every member of society was equal and deserved to have whatever any other member had;
10. Had a rise in superstitious beliefs, astrology, religion, and any other escape philosophies that promised a better world to come:
11. Entered a time of political purges and revenge;
12. Was faced with reluctant trading partners in other countries of her world;
13. Lost a steady stream of food and essential supplies because of weather reverses;
14. Gave up the pursuit of artistic and technical superiority;
15. Began a final era of corruption and intrigue that left a society in which no one could be trusted or depended upon.

Of the 32 civilizations the earth has seen, Toynbee says that over half have collapsed and half of the rest are in a terminal condition. The distinguished historian himself concluded after his impressive study "Death the Leveler will lay his icy hand on our civilization also." There is little purpose to be served by our debating the likelihood that our own nation will succumb to these same weaknesses. The indicators are present in our situation without question. The next five years will reveal whether or not society has been able to learn the lessons of history or will simply repeat them. In either case, you will need to be prepared. You will be wasting valuable resources and earning power if you withdraw into a state of readiness too quickly. On the other hand, you want to plan your trajectory so that you are prepared for the worst just before the worst arrives.

The America historian, Crane Brinton, has analyzed four major historical revolutions: the French Revolution, the American Revolution, the Russian Revolution, and the Glorious Revolution of England in 1688. Crane found that conditions preceding each of these revolutions had a striking degree of commonality. Among these were the presence of bitter class antagonisms, ineffective operation of governmental machinery, potential approaching bankruptcy of the government, and a loss among the ruling class of confidence about their traditions, with many members of the upper class moving over to support the values of attacking groups. All these conditions sound strikingly familiar to the observer of Western civilizations.

The evidence is overwhelming that our present system of dealing with populations and their subgroups has built-in self-defeating characteristics. There will definitely be a nation between the Atlantic and Pacific during the 1990s, but it is almost certain to have a different personality from the one we know today.

# THE FUTURISTS: THE FLOWERS OF ALL THE TOMORROWS LIE IN THE SEEDS OF TODAY

In view of the serious trends of world population growth, food shortages, and political tension, maybe we should arrange to get the best minds in the world together and give them free rein and plenty of resources to explore the possibilities and tell us what to expect and how to prepare for it.

It's a good plan, but it's already been done. The findings were documented, startling, and almost totally ignored. The whole effort was valuable in its ability to prove that the majority of humanity will not listen to sensible warnings. You, on the other hand, may have the kind of individual drive to prepare for your part of the world wind-down predicted in 1972 by the prestigious Club of Rome.

This highest-level think tank was founded by Aurelio Peccei, an Italian economist and management consultant who got his start as an expert by making Olivetti an international corporation. He invited the participation of the best brains in the world—from business and scientific endeavor—and began in 1968 an organization with the purpose of exploring the most basic issue confronting society: survival.

With a $250,000 grant from Volkswagen, the Club of Rome gathered data that could have impact on the world's future survival. The data included both hard statistics and subjective judgments from many of the world's best thinkers on the various component topics. All this information was fed into the giant computer at M.I.T. with an intricate program that could not only simulate the major ecological forces at work in the world but also compensate for the interlocked nature of these influences. For example, the growth of human population requires more food and less pollution. We cannot have more food without increases in industrial products to facilitate natural growth methods. More industrial process results in more pollution and fewer natural resources. Pollution ultimately interferes with everything and, according to the computer projections, everything winds to a halt with the survivors living a sort of primitive agricultural life trying to grow crops in the medians of deserted interstate highways and to capture rainwater next to poisonous, polluted rivers.

It sounds like the ravings of a wild science fiction writer, and yet these projections have been verified and cross-checked by countless computer runs. The findings have been questioned but never successfully denied. My feeling is that they may have been overly optimistic. Common sense dictates that there has to be an end to the use of raw materials that cannot replenish themselves.

### Limits of Growth?

A revelation of the Club of Rome that may prove harder for the American people to accept is the idea that continued growth is literally going to kill us. *Growth* has become a religion with our economy, and it is almost impossible for us to imagine an economic problem that cannot be solved by continued growth. If a company is selling its product below costs there is no way that the difference will be made up in volume.

According to the Club of Rome report, economic population growth has to stop almost immediately or shortly after the arrival of the next century the population, food production, and pollution curves, along with the supply of natural resources converge for a catastrophic collapse. The life-style of those who survive will center on getting food and maintaining life at the simplest possible levels.

### What about the Happy Ending?

At about this point in the story, we are accustomed to the introduction of the happy ending. We are prepared to hear a voice say, "However . . . if we will *stop* doing these things and *start* doing these we will be able to avoid the events which have been described." Unfortunately, there are no happy endings in these predictions of the future. In fact, the computer analyzed various alternative situations and in every case came back with discouraging results. What if there are other undiscovered reserves of natural resources (perhaps under the oceans)? The computer answers that industrialization will accelerate with runaway pollution. What if new technological devices are found to control pollution? Population would soar, and soon the land's food-producing ability would lose out. What if pollution were abated, the birthrate halved, and food production doubled? Even then, responds the computer, the pollution generated to produce and process the food will ultimately outdistance the earth's ability to assimilate it.

There is no happy ever after. It appears that if the M.I.T. models are correct, we may have already gone too far down a self-destructive path toward unrelenting growth. The next steps can only be those of compensating, not correcting. The breakdown of society and of the life-support systems in major portions of this planet is inevitable—possible by the end of this century and certainly within the lifetime of your children.

When the Club of Rome was pressured to re-examine its data, the same research team came out with a modified set of conclusions. They suggested that possibly if the rich nations began to give very large amounts of aid to the poor nations, it would be technically possible for us to avoid the kind of prospect described in the first report's limits to growth. If you analyze the data carefully and read between the lines, you will find that according to their projections, we are probably reaching a point of no return. Without control of population growth and economic growth, events will be set in motion that simply cannot be reversed. Eventually some major adjustment (i.e., worldwide famine or war) will be necessary to rebalance the relationship between supply and demand of the world's life-sustaining material resources.

Lest it appear that this entire case rests upon the Club of Rome study, two other major futurists reached the same conclusion while using different procedures. In his follow-up to the global best-seller, *Future Shock*, Alvin Toffler described an *"Eco-Spasm"* that has the potential of destroying the life-style which made his prior book so successful. Like any sensible observer of global trends, Toffler concludes adapting to the man-made marvels projected in *Future Shock* may not be the world's greatest challenge. Instead he comes back to the hauntingly familiar theme of survival.

An Italian computer wizard and systems expert, Robert Vacca, has predicted the collapse of technology and of modern life in his book *The Coming Dark Age*. Vacca shows how all the major systems on which we depend (transport, electrical, garbage removal, postal, telephone and so on) are hopelessly overloaded, poorly planned, badly managed and about to crack. While his homeland shows ominous signs of this breakdown, Vacca believes that the collapse will be signaled by the major failures (between 1985 and 1994) in the United States and Japan. A collapse in one system will aggravate a collapse of another, and then another—until the catastrophe becomes worldwide. If Vacca was right, the October 1987 crash may have been the first of other catastrophes to follow.

Signs to support this thesis are already apparent. These include massive power failures, fuel shortages, chronic traffic jams, deteriorating mail services, and paralyzing garbage strikes. Commenting on Vacca's book, the famous science fiction writer Isaac Asimov said, "I have never read a book that was at one and the same time so convincing and so frightening."

Other global models have presented a similar picture. A recent World Bank forecast for the year 2000 calculated that the number of people living in "absolute poverty" (without sufficient food to keep body and soul together) would rise from the present 800 million to 1.7 billion.

The *Global 2000 Report*, undertaken at the request of President Carter and delivered just before he left office, depicted conditions that were equally disturbing. According to that report, the following future conditions seem likely:

• The gap between the richest and the poorest will increase.

- Over the 1972–2000 period, the world's remaining petroleum resources per capita can be expected to decline by at least 50 percent.
- The environment will have lost important life-supporting capabilities.
- By 2000, 40 percent of the forests still remaining in the less developed countries will have been razed. The atmospheric concentration of carbon dioxide will be nearly one-third higher than preindustrial levels.
- A 100 percent increase in the *real* price of food will be required.
- To keep energy demand in line with anticipated supplies, the *real* price of energy is assumed to rise more than 50 percent over the 1975–2000 period.
- The world will be more vulnerable both to natural disaster and disruptions from human causes.

According to continuing work being done at the Carter Center in Atlanta, the *Global 2000 Report* may have been unduly pessimistic about the real price of food and energy (because the report was issued during a period of high inflation). It may be that *prices* will be lower but that the *number of hours* needed to generate the income to pay them will be greater; it is not clear that the long-term prospect for inflation will be as high as was predicted in the report.

## THE ECONOMISTS: A DISMAL SCIENCE BECOMES MORE DISMAL

*Futurist* magazine featured an important article entitled, "Smith, Marx, and Malthus—Ghosts to Haunt Our Future." The article explored the kinds of society envisioned by three key economists, Adam Smith, Karl Marx, and Thomas Malthus. While the first two presented economic models for activity (neither of which is currently in use anywhere in the world, although we assume that Smith's model is the foundation for the "free societies" and Marx is the patron saint of communist countries), Malthus was the most predictive. Known as the "Gloomy

Parson" because of his dreary vision, Malthus presents a cruel future dominated by the specters of famine, pestilence, plague, disease and war. Reverend Malthus saw a world driven by uncontrollable forces. While I was a student of economics in the 1950s, my professors ridiculed the naivete of Malthus's pessimism. Today, his concerns are widely shared by two growing camps of economic analysts, contemporary Jeremiahs and mainline economists.

The best hope is that there will be a series of minicollapses during the next thirty years that will relieve some of the strain and pressures on the over-budgeted support system of the *planet*. This is what I expect will happen during the next decade. I genuinely believe that a severe crisis is preferable to a complete global collapse in thirty or forty years. Our culture has adopted the philosophy of "Fly now and pay later." The time has come for us to make the payment. It will be painful for us to settle our debts, but if we fail, our debts will settle us.

### The Modern Jeremiahs

In the Old Testament a Jewish prophet named Jeremiah incurred the disfavor of his people by constantly lamenting the imminent downfall of his culture. Today, an impressive number of modern Jeremiahs with conservative economic backgrounds are bowing at a golden shrine and prophesying "tribulations and desolations." Chances are, this is not the first book that you have seen decrying the coming calamity or suggesting ways to survive it. The mails are filled with newsletters from a host of prophets who provide regular doses of personal opinions, evidence of trends, and tidbits of sound advice. Several of these publications are reviewed in the appendix of this book.

The new Jeremiahs do practice what they preach. The gold-silver doctrine was dramatized by Harry Browne, author of the best-seller *You Can Profit from a Monetary Crisis*, when he told a *Newsweek* reporter, "When we are in the middle of a crisis, a pound of beef may be selling for $80 million—or two silver coins. The next week, the price will be $80 billion—or two silver coins. People will realize it's not worth using paper currency and they'll switch to other media of exchange."

Browne, whose writing and investment success has enabled him to take his own advice, sold his lavish home in the mountains overlooking Vancouver, British Columbia and moved to Switzerland. He maintains a wilderness retreat from economic disaster stocked with a year's supply of food and other essentials for independence and survival.

Browne's lastest book, *Why the Best-Laid Investment Plans Usually Go Wrong*, suggests the importance of adapting your investments according to your level of concern about the probability of various economic scenarios. He warns that there is no investment plan for all seasons. Success is becoming dependent on adapting your strategy to a rapidly changing economic environment. In chapter 6, you will read about a similar concept I developed back in 1978.

Another Jeremiah is John A. Pugsley, author of the best-selling *Alpha Strategy* and editor of two monthly journals, *Common Sense* and *The Metals Investor*. Pugsley's basic position is that "wealth consists of all the real products produced by man." Thus he recommends investing in real things rather than paper representations of wealth such as stocks, bonds, and certificates of deposit that have no intrinsic worth. No matter if you have $100 or $1,000,000 to invest, you can purchase things that have real use—preferably by you. In addition to survival foods, Pugsley recommends buying extra shoes, lamp bulbs, and other basics anytime you have extra money. As you have more to invest, he believes that copper futures offer the kind of opportunities that gold and silver used to have.

Other newsletters zero in on tax havens, the purchase and holding of gold and silver, the avoidance of taxes, the best times and places to consider if you are going to leave the United States. I have personally read and reviewed more than twenty of the leading newsletters. Many of them I have found quite helpful in doing research for this book. The appendix summarizes the major features of several of these.

As I will stress throughout this book, the nature of any prediction or advice is that it remains ultimately a guess about what is going to happen. Maybe an educated guess, but it has to be a guess. Any advice can aid you only as long as you maintain perspective about your information source. No expert is able to foretell the future accurately and outline exactly what you need to do to come out on top. You can, however, benefit from the principles that are distilled from the experience and research of individuals who devote their full time to assessing economic trends and developments.

While the modern Jeremiahs generate a great deal of publicity, it is only a minor overstatement to say that the conservative economists (especially the so-called Chicago School of monetarists) are unanimous in their opinion that the monetary policy of the United States is leading us toward a collapse of the system. Most prominent among these is Milton Friedman, a Nobel laureate, who for decades has pointed out the irresponsibility of fiscal and monetary practices of the United States.

The predictions made by the conservative economists are supported by disturbing revelations about the manipulations of the Federal Reserve System to expand the money supply and thus guarantee continued inflation. They point to the juggling act of U.S. banking and make us wonder how any bank can keep from being dangerously overextended in the middle of the "rob Peter to pay Paul" approach that is standard operating procedure. They talk about the millions of dollars in U.S. accounts that come from the Middle East and, if moved suddenly, could topple the system. (This possibility was explored in Paul Erdman's best-selling novel *The Crash of '79*—later reissued under the title *The Crash of '83*—and then in a more recent new novel entitled *The Panic of '89*, which updated the same theme. They make convincing scenarios for the set of events that could create the setting for a breakdown of the economy's ability to withstand failures of banks and major corporations.)

### Mainline Economists

Underlying all the arguments of the conservative economists is the background of the Depression of 1929.
Some disturbing comparisons can be made between the
monetary policy of our time and those just prior to that
crash. Frederick Von Hayck, Nobel Laureate of 1974
and one of the world's leading economists, accurately
predicted the crash of 1929. Now he describes a coming
world economic collapse as something that everybody
should more or less take for granted. "I used to think it
would not come for many years," he maintains, "but
now I think I might live to see it." Hayck made that
statement at seventy-seven years of age.

William Simon, certainly not a moss-bound academic,
left a two- to three-million-dollar-a-year partnership with
Wall Street's Salomon Brothers to join the Nixon administration as Secretary of the Treasury in 1973. He continued in the highest levels of government policy-making
through the Ford administration. Since leaving Washington, Simon has become one of the wealthiest men in
America through his ability to buy ailing companies and
transform them into winners.

In a far-ranging interview with *Reason* magazine in
1978, Simon said:

> We are in a position now where half the people in Amer-
> ica work for a living and the other half vote for it. . . .
> We have been going through mini collapses for the last
> twenty years—going through exaggerated boom-bust cy-
> cles, with ever-increasing unemployment, ever-increasing
> inflation, and ever-increasing miseries for the people. If
> you are looking for a grand collapse that ultimately is
> going to come as a result of all these shocks, don't worry,
> it will come if we just continue to follow these insane
> policies [fiscal and monetary policies].

While it now appears in the last years of the 1980s that
inflation is under control, there is real reason to believe
that it will again become a major problem. This theme
will be explored at greater length later in the book.

Few economists can match the establishment credentials of Robert L. Heilbroner. He is a past president of

the prestigious American Economics Association, author of several best-selling economic books, including the widely acclaimed *The Worldly Philosophers*, and numerous scholarly publications. As late as 1970, he was a spokesman for economic optimism about the potential for the U.S. and world systems. Intervening events have, however, forced him to change his perspective. His book *An Inquiry into the Human Prospect* describes a future that is dismal on almost every front.

Heilbroner describes the same problem areas that other writers mention, but goes on to point out that human beings have proven themselves unable to heed warnings, to deny themselves in the present to avoid certain future catastrophes. His conclusion:

> If then, by the question "Is there hope for man?" we ask whether it is possible to meet the challenges of the future without the payment of a fearful price, the answer must be, "No, there is no such hope."

The "fearful price" that Heilbroner foresees includes "wars of redistribution," "pre-emptive seizure," "the rise of social tensions in the industrialized nations," and a number of other experiences that will allow mankind to survive, but only at the drastic renovation of the life-style we know today. Like most others who have delved into the future, Heilbroner comes again and again to attack a concept that is dear to modern man's heart, but, at the same time is the root of his survival dilemma. Growth is one of our society's favorite opiates, but the future-oriented thinkers of our time have almost unanimously identified growth as a concept that can kill.

During the 1920s a Russian economist, Nikolai Kondrateiff, developed and published a set of statistics indicating that capitalist countries were subject to fifty-year cycles of growth and decline. He accurately predicted the great depression but alienated the Marxists because his long-wave theory suggested that capitalism would bounce back. As a reward for his research, Kondratieff wound up in Siberia. In Western circles, the reception of his ideas was only slightly warmer. More recently, with the passing of another fifty-year cycle, a number of other observers are re-examining his ideas. One key scholar is J. W. Forrester, an MIT professor who invented the random access magnetic memory for computers. Forrester is world-famous for his computer simulations of complex organizations. With his colleagues at MIT, Forrester has put together a new computer model that indicates that we have passed the peak of another Kondrateiff Wave and will probably face a prolonged period of economic disarray. Forrester warns about the danger of a break-down of political stability as well as economic difficulties.

Basically, Kondratieff's hypothesis is that the free world economy fluctuates in an economic cycle that peaks every forty to sixty years. Recent scholars have tried to pinpoint the peak at fifty-four years. This long-wave concept is tied to wars and depression. At the bottom of the peak there is usually a war. The cycle will move up following a war for approximately twenty years. At the peak of this period of peace and prosperity, there may be another period of war. The peak is followed by a sharp decline and a plateau that will usually last between seven and ten years. After this warning period everything moves downhill for the next twenty or so years.

### The Sixty-Year Gloom

Ravi Batra, a professor of economics at Southern Methodist University, does not offer much hope of escape from these scenarios of gloom. In *The Great Depression of 1990* Batra rejects Kondratieff's long waves and offers a pattern based on four economic variables: rate of inflation, rate of money growth, government regulation of the economy, and the historical recurrence of depression and recession (depressions occur every sixty years).

Batra draws parallels between the 1920s and the 1980s. Both were characterized by: (1) low money growth, low inflation, and deregulation; (2) a growth in high-technology industries; (3) a depressed farm economy and lower energy prices; (4) a Republican administration with strong pro-business views; and (5) a feeling by economists that a depression was impossible.

What we are on the brink of experiencing, Batra feels, is "the worst economic crisis in history." The stock market will crash, he says, in 1989 or 1990 and be followed by severely decreased business activity and a sharp increase in unemployment. While Batra was two years off in his prediction, I believe he was correct in believing that this depression would last for seven years, with the low point in 1994. Can this be averted? Only if drastic steps are taken now. According to Batra, we must restrain financial institutions from lending money for business takeovers and increasing margin requirements in commodity and futures markets.

Alfred L. Malabre, Jr., author of *Beyond Our Means*, agrees that there is no painless way to avoid the coming catastrophe. As he sees it, there are three possible solutions to our difficulties: hyperinflation (about a 20 percent chance), deflation, which is what occurred in the 1930s (a 30 percent likelihood), or government regulation (50 percent).

According to Malabre's forecast, a recession will occur sometime in 1988. Business failures will escalate and unemployment will return to double digits. Government debt problems will result in default or confiscation of Treasury securities, as well as in nationalization of the banking system.

My own view is similar to William Simon's—hyperinflation is more likely to be an intermediate problem than is suggested here, although in the long term we may see the kind of deflation that is seen in the second scenario.

## THE PHYSICISTS: CLOSE ENCOUNTERS OF A FEARFUL TYPE

While the economists have been trying to predict the tangibles of the future by the intangible philosophies and trends of the present, the physical scientists have been inferring some of the future's intangibles from some of the tangibles of high probability.

## Is Your Underarm Deodorant a Global Threat?

We have heard about the ozone layer now until it is old hat. It was in the early seventies that scientists like Dr. Harold Johnston of the University of California at Berkeley began announcing to us that fleets of high-flying jets or sequential detonations of several nuclear bombs could create holes in the ozone layer that sits up twenty-five miles in the sky and screens out lethal untraviolet rays from the sun. Next we got the word that fluorocarbons in areosol cans could also erode this protective shield. Whenever a scientist makes a startling finding, the news media can usually find someone who will interpret the facts differently. Galileo had the same problem. The result in the case of the ozone layer is that we have all now heard the story both ways (imminent danger vs. very little danger at all) until we are confused enough to push it out of mind. The person on the street figures that ozone, for good or bad, is twenty-five miles up and totally out of his control. It's a good example of the normal human response to a warning. We assume that it's out of our individual sphere of influence and that the government will no doubt fund an extensive study of it and that eventually it will be replaced as the topic of current panic.

Another problem of "high" concern is space pollution. Since 1957, when the launching of Sputnik ushered in the age of space exploration, thousands of objects both large and small (dead satellites, rocket boosters, fuel tanks, and other assorted "junk") have created a pollution zone above the earth. Although these objects create no visual eyesore, they do pose a serious hazard to further exploration. Traveling at 17,500 miles an hour, even a flake of paint can puncture an astronaut's spacesuit or damage a spacecraft. Several unexplained satellite failures may in fact have been caused by such collisions.

# THE CLIMATOLOGISTS: EVERYONE TALKS ABOUT THE WEATHER

You've heard the old adage, "Everyone talks about the weather, but no one does anything about it." Historically this statement may be true. For centuries people talked about the weather and, fortunately for us, frequently recorded the kind of weather conditions they experienced. In recent years a science of forecasting the weather has begun to emerge. Recently that science has become critical for topics much more significant than planning a weekend picnic. Nations across the world are beginning to get some rather disturbing messages from the weather phenonema of the past decade. Record cold waves in the winter and extensive droughts in the summer are not merely unpleasant, they are potentially devastating to the world's economy. Weather scientists at the Institute for Environmental Studies of the University of Wisconsin and other key centers have become quite concerned about the evidence that appears to emerge from their analyses of historical and contemporary weather patterns. The verdict is good news and bad.

The bad news is that the earth's weather is undoubtedly getting colder. The good news is that colder winters around the world could be one thing that could reverse the downhill economic direction of the United States. While none of us is going to welcome longer, colder winters with deeper snows, we can still take some consolation. Under such conditions, the United States would become the dominant food-producing nation in a world that is not only hungry, but absolutely unable to grow enough food. According to special reports prepared by the CIA, the country that has the food is going to hold all the cards in the next few years.

Of course, every advantage has an accompanying disadvantage. What do we do when we have all the food and a frozen, starving leadership of less fortunate nations decide they have little to lose by holding a nuclear gun to our heads? The pressures of hungry masses on the judgment of otherwise sane leaders could be devastating. When the pressure begins to rise, do we give the food away, or sell it, or exploit its power to control the way other cultures must behave? Do we require birth-control practices of those who will receive our precious food? How many people are we willing to allow to starve so that we can maintain the standard of living to which we have become accustomed?

The evidence points to the fact that we will not really have the option of keeping our present standard of living. The winters of recent years have treated us all to extremes and dilemmas we had not encountered before. Some people are beginning to wonder if this bad weather was a fluke or an ominous trend that is becoming a permanent fixture. A careful investigation of the historical records of temperatures and snowfalls has now begun to reveal the unhappy news. Climatologists tell us that this weather is not abnormal—what we have enjoyed for the past fifty years was abnormal.

In a comprehensively researched, scholarly publication, Nels Winkless III and Iben Browning confirm the fact that climate in the past fifty or so years has been the warmest and most productive in several centuries. They predict that the world will soon return to harsher, more normal conditions. They also suggest that the predicted changes in climate can cause some severe disruptions in food production with accompanying political and economic pressures on countries. In fact, of the twenty-eight scholars who have published significant papers on climatology in recent years, twenty-three are in agreement that the earth will be cooler in the next years than it has been in the past few years. Thus, it appears that the weather is now beginning to return to the normal state of long, frozen winters. We may not like it, but the earth's climate cycles were in existence long before our civilization came along, and if it's time for another Ice Age, there is little we can do to stop it.

We've enjoyed unseasonably good weather during the past half-century and now we are headed back into a cold cycle that can be expected to extend hundreds of years into the future. The extent and impact of this trend on you and your family can be quite easily deduced. You want to store food and other supplies that will ensure your survival in the more likely event of being trapped in your house for a long period of time. You may need to insulate and weatherize your home for the eventualities of colder temperatures and loss of outside power support. Or you may decide that your home deserves to be sold as you seek warmer regions of the country where the temperatures promise to be colder but not paralyzing.

## THE THEOLOGIANS: IS THE END FINALLY AT HAND?

A bumper sticker on a psychodelic van put it this way, "Jesus Is Coming Soon . . . And Is He sore!" A growing number of popular religious personalities are building their followings on the claim that they are able to illuminate for us from the Bible's prophecies for the future of mankind.

Hal Lindsey is the leader of the apocalyptic club. His books on prophecy have sold well over fifteen million copies and he stays in demand as a speaker around the world. Lindsey doesn't claim that God tells him directly what will happen. His deductions come from continuing comparisons between the Bible's veiled prophecies of the events leading up to the end of the world and the events of our daily world news. Though Lindsey's conclusions have their skeptics among the more scholarly theologians, his ideas have quite obviously caught the imagination of a great many readers around the world. He estimates that some eight million people stand with him in an apocalyptic interpretation of the following political, economic, and geographical trends:

1. The growing isolation of Israel will force it to work out a mutual defense pact with the European Common Market, which will cause:
2. Black Africa to align with the Arab world against Israel;

3. A tenth nation will join the Common Market, making it fit the biblical description of the ten-horned beast described in Daniel and Revelation.

4. The beast will be led by the "Anti-Christ," an electrifying speaker who will be possessed by Satan, after miraculously surviving a head wound. Possessing almost superhuman intelligence, he will become head of a world confederacy.

5. This world confederacy will assign code numbers for every person on earth. Each number will incorporate the 666 which the Biblical prophecies established as the identity of the Anti-Christ. The numbers will be tied into computers that can read them by ultraviolet light and cut off the ability to buy and sell for those who are out of favor in the cashless, electronic banking society.

6. Famines will increase due to climatic changes and create great international tensions and crises.

7. There will be a great increase in killer earthquakes.

8. The power of the United States will decline and there will be a shift in the balance to Europe.

Hal Lindsey says that these events will (in his opinion—not in prophecy) all take place before the year 2000. Although he has been sharply critical of Jeanne Dixon, Lindsey's predictions do mesh loosely with those of the best known prophet of our time. According to Ms. Dixon, the world must return to a life of faith and prayer or else the next half century will include:

1. Russian occupation of Israel leading to: a nuclear war between Russia and the U.S. in 1999, with "fear for the survival of all mankind."

2. the victorious allied armies will then fight Communist China for nineteen years.

3. culminating about the year 2020 with the apocalyptic battle of Armageddon.

4. The Allies will win and usher in the reign of the anti-Christ who will be in full command of the world.

5. The years 2020–2037 will hail the second coming of Christ. The surviving Jews will spread his gospel throughout the world.

6. The new Judeo-Christian faith will usher in unprecedented human happiness and good will beyond the year 2037, after which Ms. Dixon's visions cease.

## YOU: THE ULTIMATE ANSWER

I realize that some religious readers will be offended by what they interpret as the humanistic emphasis of this section heading. I respect the sincere conviction of my religious friends who believe that the only solution to the problems that lie ahead is for God to intervene in our behalf. My personal religious persuasion is that God will not repeal the law of consequences that he set in motion. Rather, my hope is to remain open to receive guidance about how to direct my affairs now and throughout the future. I do not expect a miraculous vision or a still small voice in the night. I believe that by being receptive to truth from all sources, I will receive the direction that is needed.

Once you have evaluated the varied, yet similar, prophecies by the experts of many disciplines, I believe you will be impressed by the frightening prospects of the next decade. The visions of the future are not identical, but they are similar. According to probability theory, the true nature of any universe tends to be near the center of observations that fall on either side of it; thus, the phenomenon of the bell-shaped curve. I don't expect to see the fulfillment of all the prophecies mentioned in this chapter. Depression, famine, violence, and natural disasters have, however, been recurring themes.

Among the various popular futuristic novels, Ayn Rand's *Atlas Shrugged* presents a scenario which I find very appropriate for this time. She describes a society where the producers become tired of bearing the burden of everyone else. They finally refuse to continue shouldering this heavy burden. Of course, the book's title refers to Atlas's mythical duty of bearing the world on his shoulders. The shrug is the prophesied result when Atlas finally gets tired of doing his share and everyone else's too. In the novel, the producers go off to a place called Hidden Valley (perhaps a survival community like those discussed in Chapter 11?), where they are able to work and not worry about the lazy and irresponsible. Is it possible in a society where 10 percent of the population pays 50 percent of the taxes—where 7 million taxpayers work to support 155 million people who pay no taxes— that a significant number of citizens are almost ready to shrug?

Regardless of what everybody else is saying about the future, you can tell that things are not quite right. This is a gnawing kind of concern that tells most people today that there are harder times ahead. That's the reason you picked this book up and the reason that you may be one of the few to prepare for the coming stresses. Your own intuition tells you that we have gotten off the track and that there are some dark days ahead. This book is designed to show some of the ways that these hard times can be handled in a way that will be more pleasant for the people who are willing to read and heed the signs of the coming times.

## CHAPTER 3

# WHY HAS THE AMERICAN DREAM GONE SOUR?

When Tennessee Ernie Ford went to the top of the Hit Parade with his song called "Sixteen Tons," it was before the era of the protest song. People just liked the beat and the bitter-tough soliloquy of a poor coal miner trapped in the economic death grip of the company store—loading 16 tons a day and getting deeper in debt.

When the song came out in the boom-time fifties, the record-buying middle class was not worried about its soul being taken over by any company store. Of course, most families did have the kind of gradually growing debt that Sears liked to call a revolving charge account. But, why worry? Everybody has to owe money to have the things he needs.

It's no wonder the fifties have found their place in nostalgia as the happy days. They occurred just as the nation was whizzing to the top of an exciting roller coaster. The ride was still fun and the "spend what you are going to earn" myth was still keeping us up to our ears in bright, shiny things. What we didn't know then was that there was no track at the other side of the roller coaster's summit.

If we thought we were speeding going up, we will hardly believe the acceleration on the way down. The speed on the way down is not fun, though, because of the obvious fact that we cannot continue without a crash. At this moment, we are descending into a catastrophe where we will finally pay for all the lunches we thought were free.

By now, everybody is familiar with the dates and figures: On August 2, 1982, the Dow Jones Average stood

at 776. During the next five years a raging bull market
carried it up to nearly four times that level, peaking at
2722 in August of 1987. And then, on October 19, the
bottom fell out and the Dow plummeted 508 points. A
black day for Wall Street, everybody agreed. But how
serious was it? What does it portend for the future? On
such questions, agreement is more difficult to come by.

Some experts argue that the October crash will not
start a depression. Few Americans, they say, hold much
of their worth in stocks, and thus the majority will not be
personally affected to any great extent. Further, government spending accounts for more than a third of GNP.
So unless the government and the middle class stop spending, which isn't going to happen, the economy simply
cannot collapse.

Hold on, others say. The government *does* spend a lot
of money, but where does that money come from? Does
the government produce it? No. It comes from the goods
and services produced by citizens like you and me. From
this fact proceed all sorts of widening ripples. Initial
belt-tightening in the wake of the crash will dampen
consumer spending and business expansion. Credit will
be harder to come by because of rising interest rates.
Bank loans will be more difficult to arrange because the
collateral they depend on has been weakened by the
market's fall. Pension funds have been hard hit, as have
insurance companies and their ability to cover claims and
pay retirees. In short, one thing leads to another, and all
of them together are leading to a calamitous state of
affairs.

To put things in perspective, in the eight weeks beginning with the crash on October 19, the nearly six thousand U.S. stocks represented by the Wilshire Index lost
one-third of their value, or $1 trillion. In other words,
the net worth of the average American dropped by more
than $4,000 during this brief period. The biggest loser by
far was Sam Walton, founder of the Wal-Mart store
chain, who lost a total of $1.75 *billion* dollars.

On a national and individual basis, we have been over-
extended—a nice economic term for being broke! The

American dream has gone sour. We finally succeeded in cutting free from the old-time, hard-cash morality of our grandparents. We finally convinced ourselves and the world that you've got to spend money to make money. Unfortunately, we worked right through the cliché and coined another that said you can spend tomorrow's money today.

As we dig our fingernails into the rail of the roller coaster car hurtling downward, we can't understand what went wrong. We can't understand why our nation's economy no longer leads the world, why the dollar is starting to do those things that only the foreign currency used to do. Why don't the other nations love us anymore; didn't we give them millions? And why isn't the capitalism that people used to criticize for being so efficient continuing to give us worry-free goodies; what ever happened to the self-correcting promise of competition and free enterprise?

## THE DEVIL WITHIN
## AND THE DEVIL WITHOUT

There are two major causes for the dizziness you may feel whenever you try to comprehend our economic situation. One is a personal devil inside each of us and the other is an even larger demon who rages outside. Unfortunately, neither seems to be under the control of anybody.

The internal troublemaker has been on the lips and pens of theologians and philosophers forever and ever. It is the predictable, but still puzzling, enigma known as human nature. Mankind seems to possess a germ of laziness and dishonesty that hopes against hope that you can really get something for nothing. As children grow up (in any century) parents and societal clichés provide regular reminders that you have to work for what you get, the cream will rise to the top, and the free lunch is always gonna cost you. We hear the words, partly believe, but never completely drown out the inner voice that starts babbling whenever we are onto a sure thing, in on the ground floor, coming up on the chance of a lifetime, or hearing sleigh bells on the roof. When opportunity (or temptation) knocks, humans seem to forget all the things they have righteously maintained and run wild in carefully rationalized idiocy.

Human nature allows us to rant on and on about the ridiculous, irresponsible movements in which Washington is selling us down the economic river by printing paper money that is two parts money and ninety-eight parts paper, and then, in the next breath, to make personal plans to spend today the paycheck we expect to receive eight months later. Human nature is the puzzling humor that lets us laugh and say "who cares" while doing something that we know is financially suicidal. None of us wants to give up our flawed human nature because, even though it gives us daily pain, it is still our membership card to the global fraternity. Misery loves company, and the cadre of people overpowered by human greed is growing every day.

Is it fair to blame human nature for the obvious worsening situation of our economy? Since human nature has been around for millennia and the economy has only been staggering for less than a century, how can we pin the blame on human greed? The answer is simple. There was a time when society held on to the brakes that protected us from letting base human nature run wild.

Since the Constitution was framed and up to the early years of this century, the term "Christian nation" was acceptable in polite conversation. That didn't mean that everybody was a Christian, or even a churchgoer. It just meant that, generally speaking, everyone was under the restraint of a social disapproval system that was closely tied to the old-time religion. That religion may not have come from God, the Bible, or even the church. It may have been an intricate weaving of Ben Franklin's sayings, Horatio Alger's stories, and the precarious season-to-season life on the farm. Whatever its composition, it provided a set of brakes to slow us up and to say no when we were about to go for something that would hurt us.

If the idea of religion offends, we might just as well say that until World War II, we were, as a nation, far more willing to be guided and restricted by the accumulated wisdom of the ages. Obviously, there have been get-rich-quick schemes as long as there have been people, and P. T. Barnum knew long before World War II that there was a sucker born every minute. Prior to the world homogenization process that began with that war, the old-time values and warnings were still assumed to be good. Only in the last fifty years has moral goodness gone on the rack and badness been given such terrific press. While the positive and negative fringes of society are always going to be far apart, the central trust of our national character has shifted. This has turned a rising host of people loose in a world that automatically devalues anything old, trusts its feelings more than its history, and praises doing what you want to rather than what you ought to.

So culprit number one is a familiar one—the devil within—and collectively, we have abandoned the old restraints and no longer benefit from the accumulated wisdom of the past. In fact, we are proud of a newfound ability to stand on our own, distrusting tradition, and making our own decisions, but as a nation we are more in trouble than ever before.

Devil number two is both familiar and unknown. Inflation is a word that is worn from daily use, but few citizens realize what causes it, what it causes, and how little about it we are ever allowed to know. How many times have we heard someone say, "I remember when I bought my first car . . . paid $250 for it . . . but saving that $250 was like saving $2500 in this day and age."

Although inflation is not currently the problem that it once was, there is a very real possibility that it will soon become a major problem again. It is inevitable in the face of our continuing deficit spending and our woes in the international trading markets. It is a problem we were familiar with only a few years ago, and it will return to haunt us again. So what is it?

Suppose you crawl up on the beach of a deserted island. Correction: an island that is deserted, except for one coconut vendor. The stock in his coconut stand is composed of one hundred coconuts, priced at one fish each. You feel confident that, as an expert fisherman, you should be able to satisfy your need for coconuts. You catch a fish and buy a refreshing and delicious coconut. Life won't be too bad on this island. There are plenty of fish and an ample supply of coconuts. Next day, the vendor tells you that the coconuts will now cost two fish each since the supply is dropping. You don't like it, but there is nothing you can do. You fish a little longer and enjoy the same coconut satisfaction. Next day, the price is up again but this time you tell the vendor that you have established a new monetary standard and, in the future that two rocks from the beach will equal one fish. If the vendor accepts your notion, he is a fool (but no bigger fool than the U.S. public and the host of foreign buyers who have accepted the dictum that paper is as good as gold). The cycle continues, but there is no feeling of ease because of the obvious fact that no matter how many fish or rocks you have, there are no more coconuts. In fact, there is an ever-decreasing amount of the basic resources.

The word "inflation" has the sound of hot air filling a balloon. Balloons are relatively simple but our understanding of monetary inflation leaves us wondering. Actually the same thing happens. When you blow into the balloon, you appear to create a bigger balloon, but you don't. You are in reality only stretching the same balloon over a bigger area. There is no additional rubber in the balloon, only hot air to make the same amount of rubber appear to go farther. Of course you cannot stretch the balloon indefinitely. Hot air can push the balloon beyond its limits, and the hot air of inflation is pushing the economy beyond its limits.

## INFLATION—GETTING LESS WHILE EARNING MORE

The reason we have economic problems today is that we quit doing what we were doing when we didn't have these problems. "Thanks a lot," you say, "what does that doubletalk mean?"

The beginning of the problem corresponded directly to the beginning of some specific policy changes. Specifically, we left the gold standard and started printing paper that said it was gold. This was about like calling a rock from the beach a fish. It makes you feel wealthy but it creates no actual wealth.

The deficit-spending disease began to spread at the point the nation said, "Either we are going to have to spend money we don't have, or some of us will have to do without." That simple change in policy created the fantasy-land roller coaster that was so exhilarating through the fifties, but is now becoming a terrifying nightmare. At first, it was fun for the nation to spend money it didn't have. People in need were getting what they wanted. Everyone seemed to have more, and there was still the optimistic anticipation that eventually we would be able to pay it all back. The hope of being in the black again enabled us to maintain our self-respect at the beginning. But, as we have continued to spend more and more that we did not have, gradually, like a junky who accepts his need for larger and larger fixes, we have come to think that life in the red is normal.

It was a simple habit to acquire. And once a policy of monetary inflation was adopted, carrying out the policy was taken out of our hands. Government grew. It seemed natural to take over and administer the care of people in need and protect us from every danger. After all, someone had to keep the nation safe for deficit spending. The cycle continues today as the bureaucracy, the politicians, and the taxpayers look for someone else to bail them out of their baffling problems. More than anything else, everyone wants to avoid the personal pain required to kick the habit and fix what is wrong. We are all desperately over-extended in debt and hoping that there will be some way to get right again without pain or sacrifice or surrender. It is not possible. We are where we are because we have put off for years the daily sacrifices and discomforts of getting along. The price must be paid—either a day at a time (which is called life) or all in one terrible lump (which is called the crash). Balloons can only stretch so far.

Because of the massive amount of debt held by the Japanese and other foreign nations, there is a great temptation for us to reduce that debt in real terms by allowing inflation to take hold again. It would be a great opportunity for the U.S. because we could repay those debts with cheaper dollars. We are already seeing the Federal Reserve Board increase the money supply in order to hold interest rates down and keep the economy active. But this can be only a short-term action. Ultimately we are going to have to deal with the inflation created by that. To many people this seems a positive direction. The only problem is that the resulting inflation could easily get out of hand.

# A BRIEF HISTORY
# OF THE CRUELEST TAX

There is little encouragement when you look at the history of inflation. Like heroin, inflation is not a new addiction. It has existed in many societies and for many centuries. It has not always existed, which counteracts the idea that inflation has always been with us and is inevitable. However, when inflation *has* existed in history, it has always been caused by the same types of human weakness. Someone avoided the unpleasantries and left them to be handled by those who came after. And, without fail, the unpleasantries did get handled. The bill always gets paid and somebody always loses. History tells us that we have the option of either biting a bullet each day or swallowing the bombshell all at once.

### Nero Fiddles While Inflation Burns
By our political standards, Nero was not a bad leader. He was well liked by the people because he was always giving the exciting shows at the Coliseum and providing public works and services that cost far more than people paid in taxes. What more could the people want? What could be better than a leader who charged you 10 denarii

in taxes and gave you 20 denarii back in goods and services? What would have been better was honesty, even honesty that painted a bleak picture.

No accounting was ever done of Nero's fiscal income and expenditure. Historians suspect that in the beginning Nero was able to do his wonders by simply paying for them out of his own pocket. Admirable, but laying the groundwork for future problems. Next, Nero discovered that if the rich were found guilty of treason, condemned, and executed, the state could confiscate their wealth. He did so. (Today we accomplish the same goal by confiscatory estate taxes.)

Nero's final stroke of fiscal genius set a precedent that has been emulated in every economy in trouble. In A. D. 60 he changed the nature of the coins the Romans used. There had always been 42 gold coins to one pound of gold and 84 silver coins to one pound of silver. Nero discovered that by mixing in baser metals, he could make each pound of gold produce three extra gold coins and each pound of silver produce 12 extra silver coins.

It was like creating money from nothing. It was the literal devaluation of the money, and it has been repeated by nations in financial trouble ever since. The United States has continued to devalue simply by letting the dollar become weaker and weaker relative to other currencies such as the Japanese yen. Like Nero, we devalue because we want more than we can afford. This is a not-too-glorious tradition in North America.

When the colonists started a revolution to gain freedom from England, there was not enough money to pay for the war. The Yankees used their printing presses and printed up a supply of money that paid for the war but left the American money with only about one-fortieth its face value. The expression that something is "not worth a Continental" grew out of these times when there was American money with nothing to back it up.

### Don't Save Your Confederate Money

The Civil War in America produced its own horror stories of inflation. The Union paid for its side of the war by printing up $450 million in special bills which gained the nickname "greenbacks." The greenbacks ended the war at a value of 74 greenbacks for one real dollar. People were pretty upset when the issuing government began refusing to accept them as payment. The government paid its debts in greenbacks but wanted real dollars when it was paid.

The Confederate States in the Civil War cranked out over $2 billion on their printing press. When the war was lost the Confederate money was all people had. Its value was so low that it took $1,000 to buy a barrel of flour.

After the Civil War the U.S. government eventually bought back all the greenbacks for gold. It was difficult. It put a lot of strain on the economy. Many people were out of work, since there were so few dollars available for the same amount of goods. It was a painful time, but it put the U.S. dollar on firm footing in the world's money market. The dollars then continued to gain in strength, because the people were working hard to get the country moving again after the war. There was a steadily increasing productivity. A lot of new and valuable commodities were being created, grown, and manufactured. With that creation, there was strength behind the new dollars that were printed.

### Inflation: Prelude to the Goose Step

The most spectacular inflation story is that of the Germans in the years following the First World War. Germany's industry and agriculture were destroyed, and there was nothing to swap for the goods needed from other countries. At the same time the truce placed a reparations payment on the Germans they could not possibly meet. The value of the German mark began to drop. One mark had been equal to about 25 American cents in 1914, but by 1923, one American dollar would equal 4 million marks. This meant that the prices of things in marks were almost unbelievable. Prices were going up so fast that many companies would pay their employees three or four times a day so that they could spend the money before it lost its value. In order to supply enough marks for this madness, more than 2,000 printers and 300 paper mills were working 24 hours a day to supply bank notes to the Reichsbank. Eventually, there were bills in general use for one billion marks and for one trillion marks. This unbelievable situation finally began to stabilize when the Dawes Plan eased the payment of Germany's war debts. However, it was out of the dissatisfaction in Germany that Adolf Hitler found a foothold and eventually led Germany into World War II.

### A Fast Deal on Dollars

In the United States, the strong, well-founded economy became the basis for more and more risk-taking. The stock market was rising so continuously that many people began to speculate on the rising stocks. They would purchase shares of stock with money they did not have. Then the stock would rise in value and they would sell, pay the money they had borrowed, and make a handsome profit. It was easy money. Everybody got into the act. More and more people bought more and more stock with money that wasn't real. The banks loaned more money than they actually had, since it was all on paper anyway and no one ever called for the real money. As the market's rise hesitated, everybody seemed to panic and sell. The market stopped going up, so people stopped making profits and could not pay what they owed the banks. The banks were in trouble already when everybody got worried and rushed to take their money out of the bank. In effect, the people demanded more money out of the banks than the banks had. The crash which occurred in 1929 left banks broke, individuals in financial ruin, and the government seemingly helpless to get things moving again. People were out of work—they couldn't buy till they were working again—and the companies couldn't hire them until people started buying again. It was a depression of the most basic kind—the sort that is necessary to get things level again. The government could have suffered with the people, tightened the belt, and ridden out the depression as it did following the Civil War. Instead, it took a turn from which we are yet to recover.

In 1933 Franklin Roosevelt took office. He adopted the economic policies of John Maynard Keynes (pronounced kaines), an English economist. Keynes' basic idea was that there was no reason for countries to have to back their money with gold. In fact, Keynes suggested that the responsibility of government was to get the ball rolling by spending money, even if the government was broke. His plan was to create money by deficit spending.

Roosevelt bought the idea. He took control aggressively, pumped money into the economy by creating government jobs for millions of Americans in public works. It was good news—people were going back to work. There was money in circulation again and the wheels of the economy began to turn. The wheels spun faster and faster. At least, they appeared to spin faster and faster. In reality, there was more money around but not that much more productivity.

Roosevelt became one of the most popular presidents ever. People were happy. They were working. But at the same time they weren't too happy about the way government and taxes were growing. And they didn't like the fact that they were paying more all the time for the same goods and services. The inflation roller coaster had been boarded. The inflationary ascent would be gradual at first, but ever increasing. Nobody stopped to recognize that the idea of spending money without having it had been tried repeatedly in the economic history of the world and had never worked.

### What We Haven't Been Told

When Keynes recommended that nations spend their way back to prosperity it sounded good. Most drunks like the idea of taking a couple of snorts to end a hangover. The prescription seemed to work at first. But the inflation that was begun at that time may eventually be the final undoing of America's economy. Priming the pump was one thing. It is quite another to continue to prime the pump (and other countries' pumps too) after the water has begun to flow. Too much pump priming means that everyone gets soaked!

People and their governments have simply become unable to say no. When we want something, we buy it regardless of our debts or ability to pay. What difference will more debt make when you never plan to pay? The government borrows money to meet its obligations. When those loans come due, it borrows more money to pay. By 1987 the interest alone of the national debt was almost $370 billion.

Because the politicians want the American public happy at any cost, the figures that would reveal the alarming trends are doctored on a continuing basis. The official Consumer Price Index (CPI) is published every month by the Department of Labor. It calculates and explains the monthly changes in the prices of all items forming the CPI. This comparison system began back in 1934. It gradually increased each year. By 1947 the index (which considered the period 1934–39 to equal 100) was faced with a comparative index of 159. Because a 50 percent increase is terrible politics, a little statistical lie was told and accepted. 1947 became the year to which we would compare all subsequent years. Thereafter, the year of comparison has been changed at regular intervals. *If we were still stuck with comparing to 1947 levels, we would have to announce a CPI of about 520 percent in 1988.*

Most people don't realize that the statistics get this cosmetic treatment every decade or so. But one suspects that if the true figures were revealed, there would not be much of a public outcry. There would be many words but little impact. Inflation is an addiction that our nation does not want to take the cure for. We will content ourselves with inaccurate statistics and myths like "things do cost more, but we all have more" rather than pay the price of reversing the trend.

## WHY WE WON'T LEARN

Inflation is the universal enemy. You will never hear anybody stand up and say that inflation is a virtue and makes life better. But history makes it quickly clear that the voting public demands the inflation-producing behavior of its elected representatives. A President could, for example, decide between reduced inflation next year and one million additional people unemployed. Not much of a choice! One alternative would halt inflation and end a political career. The other alternative will continue the spiral of inflation, reduce the price of the dollar, and spell slow death for all.

The anathema against putting people out of work is relatively new. Prior to the Roosevelt era, there was no general assumption that everyone deserved a job or had any innate right to a given income or standard of living. The processes of protecting every person from every eventuality have increased the size of government and fed the fires of inflation. The year after World War II ended, Congress passed the Full Employment act, stating that the government would vigorously promote two goals which were and are basically inconsistent—price stability and full employment. Ever since that time we have opted for the full employment half of the equation whenever there was a conflict. That's not totally bad. It is based on the humane idea that it is better for everyone to hurt a little than for a few to hurt a lot. Unfortunately, the number of people who are willing to give has declined in inverse relationship to the people who want to get.

Throughout the history of the world, nations have followed wars with inflation and then deflation until things stabilized. Thanks to Keynes' theories and the United States' world leadership, World War II and the Vietnam War have been followed by nothing but runaway inflation. The inflation has been worse. Does it stand to reason that the deflation when it comes—and it must come—will be worse?

As the rate of inflation increases, everyone thinks he is getting more. But average price increases of 2 percent in the 1950s, 2.3 percent in the 1960s, and 6.1 percent in the 1970s produce no more goods and services—just higher prices for the same goods. Can you accurately say, though, that as long as most people *feel* good about the economy, the economy is good? Of course not, Aspirin never cures a headache. It simply keeps us from feeling the pain that in the case of real disease would be a valuable warning to us.

When a major employer like Lockheed or Penn Central goes broke, the government has two options again. They can let the mismanaged company go under (putting thousands of voters out of work) or they can bail the company out (with dollars the country doesn't have). Sound economic direction would say, "It's sad, but the company is not justified by the economy. It will have to die." Popular politics would say, "We are already in debt. What difference will a little more debt make? Besides, my brother-in-law works for that company."

Inflation becomes an international way of life. If the Arabs charge us more for oil, we no longer consider responding by marching in with troops and tanks under the pressure of some international affront. Rather, we now pay the price and charge them higher prices in return. It's automatic—the oil costs us more so the things they need are going to cost the Arabs more. Air conditioning and computers are going to come at higher and higher prices.

Inflation is much more popular than any world leader will ever admit. More than anyone else, the U.S. government benefits from inflation, at least in the short term. Inflation means that massive debts can be repaid in cheaper dollars. Inflation pushes people into higher tax brackets and they send an even larger share of their shrunken dollars to Washington. No wonder governments prefer inflation to unemployment. Inflation is popular because it provides a device for staying popular with the electorate. The man on the street needs a financial fix and wants to believe that he has more money when he actually has less. Inflation is only unpopular with those who recognize the historic economic implications. A fresh fix seems to make everything more pleasant, but each cycle requires a bigger dose. Breaking the habit sounds so simple. There seems to be little reason to worry. In reality, the addiction is frequently lethal for a culture.

When you blow a tiny balloon full of hot air, it inflates. Reverse the flow of air and you have to swallow a lot of unpleasant carbon dioxide. Continue blowing in the air. The balloon won't get bigger but the space it must cover will, and the balloon will find its own way of relieving the undue stress. However, after the balloon (and our economy) fixes itself, it will never be the same again.

# CHAPTER 4

# THE WORST
# IS YET TO BE

When the romantic poet Robert Browning contemplated the future, he wrote in "Rabbi Ben Ezra":

> Grow old along with me!
> The best is yet to be,
> The last of life, for which the first was made.

In addition to his poetic genius, Browning was an optimist. He also lived in an era when a positive view of the future was much more reasonable than it can be today. The best I can offer you is "come read along with me, for the *worst* is yet to be." In this chapter I will provide you with a general scenario of how the coming crash will probably occur. This vision is not based on hallucinogens or a crystal ball. Instead, it reflects the accumulated lessons of a life spent observing and participating in the economic determinations of our time. This analysis is based on a consideration of practically every written projection of the future. I have discounted a great deal of it, and stirred in some knowledge of the historical responses of other societies when confronted with the same dilemmas we face. All of this input has been filtered through my own common sense and judgment—two key traits which each individual must develop if he or she is to wade through the flood of gurus, seers, and saviors to survive the coming trauma. This is an important scenario because it has a direct relationship to the type of preparations you will want to make. In considering the possibilities for the coming decade, my vision is not an extreme one. Some observers believe that the catastrophe will be so great that only 20 percent of the total population will survive. They foresee an era of runaway famine, pestilence, plague, and massive armed violence. If this is your vision, you will need to make much more extensive retreat provisions.

I feel that this is a reasonable scenario because it will provide the flexibility to deal with a situation more intense than I anticipate while at the same time providing personal and financial advantage if conditions do not deteriorate as drastically as I anticipate.

## THE SHORT TERM: THE CRASH HAS BEGUN

As we have already mentioned in discussing the Kondratieff Cycle theory, business cycles will experience wider and wider swings. We have just finished a swing that brought the most dramatic increase in wealth in history because of the recent bull market, and then ended in an equally dramatic sell-off—or "meltdown," as the chairman of the Securities and Exchange Commission so colorfully phrased it.

My prediction is that within a few months we will enter into another period of inflation that will make the last inflationary period of the early 1980s look pale by comparison. Following that, there may be another period of illusionary profitability. But inevitably a crash will occur, a crash that will jolt the very underpinnings of our society. Each swing is coming in wider amplitudes and occurring in shorter time frames.

### Less Service for More Money

The level of police and fire protection will have to decline because of the inability of municipalities to pay the rising bills for declining skills. The faster inflation grows, the less likely there is to be any remaining fat to be trimmed from the police, fire, or garbage collection operations. City councils will have to choose between purchases of modernized equipment or higher pay for existing personnel. Equipment purchases usually get press coverage, but they do not lead to contented personnel or satisfied, well served clientele. Given a choice, most of us would rather have a working police force with old walkie-talkies than the best equipped strikers in the United States. But that choice is still a dilemma and either alternative provides a decline in the level of service at the time that a demand for these services will reach critical highs. Already most major cities are trying to fight rising crime rates with a declining number of paid employees.

### Whatever Happened to Private Enterprise?

While public agencies are taking their licks, the activities we mistakenly refer to as private enterprise will be suffering similar throes. We seldom stop to think of the extent to which many private companies are dependent upon government contracts, purchases, and protection. We can no longer support the fantasy that the role of government is merely to provide necessary protection to its citizens and to stimulate private activity. We have already passed the point where one out of every three Americans is on the public payroll. Gradually, the strength of the private sector has been sapped by the same disease that has eroded the moral fiber of our individual citizens. The private sector no longer has the strength to "save" the public. Businesses that do not sell all of their output to government purchasers certainly depend for buyers on at least one of every three customers who are dependent on the government. Capital and credit will become two critical criteria for business survival. Already, the quality of U.S. plant and equipment has slipped well below that of many international competitors. Firms are asked to depreciate their assets on the basis of prices that are obsolete immediately. Most companies are not able to finance "sinking funds" to offset the deterioration of their equipment, and the typical depreciation allowance simply does not provide enough money to purchase replacements when they are needed. Many observers feel there simply is not enough capital to maintain industrial productivity in the next decade.

In order for business to prosper, sufficient credit and capital must be available to finance new ventures and expansion of successful activity. While we can anticipate a strong demand for capital, there will be a relatively weak supply to meet this need. As a result, interest rates will be quite high. Extremely large sums of money will be needed to finance pollution controls, energy developments, modernized transportation, making factories more efficient, and salary increases for workers. Because of increased inflation and higher deductions for social security, income taxes, and other public services, our personal savings will drastically decline. This, of course, will reduce even further the amount of capital available for business borrowing and investment.

As it becomes more difficult and expensive for corporations like General Motors and IBM to borrow money, imagine how consumers' credit will be affected. As interest rates for mortgages and car loans skyrocket, you will see a recession in the housing sector that will filter throughout the rest of the economy and accentuate the problems of unemployment that we mentioned earlier.

### The Demise of Middle-Class Affluence

As we pointed out in the first chapter, middle-class affluence has already become something of an illusion. As an individual consumer, you will continue to spend larger and larger percentages of your income to obtain the basic necessities such as food, housing, and energy. Little money will be left to spend on frills such as travel, entertainment, dental work, and medical checkups. If you have thought that you have been on a treadmill, running hard to just stay in place, imagine the sensation as the treadmill continues to gather speed.

Filled with dreams of the Great Society and the New Frontier, we really believed that we could eliminate poverty and make everyone prosperous. The black, the young, the middle class all bought the notion that everything was going to be better. Even education no longer offers an avenue to a better life. Numerous college graduates are finding it almost impossible to find employment unless they major in fields like business, education or engineering. Enrollments are dropping in the liberal arts as students move to more practical disciplines in hope of being able to find a job.

We can see evidence of growing disenchantment among men and women who face menial jobs or unemployment and who, in addition to their frustration about lost income, must accept the loss of anticipated social status and their claim to a good life. The near future is almost certain to see great hostility and suspicion directed, not only against the government, but also against others who are seen as being wasteful and nonproductive. The gulf that already exists between rich and poor, black and white, even doers and watchers, will accelerate. Indeed, all the stress points of human relations can be expected to intensify when critical financial stresses are introduced. The seething discontent of both sides of the economic equation will lay a foundation for some event that will trigger the collapse. Inflation has already created social tensions that fill our social atmosphere like an invisible gas vapor waiting for some chance catastrophe to strike a match. Severe weather—extremely cold winters and shorter growing seasons and droughts in the summer—will create scarcities and higher prices for food that will further aggravate social discontent.

### The Straw to Break the Economy's Back

The crash of October 1987 has probably been the triggering mechanism for economic failure. We can expect other factors to add complications. Recently a disappointed investor shot his stockbroker before killing himself. Earlier in the summer, frustrated motorists in Los Angeles declared open season on each other and began roving the freeways with guns. Another incident could be just around the corner. It could be a series of inner-city riots brought on by declining support for the welfare ethic. It could be a plane crashing into a key electrical relay station in New York, Chicago, or Boston during the middle of a winter storm that sets off a chain reaction resulting in a nationwide paralysis of transportation and communication. Another major possibility is a series of natural disasters such as earthquakes striking two or three major cities at the same time. Nuclear blackmail from some minor power becomes more possible every day, even though this trigger is less likely, in my opinion, than the other alternatives.

Almost without exception, the equipment and procedures that are highly touted as modern means of meeting urban disasters can be immediately crippled by the obstruction of public roads or by the removal of power. The national interstate highway system was justified by the rationale that it was built primarily for purposes of defense and public safety. Many Californians can testify that a relatively minor earthquake can raise or lower the slabs of concrete in an expressway by eighteen inches and render the freeway impassable to any vehicle other than trucks. How well will modern fire engines or police cars perform in a city with its streets clogged with cars that have run out of gas and are stuck in a twenty-inch blizzard? How many of our gasoline-powered vehicles can function when there is no electric power to run the gas pump? Not only is our security highly vulnerable to a multitude of likely natural disasters, we are even dependent on highly vulnerable emergency equipment and contingency plans.

The components for paralysis already exist in most cities with populations above two million. The only thing that remains is for the right combination of catalytic agents to come together at an appropriate time.

### Chaos in the Cities

Several of our large cities have already been through blackouts and lived to laugh about them. But we have not yet seen the impact when several metropolises are hit at the same time, and it all arrives in the middle of the policemen's January strike. The domino effect will rock the entire country. We can count on public disorder, looting, and the essential outside authoritarian solution to the chaos.

Economist Thomas Muller of the Urban Institute in Washington lists several "municipal danger signals." These include: substantial long-term out-migration, loss of private employment, high debt service, high unemployment, high tax burden, increasing proportion of low-income population. Do you know any major city that doesn't have a perfect score on this list of imperfections?

Americans were shocked at the looting in Watts two decades ago and later during the blackouts in New York City and the 1978 snowstorm that immobilized Boston. Although we have seen no similar major riots in the past decade, the conditions that led to this unrest have hardly changed, continuing to smolder until some incident ignites another conflagration. We used to assume that these types of civil disobedience were reserved for less sophisticated nations. But every day we move into a more desperate condition than we have ever been in before. Many people identified with Howard Beale, the deranged newscaster in the movie *Network*. They are "mad as hell" and don't plan to take any more. More important, people believe that authority is probably wrong. No longer is "our friend the policeman" respected as a public servant with the public well-being at heart. Today, public servants are assumed to be out to serve themselves first, last, and always. Has your city experienced a police or fire fighter strike? At the local level, they're caught in the crunch, too.

We should well expect that during the critical first days when urban America is really beginning to fold and people have begun to get the idea that they are on their own, looting will become the order of the day. Those whose consciences might discourage them will be able to rationalize that the supermarkets and gas stations have taken more than their share for years and that looting is only evening the score. Besides, they will reason, the big companies can stand to take the losses anyway, and they probably have insurance to take care of it. Supermarkets will be hit hard and fast. Rioting will break out quickly. You should expect to see some type of guerilla warfare and massive sabotage, as those who got to the store late proceed to take it away from those who looted early in the day. (Secondhand looting is easy to rationalize; imag-

ine the simple mental steps required to justify stealing
something from someone who stole it in the first place.)

Food and welfare riots will continue. Remember that
some of the riots of the 1960s were triggered by relatively
minor events. Howard J. Ruff reports that he has encountered massive fear on the part of white surburban
Americans and believes that this fear and the lack of real
progress for blacks will trigger massive black militance
and signal the beginning of a race war. Given the dependence of much of the black population on public funds,
the high rate of crime and unemployment among black
teenagers, the growing alcohol and drug addiction as well
as the "hate whitey" rhetoric of the past, this vision isn't
difficult to conceive. Yet Ruff makes two excellent points
concerning the containment of this activity. He believes
that the resulting violence will be contained within the
city limits. If you assume a ghetto 6 miles across with
500,000 population, there is a 28-square-mile area with a
population density of almost 18,000 people per square
mile. Obviously every ghetto resident will not be ready
to go on the warpath. The attack group will be mostly
adult males and teenagers on the loose. If 100,000 people
decide to spread out in a radius of 15 miles from the
center of the ghetto, they have to occupy 706 square
miles, leaving only 141 people per square mile. A 40-mile
radius reduces the intensity to 20 raiders per square mile.
The farther you move out from the ghetto, the less of a
threat exists.

As Ruff points out, full-scale rioting, looting, and burning in the context of a full-blown depression and monetary crisis "will be a tragedy for America's black people,
as the numbers and the guns are against them." Violence
and looting in the ghettos will probably die down within
one to three weeks when there are no more food stores
to loot and liquor stores' supplies run out. Spoiled food
and stolen liquor are not a sustaining diet. Streetwise
blacks will realize that they can't hide in a white community, so they will come back to their own environment,
where their survival skills prove more valuable.

The intensity of the initial reaction will probably stimulate many urban whites who have managed to hold on to some of their money to exodus toward small cities that they believe will be safer. There will be a short-lived boom in land, farm equipment, and home furnishings. Although the intensity of the initial looting and rioting will subside, violence and robbery will become increasingly common. I believe that Ruff is mistaken in his assumption that people living more than 15 miles from a ghetto will be relatively safe during this crisis. Already the suburbs are being plagued by a dramatic increase in burglary and theft. People who have to satisfy a drug addiction (or even an addiction to food) learn quickly that you can't steal money from people who don't have it. They will consequently move in increasing numbers to any area where they believe that people still have food or other valuables. Such criminal acts will be driven by more desperation than is typical today. I expect a great deal of violence on the part of perpetrators and the victims.

### Hungry People are Not Polite

Food shortages will become critical. We have become a nation where few individuals can grow or kill their own food, even in the best of times. As the chaos spreads and the meaning of money become less clear, food itself or old silver coins will become the best medium of exchange. People will revert almost overnight to some of their basic drives for the basic requirements of food, water, and shelter.

As the initial rash of looting, burning, and violence subsides, authoritarian control will be imposed in an attempt to sustain life and public safety. Another totally unbelievable stage will be entered. For a relatively short period, prices will accelerate to unimaginable levels due to the scarcity of food and other necessities. In this period of runaway inflation, people who have supplies of paper dollars will buy any kind of luxury goods that is available because they see the prices rising so quickly. This will be a very short-lived boom. During this period I would encourage you to unload your paper dollars as quickly as possible. You may be paying $500 or $1,000 an ounce for gold, but it will hold its value better than any of the gadgets you might buy.

Black markets will return us to the sort of unbelievable prices we have heard of in post-World War I Germany, but never could quite believe. But we *will* believe them when the only way to get a loaf of bread and a quart of milk is to pay out $16 in greenbacks or one gallon of gasoline or two genuine silver quarters. This last sentence suggests how the transition from runaway inflation to a full-blown depression will take place. Prices in paper dollars will continue to skyrocket for a while, but concurrently, there will be a second and much lower tier of prices for real money.

The stock market will plummet out of sight—after having produced at least one late-inning rally which will keep some people thinking that the market will muddle through. But it will be some time before it becomes a reasonable place for prudent investors.

There will be another attempt at price controls and official action to force people to make goods available. But these approaches have never been able to control the black markets which spring to life almost automatically whenever there is a low supply and high demand. Paper money will be a highly suspect medium of exchange. Initially, the government will try to force people to accept and use paper dollars. However, most merchants will learn to say the requested item is out of stock and save it for the buyer with gold or silver. Shop owners will quickly learn that, no matter how many dollar bills they receive for an item, inflation makes it impossible to buy replacements for that price. The natural stability of gold and silver will return regardless of government monetary policy. It always has.

Even before the final crunch of the crisis arrives, the dollar bill will continue to falter on the international scene relative to the more stable currencies of Switzerland, Japan, Germany, and Holland. This will mean that we will be able to sell our goods abroad, but it will be very difficult to buy foreign-made items. Foreign-made cars and parts will be extremely expensive, and anything else made abroad will be hard to purchase.

Two other significant developments on the international scene are almost inevitable. We can expect an increase in the terrorist activities of other countries, and their spread to the United States has already begun. We need to reckon with the existence of groups throughout the world who view themselves as united in behalf of the creation of international chaos as a step to international renovation. The "Revolutionary Army" has volunteers in practically every country throughout the world. There have been at least two training schools for revolutionary activity within the United States where recruits are taught the basics of guerrilla warfare, terrorism, and even torture. Additionally, we have thousands of disillusioned Vietnam veterans who have been taught these concepts in an optimum laboratory environment. It isn't hard to understand why someone who was prevented from entering a career while times were good, and who was trained and armed efficiently and then sent out to fight in a godforsaken quagmire where he was told to be careful not to win, might resent a society that returned him home where it was difficult to find a job and then asked to endure the cruelest inflation in the history of the country. Remember, too, that the more than 460,000 in the Air and Army National Guards have ready access to high-powered, sophisticated weapons of destruction. Those who prophesy marauding bands of terrorists sweeping through the countryside may have only a slightly exaggerated picture of future events. You can rest assured that terrorists in this country will have financial and moral support from their comrades throughout the world.

The other international development is the likelihood of one or more bad crop years abroad, which will lead to certain famine and create pressures in the poorer nations to consider a nuclear blackmail. They would have little to lose by demanding food from the United States in exchange for sparing the District of Columbia. Some observers cite the probability of nuclear blackmail as being as high as 40–50 percent within the next five years.

# THE MIDTERM: THE DARKEST BEFORE THE DAWN

In ancient Egypt, the pharaoh of Moses' time was warned that his country was to endure seven years of great suffering. Only by making provision for these seven lean years could his country survive. And only after enduring this period of deprivation could the Egyptian nation go on to achieve its ultimate destiny. Similarly, I believe that this country must endure seven years of full-scale depression with large numbers of people unemployed, shortages, and the pervasive inability to get many necessities. Luxuries will be only bitter memories for all except a fortunate few who have been able to preserve portions of their predepression resources.

Cities will deteriorate rapidly and to overwhelming degrees. Criminal elements will prove more dependable than police, and there may be a revival of the old protection games. Citizens will be afraid to walk the streets of most American cities. Services within the cities will become almost nonexistent. There will be rampant fear, hostility, hunger and despair.

The government will attempt to provide control, but neither the National Guard nor the military forces will be able to restore order once the public at large becomes convinced that its survival is not the primary interest of these authoritarian forces so representative of the government that let them down before.

## A Perpetual State of Emergency

To stave off a complete collapse of order, the President will be forced to use some of the emergency powers at his disposal. Most people do not realize that the President has near dictatorial powers to issue orders changing the course of foreign and domestic affairs. Often this can be done without consulting Congress. The most impressive weapon in the President's arsenal is the broad power given him under the National Emergency provisions. It is with this authority that presidents have issued wage-price controls, imposed import taxes, called out troops to deliver mail during a postal strike, and reorganized the nation's banking system. Under emergency circumstances, the President can at any moment:

- Call up retired or reserve members of the armed forces and send them anywhere he chooses
- Seize foreign ships in U.S. waters and requisition and arm private ships
- Restrict production of explosives
- Refuse the right of any person to leave or enter the United States
- Take back former federal installations which have been transferred to state and local governments.

Any time the President declares a state of emergency, there are more than two hundred laws which permit him to take decisive action without waiting for the approval of Congress or anyone else.

In case you may wonder what constitutes a state of emergency, the answer is that one exists whenever the President says it does.

### Survival and Security for the Duration

The people who will function best during this crisis will be those who have had experience in taking care of themselves, whether on a farm or in an urban ghetto. Flabby members of the middle class will probably suffer more than anyone else. The poor have always had to worry about survival, and poverty may prove good practice for developing the skills needed for survival. The middle class, on the other hand, will survive only with deliberate preparation and practice for the time of stress.

The development of citizens' police groups to protect subdivisions and neighborhoods is likely. Security is already a major expense for American business. During the next ten years it will surely increase in an attempt to protect against increased robbery attempts and crimes of vengeance or simple hostility. This latter category will be the characteristic crime in the war of the haves and the have-nots. Racial and class hatred will continue to become more pronounced during this time.

The subterranean economy will become significant as more people do business and never report it or swap products between themselves with no money changing hands and no resulting tax records. This will be a time when individual initiative and ingenuity will once again be rewarded in America—not with wealth but with survival.

During this period it is likely that churches will become very introverted. Religion will offer solace for the righteous, but will tend to ignore the "heathen"—which will mean everyone else. True believers will find unity and brotherhood in their abhorrence of the wicked who are responsible for this calamity. When any group wants to deny responsibility for mistakes, there is always a convenient scapegoat. Familiar sermon themes will be "God Helps Those Who Help Themselves" and "If A Man Won't Work, Neither Let Him Eat." The rise of the Moral Majority is frightening to many observers who worry about the group's tendency to see people who don't share their views as enemies.

The mood of the times will make the country susceptible to a popular takeover by a demagogue who appeals to the popular paranoia and offers a simplistic solution to the nation's plight. I fear that Hitler's rise to power on the frustration of people racked by runaway inflation will be a tempting model. A charismatic leader will have a unique opportunity to rise on the political front of the country as popular opinion is drawn to anybody who can optimistically, enthusiastically, and authoritatively present a way out, even at the surrender of some previously treasured civil rights and national values.

During this period, people who live on farms will be in the best shape of all. This will not be equally true for people who live *near* farms, as many commuters do today. They will be isolated from the place of earning and yet unprepared to create a self-sustaining farm on their half acre with split-level home and pool.

Farms will rise in value but not price, for a couple of

obvious reasons. They have food that will be in demand. But, more important, farm life tends to imbue its people with a greater degree of self-sufficiency. Small towns, with their closer social ties and more conservative values, will see less suffering than the major urban areas, which are so totally dependent on public services.

Some manufacturing and service businesses will do surprisingly well even though there is limited money around. Luxury merchants who prospered during the hyper-inflation will fold, but those providing basic services will prosper. Individuals with skills will do well. Diplomas and certificates that *say* you have skills will be as worthless as paper dollars unless the pieces of paper have solid backing. Survival may depend on real and required abilities that are useful enough that people will value them more than their limited financial resources.

Many of my former colleagues in academia will find that idyllic university towns are not suitable locations for riding out the storm. Since most of the jobs in these towns are oriented around a university that may close (and certainly cut its staff to the bare bones), it will be hard to make ends meet unless the town has more seed stores than pizza parlors.

Overall, the surest place to be in the midterm crisis is on a farm where there are self-sufficient people with plenty of preparation and substantial practice at keeping wishes in line with means.

## THE LONG TERM: THE DAWN OF A NEW ERA

Just as gold or iron ore is made more valuable by a fiery refining process, human beings are also able to grow as a result of suffering. Many psychologists feel that there is little emotional growth without pain. If this is true, as I believe it is, this period of refining will strengthen our national character and provide hope for the future.

While it is doubtful that the United States will ever again have the degree of world dominance it knew during the 1950s, there is hope there will be an even greater nation. As the country works through its problems and some of our individual expectations are scaled down, we can anticipate a repudiation of national debts and a start over again with at least a modified gold standard.

People eventually find themselves returning to an old-time morality with the pace being slower, simpler virtues being emphasized, greater respect for nature, and more reliance and trust in the free market system rather than a naive trust in the power of government to solve our individual or collective problems.

This does not imply that there will be a return of life as it existed around the turn of the century. Technology will still be with us. Computer and laser technology will eliminate much of the repetitive nature of manufacturing activities. New forms of energy will be utilized that are less damaging to the environment. I anticipate that solar energy will be even more widely used than is currently anticipated.

We will emerge from the crisis holding fast to the idea that reward should be directly related to how much a person is willing to contribute—not what their educational credentials are or what status symbols they possess. While there will be compassion for those who are unable to work, there will be much less sympathy for people who choose not to contribute to society. Because of the thorny problems of how to deal with the innocent children of irresponsible parents, I believe that society will conclude that parenthood is not an inalienable right and consequently there will be many more cases where parental rights are terminated in order to break the cycle of dependency. Punishment for crimes will seem more severe compared to current standards. We will, I hope, have learned a lesson that there is an immutable law that people must reap what they sow.

There will be less emphasis on growth. We will be more content with smaller cars, smaller houses, and fewer status symbols that serve no purpose but to merely demonstrate wealth. Skills will be respected more than useless knowledge. In the words of John Gardner: "A country which respects a poor philosopher more than a fine plumber is in trouble. Neither their ideas nor their pipes will hold water!"

In this period of time we will move toward an emphasis on the *complete* individual versus the *specialized* person. A person who is able to take care of his problems—whether it be a leaky faucet or a faulty relationship—will know prosperity, peace of mind, and respect of peers.

Sex roles will be far less pronounced than they have been in the past. Household tasks and contributing to the economic well-being of the family will be shared by all family members. The family itself will be forced back to old-time closeness by the common survival needs of its members and memories of the past.

Although the last chapter in this book will emphasize our ability to *make* the future a positive thing, I am basically optimistic about the long-term prospect. There will be a great deal of suffering in the short- and mid-terms for people who are not prepared—and a great deal of painful readjustment is going to be necessary to get the nation's economic ecology in balance again. A certain amount of suffering will be healthy, but you and I won't be stricken by the worst of it if we plan ahead.

In the late 1990s and the early part of the next century, life will not be as rosy as it was in the happy days of the 1950s or even the '60s. The average standard of living will not be as high and few people will have the luxury of naive optimism as in the recent past. We will still be plagued by climatic problems, but there *is* light at the end of the tunnel we are going through. Whether or not you and I make it into the light will be determined by our wisdom as well as the way those around us react to the trauma of the times. The sad events that have been described in this chapter are the specifics of the "abominations and desolations" suggested in Chapter 2.

On the international level, there will be a massive number of people who will die of starvation and exposure. The big question in the long term is how we are going to fare with the world's suffering. There may be events over which we have no control. There may be power plays that make it impossible for us to go back to this period of tranquility. The Soviet Union, because of its vast store of natural resources, extensive space, and military power, may emerge as an even more significant world power than it is today. A lot will depend on how aggressive its tendencies are and whether or not we are able to develop a position of strength while fighting off the monster of inflation.

It is likely that as we rise from the ashes of economic collapse, we will seek a position of strength based on soundness and wealth and integrity rather than the "might makes right" philosophy that seems to have motivated us during the early days of the Cold War.

## Section Two

---

# HOW TO ACHIEVE PROSPERITY AMID POVERTY

# CHAPTER 5

# WHAT WILL HAPPEN TO YOUR TRADITIONAL INVESTMENTS?

The fact that you are reading this book indicates that you are one of the minority of thinking people who can see through the disastrous impact of tradition on day-to-day activities. Without becoming a jaundiced cynic, you've learned to carefully evaluate the enthusiastic investment recommendations that you regularly receive. It never hurts to ask a few extra questions or to seek the undisclosed bias that influences the person making a recommendation. Have you ever wondered why your stockbroker almost always says your portfolio needs more stocks or bonds? Has he or she ever recommended that you buy a "no-load" mutual fund? An insurance agent may do a computerized analysis of your financial situation, but almost inevitably will conclude you could use a little more whole life insurance—not term insurance, but the more expensive, more commisionable whole life policies.

Even some of the excellent advice given by such astute advisors as Harry Browne and Howard Ruff tend to reflect their own individual backgrounds. For many years Harry Browne was affiliated with Economic Research Counselors and was involved in setting up Swiss bank accounts for persons who resided on the West Coast. Similarly, Howard Ruff's emphasis on the possibilities of famine in this country is somewhat influenced by his years as a nutritional counselor representing Neo-Life, one of the nation's largest food storage companies and his role in setting up Reliance Products Company.

One of the major advantages of this book is the relative degree of objectivity which it provides. As a professor and consultant, I had to evaluate a vast amount of material relating to each of the subjects discussed in this book in order to make recommendations to students and clients. Nevertheless, I have never received income from any of the investment media that are being discussed.

To be perfectly fair, I need to point out that a person who has spent several years representing a particular investment media is much more likely to know the intricate details of that particular concept than I am. In writing this section of the book, I have attempted to steer a middle course, assuming that the reader is neither a completely uninformed oaf nor a super-sophisticated multimillionaire. I will not take time to explain the difference between common stocks and preferred stocks, since I assume that anyone who is willing to invest in a book like this is already sophisticated enough to make some good decisions concerning his or her financial objectives. And since the book is aimed at a wide audience, I don't intend to explain the difference between puts and calls, selling short, and straddling an investment. There are a number of excellent specialized books and consultants who are willing to provide this type of assistance. My feeling is that if you wish to use some esoteric investment technique, you will be better off talking to a professional in that area. This book is designed to give you some general guidelines—some principles that will help a person with above-average intelligence plot a practical course during the coming period of financial disorder and uncertainty.

Traditions are a valuable part of our society. They give stability and the ability to remember lessons learned by our predecessors. Any tradition, however, is cursed for those who accept it blindly. Traditions can help you if you accept their wisdom while questioning their assumptions and applications. They can destroy you personally and financially if you swallow them indiscriminately.

In this chapter I will review the traditional means of investing. I will discuss the likely impact of chaos in the financial markets on the standbys like banks, bonds, and the bull market. I will also ask you to consider the likely results of devaluation and other natural disasters.

Most investors seek absolutes when looking for an investment philosophy. If this is your goal, you'll find plenty of books and advisers who will tell you the one best way. Doubtless you've heard people say, "Bank accounts are insured, they're solid as the United States"; or "The stock market reflects the health of the nation"; or "Treasury bills are as safe as the federal government." Frankly, none of those clichés is particularly reassuring to me. Even in the best of times, such absolute statements lead to narrow-mindedness, inflexibility, and inability to learn. In these troubled times such clichés will almost certainly lead to financial ruin.

If you're assuming that this chapter will tell you specifically how much to invest and where, you're looking for the impossible. There are people who will be willing to give you the certain answers you seek. But I am writing to people I hope will be my friends after we have worked through the problems of the next decade or so. My conscience requires me to give up any hope of simplistic formulas for financial success. Even if I were willing to dole out simplistic answers, they could hardly be expected to be trustworthy, as each case has its constellation of specific circumstances. The key to financial success or failure requires the proper understanding of your resources, goals, and temperament. This chapter will be full of principles and concepts that can enhance your ability to evaluate investment options. But ultimately, your challenge will be to filter out all that you've learned through your own intellect and judgment, then weigh the apparent consequences against your gut-level feeling for what is best for you.

You'll never get where you want to go by blindly putting all your eggs in the most highly touted basket. You cannot follow any one adviser's counsel to the exclusion of all others, your own common sense, or your emotional evaluation of the situation under consideration. I will attempt to share with you my experience and insight concerning several major investment media. I'll even provide some guidelines for various sizes of investment portfolios and timetables to keep in mind. But you

are the star of the show when it comes to planning and
determining your investment future. When you think
about it, would you really want it any other way?

## FRUIT JARS AND BANKS

You would probably be surprised if you could know the
number of people who have buried money in their back-
yards, packed it away in fruit jars, or hidden it in mat-
tresses. The *Wall Street Journal* has carried front-page
articles on the so-called "subterranean economy," which,
as the name implies, is that part of our nation's economic
activity that cannot be seen. Estimates put the value of
the underground economy at about $1 trillion in 1985.

A significant portion of that economy is devoted to
illegal use. According to Peter Gutmann, an economics
professor at City University of New York, this currency
also "lubricates a vast amount of non-reported income
and non-reported work." In all probability, continued
inflation, high taxes, and pervasive government regulations will guarantee the continuing growth of this component. Additionally, large numbers of people are simply
hiding away currency because they do not trust banks. In
some instances, they do not trust the banks to protect
their income. In other cases, it is because they do not
trust the banks to keep their possessions secret from the
government.

The traditional middle-class response to stories about
misers and pack rats is that these people are leftovers
from the Great Depression and simply don't know any
better. It is generally assumed that if you have any money
at all above your immediate needs, it ought to at least be
in a savings account where it can be safe and earning a
little interest. Perhaps this is true if you are talking about
the $156 in the PTA's checking account. However, the
bank is one of the poorest locations for any sizable amount
of money that is supposed to be working or even safe.

An important distinction that is seldom made by investment advisors is that some savings are mainly needed
to provide emergency backup while others are thought of

as investments. Banks and other savings institutions are probably the best ways to store dollars that must be kept liquid and ready to jump into service in the very near future. But if the money is considered to be *earning* investment—one that is made up of dollars that are not critical to week-to-week survival—then the savings account ranks at the bottom of the list of places to put your money. Banks are probably currently a safe place to deposit money that you are going to need in the short-term future. As I will point out, however, you need to be alert to signals which will indicate that it is time to take anything you have out of the banks.

Those who defend banks and savings and loan institutions like to point to the fact their deposits are "fully insured." The letters F.D.I.C. and F.S.L.I.C. are featured in every commercial or savings account book because people feel at ease knowing that the government's Federal Deposit Insurance Corporation and the Federal Savings and Loan Insurance Corporation guarantee up to $40,000 of the account. By putting multiple accounts in the names of various family members, you can have a large amount of your savings insured in this manner. Once a person is infected with the Federal Insurance idea, he or she can glibly respond to any subsequent mention of a high-return investment by saying, "I know there are places where I can earn more, but I need to know that my money is safe. I'd rather have my sure five percent than some pie-in-the-sky fourteen percent on a less secure deal."

Unfortunately, the savings accounts are not as securely guaranteed as you have been led to think. In 1986 the total transaction value of banks was twenty-four times greater than the amount of reserves banks had on deposit with the Federal Reserve. More and more borrowing is taking place beyond the reach of the safety net provided by the Fed. Also, the globalization of the banking system is bringing new participants with unknown reliability. Since banks must settle their accounts daily, the failure of even one of them to pay up could cause a chain reaction.

The best strategy, of course, is to have your savings in one of the first banks to go under. For obvious public-relations reasons, FDIC is going to be on the spot in a hurry doing everything possible to inspire public confidence by paying back dollar for dollar. But FDIC cannot survive many bank failures in a row. I can assure you that their broad smile of confidence when a large bank fails masks the private knowledge that the amount they are paying out represents a very large percentage of their total insurance fund.

Obviously, it is just in jest that I recommend finding the next bank to go. You should use banks for the things they can do well for you but not be tied to them by traditions. It is highly unlikely that when things start to collapse, the banks will go out in one united flash rather than one by one according to strength. Few people realize it but the nation's banking system is dominated by no more than fifteen banking groups, most of them controlled by giant holding companies. Though that may seem strange to you, stop and think where *your* bank gets its loans. The pinnacle of the pyramid is in New York City, and the domino effect is all set for one spectacular chain reaction. The chairman of the Senate Banking Committee has admitted, "A relatively limited economic setback could result in the failure of some of the nation's largest banks."

Not only are the banks interlocked to pull each other down, they are not even individually sound. They are in fact made out of money that does not exist—not just living on borrowed money but living on non-existent money. Suppose you're the bank; I'll give you a $1,000 deposit. You turn around and loan out $750 to someone. How much is your bank worth? $1,000? Not the way bankers see it. You have $1,000 in deposit and $750 in outstanding loans. That's $1,750! Maybe you can even borrow additional funds on the strength of the numbers. Our banking system is sophisticated, but it is still involved in this same kind of exercise—creating money on paper and even loaning out the blank spaces between the lines of figures in their ledgers. And this practice doesn't scare me as much as the shaky loans that have been made to U.S. real estate speculators, almost defunct municipalities, and questionable foreign operations.

Even if banks were as strong as we have always been told, they are lousy places to get a return on your money. Anytime the rate of inflation in the economy is greater than the interest you are earning, you can be sure that the end result is a loss for you. Your savings passbook will *say* you have more dollars, but the purchasing power of the total will be less than the purchasing power of the money you originally deposited.

Banks can help you. The cash you stash in the fruit jar may even have its appropriate place in your financial plan. Banks are valuable in the day-to-day handling of money and rainy day savings for emergency use. If you wish to put money in a fruit jar, remember that currency draws no interest and will lose value daily. While I would recommend something more secure than a fruit jar, be sure that any money you squirrel away is "real money," that it has some gold and silver content. More about that subject, however, in the next chapter.

In summary, you should neither trust banks implicitly nor distrust them altogether. Keep close to your bank until danger signs (such as a few bank failures or the default of a couple of cities on their bond obligations) tell you that you should be losing interest in them. Use them for your day-to-day dealings, but look elsewhere for a place to develop your money's greatest earning power.

## THE STOCK MARKET

The first thing to remember about the stock market is that you are competing with some of the most intelligent and sophisticated money managers in the world. Pension funds, insurance companies, and trust departments of banks account for a majority of the trades made each day. These funds are managed by teams of full-time professionals who follow every piece of financial news, often monitored by sophisticated computer systems, to anticipate the impact of any news event upon the perfor-

mance of various stocks. In other words, it's awfully hard
for the average dabbler to outperform the market—or
the funds.

One popular method of being in the stock market
without competing with the professionals is to work with
the professionals via mutual funds. By pooling your
funds with many other investors, you can hire experienced professionals to buy and sell a large, diversified
portfolio of stocks and bonds. You can even choose
funds which reflect your particular investment philosophy. There are funds that emphasize income and those
that emphasize capital growth; funds that stress old-line,
blue-chip firms; and funds that concentrate on relatively
unknown over-the-counter stocks. You pay your money
and take your choice.

At face value, mutual funds seem to have a great deal
going for them. There is the security of being in a large
group, the security of a professional investment team,
and the security of a diversified placement of money. It
must be remembered, however, that no mutual funds
have consistently outperformed the market. There have
been many short-term managers who have provided dramatic returns to their investors. When you put them all
together, they tend to move in the general direction of
the overall market.

If you want to be in the market but have neither the
time, patience, or confidence to play the role of the
swashbuckling risk-taker, mutual funds may be for you.
If you want to give your money the no-holds-barred
potential to hit the sky or drag the bottom, invest in one
or two stocks at a time. Somewhere in all the literature
about the stock market, someone needs to admit that
one of the factors which encourage people to participate
in this gigantic crap roll is that it is exciting fun. You
really don't have to go to Las Vegas or Atlantic City to
gamble. Moreover, you can gain the added dignity of
being a member of an exclusive club with a dramatic
history. The fact remains that there is a bit of the dreamer
in each of us. Everyone wants to strike it rich.

To admit that the stock market can be fun is not to

exalt it or condemn it. My purpose is merely to provide better perspective. The funds invested in the market should be discretionary funds. The market is the last place for money which you and your family may need in an emergency.

If a person has any significant assets (a minimum of $50,000 to invest), he or she might be wise to have a portion in the stock market, particularly in small, local companies that have a potential for growth. Rather than going by the sound of a corporate name or the national advisement services, the sage stock trader will look to small companies that he or she knows something about. Ideally, you can find a regional company that is in some field that is likely to do well during the period of a faltering economy. For example, certain companies in agriculture and energy are going to have good prospects even when the nation's consumers begin to tighten their belts. These types of "basic human needs" stocks are the surest bets. And the more basic the company is, the more potential they have. In other words, I'm not as optimistic about the long-term future of the nutritionless convenience food companies as I am about companies that are involved in planting and harvesting real food.

By emphasizing regional companies, the small investor has a chance of being at least as knowledgeable as some of the competition he faces. One of the few individuals I know who has been consistently successful in the stock market uses the following rules as a guide:

1. Emphasize companies you know something about.
2. Choose companies that perform or deliver a worthwhile product or service.
3. Watch for young companies that have a record of growth (or evidence that they are making a dramatic turnaround).
4. Prefer stocks priced under $25 per share. (It is easier for low-priced stocks to double than for high-priced stocks.)

5. Divestment is as important as investment. (Don't expect a stock to double in value every year. Sell when you've earned a reasonable return. Don't be greedy.)

David Rhoads estimates that 65 percent of an investor's profit comes from being on the right side of the market moves and 25 percent of his potential comes from picking the right industry. You should still remember that each stock reflects the fortunes of an individual operation, and in all cases anticipation is the key to market success. While you hope that your stocks will outperform the market, it is an unusual company whose stock moves in opposition to the market.

If you try to stay up with the stock market, don't make the mistake of using the Dow Jones Industrial Index. This is the most widely quoted index. Yet it is based on only thirty old-line, blue-chip stocks that most of my readers will not be interested in. For overall assessment of the market, the New York Stock Exchange Composite is a much better reading. If your portfolio emphasizes stocks that are traded over the counter, the NASDAQ OTC Composite is a better index. Since the Dow Jones Company publishes the *Wall Street Journal*, you would expect the Dow Jones Average to receive special attention. Yet the next-to-the-last page of each *Journal* contains several indexes which are much better suited to monitoring the activities of your portfolio.

### Consider Your Taxes

For most people it is important to consider the advantages of tax-free municipal bonds for your short-term portfolio. These bonds, which are promissory notes offered by various municipal agencies, pay a return that is not subject to federal or state income taxes. The higher your tax bracket, the more this feature can mean to you in April.

Unfortunately, municipal bonds are no longer the conservative domain of widows and orphans who wish to commit their money for long-term periods of time without worry or concern. The financial solvency of large cities is certainly suspect. As with many other investments, pick your choices with care. If you prefer to let someone else evaluate municipals for you, there are several municipal bond funds that provide regular tax-free income. There is a ready market for units of these funds should you decide to sell, but you may have to accept a slight loss in your capital.

## YOUR INSURANCE INVESTMENTS

Even if you don't own stock in Prudential or Metropolitan Life, you probably have a significant portion of your investment funds tied up in insurance. But what most people don't understand is that a major part of the premium for ordinary life insurance is an incredibly poor investment. The old argument that insurance is a good way to force you to put aside for a rainy day is totally fallacious for anyone with the good sense and discipline to read this book. To meet family needs for a young wage earner, there is no question that term insurance is by far the best alternative. Young people who need an insurance agent to force them to put some money aside for investment deserve the 3 to 4 percent return they receive.

Since not many people like the idea of sickly 3 or 4 percent return, this fact is not highly publicized by insurance agents. There is a simple solution, but it requires a measure of self-discipline. Instead of buying an ordinary life policy, buy the same amount of term insurance. Find out the difference in the two premiums and then invest the difference as regularly as you would have paid the insurance company.

Consider, for example, the case of a thirty-five-year-old male (the rates are the same for a forty-year-old female because of her higher life expectancy) who needs $100,000 of protection until his two children are grown. Using 1987 rates of one large company, he can spend $313 per year for a twenty-year term insurance policy, or $1,737 per year for a whole life insurance policy. If the individual's protection needs end at the conclusion of 20 years, he will have a cash value of approximately $29,580 in his ordinary insurance policy. On the other hand, if he takes the difference between the premiums and invests it—yield 12 percent—at the end of twenty years, his nest egg will be worth more than $100,000.

Another factor to consider when taking out insurance for protection needs is a cost-of-living adjustment. For example, some policies give you an option each year to purchase additional insurance that will keep your coverage comparable to the amount you had when you bought the original policy. For example, a major insurer recently provided a policy holder with a notice about his term insurance which read, "For the year beginning May 1, 1986, you have $22,785 as the contractual amount of insurance under this policy. During the period used to measure cost of living changes for this policy, the Consumer Price Index increased by 123.30 percent, making $28,105 of insurance available to you for the coming year in addition to the contractual amount. The year's premium for this additional insurance is shown above."

If your objective is to provide liquidity for your estate, an important way to gain maximum advantage is through *minimum deposit insurance*. Under this arrangement you take a whole life policy because you want it to last for all your life, not just a specified term. If you pay the full premium in four of the first seven years of the policy, you can in the other years borrow against the cash value of the policy to pay the premiums each year. This has three valuable results. First, the rate of interest is very low for this loan, and the interest is tax-deductible. The premium is fixed so you always pay back with inflated dollars, which makes the cost less than it would appear. Finally, the overall cash outlay is quite low. For a $100,000 policy the average annual net outlay will be approximately $400 per year (see Table 5.1). This is still not quite as good a buy as term insurance.

A relatively new concept that puts the emphasis on the wishes of intelligent buyers rather than the persuasiveness of the agent is called "agentless" insurance. A few

TABLE 5.1

EXAMPLE OF MINIMUM DEPOSIT LIFE INSURANCE
Age 35 Male Face Amount    $97209.00
BASIC PREMIUM    $2120.38

WHOLE LIFE POLICY

| YEAR | NET ANNUAL PREMIUM* | LOAN INTEREST* 6 PER CENT | PAID BY LOAN* | ANNUAL CASH OUTLAY* | NET ANNUAL CASH OUTLAY* | CUMULATIVE LOAN* | GUARANTEED CASH VALUE | NET DEATH BENEFIT* |
|---|---|---|---|---|---|---|---|---|
| 1 | 2121 | 0 | 731 | 1390 | 1390 | 731 | 778 | 96478 |
| 2 | 2121 | 44 | 1553 | 612 | 590 | 2284 | 2430 | 94925 |
| 3 | 1969 | 137 | 1645 | 461 | 392 | 3929 | 4180 | 97460 |
| 4 | 1915 | 236 | 0 | 2151 | 2033 | 3929 | 5930 | 99210 |
| 5 | 1862 | 236 | 0 | 2098 | 1980 | 3929 | 7680 | 100960 |
| 6 | 1810 | 236 | 0 | 2046 | 1928 | 3929 | 9526 | 102806 |
| 7 | 1756 | 236 | 0 | 1992 | 1874 | 3929 | 11276 | 104556 |
| 8 | 1706 | 236 | 8406 | 6464CR | 6532CR | 12335 | 13123 | 97997 |
| 9 | 1655 | 740 | 1736 | 659 | 289 | 14071 | 14970 | 98108 |
| 10 | 1605 | 844 | 1736 | 713 | 291 | 15807 | 16817 | 98219 |
| 11 | 1561 | 948 | 1645 | 864 | 390 | 17452 | 18567 | 98324 |
| 12 | 1516 | 1047 | 1737 | 826 | 302 | 19189 | 20414 | 98434 |
| 13 | 1473 | 1151 | 1645 | 979 | 403 | 20834 | 22164 | 98539 |
| 14 | 1432 | 1250 | 1736 | 946 | 321 | 22570 | 24011 | 98650 |
| 15 | 1393 | 1354 | 1644 | 1103 | 426 | 24214 | 25760 | 98755 |
| 16 | 1358 | 1453 | 1736 | 1075 | 348 | 25950 | 27607 | 98866 |
| 17 | 1326 | 1557 | 1736 | 1147 | 368 | 27686 | 29454 | 98977 |
| 18 | 1298 | 1661 | 1736 | 1223 | 392 | 29422 | 31301 | 99088 |
| 19 | 1275 | 1765 | 1737 | 1303 | 420 | 31159 | 33148 | 99198 |
| 20 | 1256 | 1870 | 1736 | 1390 | 455 | 32895 | 34995 | 99309 |

SUMMARY TO AGE 55

NET SURRENDER VALUE AT 53    1365*

| YEARS | AVERAGE ANNUAL GROSS OUTLAY | AVERAGE ANNUAL NET OUTLAY 50% TAX BRACKET | ANNUAL SURRENDER NET COST 50% TAX BRACKET |
|---|---|---|---|
| 1– 5 | 1342 | 1277 | 482 |
| 1–10 | 565 | 418 | 300 |
| 1–15 | 691 | 401 | 284 |

companies have developed very low-cost programs that allow you to choose exactly how much and what type of coverage you want. A forty-year-old nonsmoker would pay $151 per year for a $100,000 policy. You complete a simple application, someone comes to your house or office to collect basic medical information, and you need never talk with an employee of the insurance company. You pay only for insurance, not for sales commissions, massive advertising, or bad investments.

## THE GOOD EARTH

There is probably no area of investment that is more victimized by the traditional clichés than real estate. You have heard the old saws that "God has quit making land but he's still making people" and "real estate prices always bounce back eventually."

These little ditties sound good, but there are plenty of examples of ways they have been proven wrong recently. The U.S. population has hovered near the zero-growth level since 1973.

Land prices which have suffered after a particular speculative wave may come back up in the long run, but as economist Maynard Keynes once said, "in the long run we are all dead." There are a startling number of locations in urban centers where demographic shifts have left property owners with holdings that were useless for the production of income or capital gains. Most major cities have areas that have been literally abandoned by owners rather than paying the taxes that already exceed the earning power of their property. The number of these urban wastelands will certainly increase during the next decade.

Studying migration trends can be helpful. At the present time, it appears that people are moving away from the large cities. The Conference Board, a New York-based business and economic research organization, predicted that the metropolitan areas with populations above 2 million will continue to decline rather than experiencing the growth of smaller cities. Conversely, they suggest that cities with populations between 100,000 and 2 million will experience considerable growth. Personally, I would prefer to risk my money (and life) in cities that are closer to the 100,000 level—particularly if these are in the so-called Sun Belt. It's not merely that the weather is better in these locations, they're going to be safer and have lower energy costs. Consequently, jobs and business opportunities are more likely to be found in these situations and along with them a demand for housing and office space.

For many people their home is the largest single investment they ever make. While I believe it is a mistake to view a house as an investment, certain real estate principles need to be considered in making this purchase. Many individuals make the tragic mistake of computing their net worth based on the appreciated value of their house. This has the intoxicating effect of making them appear to be much better off than they really are. As things now stand, you might be able to sell your house for a substantial profit. But what would you do about another place to live? Chances are you would buy an even more expensive house in order to move up the materialistic ladder. Once we are faced with a massive deflation, that overpriced house will offer only shelter as a major advantage and little hope for further capital gains. Already the average price of homes has declined from the heights reached in September 1987.

Consequently, you should choose a house based on your plans to live in it. I would further recommend that you not buy the largest or most expensive house you can afford. Large houses cost a great deal to maintain today. But maintenance is going to be a major problem throughout the future. Repairs and upkeep, as well as energy, make a big house a questionable investment, unless you have a big family. The place you live in is a necessity, not an investment.

What then about real estate as an investment if you have funds beyond those that are required to provide lodging? Here we're talking about income-producing real estate and property held for potential appreciation. Like every other investment, your success in making these investments depends upon your ability to assess the changing situations and time your commitments correctly. If you already own rental units in locations that are safe for the long term, you would be well advised to hold onto them. I wouldn't recommend shopping for a new acquisition, however, because it will be very difficult for you to get a long-term return if, as I anticipate, the long-term prospects for housing include continued declines. If your rental units are in a location that you think might be shaky for the long term, start looking for a buyer who is less realistic about the long-term economic future of this country.

As far as I'm concerned, the bloom is off the rose as far as holding raw land for appreciation. *Business Week* has reported that farm prices have been declining in certain parts of the Mid-west. In Kansas, for example, irrigated farmland that had reached a peak value of $1,200 an acre is being offered for $600 to $700 an acre. As a general rule, it's a good time to start unloading some of your nonliquid investments. Prices will probably go a little bit higher during the next couple or three years, but it's better to be a year early than a day too late. If you are able to convert your money into gold or silver that will continue to appreciate with inflation, you'll find yourself in an enviable situation when real estate prices hit the bottom—probably in another two to three years.

Incidentally, if you happen to have some basic carpentry and plumbing skills, buying distressed properties will continue to be a wise move during depression times. Find a property that has been on the market for a while and needs repairs, make a very low down payment, and quickly spruce up the property, keeping the improvements primarily cosmetic and noticeable to prospective tenants. Don't redecorate to your own tastes, but to the standards of comparable units in the surrounding neighborhoods.

Since you've put a small amount of money into the property, you can allow the rent to make the payment, support the upkeep on the property, and pay your increased taxes. And since you can depreciate the house as a business expense, this will provide a limited tax shelter. Most of the innumerable books on how to make big money in real estate suggests this approach with the profit from each transaction becoming the down payment for the next, larger investment. If this has been your plan during the past, the next few years will be a good period for you to take a brief rest from your labors so that you can start over when prices are lower and prospects are brighter.

In facing our cloudy future, debts pose a complex dilemma. With the prospect of renewed inflation during the next few years, there is an incentive to borrow as much as possible and to pay back the obligation in cheaper dollars. If your income doubles, it would appear to be relatively easy to pay off a debt that may have been almost too much for you to handle at the time it was made. If, however, the cost of food, services, and energy have tripled in that time period, paying off the debt may be even more difficult in the future than it is at present.

The other major problem with debt is what will happen when inflation tops out and is followed by the almost inevitable deflation or depression. With an ordinary home mortgage, all of the buyer's assets are pledged as security against that debt. If the borrower is fired from work and defaults on the house payment, the lender can foreclose on the mortgage. If the proceeds aren't enough to discharge the obligation, the mortage holder can get a deficiency judgment and take other of the homeowner's assets. This feature is typical in most debt agreements. Be wary lest all your possessions be subject to seizure for the satisfaction of any debt that may default. Unless you carefully read your loan agreement, you may not be able to simply let the bank or finance company take back the item that you borrowed against. It is quite possible that your income and the value of your investments will be declining while the prices for services, food, and energy will be increasing.

Have your attorney check all of your loan agreements to see what options are open to your creditors in the event you are unable to make any of the payments. Then work with him to restructure your debts so that you can protect yourself as much as possible. On future obligations, be sure that you have limited your liability to the property under consideration. This may be done with a sales contract, a purchase money mortgage, or a clause specifically inserted in the loan agreement which identifies the limit of your liability. A sales contract merely says that the title stays with the seller until he has finished paying for the property. You can resell the property under certain conditions, but if you are unable to make future payments, you simply return the property back to the original owner. You lose your down payment and whatever else you have paid toward the mortgage, but your other assets are protected.

A purchase money mortgage is a loan that is made by the seller of the property. Instead of using a third party such as a bank or savings or loan association, you may be able to persuade the seller of the property to make a loan directly to you. In this instance, the seller is protected because of your down payment and the inherent value of the property. Even if the seller still owes money on the property, you may be able to make a down payment that will cover his indebtedness. Then the only debt you will owe is to the seller. In other instances, you may be able to "assume" the mortgage. Frequently, under this arrangement, you will be able to limit your liability to the property itself. If, for example, you assume a VA "guaranteed loan," the individual you bought the property from still maintains a degree of liability. This means you should be extremely careful if you happen to have obtained a government guaranteed loan and wish to sell the property to someone else.

If you are able to obtain the services of an attorney who will work with you to protect your finances in the event of economic distress, his fees will be a worthwhile investment. If an attorney, no matter how prestigious the firm, tries to tell you that you don't need to worry about things like this, look around for somebody who's willing to work for you. The best attorney is the can-do type who will work things out for you, rather than telling you all the things that are impossible. You may want to look for a one-armed lawyer who isn't always saying "on the other hand . . ."

## CHAPTER 6

# BEST BETS
# FOR YOUR MONEY

The basic dilemma confronting each investor is the trade-off between risk and return. Every investment in an uncertain world involves risk. Generally speaking, we expect our return to increase in relationship to degree of risk. This simplistic formula assumes that an investor can anticipate the returns from a particular investment and accurately estimate the risk involved. There is also the assumption that the wise investor knows to put the right kind of money into an appropriate investment. He or she never puts grocery money into long-term or highly speculative investments. Neither is it prudent to keep stashing money in a low-yield investment when safety is not the primary consideration.

Every investor must recognize that the basic principles which existed ten or twenty years ago are no longer valid today. If circumstances are substantially different today than when you first learned your investment principles, you need to reevaluate your principles and the premises on which they are based.

An awareness of the concurrent economic crisis and the impending collapse can provide you with a keenly focused sense of perception that all investors should strive for. More than ever before, you should be exactly sure *which money* is going into a particular investment and what return you expect that investment to generate for how long a period of time.

While this single-mindedness will add strength to your pursuit of specific goals, it will also mean that you must have the courage to move contrary to traditional investment philosophies. For example, you may put retirement funds into gold certificates rather than the common stock of blue-chip companies. Or you may pay record high prices for diamonds even though you are not particularly interested in jewelry.

On application of the new perspective suggested by this book you can expect some scorn from some of the experienced professionals in the investment field. Unfortunately, their experience will have been gained in the wrong era to assess the performance of the emerging economy. Even more difficult for you to handle will be the difficulty in shaking free of the investment instinct which you evolved when growing up in a prosperous America.

In many ways the self-discipline required to cope with the challenge to your commitment will be a preview of the type of determination that will be required for long-range survival. Living through the actual depression will be much easier for people who have had the determination and stamina to survive the trauma of preparation. In an athletic contest, a great deal of attention may be directed to a final free throw or extra point attempt. In reality, those crucial plays are no more important than all of the previous plays that led up to the final climactic moment. Similarly, the final stage of your survival plan may involve a dramatic move to a survival retreat or some other highly significant activity. Still, your game plan leading up to that final moment is just as important as the grand finale. As you move toward that critical moment, expect considerable conflict between your long-range strategy and objectives and your short-term instincts. The difference between you and other investors will be that they expect the future to follow in the footsteps of the past. The timid souls who choose to run with the herd fail to see that circumstances have rendered time-tested clichés invalid and dangerous. The old principles are quickly becoming clichés. Can you remember when people used to say that something was "sound as a dollar"?

The national outlook would not be so frightening if we merely had to worry about the gradual shift of our national fortunes. Even though inflation is a demoralizing, debilitating malady, economic strategy might help us cope with its impact for another decade or so. Predictable changes are much easier to handle than major surprises. In assessing the future, we need to be prepared for what Peter Drucker has called the major "discontinuities." In my opinion, these may be brought on by a widespread famine associated with severe climatic changes, earthquakes, or a major breakdown in the electrical system so that a heavily populated segment of the country is without power during a heavy winter blizzard. Rampant frustration and economic weakness resulting from chronic inflation combined with such a catalytic catastrophe will create changes that only the most prepared will be able to handle.

## OUR DEADLY ASSUMPTIONS

Most investment philosophy and most business disciplines, including economics and marketing, are based on the assumption that everybody will continue to experience higher standards of living indefinitely. Against all logic we expect to continue an unbroken stream of economic progress even when we see evidence that the progress has already ended. We assume that somehow there will be an availability of resources for investments and paying inflated bills for food, shelter, energy, and government. We also believe that there will be sufficient natural resources to meet this demand that a higher standard of living would create. In spite of previous shortages in several key areas, we plan for "progress" that would place even higher strains on our natural storehouses without paying an exorbitant price for this recklessness.

Another assumption is that we can predict and control the economy. We seem to think that our civilization is basically stable, and that the immediate future will dependably mirror the past. If the study of history teaches us anything, it shows that historical themes repeat themselves but *never* with dependable predictability.

As suggested previously, there is a common misconception that any changes that take place, will evolve gradually. This reminds me of the assumptions we make about being in an automobile accident *until we actually are in one*. You have probably watched those slow-motion movies of dummies being bounced around inside the test cars. Somehow the slow motion is deceptive and you can imagine having time to brace for such an impact and ride out the crash without injury. But when you are in your first real crash, you realize that it does not occur in slow motion. Indeed, it happens faster than your eyes and brain can register impressions. It's over before you know what hit you. Many victims never know they hit the dashboard—they merely begin to wonder first why there is suddenly blood on everything.

You can anticipate this type of shocked belief when you experience an economic crash. There will be no slow-motion documentary accounts before the fact, no last-minute chance to brace for the crash. Rather, you will wake up to discover that yesterday's rules no longer apply. The crash will have happened and left its victims injured before they have a chance to see it coming. As the collapse nears, the government will initiate a last-ditch media campaign of lying optimism in a final attempt to turn the tides. Our leaders at the FDIC will be telling us that first bank failures have been paid off in full. They will calm our fears with their confident news conferences on the very night before massive bank closures and the FDIC announcement of its own bankruptcy.

Don't waste time trying to explain your mistrust of the system to your stockbroker, insurance agent, or most business friends. The ones who will understand or even listen will be few. More likely they will lock arms and reassure themselves by unanimously denouncing your pessimism. They will hurry to remind you that the American system will "always find a way" and even profit in the development and marketing of the new ways. They may tell you that too much negative talk about the economy can become self-fulfilling and that you have a moral obligation to the country to express confidence in the system by staying in your traditional investments and letting this invincible system heal itself. Just save your breath. The majority of your friends are too afraid to see what is happening. They are unwilling to see that growth cannot possibly continue indefinitely and that the limits of growth are becoming apparent in almost every aspect of our society. A major readjustment is inevitable: there is going to be a realignment of the goods, services, and values in our world. You will never explain it to your friends, but if you have read this far in this book, you may have the kind of objectivity that allows you to see and prepare for history's most obvious surprise.

Despite the selective deafness of the majority, your major responsibility is to set your own house in order and prepare for the problems you see on the horizon. In this chapter we will discuss the investment approaches that are capable of preserving your wealth whether the system collapses or continues. You have everything to gain and nothing to lose by shifting into an inflation-resistant, crash-proof form of investing. This is as logical as it can be, but don't try to explain it more than once to people whose heads are stuck in the sands of foolish optimism.

### The Meaning of Money

Have you heard the story about three wealthy play-boys who were trying to impress a pretty blonde at a cocktail party? One lit her cigarette with a $50 bill. The second lit her cigarette with a $100 dollar bill. But the fellow who took her home was the one who lit her cigarette with his personal check for $1 million!

He knew (whether she did or not) that it was only paper that was worth nothing. Incidentally, there are about 200 million people in the United States who appear to be as gullible as the naive blonde in the story. Money only has value because of what it represents. Dollar bills began steadily losing their value when the United States quit letting each dollar bill represent a specified amount of gold that was kept on deposit in the U.S. Treasury. Without increasing the supply of gold, the government increased the number of dollars. Somehow public valuation of paper money always manages to adjust itself to stay in step with the true value of the paper. For example, the purchasing power of one work-day or hour is a valid yardstick that remains fairly constant no matter what somersaults paper money might take. It still takes the average worker approximately the same number of working hours to buy an ounce of gold as it took ten years ago even though the pay for that hour is expressed in much larger numerical terms.

Historically, money usually is relatively rare, has real value of its own, is easily carried, is widely accepted everywhere, and does not deteriorate. Money is most often not sought for itself but for the power it represents. You can exchange it for many specific things that you want.

Picture yourself as a shepherd in the old days before greenbacks. Someone visits your flock and wants one of your sheep. He offers to trade you an ivory zither for a sheep. Since you don't play the zither, you are reluctant to make the trade, but your visitor eventually convinces you that the zither is going to be quite usable to people so you let him have the sheep. When you go to town to purchase a new toga, the tailor tells you that he has no use for the sheep since he has given up making woolen togas. You try to convince him to trade you a double-breasted robe for the ivory zither. He finally agrees even though he doesn't play the zither and has no intention of learning to play. That zither has become *money* in this basic society. Though it has some value as an instrument, it is really just moving from person to person representing value—the value of a sheep, a toga, or whatever the tailor trades it for. Somewhere along the line, folks are going to get tired of carrying their zithers around. They will leave them with the local zither-keeper, who will give them a receipt on a piece of paper that can be redeemed for one zither. From this point, people can trade that piece of paper for one sheep or one toga. Major problems will begin, however, when the zither-keeper gives out more than one piece of paper for the same zither. Then, if the tailor is smart, he's going to require *two* zither notes for one toga. And you will expect *two* zither notes for one sheep. There is only a certain amount of value around. Calling it twice as valuable doesn't make it so. The value of any money is held in natural check by the real value of the thing it truly represents. If the zither-keeper keeps printing worthless receipts, people will eventually quit giving two hoots for them. Perhaps this foolish zither-keeper will help you understand why the U.S. dollar has lost so much ground on the international market.

### When Is Money Not Really Money?

In 1939 one dollar of U.S. currency could buy 2½ ounces of silver or 12 loaves of bread. In the almost fifty years that have passed since those "good old days," the quality of the dollar and the quality of the bread have both deteriorated. Today it takes about $17.00 to buy the same approximate amount of silver or bread (if you want bread with comparable quality without the empty calories or chemical additives that most of today's bread contains).

The conclusion is obvious. Compute your wealth in dollars and you will never know for sure how much you have and you'll never be able to predict your future wealth or what you will be able to buy in a few years. Silver or other "solid currency," on the other hand, remains an almost consistent monetary element—one which *gains* in relation to the dollars and *holds* in relation to the goods and services to be bought.

This illustration about silver, dollars, and a loaf of bread capsules the way in which silver, gold, and other hard currencies remain a solid way of providing protection. There are several currencies in the world today that have some direct relationship to gold. Of those the Swiss franc, while not having the highest degree of gold backing, is probably the most stable. For a beginning portfolio, some form of currency that has both gold backing and also is recognized as a medium of exchange is desirable. Later in this chapter some sample portfolios will be suggested, reflecting this component.

For anyone with additional assets, the investment commodity with *security* to equal its fame is gold.

## THE GOLDEN RULE

The use of ivory zithers as money somehow never got off the ground. But since 4000 B.C., mankind has been fascinated by the glimmer of gold. Gold has always had its own intrinsic value as a metal for fashioning things; its greatest appeal since the beginning of history has been that everybody *perceives* it as money.

Gold is virtually indestructible. If you have visited an exhibit featuring King Tut and his possessions, you will know that gold holds its beauty and rich appearance century after century without interference from moths, rust, or corrosion. Even though our nation has officially abandoned the gold standard, the phrase "good as gold" holds its impact long after the demise of "sound as a dollar." When large American banks saw their dollars shrinking, many of them began switching more of their assets to gold. And if you wonder where excess petrodollars go, you may be interested to know that the Arabs are the world's largest purchasers of gold today. Those who have the option of any of the investment avenues are, without exception, depending on gold as the sure thing to hold value through thin and thinner times. Gold has been called a "magic time machine" because it is the one commodity that can dependably transport wealth from the present, across uncharted chaos, and into the world of the future where economic waves have finally been calmed.

### Why the Fabled Appeal of Gold?

As a metal and as an investment, gold can do things that other metals can never do. It is one of the most malleable, permanent, and beautiful of metals. And despite the demand by dentists and the jewelers who are using it in record quantities, the supply is diminishing. The world no longer produces as much gold as it used to—the productivity peak was reached and passed a few years ago. The demand continues to grow yet there are no new gold fields being discovered or mined. The great majority comes from either South Africa (60 percent) or Russia (30 percent). Either of these countries could clamp down our gold supply completely should they decide this was to their political advantage. Our nation could be denied a supply of gold at any price. In this event, we could probably find suitable substitutes for the industrial and jewelry applications of gold but the international economic consequences would be frightening. We could find ourselves completely out in the cold without gold.

Countries that are under a threat of impending political turmoil invariably experience a sudden rush in the buying and storing of gold. This has happened recently in Italy, France, and the United States. Private citizens have been buying and storing gold, even at what appears to be highly inflated prices. Though the traditionalists ridicule purchasing gold at the current high prices, alert citizens in France, Italy, and the United States are purchasing and salting away gold. They know that if there is any money that can safely get them to the other side of their nation's crisis, it is gold, mankind's most historical money.

Another reason for gold's appeal is its scarcity. All the gold that has ever been produced in the entire history of the world could fit comfortably in a large barn. Its rarity is part and parcel of its myth.

In 1946, at Bretton Woods, New Hampshire, a new international monetary system was established with gold as its basis. Its primary purpose was to keep the U.S. dollar close to the gold standard since all the participating nations recognized the pivotal nature of the dollar. The system lasted until 1971, when the United States could stand it no longer. The temptation to print two certificates for every ivory zither was just too great, and the U.S. left the gold behind and rushed off into a sunset of inflated (and therefore deceptive) prosperity.

The appeal of gold is a fact of life. The factors we have discussed can help us understand it but none will explain it fully and simply. The most persuasive reason is that gold has gained too much strength (through many centuries as the world's ultimate money) to ever be placed or unseated due to some minor historic occurrence like the economic collapse of a single century.

Owning gold will cost you a bundle of paper dollars, but that paper bundle is going to be worth a lot less next year. If you are investing to turn a quick profit, gold does not have the same potential as it did when the first edition of this book appeared. Gold was selling for around $200 an ounce at that time, and had tremendous upside potential. There still will be opportunities for investors to make money in gold, but the major reason I am recommending it at this time is to provide you with something that has lasting value. Once you are sold on the idea of gold as a hedge against disappearing money, your basic questions are: how do I get some and where do I put it? With the exception of a few television ads for gold coins and regular ads in the *Wall Street Journal* and other financial publications, the gold market has remained largely the arena of the insiders. The mental image of yourself driving a lift truck with several pallets of gold ingots will soon disappear as you consider the density and price of this truly precious metal. You will have to be in the top one half of 1 percent of investors to buy more gold than you can carry. And if you have these resources, you'd be much too smart to carry it anywhere. You would more likely "take possession" of it by signing a paper that causes it to be moved a few inches in somebody's vault and labeled with your name.

Although this is sound strategy for major purchases, I must warn you against the dangers of trusting anyone with a vault and a receipt book. If you want to own over $100,000 in gold, consider the advantages of storing it in a Swiss bank, where your worries of financial failure or government seizure are much less realistic.

There are numerous ways you can purchase gold today. There are plenty of people waiting to make a profit when you are ready to buy. Once you begin to consider the ways you might wish to make your purchase, you need only to request a free brochure and the sales representatives will begin to telephone to give you the latest tips and recommendations. Some of the major alternatives are discussed in the following pages.

*Gold Coins:* Gold coins are an outstanding medium of exchange that will become immediately visible in the event of a collapse of the established currencies. Dollars will still be used after the crash, but it will take astronomical numbers of them to equal the buying power of a single gold coin. When the crash comes, you may be swapping that single gold coin for a food supply, wardrobe, perhaps even a car.

While gold coins are not likely to become a total medium of exchange, they will most certainly enable you to purchase necessities when merchants begin to turn down offers of dollars in any amounts. It may be hard for us to imagine, but quite likely that day is coming when all the paper money in the world will not buy what you need. If you don't believe it, ask some old Germans what they used their money for in the 1920s.

There are two basic categories of gold coins when you begin to consider owning them. The coins that are of special value to coin collectors have numismatic value and their prices are set by a combination of the amount of gold in them and their rarity as collector's items. If your primary interest is getting the most gold protection for your money, you will probably avoid the numismatic treasures since you may be hard-pressed to find a healthy coin collector in the midst of social chaos. During a crisis the rarest gold coin might be reduced to the value of its gold content.

There are, however, a number of coins that are minted and available today in coin shops, banks, and even some department stores. Because they are current coins, the premium to be paid to buy them tends to be far less than for the antique and rare coins. The term "premium" refers to the extra amount above the face value of the coin that you may pay as profit and handling costs to a dealer. The more coins you buy, the less premium you should have to pay.

Of those coins available to Americans, the most popular are American Eagles, Canadian Maple Leafs, Chinese Pandas, and South African Krugerrands. Generally, you should not expect to pay more than a 10 percent premium above the quoted price of gold on one of the major exchanges to buy non-numismatic coins. They will store easily and allow you to carry a significant amount of purchasing power when you begin your retreat. Because of sanctions imposed against South Africa, it is more difficult to import Krugerrands now than when this book first appeared. Because the market changes quickly, I recommend checking with the traders at a large bank— such as LaSalle National in Chicago.

Other gold coins that often sell at attractively low premiums are the Austrian 100-crown piece, which contains just less than a full ounce of gold, and the Mexican 50-peso piece, which has a bit more than an ounce. Most of the other coins tend to have prohibitively high premiums for the limited amount of gold content—for example, the American $20 "double eagle," which contains less than an ounce and carries a premium of around 70 percent.

Some coins of numismatic importance have premiums as high as 575 percent. If your interest is beating inflation and assuring the security of your wealth, you want the coins that will have low premiums, high credibility, and immediate liquidity after the crash.

Gold coins are not the best or even the first thing to buy for escaping with your money, but they certainly have their appropriate place in your survival portfolio. Their primary weakness is that they are worth so much that they are not likely to be very good at purchasing bread and milk when you have to have them. But gold represents the near ultimate in doomsday security, and when you are buying gold for the crash, I don't think there is a more efficient, flexible, secure, liquid way to get it than in the form of gold coins. They don't come cheap, but neither does survival.

*Bullion:* Gold bullion evokes exciting images of Wells

Fargo and the Old West during the mid-1880s. Gold is exciting to see, touch, and own, but it has some major disadvantages relating to security.

The disadvantages of bullion are that you do have to pay for storage, insurance, shipping, and assaying—either when you buy or when you sell and sometimes on both occasions. There are a lot of carrying costs associated with owning bullion. On the other hand, if you have substantial resources, these costs may be justified in order to store a lot of wealth with little worry about devaluation. In the short run, you may leave bullion with the conventional storage places. But if you have more than $100,000 in gold, you should begin moving it to private storage or a Swiss bank. If you expect to store it in a Swiss bank, then you should make your purchases from that bank in the first place (see Chapter 8). In this manner you will save the costs of assaying, shipment, and insurance and pay only the minimal storage charge.

*Buying Part of a Gold Mine:* One of the easiest ways to get into the gold business is to purchase stock in one of the world's gold mining companies. Shares may range in price from less than $10 to over $100. This process works like any other stock ownership.

Although some advisers talk about gold stocks as an inflation-proof investment medium, I generally don't recommend them because of three basic kinds of uncertainty that can influence the success of the stock. The first factor is the stability (or lack of it) of the country in which the company is located. Most gold mining operations that you can invest in are located in South Africa, where the political turmoil and uncertainty make them a rather shaky investment. Second, there is the question of the firm's management capabilities and how well they are able to utilize the valuable resources they control. My final reservation deals with the overall problems of the stock market. Many negative factors can influence the price of a stock that have little to do with the nature of the investment. During a bear market, factors that may discount a stock's price might not have any relationship to the real value of the ownership represented by the shares of stock. For that reason I'd recommend moving into some actual ownership.

*Futures:* While investing in the futures of gold and silver is very different from buying future contracts for soybeans or pork bellies, all these contracts are technically classified as commodities. By utilizing the commodities market, you can put some of your dollars for speculation into precious metals.

The commodities market was developed to help farmers eliminate some of the risk in the production of their products. Cattle ranchers or cotton planters can make agreements to sell their crop at some specified time in the future. This eliminates some of the uncertainty associated with estimating probable return for their time and effort. It also enables them to do a better job of determining the amount of a crop to produce. Commodity traders are willing to make advance agreements with farmers because they think the price at the time the commodities are available will be higher than the price they negotiate through the futures market.

In a similar way you can agree to sell gold that you own or to buy gold that you may wish to acquire at a specified price on a specific date in the next couple of years. Gold futures are less a barometer for production than a place where some high gains and losses can be made in the area of predicting the price of gold. Basically, it is a form of speculation. Ninety-five percent of the people who speculate in commodities lose their money because of the wide swings and fluctuations in the futures market. The producers and the specialists are the people most likely to find this market useful.

If you recognize that precious metals do experience wide fluctuations, you can study the charts for long-term directions and get a feeling of whether or not it is a bull or bear market. Overall, the market for precious metals is going to move in an upward direction, but there will be a number of adjustments as we move through the treacherous nineties.

One minor disadvantage of buying gold futures is that a monthly fee for insurance storage is included in the quoted price. This explains why a futures price for one year from the present is always more expensive than the future price for six months from the present. This is not because the price of gold is going to go up every month. There is simply a recognition of the storage cost associated with holding gold.

On the other hand, the purchase of a gold future represents the least expensive method of gold ownership. Compared to other forms of buying gold, a futures contract affords low transition cost, relatively inexpensive, safe storage, and ease of disposition (no inspection required and immediate liquidity available). The carrying charge associated with your contract can be recovered for the unused portion of time if you sell before maturity.

Most futures are purchased on approved margin accounts. This means you only have to put up about 15 percent of the money represented by your contract. My rule of thumb is: "Never buy when the price is within 90 percent of the season's high." Some people do make money by making purchases at record highs, but I feel better buying gold coins at high prices than gold futures. Generally, motivation in purchasing coins is very different than when speculating in futures. Unlike coins, futures are not a medium for long-term buy-and-forget investment decisions. If you have the patience to wait for market fluctuations, the futures market can be a stimulating place to put some of your speculative dollars. The biggest temptation for you to watch for is the tendency to become euphoric about the paper profits that you may be able to make on your first purchase. If you time your purchase near the beginning of an upward swing in prices, it is easy to see your original investment double or triple in a short period of time. There is a strong temptation to keep redoubling your bets until the market downturn catches you heavily leveraged with high-priced contracts. It takes a special kind of discipline to take your profits and keep a substantial amount of your resources liquid for a time as you wait for another downturn. Of course, if you are interested in storing bullion, but don't wish to take immediate possession, properly timed purchases of gold futures might be an attractive way to accomplish this objective.

*Options:* On June 1, 1978, the sale of gold options became illegal in the United States because so many people selling the options were unreliable. One spokesman in the industry said that there were basically "bucket operators who had a telephone, a brochure, and a willingness to sell options." When the buyer was ready to exercise the option, however, the operator had disappeared.

Because of the abuses and the inability of the law to control the situation, options have been outlawed as of this writing. But they can still be purchased through Swiss firms like Valeurs White Weld of Geneva.

The bottom line of any discussion about gold is that "gold is good." It is a sure bet for getting your wealth across the time chasm from one side of the collapse to the other. Own some gold—it is a value holder. However, there are some other commodities you may also need to round out your portfolio—silver for daily bread, and diamonds for the road.

## LOOK FOR THE SILVER LINING

The history of silver's value is a representative story of economic theory with special emphasis on the relationship between price and supply and demand. For thousands of years, silver maintained a fairly consistent relationship to gold. Between ten and fifteen ounces of silver could be counted to equal one ounce of gold. But the respective supply factors and new industrial uses for silver began to change that tie.

In the 1800s the United States knocked the price of silver off its even keel and the metal has never recovered its old relationship to gold. In 1890 the Comstock Lode in the American West began to flood the silver market of the world. Eventually the number of ounces of silver required to equal an ounce of gold rose to forty. Then, with the 1930s Depression, the number rose to seventy. Since that time the rate has declined as the value of silver in relation to gold has risen steadily because the supply of silver is now being used up instead of simply stored and swapped.

The United States government has been a major manipulator of the value and availability of silver. For years the government agreed to contracts that purchased silver from western mines at prices far above the going price in the rest of the world. This resulted in the U.S. government being the leading stockpiler of silver and therefore a key factor in the world price. The pattern-changing policies that evolved thereafter appeared to be erratic and contradictory, but almost always made sense at the time. Basically, the government was storing and releasing silver at different rates in an effort to keep its silver coins at a fairly consistent value. The effort finally became unmanageable because the use of silver in the industrial world began to increase so dramatically. Now the U.S. government has lost its silver stockpile and the world is heading into an unavoidable silver shortage.

While silver is a positive hedge against inflation, it is also a very promising speculative investment because of several prevailing conditions. The simple fact is that the world is using up over 400 million ounces of silver a year while it is producing a little over 200 million ounces! The difference is being made up from the silver stockpiles of the world and they are just about empty. The largest stockpile is probably in India, where silver jewelry remains the most prevalent national method of storing individual wealth. The future is unsettled in fields like photography, electronics, and pollution control since they are dependent on a ready supply of silver. The one certainty is that they are going to be paying higher and higher premiums for the disappearing metal.

Silver is not an inexhaustible resource. We are rapidly approaching the end of its availability. The U.S. Treasury finally had to give up minting silver coins because people were likely to melt them down for their silver content, which far exceeded their monetary value.

If you have silver, hold it. If you get a chance, buy it. It will be easiest to handle in the form of coins, but you will find that silver tableware and silver trays will continue to appreciate in value. Some authorities even suggest that old X rays (which are coated with silver) will eventually become objects of value.

There is probably less than a billion ounces of silver in the world's stockpile and it is being used up rapidly. The supply is being coddled and collected with the greatest of care. In view of the effects of the current financial turmoil on the price of gold and the effects of diminishing supply on silver, the race of gold and silver prices will be an exciting one—especially for those sitting on personal stores of each.

### Usage and Demand

In economic theory and practice, whenever the price of a commodity gets too high, users will be forced to find alternatives to substitute. The methods of reclaiming and recycling also become much easier to justify and develop. However, this law does not seem to apply to the impending silver shortage since there are many industrial applications where no suitable substitute has been developed.

In photography, silver salts are the only elements with suitable light sensitivity. For twenty or more years, researchers have been trying alternatives, but none work as well. Projections are that silver will continue to be bought and utilized in photography and X-ray processes even if the prices continue to rise. The newest inventions in the realm of instant self-developing film processes are not likely to change the picture since there is no recycling potential with instant films. Silver is in the photographic picture to stay and the industry anticipates tremendous expansion over the next decade.

In electronics, silver's utility as a conductor has caused it to be in great demand by manufacturers of circuitry. About 75 percent of the silver used in electrical equipment goes into high- and medium-voltage connections where there are no known economical substitutes for silver. Other irreplaceable uses of silver include catalysts in the manufacture of plastic, reflecting surfaces in mirrors, bearings and brazing alloys, coinage, medicine and dentistry. New uses are being added constantly in spite of the irreversible loss of the world's silver supply.

There is currently a yearly deficit between production and consumption of approximately 100 million ounces. This difference is made up by sales from existing stockpiles that have dropped from 2 billion ounces in 1968 to less than 1 billion at the present time. Although there is some debate about these figures and their meaning, it appears obvious that the demand for silver can be met only when prices are sufficient to encourage the current holders to part with their treasure. Consequently, I expect silver prices to have a bullish future for the next decade.

Geologists estimate that in every million pounds of the earth's crust there are 50,000 pounds of iron, 80,000 pounds of aluminum, but less than 2 ounces of silver. To make matters worse, we know that silver is always found near the surface of the earth and all the available large silver sources have been mined. The future for silver discovery is not promising—even according to the most optimistic of authorities.

When any commodity grows scarce, the price goes up and spurs the search for substitutes. It's already happened with silver. No suitable substitutes have been found and the price continues to rise. The higher the price, the more incentive there is to start up new production. Yet the new production of silver is not so much a matter of demand as a question of availability. At some price level, supply usually comes to equal demand. But, given the collision courses of growing demand and shrinking availability, the final balance can be achieved only at a phenomenal price level.

### Gold versus Silver

There is some feeling that silver may be a better investment than gold in the next few years because silver has so many demands in the industrial world and because the historical ratios are somewhat out of kilter. Gold is affected more by speculation than silver is. As a result, there will almost always be wider swings in the gold market, but the prospects for silver values cannot help but be bright.

Metals are generally safer than any other commodity investments. But for those who are looking to gold and silver as "stashing agents" they can hardly be beaten. And now, after years in which the decision between the two hinged on their portability and relative values, it appears to me that silver offers more stability, but gold affords more inflation protection. While silver is cheaper than gold (and therefore more flexible as a bargaining commodity during economic chaos) it also involves considerably more storage and transportation problems.

As chaos money, silver remains number one for day-to-day exchange and for purchase of the necessities of survival. Gold remains the sure thing for holding and adding to value invested in larger amounts. You will need both to have a well-rounded preparedness.

### Ways to Weave Your Silver Lining

There are four basic ways to invest in silver. The same principles apply in silver purchases as in gold purchases, though some of the specifics will differ due to the mere bulk of silver required to equal the same value as gold.

You can buy stocks in a silver mining company. They are available on the major stock exchanges throughout the world. The problem, in fact, is that there are too many companies on the stock exchanges that are involved in silver mines. Only a few are worth considering—and they are questionable. These companies rarely mine silver only. They usually are after copper, lead, and zinc with silver as a by-product. Copper, lead, and zinc are all plentiful, so the companies are not usually aggressive. You can buy their shares quite inexpensively, but there is little likelihood that you will be getting dependable, high dividends or capital appreciation in the near future. You don't have to worry as much about the mining being in South Africa or Russia (as with gold mining stocks); on the other hand, it will take much higher prices to make the mining of silver only highly profitable. I would not advise silver mines as a short-term stock investment, but if you have money for the long term, the prospects for the eventual resumption of lucrative silver mining are quite promising in light of the dead-end course of current silver supply and demand.

You can buy silver futures contracts if you are interested in speculating in short-term silver price movements. The same principles apply here that we discussed in the section on gold futures. For your investment strategy, you will be more interested in purchasing and holding silver instead of in these speculative "paper markets," where you rarely will see any actual silver. If you are interested in some short-term speculations you can get into futures by checking with any stockbroker who is represented on the Commodity Exchange, Inc. (in New York) or on the Chicago Board of Trade. While this is primarily a market for full-time professional traders with nerves of steel and reflexes of silver, small-timers who can tolerate substantial risk have made substantial returns in this manner.

You can buy silver bullion in America or Switzerland. If you do not plan to take physical possession of the silver investment or if you are apprehensive about the U.S. government confiscating your precious metals, you can contact the American representative of a Swiss bank and order a specified amount of silver either by weight or by dollar amount. You can also write, phone, or wire a Swiss bank directly if you prefer. Your privacy is more likely to remain protected in this manner. The bullion will be set aside and labeled with your name and account number. While you will have to pay a small storage fee, you will not have to be concerned with costs of assaying or insurance.

If you intend to take possession of your silver, you will be better off buying it in this country and storing it in a private vault or in a non-banking safe deposit box. Bullion is available through banks, coin shops, and some specialized companies like North American Coin & Currency, Ltd., Monex, or major banks. Owning bullion is the most direct and low-risk way to profit from the expected long-term price advances in silver. There are some storage and exchange problems for the survival buyer, but even these may be more than offset by the promise of silver's skyrocketing future. As will be quickly apparent, however, my personal preference is that your basic stock or silver be stored in the form of coins since they will be that much more recognizable by the grocer after the economic system comes unglued.

You can buy silver coins. United States dimes, quarters, and half-dollars minted prior to 1965 are 90 percent silver. If by some quirk you get one in change, hang onto it, because it is already worth almost four times its face value. Almost any silver coins you own will have to be bought from a coin dealer and you will have to pay a premium for them. The traditional way to buy this "junk silver" (meaning without numismatic value) is in large canvas bags about the size of a bowling ball but weighing over 50 pounds. You order one of these bags from your supplier. The coins will have combined face value of $1,000 and, of course, always will be worth at least that much, even in the unlikely event that the bottom should drop completely out of silver.

In my opinion, the best investment for those with small assets would be bags of silver coins. It is a basic inflation hedge for the small investor. While silver coins can be bought from almost any dealer, it pays to shop around. Anyone who is interested in this ought to make three or four telephone calls to compare. Check prices and delivery terms from competing suppliers. Unless you know someone personally who is involved in silver sales or you live in a city that is large enough to have a major dealer, I would recommend sticking to an established organization that has a history of performance. There are a number of reliable dealers who perform this service and you may have some reasons for preferring to work with them.

A reasonable goal is for you to have one bag of silver coins for each person in your family or survival group. While it is a very good investment, I view it more as a survival kit. When I talk later about your investment portfolio, I will stress that the most basic component of a portfolio is *survival*. If you don't have enough money to need an ounce of gold, then silver coins can be extremely helpful. Silver coins are an investment that will continue to appreciate, be readily recognizable, and be fairly easy to acquire. For most people silver is much more easily managed for day-to-day purchases than gold coins. Purchasing, taking possession of, and sorting a bag of silver or two is your first investment priority. Do this before you begin to look at any of the other investment opportunities discussed in this chapter.

## ARE DIAMONDS A SURVIVOR'S BEST FRIEND?

While Wall Street brokers are depressed, diamond merchants around New York's West 57th Street are scarcely able to conceal their excitement. The wholesale price of a one-carat, high-quality diamond ("D" color, internally flawless) has risen dramatically over the past decade. Normally these stones are purchased immediately, as soon as they hit the diamond market, but if they were sold retail the price might be twice that amount. Diamond merchants assert that the price of their product has been remarkably stable except for 1980–81 and has almost always moved ahead of inflation. Moreover, history is filled with examples of wealthy people and royalty who have survived natural and political calamities because they possessed the world's most concentrated form of wealth.

An acquaintance of mine was a Jewish diamond dealer in Berlin before the Hitler regime. When he saw the handwriting on the wall, he took a snuff can full of quality diamonds and beat the SS troops to the border. His canister was worth about $100,000. The diamonds enabled him to travel around the world until eventually he reached the United States. He settled in San Francisco with less than half of his original horde. Now he is a retired millionaire living on the Monterey Peninsula.

### The Diamond Sheiks

The major reason, in addition to their historical survival potential, for the tremendous appreciation in diamond prices comes from the control exercised by one of the world's most powerful cartels. Long before the Arabs organized their petroleum cartel, the South African company, DeBeers Consolidated Mines, staked a claim to most of the world's diamonds. Although their own mines produce less than a third of the worldwide production of uncut and unpolished stones, they virtually control worldwide rough prices. They are the sole distributor for almost every other major producer of rough diamonds, including the Soviet Union.

Through their subsidiary arm, the Central Selling Organization, they distribute stones to around 250 to 300 key clients throughout the world. They decide how many diamonds will enter the market and at what price. If demand weakens, DeBeers simply cuts the supply and maintains the price. When diamond demand peaks, they release larger amounts of the stones. During the investment fever in diamonds, DeBeers slapped a 40 percent premium on its stones to reduce the speculation. Diamond brokers were selling (mainly to Israeli speculators) uncut diamonds at 30–40 percent above the going rate. Russia was getting upset that it was not getting its fair share of the profits. DeBeers also felt it should get more of this profit; therefore, the surcharge was placed on these goods as a warning to the speculators.

Interest in diamonds reached a fever pitch in the early 1980s. As is always true, when speculative fever sweeps through an investment medium, abuses will occur. People were buying diamonds without ever seeing them in the anticipation that there was no way the investment could fail. But declines have hit the diamond market. DeBeers has lost some of its clout in setting prices. Diamonds are still important instruments for the movement of large sums of money without attracting attention, and I believe they still have appreciation potential if purchased wisely. Nevertheless, an investor in these

TABLE 6-1
DIAMOND GRADING SCALES

## GIA COLOR SCALE

INVESTMENT QUALITY

| D | E | F | G | H | I | J | K | L | M | N | O | P | Q | R | S | T | U | V | W | X | Y | Z | | |
|---|---|---|---|---|---|---|---|---|---|---|---|---|---|---|---|---|---|---|---|---|---|---|---|---|
| Colorless | | | Near Colorless | | | | Faint Yellow | | | Very light Yellow | | | | | | Light Yellow | | | | | | | | Fancy Yellow |

## GIA CLARITY SCALE

INVESTMENT QUALITY

| FLAWLESS | VVSI-1 | VVSI-2 | VSI-1 | VSI-2 | SI-1 | SI-2 | I-1 | I-2 | I-3 |
|---|---|---|---|---|---|---|---|---|---|
| | Very, Very Slight Inclusions | | Very Slight Inclusions | | Slight Inclusion | | Imperfect | | |

troubled times should be more interested in preserving value and survival ability than in making a quick killing.

### Evaluating Diamonds

Diamonds are evaluated or graded on the basis of the four famous C's: color, clarity, cut, and carat (weight). Their total value is determined in an overall evaluation of these four factors.

*Color:* In diamonds, the absence of color is ideal. These blue-white (technically called "colorless") stones are virtually transparent. Less than 1 percent of all diamonds have this characteristic. Poor-quality diamonds have a distinctly yellowish cast. The Gemological Institute of America (GIA) trains jewelers to be more knowledgeable about grading diamonds and, if they desire, to become registered gemologists. The Institute is one of the most highly respected for its grading criteria. This organization classifies colors into twenty-three variations. Investment-quality diamonds are H or better. Z is distinctly yellow and is at the bottom of this spectrum.

*Clarity:* The number of inclusions or imperfections in the diamond determine its clarity. The fewer the imperfections, the rarer and more valuable the stone. A perfect stone would be free of all blemishes, flaws, or specks. Although some retailers are prone to advertise their diamonds as flawless, the FTC regulation limits this claim to diamonds that show no blemishes or inclusions under a magnification of ten times. As shown in the preceding table, clarity ranges from flawless through imperfect and is divided into ten categories. If you can see flaws in a stone without magnification, the stone is probably graded imperfect and is not a good investment. If you have to use a magnifier to see the imperfections, the stone would probably rate a "slightly imperfect" grade. Generally, diamonds from grades flawless to VVSI-2 (very, very slight inclusion) are generally recommended for investments. In reality, any stone bought at the right price is a good investment.

*Cut:* Most investment diamonds have fifty-eight facets

and are cut out to precise calculations. Style, fashion and preference will affect the desirability of various cuts. Less desirable cuts are often utilized to avoid wasting a flawed stone.

*Carat:* Each cut and polished diamond is stated in carats. A diamond described as 1.53 carats means that it has one and 53/100 carats. The larger the stone, the more rare it is. Depending on color, clarity, and cut, one-carat stones can go anywhere from $400 (at your local pawnshop) to almost $50,000.

For investment purposes, seek out the best stones available. The novice investor should watch out for diamond imitations. Modern technology has made it sometimes difficult to spot a fake. You don't need to worry about this if you purchase through reliable channels. Stones appraised by the GIA are generally required for investment purposes. A jeweler's appraisal certificate should not be taken for investment purposes. The GIA certificate is accepted in all the cash markets around the world.

### The Advantages of Diamonds

While most of the advantages of diamonds as an investment medium have been suggested by the preceding paragraphs, we can summarize these key concepts: durability, portability, stability, and appreciation potential.

Although many people have heard that diamonds are the hardest of all substances, they cannot comprehend the degree of its superiority. A sclerometer, an instrument that measures the hardness of materials, gives corundum (rubies and sapphires) a hardness value of 1,000. With a hardness value of 140,000, it can be said that diamonds are 140 times as hard as their nearest competitor. The reason for this significance is that if a gem breaks in half, it will lose much more than half of its value. You should not expect to survive any type of holocaust and find that your diamonds have been destroyed.

Because of the portability of diamonds, demand has grown dramatically in France and Germany during periods when citizens feared that the Communist Party might come to power. In the United States, diamond specialists estimate that more then 20 percent of the diamonds now sold are for investment. There are over 200 firms in business whose sole business is selling investment diamonds to the public.

With this impressive historical performance, the potential for diamonds continues to be real. Increasing worldwide interest in investment diamonds, as well as the strong and growing international jewelry market, constitutes a healthy demand situation. George Switzer, director of the Mineral and Gem Department of the Smithsonian Institution, estimates that known diamond supplies will be exhausted by the year 2000 or shortly thereafter. There is little likelihood that any large new deposits will be discovered in the future. Further political unrest in South Africa, which supplies over 80 percent of all rough carats produced annually, could produce a drastic reduction in the availability of diamonds. In Angola, production has dropped from a high of 1.5 million carats to about 300,000 carats per year.

### Disadvantages of Diamonds

Although diamonds have many factors that recommend them as investments, there are some problems. Dealers agree that individuals buying stones as an investment should exercise extreme caution. It is very difficult to buy from a retail jeweler and sell it back to him at a profit. The retail markup is anywhere from 30 to 100 percent of the wholesale price. Investors must also pay local sales taxes and usually an annual insurance charge that may be 5 percent of the stone's value. Selling isn't simple either. The retail jeweler would probably offer even less than the current wholesale price.

These high markups in the usual marketplaces have provided an opportunity to the diamond-investment firms. These firms claim to sell their stones at the prevailing wholesale price plus 10 percent. A number of them, however, are selling at twice the wholesale price. I have reviewed price lists and found some of them to be ridiculously high. For example, one firm was selling at about double the true wholesale price. It is easy to get in touch with these firms. They advertise aggressively in the major financial publications. Many maintain WATS lines with a staff of personnel who aggressively work their prospect lists. Even if they have GIA certificates and insurance, I am still dubious when a high-pressure salesman says, "If you'll send me ten or twenty thousand dollars I will pick out the best diamond we have available." It's a nice offer, but it requires more trust than I can afford to exercise with my family's survival money.

In summary, diamonds pay no interest or dividends and are not likely to experience a stock split. You must be responsible for insurance and storage costs as well as the expense in selling the diamond. Despite the promise of many firms to buy them back at their original invest-ment price or better, these promises are only valid as long as the firms survive and there is no sweeping politi-cal or social upheaval in the country.

Diamonds do have a place in any significant invest-ment portfolio, but their greatest advantage is to the wealthy individual who needs to conceal or carry large amounts of wealth in an inconspicuous manner. It is difficult to carry $100,000 in gold without being a prime target for a hernia or a holdup. Yet $1 million in dia-monds can be carried without notice. Unlike gold, it does not show up on X-ray scanners that are used at most airports.

The DeBeers control of the market protects the dia-monds from depreciating in price during a depression. Inflation and the historical track record of diamonds protect the buyer on the up side. In my opinion, anyone with an investment portfolio of about $80,000 should consider putting a small amount of his resources in small, high-quality stones.

### How to Buy and Sell

As we have indicated earlier, one of the major disad-vantages of most diamond dealings is the difficulty of making purchases at acceptable prices. Most people buy their diamonds at retail prices and sell them at wholesale.

Small stones (anything under a full carat) usually have a markup of at least 100 percent. The larger your purchase, the smaller the markup you should be able to negotiate. If you are going to invest a quarter of a million dollars, you should investigate the possibility of buying a box of assorted rough-cut stones from one of the DeBeers brokers. The various diamond brokers, investment firms, and auction houses are possibilities that may provide alternatives for smaller purchases. Regardless of which approach you use, check the reputation of your seller and insist on a GIA certificate. You need to know your dealer, however, to make sure that you are getting the diamond that the certificate describes. Most of the reputable dealers will allow you a five-day appraisal period. Unfortunately, local appraisals are seldom objective. If you take a stone to most local jewelers, there's a strong possibility that they will downgrade your acquisition in hopes of replacing it with something from their own stock. Plan to spend some time in shopping before you make your initial purchases. After several sessions with a jeweler's loupe, you will be able to tell what constitutes a top-quality stone. My best experience has come from looking in the telephone directory under "Diamond Wholesalers." Talk to two or three dealers before you make a decision. After considerable shopping, I have made most of my purchases from the nearest representative of SIDIAM (Society International Diamonds), a Belgian diamond company. This firm imports and purchases directly from diamond-cutting factories.

### A Sparkling Review

Massive speculation is always a dangerous specter. If you feel that your financial situation warrants this type of investment, the following guidelines summarize the main points that we have discussed.

1. Diamonds have appreciated faster than most other investment vehicles. Of the over 2,000 separate categories of stones, only one percent—the finest-quality

gems—have historically appreciated faster than 15 percent per year.

2. Be sure that your diamond has been graded by a bonded and insured gem laboratory such as GIA.

3. Shop and compare prices and grade categories. Do not buy a 1-carat stone just because it is cheaper than any other diamond of that size you have seen. Insist on inspecting the diamond under magnification and make your purchase only from established companies whose references you have checked. Buy only from firms which agree to repurchase your stone within a specified time period if you are not completely satisfied.

4. Pick a stone that fits your financial requirements. While most advisers recommend buying the largest and highest-quality stones available, I believe that ⅓-to-½ carat diamonds are probably the best choice for individuals with less than $100,000 to put into gems. It is true that the large, top-quality diamonds appreciate faster, but these are very difficult to find and are usually not very liquid. Good-quality gems between ⅓ and ½ carat are the most liquid when you need to change your stones for a more commonly accepted medium for exchange.

### A Sparkling Alternative

Many industry observers believe there is now more safety *and* upside potential in investment-grade colored gemstones than in diamonds. The October 1987 issue of the jewelry industry trade journal featured a cover story on "Jewelers for the 21st Century." This survey of young professionals, officers, and managers of jewelry specialists in every region of the United States painted a fascinating portrait of an industry in transition. The article concluded, "The big news is the strong vote of confidence in colored stones." Over 75 percent of the respondents believed that colored gemstone jewelry will become a more significant part of their volume and profits during the next decade. According to the experts, "Sparkle isn't limited to the big three colored stones (rubies, sapphires, and emeralds). Over three-fourths of the respondents are committed to a growing market for lesser stones as well."

As is true in any investment alternative, the key to potential appreciation is the ability to purchase high quality items at prices that represent investment value. The rule to follow just as in the equities market or with diamonds, is "buy low and sell high." One means of achieving this is to eliminate several of the ten to fifteen middlemen in the gemstone's path from the mine to the North American marketplace.

A small group of hardy entrepreneurs travel on a regular schedule to remote sites where precious and semiprecious gemstones are mined. They buy the "brute" or rough stones (emeralds, sapphires, topaz, alexandrite, aquamarine, citrine rubelite, and tourmaline). They then have the stones lapidated (cut and polished) by Amsterdamtrained professionals and bring them back to the States for sale through network buyers or investment pawners.

One entrepreneur who has impressed me most favorably is Charles Knechtel, founder and president of Brazilian Gemstones U.S.A., Inc. (see Appendix B). A former bank executive, Knechtel swaps his pinstripe suits for bush clothes four times a year and goes directly to the remote provinces, where he purchases large numbers of rough stones and personally brings them through the distribution chain eliminating an estimated eleven middlemen in the process.

## INVESTMENT STRATEGY

Without knowing a great deal about you and your personal situation, I cannot make specific recommendations about how you should invest your wealth. Yet there are some general principles that will help you finance the voyage through the troubled waters ahead.

In approaching this challenge, your strategy should reflect a combination of three important variables: the amount of your wealth, your station in life as reflected by your age or family responsibilities, and your asssessment of the immediacy of a major depression. Table 6-2 at the end of this chapter summarizes my basic recommendations by breaking your portfolio into three types of dollars you will be investing.

*Survival dollars:* The first order of priority is a good food supply. If your getting-ready capability is no more than $10,000, then you are going to deal first with that six-month supply of food and a bag of silver coins. You'll also put some of your money into the services of a locksmith to make your residence as secure as possible and purchase a gun for hunting or protection. The lower your income level, the larger the percentage that should be allocated to survival needs and the fewer investment concerns you will need to worry about. It is important for you to recognize that some of the items in the survival category are really depression-proof investments. Diamonds and silver will appreciate; gold coins will buy more each year; and any money that has been placed in the right kind of retreat will be an investment that will pay off more than traditional real estate investments. This is true since your consideration of water, weather, and fertility of the land in choosing retreat property will become key determinants of land values during the depression even more than they are today.

*Traditional Investments:* Beyond survival needs, you will need a couple of months' income in a savings account. If your assets are limited, you may want to put some of this into a Swiss bank account (see Chapter 8). By doing this you accomplish dual goals of having ready liquidity and in a depression-proof medium. Even if you share my reservations about the long-term safety of savings institutions, you should keep some of your funds where you can get to them quickly in the event of a personal crisis.

After providing for your liquidity needs, I would recommend that your next group of traditional investment dollars go to buy some stock in a company, preferably local, that you know well. As your income increases, you will probably want to shelter some of your investment earnings from income taxes by purchasing some municipal bonds. As suggested in Chapter 5, this can be tricky since many of the nation's cities could be experiencing grave financial problems during the next decade. As a short-term consideration, I think you can make some good choices with the debt obligations of some healthy medium-sized cities. When you start moving most of your resources out of the traditional into the depression-proof categories, your municipal bonds will be one of the first categories to cash in.

Until you have assets in the quarter-million-dollar category or extremely high earned income, I recommend that you avoid traditional real estate investments. In my opinion, it is almost impossible for the small investor to make a significant return in real estate. With adequate resources and the principles identified in the previous chapter, you can enjoy some excellent (and partially tax-sheltered) returns from properly situated real estate holdings.

*Depression-Proof Investments:* Although most other writers who recognize the probability of imminent economic chaos will disapprove of my recommendations for traditional investments, I believe that there will be substantial profits to be made in these investments in the pre-depression period. Government officials and financial executives will do everything in their power to keep the sinking system afloat. Their efforts will create some excellent opportunities in the investment area.

With each passing year you will probably want to move more money out of traditional investments. As the signs continue to confirm the predictions throughout this book, you will want a larger and larger proportion of your wealth in depression-proof investments. During any period of relative stability as we approach the brink, take advantage of every opportunity, but only on a short-term basis, never diluting your security and depression-proof investments. In deciding how to balance the amount of commitment in traditional versus depression-proof investments, ask, "What is the probability that the crash will occur during the next two years?" Anytime you think there is more than a 50 percent probability of disaster within twenty-four months, multiply your estimate of that probability times the total amount you have to invest in nonsurvival categories and move in that direction. In other words, I now believe that there is approximately a 50 percent probability that the crash will occur within two years after the publication of this book. Consequently, I have recommended that you place approximately equal amounts of dollars in the two major nonsurvival categories. As I become more convinced that the depression is closer at hand, I will want to move more of my assets in the depression-proof category.

*Amount of Wealth:* Obviously, a person's investment strategy will be determined by the amount of his wealth. Until a person's investment portfolio approaches $25,000, survival will demand the largest share of wealth and attention. I have provided percentages of the various investment ideas that should hold true between the categories identified. For instance, if your investment portfolio is $75,000, I would recommend that you use the percentages recommended for a $50,000 portfolio. Above $100,000 you can use the recommended percentages as guidelines, but I would suggest that you sit down with a specialized adviser from each of the purchase areas to help you select optimal choices within that category.

Typically your portfolio should exceed $100,000 before you should begin to think in terms of a retreat that is separate from your major residence. Consequently, you may want to plan your major residence with survival in mind.

If you are able to sell your house in the city, try to make your housing investment in a safer location. This would, of course, provide more flexibility in your financial planning. The retreat figures I have suggested do not take into account the basic cost of primary housing.

Your "monetary depression proof" investments might be acquired and held in the following order of priority:

1. Set up a small account in Swiss francs so that you have money that will help protect you against further dollar declines. The Swiss franc is gold-backed and is therefore likely to continue to appreciate in relation to the dollar.

2. Watch for downward movement in the price of gold futures. When they are less than 90 percent of their past year's high and 10 percent above the year's low, you should consider making investments.
3. Small diamonds should be added whenever your investment resources reach the $60,000 level.
4. Wait until you can afford 100 troy ounces before getting into gold bullion. The rising price of gold will provide its own barometer for your ability to get this investment with safety.

## A SUMMARY OF PRINCIPLES

1. *Your life and security come first.* Your first available dollars should go to make your home secure and to provide a basic food supply.
2. *Be sure that you can buy a quart of milk.* One bag of pre-1965 silver coins should be safely stored where you can have ready access to them before you put money in the stock market or even a savings account. Don't worry about losing interest. Silver coins will probably appreciate faster than a savings account will and have much greater interest during a crisis.
3. *Invest in the future and not the past.* A company's record in the stock market may be important, but not nearly as significant as what you see as its prospects. I'd rather buy stock in a company that has had some difficulties but has turned them around than in a firm that has been successful for twenty years but is now coasting on the laurels while losing market share and return on investment. The same principle applies to any investment medium. If gold were to have a couple of years like most blue-chip stocks, I wouldn't hold on to it just because of its fantastic record.
4. *Don't worry about hitting the highs and lows, but try to move with the market.* It is important to get all the good advice, but then trust your feelings. I would not recommend investing in anything that

TABLE 6-2
SAMPLE INVESTMENT PORTFOLIOS

| PORTFOLIO SIZE | SURVIVAL | TRADITIONAL INVESTMENTS | DEPRESSION-PROOF INVESTMENTS |
|---|---|---|---|
| $10,000+ | **50%**<br>Food Supply (Up to 6 months supply)<br>Portable Retreat $500<br>Locks & Protection 500<br>Silver Coins one-half bag | **25%**<br>Up to two months income | **25%**<br>Swiss Francs |
| $50,000 | **40%**<br>Food Supply<br>Retreat<br>Silver Coins | **30%**<br>Savings $3,000<br>Municipal Bonds 7,000<br>Local Stocks 10,000 | **30%**<br>Swiss Francs 6,000<br>Gold, Silver or Copper Futures 4,000<br>Precious Stones 5,000<br>5,000 |
| $100,000 | **36%**<br>Retreat & Food<br>Silver Coins<br>Gold Coins | **32%**<br>Savings 15,000<br>Bonds 12,000<br>Stocks 9,000 | **32%**<br>Swiss Francs 6,000<br>Gold, Silver, or Copper 12,000<br>Futures or Options 14,000<br>Diamonds 12,000<br>10,000<br>10,000 |

6-2 Cont'd.
## SAMPLE INVESTMENT PORTFOLIOS

| PORTFOLIO SIZE | SURVIVAL | TRADITIONAL INVESTMENTS | DEPRESSION-PROOF INVESTMENTS |
|---|---|---|---|
| $250,000 | 30% | 35% | 35% |
|  | Retreat & Food 50,000 | Savings 10,000 | Swiss Francs 20,000 |
|  | Silver Coins 11,000 | Bonds 30,000 | Metal Options 23,500 |
|  | Gold Coins 13,000 | Stocks 30,000 | Bullion 20,000 |
|  |  | Real Estate 18,500 | Precious Stones 24,000 |
| $1,000,000 and Over | 14% | 43% | 43% |
|  | Retreat & Food 100,000 | Savings 20,000 | Swiss Francs 20,000 |
|  | Silver Coins 14,000 | Bonds 140,000 | Metal Options or Futures 100,000 |
|  | Gold Coins 26,000 | Stocks 140,000 | Bullion 130,000 |
|  |  | Real Estate 130,000 | Precious Stones 180,000 |

makes you rush to the newspaper every day with trembling hands to check the latest quotation. Whether it is stock prices, mutual funds, or gold futures, you want to maintain your peace of mind. If you can buy *toward* the beginning of an upward market movement and sell *near* the onset of a decline, you'll do much better physically and financially than if you stay tensely poised waiting for the peaks and valleys.

5. *Stay up to date.* No matter how good your research is at a given point, circumstances can change rapidly. So you need to seek out the kinds of news sources that will enable you to monitor the significant developments on a daily basis. If you don't have time to keep up, then you need to be willing to pay somebody to do this for you.

6. *Don't be afraid to pay someone for help.* If you are a plastic surgeon who charges $5,000 for a simple face-lift that takes an hour of your time, you will probably be wise to pay someone else to do your investment research. It's not likely that the best researcher in the country will cost $5,000 an hour. Find a professional adviser—perhaps several—and make sure that you recognize when their advice may be serving their own purpose. You may be wise to let them know that you are buying the advice from them but intend to go somewhere else for the actual services they recommend. (It works with auto mechanics; it ought to work as well with other diagnosticians and prescribers.) If your assets or income warrant professional assistance, check with a member of the rising profession of "financial planners" who charge on an hourly basis for a complete assessment. Only as a last resort would I ask a stockbroker or insurance agent to evaluate my investment program. The broker knows stock and the insurance agent knows policies. But only *I* know my personal priorities.

# Section Three

# HOW TO SURVIVE ADVERSITY IN LUXURY

# CHAPTER 7

# YOURSELF:
# THE BEST INVESTMENT

One of the major purposes of this book has been to evaluate several important types of investments in view of their probable performance during a period of economic turmoil. As you might expect, most of this investment advice has been directed toward your money and how to use it.

I don't mean to imply that money can bring happiness. I have known people with $9 million who were just as happy as the people with $10 million. But I can't help but remember the words of the great philosopher Sophie Tucker, who said, "I've been rich and I've been poor—and I'm here to tell you that rich is better!"

Much of my advice is predicated on the assumption that rich is better than poor. I won't even try to make you believe that poverty is just a state of mind. Money (especially real money) has a great deal to do with concepts such as poverty and riches. One of the real tragedies of poverty is that people have to spend so much time worrying about money. Even P. T. Barnum recognized, "Money is a terrible master, but an excellent servant."

I hope you will have invested some of your hard-earned money according to the principles identified in Chapters 5 and 6. Now I am about to describe the best investment you can ever make. Investment in your own knowledge or well-being is more stable than gold and will shine brighter than diamonds when the stock market collapses and the dollar explodes.

## INVESTMENT FOR PLEASURE AND PROFIT

Some authorities recommend investments in jewelry and art because they can bring pleasure along with their potential for appreciation. I have not dealt with these as investment media because of the specialized knowledge it takes to evaluate acquisitions and because there is a very limited market for these items during a period of economic depression. Nevertheless, the concept of enjoying your investments is an important one. Where can you put your money that will provide more pleasant returns or be more valuable than by investing in that person who smiles back at you in the bathroom mirror each morning?

An investment in self-sufficiency pays dividends regardless of the economic environment. Diplomas and other paper evidences of achievement may become worthless, but skills can never be confiscated. There is a Chinese proverb that suggests, "Give someone a fish and you teach him to steal because he will be hungry tomorrow. Teach him to fish, and he need never be hungry again."

In order to gain the maximum benefit from this chapter, you may have to rearrange your thinking about the Christian virtue of humility. None of the cardinal virtues is more widely misunderstood. You remember how St. Paul wrote to first-century Christians in Rome not to think of themselves more highly than they "ought to think" (Romans 12:3). Many ministers have utilized this verse to prove that people ought to be self-effacing. They fail to notice that Paul continues by saying that each person should recognize that "God has given to every man a measure of grace." Rather than endorsing the practice of depreciating your abilities, the apostle was really saying, "Be honest about the gifts you have been given." A street corner philosopher has expressed it, "God don't make no trash."

In the Broadway musical *The Unsinkable Molly Brown* the lead character finally admitted, "I mean more to me than to anybody else I know." You will be able to avoid considerable guilt if you can make this same declaration for yourself. You are important. You deserve respect and attention—most of all from yourself.

### The Virtue of Selfishness

Selfishness is the second virtue that is widely misunderstood and abused. Nothing could be more arrogant than for an individual to assume that he is so important in the total scheme of things that he must put the happiness of other people always ahead of his own. When you get right down to it, everyone is basically selfish. One person spends every available hour helping underprivileged children. Another becomes the Mafia's most proficient hit man. Still another develops a new drug that she hopes will relieve suffering and earn several million dollars. In each case the motivation is the same. Each individual is choosing, without force or coercion, to do whatever he or she believes will provide the greatest happiness and satisfaction. The difference lies in the paths they have chosen to achieve this goal.

The sermons on self-sacrifice assume that there are only two roads to happiness. One requires that you give up what you enjoy for the benefit of others. The other option is to take advantage of others and exploit them for your own good. Fortunately, there is a third avenue that provides a greater potential for genuine contentment. This requires that you accept the responsibility for your own well-being and grant other people the right to pilot their own course through life. No one has the ability to provide happiness for you. Similarly, no matter how great you are, you cannot give happiness to someone who is unwilling to seize it for himself.

This is one of the most difficult concepts that parents have to accept as their children grow up. No amount of formal planning, investment, or cajoling can provide happiness, good grades, or wise marital decisions. You can tell your child how much he or she should enjoy a concert, a good book, or a trip with you. Your assurance will, however, provide no guarantee. Enjoyment, success, and happiness can only be achieved by the person who wants them for himself. If you really want to make someone happy, my best advice is to use your time, talent, money, and effort to help the one person you know well enough to make good decisions about his or her happiness—yourself. The remarkable thing about this formula is that if you are able to gain true happiness and contentment for yourself, other people gain much more pleasure by being around you than if you are constantly trying to manipulate them into having a good time.

Ayn Rand uses a dramatic illustration to show how her selfishness would lead her to actions that many people might describe as heroically unselfish. If someone were about to shoot a husband whom she loved dearly, she admits that she would readily stand between him and the bullet in order to spare his life. A noble gesture? According to Rand, this would be the most selfish thing that she could do. Life would be difficult without this person whom she truly loved, especially if she had to live with the knowledge that she could have spared his life. On the other hand, by stepping in the bullet's path, she dooms her husband to suffer the feelings of loss, pain, and guilt. Instead of a noble act of altruistic concern, her heroism would be the easy way out and the most selfish thing she could do.

When you make any purchase, you are deciding that you prefer that item to the money that it takes to acquire it. Similarly, the merchant wouldn't sell you the item unless the price seemed fair. Under the basic values of a private enterprise society, no one has to sacrifice himself or his possessions for any other person. Exchanges are made only when they are mutually beneficial. The same thing ought to be true in human and social relationships.

People who practice enlightened selfishness will not be insensitive to the needs or feelings and desires of other people. Neither do they accept those wishes as absolute demands. In most instances the wishes of other people can be seen as opportunities for potential exchanges that are mutually beneficial.

Planning for survival in a changing world does not require that you sacrifice your own needs for other people. It cannot be built on the assumption that other people will forfeit their best interests for you. Yet it is possible, even probable, that several people will find that their own self-interest will lead to extensive cooperation via mutual investments in property and protection.

## A NEW YOU

The American Dairy Association a few years ago sponsored a major advertising campaign that stressed the theme, "There's a new you coming every day." Based on the idea that the body generates millions of new cells each day, these ads emphasized the importance of proper nutrition in creating this new you.

Today, we find dinosaurs only in museums because these marvelous creatures lacked the adaptive powers to survive in a changing environment. Because they could not adapt, they became extinct. Our way of life faces a similar challenge today. The old you may have functioned efficiently in a world of economic growth and prosperity. But unless you can acquire new skills and new attitudes, new realities could create insurmountable obstacles to survival.

### A New Mind

A great deal of what modern psychology has discovered is summarized by the great king of Israel, Solomon, in the proverb, "As a man thinketh in his heart, so is he." For centuries scholars and philosophers have attempted to establish a definition of reality. Still, the most brilliant argument will not convince a miserable man that he ought to be happy. During the past decade several mystical writers, such as Carlos Castaneda and Jane Roberts, developed major underground markets by explaining the transient nature of personal reality. An eight-ounce glass with four ounces of water is half full or half empty depending on your perspective. So it is with our financial resources. Many of the discouraged financiers who jumped from window ledges during the crash of 1929 were far from penniless. Life just didn't seem worth living without the wealth they thought they possessed.

A former colleague who taught economics at Columbia University conducted a long-term research project in which he asked groups of people ranging from students to successful business executives how much money they thought it would take for them to be truly happy. He found that it made little difference how much money the people were making. They seemed to consistently report that they needed about 15 percent more than they currently were earning.

A New York attorney gave an interesting example of this principle of need. For many years he had handled a large trust for a young man who received $2 million a year in income. Since this individual had expensive tastes, he was able to spend the entire proceeds of his trust. In a few years the value of his inheritance was reduced because of economic conditions and eventually his income dropped to approximately $200,000 per year. The attorney reported that he received many phone calls from his distraught client who complained, "Life just isn't fair. It's impossible to live on $200,000 a year!"

Before you judge that individual's greed too harshly, ask what life would be like for you if you were to be suddenly receiving 10 percent of your current income. Doubtless it sounds like a pretty bleak picture, but in all probability you can remember a time when you made only 10 percent of your current income. I would even be willing to bet that you were about as happy then as you are now and maybe even saved a larger percentage of your income. Abraham Lincoln was very perceptive when he commented, "I have about decided that people are just as happy as they decide they want to be."

No truth exists apart from the perception of the person who is experiencing it. While you have only limited control over your future environment, you have absolute control over your attitude about it. Norman Vincent Peale has become wealthy by preaching the gospel of the power of positive thinking. More importantly, he has helped many other people become wealthy by following the simplistic formula that he outlines.

Events always grow from thoughts. We can view these thoughts as seeds and the events as harvest. Whatever happens to you is a consequence of your conscious and unconscious thoughts. Accept circumstances as a result of your own thoughts and actions rather than blaming them on greater outside forces, and you can reduce your dependency and open up new options to change your life.

You cannot increase your strength, awareness, potential, or happiness by thought alone. It takes determined effort. Deal with circumstances by concentrating on what you may have done to create the situation. More important, focus on what you can do to make things better.

Don't spend too much time in your analysis of the past. Accept your mistakes and your limitations. Adversity and pain almost always create new strengths if you have the will to win. Invest in a new attitude by thinking of your strengths and abilities. Concentrate on the opportunities for improvements that exist around you. You can collect dividends for many years from these investments of time and money.

In the biblical account of Creation, man was given dominion over the earth and everything within it. We have the power to overcome disease, poverty, war, and crime. Power over these and other problems exists only for those people who feel self-sufficient. Without this attribute we are dependent on our ability to exploit or emulate others. As Arthur Schopenhauer has said, "We forfeit three-fourths of ourselves in order to be like other people." The person who is dependent and must rely upon the crutches of other people can go no faster or farther than those crutches will carry him.

Obviously, self-sufficiency must be developed. Children come into the world with a total dependence upon others. The degree to which they achieve maturity can be measured by the extent to which they overcome this dependence and are able to rely upon their own skill, ability, and judgment.

Unfortunately, many individuals learn at an early age to manipulate others into taking care of them by appearing to be dependent. We do our children a disservice when we do for them those things that they are perfectly capable of handling. Similarly, we do a disservice to the poor and perpetuate their poverty by giving them things rather than opportunities.

The greatest gift that any parent can give a child is independence. It is also the greatest gift that you can give yourself. Self-reliance has been a constant thread throughout the fabric of this book. The need has been evident in every society, but it is becoming more apparent as the clouds of hardship gather around us.

One technique that many people have found useful in creating a more positive outlook and instilling self-confidence in their ability to handle problems is called autosuggestion or subliminal programming. Drawing on the techniques of Transcendental Meditation, yoga, and biofeedback, you can use the positive programming of your subconscious to enforce your belief in goals and yourself. One approach to subliminal programming involves sitting quietly in a darkened room and allowing yourself to move to a dreamlike state by focusing your attention on a picture of yourself in an extremely pleasant environment while consciously relaxing each part of your body from head to toe. After three to five minutes of this form of relaxation, your brainwave activity has moved from an active conscious state of what psychologists describe as the "alpha level." This state of calm relaxation reduces anxiety and provides a receptive environment for positive suggestions. Impressive results have been achieved by people who merely repeat precisely worded statements of personal objectives five or six times. A series of up to eight statements can be effectively repeated in this manner.

These exercises focus concentration and in controlled experiments have proved to enhance recuperation, create self-confidence, help decrease stress, and overcome destructive habits. I realize that many people will find the simplicity of this description somewhat distracting. It all sounds just a little bit hokey. Nevertheless, the some-what stuffy *Harvard Business Review* has reported on the positive effects of these meditative efforts. Why not invest fifteen minutes a day for one month in your private research project?

### A New Body

Perhaps you have heard the axiom "You are what you eat." If this is true, and I believe that it is, Americans are becoming a thoroughly processed, packaged, and preserved people. In 1971 we bought more processed food than fresh food for the first time in history. Since that time the proportion of healthful, natural food has declined steadily. We now spend more than $100 billion each year for convenience foods that provide little nourishment and are potentially damaging. The average citizen consumes almost five pounds of chemical preservatives, stabilizers, coloring, and other additives each year. The use of artificial substances has tripled in the past twenty years to a total of over 1 billion pounds per year. Today there are more than 3,000 chemicals that are deliberately added to your food. The long-term effect of these chemical additives on your body has not yet been determined, but a significant number of nutritionists feels that this chemical feast accounts for the almost epidemic increase in cancer in the United States.

*Food:* The devaluation of foods began when people began to leave their farms and move into cities. As part of their "progress," they turned their back on the nutritious, whole-grain bread that they associated with their rural heritage and replaced it by more elegant, refined white bread, which was associated with wealth.

To make bread more attractive, the nutrients of the grain contained in the germ were removed and fed to cattle. The livestock grew healthy on it. The remainder of the hull (largely starch) was bleached chemically and fed to people, who grew ill from it. Eventually the national health was so affected that a national program of enrichment for white bread was begun. Chemical vitamins were put back and most people relaxed. More cautious nutritionists remained concerned.

These scientists continued to look for relationships between diet and health. Dr. Weston Price embarked on a major study of what healthy people around the world ate. He found pockets of exceptional health in the Swiss Alps, Northern Italy, and isolated locations within Australia, New Zealand, Central America, the Soviet Union, and certain northern portions of Canada and the United States. These people stood straight and tall, had exceptional physical endurance, and good dispositions. There was no evidence of most of the diseases modern civilizations experience. Some of their diets emphasized yogurt. Others drank goat's milk. Some emphasized whole-grain foods. A few had eliminated animal meats.

There were only two things that their diets had in common. First, they were nutritionally balanced. Second, and perhaps more important, none of these healthy cultures knew how to refine foods. They ate them in their natural state.

Today, the United States has become one of the most overfed, undernourished nations in history. Of the approximate 8,000 products on the shelves of the supermarket, over 5,000 have been invented by biochemists in the last thirty years. We now enjoy synthetic flavorings, synthetic foods such as eggs and cream, synthetic colorings, and chemical preservatives. In many instances, chemistry has provided food that is more attractive to the eye than the real thing. But remember that your eye is more easily impressed than your stomach by appearances.

When you begin to stock your survival larder, don't overlook the importance of good nutrition. Even better, start practicing it now. In some instances, health foods may cost a little more, but if you eliminate the junk food, you will find that your total grocery bill remains about the same. There will be an added dividend as well. You will feel better, be healthier, and have lower doctor bills. Within two years of adopting a program of healthy eating, I've seen doctor bills for families drop to less than a third of their former level.

Just for the fun of it, take out some of your old doctor's statements. What are you billed for? You will probably find charges for Billy's bronchitis, Tommy's tonsilitis, and Freddie's flu. Do you find a single item on any of the statements that promotes good health, for avoiding colds or coronaries, or for making you feel healthy, happy, and vigorous?

Unfortunately, the economic incentive for physicians is backwards. We don't pay doctors to keep us in good health. We pay them to make us feel better after we get sick. The ancient Chinese had a much more practical system. They paid their physicians to keep them well. As soon as they got sick, the physician went off the payroll. Since we are not likely to win the endorsement of the American Medical Association for this compensation program, good health for your family is up to you.

If you are looking for a simple formula for healthy eating, let me propose a two-sentence recommendation for nutrition for health. First, eliminate everything from your diet that has refined flour, sugar, or chemicals in it. Secondly, eat as many natural foods (especially fruits, vegetables, and nuts) as you can and two teaspoons of miller's bran per day.

There are some excellent books that have been written on the subject of healthy eating. Obviously, my simple summary cannot provide the detail that these more thorough analyses will offer. Another excellent investment would be to purchase a couple of the nutrition books described in the bibliography. Jane Kinderlehrer's *Confessions of a Sneaky Organic Cook* offers a concise but slightly more involved summary than mine:

*HOW TO HAVE A HEALTHFUL KITCHEN*
(No harmful things and all of the essentials)

The "Good-Nutrition" cook rids her pantry of these foods:

1. Bleached white flour
2. Refined sugar
3. All shortenings that are solid at room temperature

4. White rice
5. Maraschino cherries (they're loaded with harmful preservatives)
6. Any product loaded with BHA or BHT (freshness preservers)
7. Fruits canned with sugar syrup (there are some that are not)
8. All synthetic sweeteners and products sweetened with them (Saccharin as well as cyclamates)
9. All sugared dry cereals
10. Hydrogenated peanut butter (use the natural)
11. All candy made with refined sugar
12. Commercial breads that are loaded with emulsifiers and preservatives
13. Refined table salt

The "Good-Nutrition" cook keeps on her pantry shelf:

1. Raw honey
2. Raw sugar
3. Date sugar
4. Soy flour
5. Whole wheat flour (stone ground)
6. Carob flour (chocolate substitute)
7. Wheat germ (in the refrigerator)
8. Wheat germ oil (in the refrigerator)
9. Soy and sesame oils (cold pressed) in the refrigerator
10. Nutritional yeast (sometimes called brewer's yeast)
11. Sesame seeds (unhulled)
12. Sunflower seeds (raw)
13. Pumpkin seeds
14. Kelp (as a salt substitute)
15. Unsweetened coconut
16. Seeds for sprouting (wheat, rye, oat, mung beans, alfalfa, etc.)
17. Raw nuts

Another simple rule of thumb is never to purchase a product that has any ingredient listed on the label that you can't pronounce. With this restriction William Buckley might have a more extensive diet than most of us, but almost without exception, those complicated words and strange initials signify a chemical that isn't going to do you any good.

*Fat:* Maintaining a proper weight level is easier for people who eat well. Obesity is not an evidence of too much of a good thing. Typically, it means that there has been too much of some bad things. Today, combating fatness has become a $11.5-billion-a-year industry. There are over 30 million people in this country who are seriously overweight and 15 million obese Americans. If you'll pardon a pun, obesity is becoming widespread. Unnecessary weight puts a strain on most of the body's organs and is a contributing factor in a large number of serious illnesses.

Losing weight is not incompatible with enjoying life—or food. If you are willing to invest a little extra effort in developing a healthy body that will serve you more efficiently, consider the following simple suggestions:

1. Take time to learn a little bit more about the requirements of good nutrition.
2. Study your eating habits and requirements. Do you have to eat at precisely the same time each day? Could you eat four nutritious snacks rather than three large meals?
3. Don't eat leftovers. It is no more wasteful to dump something in the garbage than it is to dump it into your stomach. If you are really hung up about waste, get a dog or start a compost heap.
4. Always eat a nutritious, high-protein breakfast to get you started. This may be simply a glass of milk fortified with a tasty protein compound.
5. Never eat empty calories. Don't eat anything made with sugar or refined flour. This especially includes donuts, macaroni, frosted cereal, and chocolate candies.
6. Never eat until you are comfortable. Eat slowly and give hunger pains a time to subside.

7. Keep plenty of carrots, radishes, and cucumbers ready for between-meal snacks.
8. Be sure to include lecithin in your diet. Lecithin helps you feel well fed with less food. It also helps to avoid some of the health problems associated with dieting, such as cholesterol deposits and gall bladder complications.
9. Avoid coffee. Drinking black coffee during a diet leads to added production of insulin and actually increases hunger pains.
10. Don't use artificial sweeteners in an effort to reduce calories. One of your objectives should be to retain your taste buds so that you no longer crave sweets. Moreover, artificial sweeteners of all kinds are highly suspect from a health standpoint. If sweets are absolutely required, use honey as a substitute. With most recipes and for most purposes, you can substitute one unit of honey for three units of sugar.
11. Weigh yourself every morning. In this manner you can observe the close relationship between food intake and weight.
12. Start an exercise program. Exercise combined with good nutritional habits is essential for permanent healthy living. More about the exercise regime later.

*Fitness:* One positive aspect of contemporary life is the current emphasis on physical fitness. It doesn't make a great deal of difference what program you use as long as you have a regular routine that provides a workout for your respiratory and circulatory systems and develops some degree of efficiency and endurance. The best exercise you can do is the kind of exercise you will do.

Finding something you enjoy that gives you a real workout is the only rule you have to remember. The benefits are numerous. Regular exercise makes you look and feel infinitely better. It reduces your chance of heart attack or other circulatory or respiratory ailments. It enables you to work harder and more efficiently. It tones up muscles throughout the body, improves general circulation, muscle tone, skin appearance, and overall well-being.

Before jumping into the middle of a rigorous program, you probably should check with your family physician—especially if you have a history of medical problems that might conflict with the exercise. If you are over thirty, you should have a checkup that includes an electrocardiogram (EKG). If you are over forty, you should request a Master's EKG, that monitors your heart while exercising. A regular EKG determines if you have experienced cardiac damage. The second records the conditions of your heart under stress.

Try to choose a regular time for your workout and make it a part of your daily routine. Physicians recommend that you wait a couple of hours after a meal. Before your evening meal is an ideal time. Don't try to start off with too rigorous an activity the first day. Stiff muscles discourage follow-up exercise. Start off with just a few minutes of exertion and add as your fitness improves. George Burns used to say that he got his exercise from serving as a pallbearer for his friends who tried to exercise too hard. Try to keep a chart showing your progress. It will not only help you remember where you are, it will serve as a motivator.

Perspiration isn't a danger sign, but you shouldn't push past the point of discomfort. Signs of overexertion during exercise includes tightness in the chest, severe breathlessness, dizziness, and nausea. If you experience these, you should stop exercising immediately. Count your pulse about five minutes after you have completed your workout. If it is still over 120, you are pushing too hard for a person in your condition. Ten minutes after the end of your exercise, the pulse should be below 100.

Don't get discouraged if you don't make immediate progress. It took a good while to get out of shape. Getting back in shape will take a while, too.

Most people recognize the importance of a warm-up period. Unfortunately, few people understand that the body also needs a cooling-down period after exercise.

Moving into complete relaxation immediately after exercise can cause dizzy spells, fainting, and even more serious problems. Five minutes of walking will ease the transition between vigorous exertion and relaxation.

Many fitness specialists suggest that your goal should be to keep your heart beating at about 60 to 70 percent of your maximum heart rate for close to fifteen minutes. A person below forty can view 140 to 125 as his optimal range. The younger you are, the higher sustained heartbeat you should tolerate. For individuals between forty and sixty, the range will be between 110 and 125 heartbeats per minute. Again, the older you are, the less stress you should plan to experience. For those above sixty, a heartbeat between 100 and 110 should be viewed as reasonable maximum level of exertion.

Remember, there are practical reasons for developing the type of health habits described in the preceding paragraphs regardless of your economic environment. It only follows that good health will be even more important during a period of unusual stress, tension, and independence than ever before. With a new, improved body and mind, you will be able to cope with the challenges of a chaotic future with calm, confidence, and strength.

## NEW RELATIONSHIPS

We live in a world of transient relationships. Friendships, jobs, and marriages are frequently viewed as short-term commitments. Dr. Eli Ginsberg of Columbia University has predicted that we are all on the verge of becoming metropolitan people without ties or committed long-term friends or neighbors. In a scholarly paper entitled "Friendships of the Future," psychologist Courtney Tall suggests that "stability, based on close relationships with a few people, will be ineffective due to high mobility, a wide interest range, and growing capacity for adaptation and change found among members of a highly automated society. Friendship patterns of the majority in the future will provide for many satisfactions, while substituting many close relationships of shorter duration for the long-term friendships formed in the past."

While many Americans have a pool of acquaintances ranging from 500 to 2,500, most have only a limited number of people who can be referred to as friends. One study of middle-class couples in the Midwest found that the average couple listed approximately seven friendship units. Jess Lair, Professor of Psychology at the University of Montana, has suggested that it is far better to have six good friends than it is to have a host of casual acquaintances. As we will discuss in Chapter 13, unique meaningful friendships will be far more valuable in your quest for survival than an impressive list of mere acquaintances. When you get right down to it, how many people do you feel free to talk to candidly about your concerns for the future? If you are embarrassed to share your anxieties with an acquaintance, that is pretty good evidence that you don't have a genuine friendship. There are practical as well as psychological reasons for having a few people you can depend on in any emergency rather than a multitude of fair-weather friends.

A key test of the quality of a relationship is whether the advantage and benefit are mutual. As we have stressed before, some of the best relationships are practically selfish for both parties involved. Openness, honesty, and integrity are the foundations of strong relationships. If you are afraid to talk to someone about your concerns, it is probably because you fear rejection. Fear of rejection really means that you do not have much confidence in the strength of a relationship. In all cases, close relationships require considerable effort and honest, open communication.

According to the psychologist Dr. Ari Kiev, "Human misery usually results when we encounter unexpected events unprepared. At times of crises, people with a natural affinity are drawn to each other as if they had prepared for the eventuality." In a similar way people who are inclined to prepare for certain eventualities are naturally drawn together. If you don't already recognize that you share concerns with some of your acquaintances, I believe that the material contained in this book can serve as an important catalyst in strengthening your relationships.

## PERSONAL INVESTMENT STRATEGY

The same principles you employ in handling your financial investments are appropriate for personal investment. The serious investor will not put a great deal of money in the stock market without checking the financial pages of the newspaper on a regular basis.

If you are interested in personal survival, you'll want to do a great deal of research and reading. A complete library of important resources is contained in the bibliography of this book. I have added an asterisk to the ones I think are practically essential.

In addition to the survival library, you will want to stay on top of current events that affect your social and economic environment. Subscribe to at least one of the major newsletters reviewed in Appendix B. Subscribe to a couple of practical periodicals or financially oriented newspapers, such as the *Wall Street Journal, Business Week,* or *U.S. News & World Report.* These sources will often help you read between the lines written by your daily newspaper.

Get involved with your reading and approach every subject from a practical standpoint. Don't read to be discouraged, read to decide how you can best cope with situations as they arise. Make notes and underline freely. Check side-headings and topics to select those that you feel are more important to you. Few magazine articles and books are written in such a way that every page is equally valuable for you. Look for the items that will make your reading more challenging and rewarding.

No matter how long you have been out of school and regardless of the advanced degrees you may hold, your education isn't over. It had better not be. Once a person has finished learning, he or she is really finished!

Call your nearest university or community college and

find out what types of courses are offered through continuing education. Make a list of all the courses you think would help you achieve self-sufficiency. Plan to take at least one course each term until you have increased your arsenal of survival skills. Most of these courses will meet only once a week. It is worth trading an evening of mind-deadening television for stimulation and practical learning.

I am probably the world's worst handyman. Some time ago I decided that I needed to correct this deficiency in case the services I was dependent upon were to become unavailable. I made a list of the courses that I felt would be useful to me during the coming decade. Mine was a rather extensive list, and I am still taking courses. I don't expect to complete this project before I am forced to start using some of the things I have learned. Many of the concepts have already proved valuable.

My first course was a standard first-aid program offered by the Red Cross. It dealt primarily with the type of skills that are required for accident prevention and the treatment of minor accidents. It helped provide preparation to treat several injuries and to meet most emergencies when medical assistance is not readily available. This course took only one day of my time and was one of the best investments I've ever made.

Next I took a program on home repair. The knowledge provided by this course would be virtually essential in the kind of society I envision. This expenditure has already returned many times the original modest tuition investment because of the newly acquired ability to solve minor problems without calling for the friendly neighborhood plumber and his gold-plated invoice pad.

My original list of courses included small engine repair, automotive repair and maintenance, home remodeling, organic gardening, living off the land, wilderness experience workshop, environmental education, landscape design, basic gardening, furniture upholstering, self-defense, and speed-reading (just to stay up with all the new areas I am interested in). I have not finished with working my way through the original list, but have discovered at least a dozen new courses that I am anxious to add.

If you are involved in team preparations, practice division of labor. If you are working as a couple or an extended survival community, try to split up the responsibility for areas of knowledge or types of expertise. In this manner some people can specialize in the area where they are most interested or skillful. It will also allow you to accomplish your goals more quickly. In many instances my wife and I would enjoy taking some of the classes together. Unfortunately, I don't feel that time provides us the luxury of this type of duplication.

My final investment advice is to begin immediately practicing the concepts we have talked about. Invest a little time in acquiring your skills and keeping those skills up to date. The worst mistake you can make in reading this book is to agree with the concept, but to decide that there is plenty of time to prepare when things get a little less hectic for you. Your life will not become less crowded until you rearrange your priorities or until circumstances rearrange them for you.

Even with food prices becoming more exorbitant every day, I still believe that I can receive a larger financial return by writing another book or conducting another seminar than practicing my organic gardening skills. By short-term return on investment analysis, I can't justify the time I spend with the garden. Still, I don't want to face the coming crisis with only some excellent books and pamphlets about survival. Right now it is fairly easy to find people who are able and willing to offer advice and assistance. Supplies are readily available and less expensive than they will be again until after the crisis becomes less acute.

Today's mistakes are not catastrophic. Learn to trust your hunches and rely on your intuition. For important issues, this may solve more problems than logic or intelligence. Learn when to seek the counsel of others and when to ignore advice that doesn't convince the jury of your own judgment. Don't assume that other people have better insight about what your objectives should be or how you should go about achieving your goals.

You are your best investment. Respect that investment, and your dividends will be generous and long lasting.

# CHAPTER 8

# SETTING UP
# A FOREIGN HAVEN

When I was an undergraduate, there was one professor who stood out from the rest in that he really seemed to be headed for the big time. With his boundless energy, he always had a number of projects whirling. Within a few years he used his technical expertise to create a product that was in great demand. Today, that product is in almost every school in the nation. The professor no longer works for the university but is employed by his own company, which is headquartered in the Bahamas. Though you are likely to see him anywhere in the States, a majority of his earnings flow through the Bahamian company.

That innovator has done what many others only dream about. When the conversation turns to talk of rising taxes and increasing government control, someone always pipes up to say that he has heard that with the right legal maneuvers a person can shelter his money by the use of some other country's special tax laws, banking system, or unique concessions to the money from outside.

Most people, however, conclude that such arrangements are too good to be true and that if they were for real, everybody and his brother would be making use of them. And so my guess is that while you may like to joke about having millions stashed safely in a Swiss numbered bank account or setting up a business in some exotic tax haven, you haven't done much checking into the matter.

# REASON FOR INTEREST (AND PRINCIPAL) ABROAD

In actual fact, there *are* foreign havens for your money. They *do* provide situations in which you can profit while keeping your money secure. As our own nation's economy continues to worsen, the impetus for setting up protective foreign custody for part of your wealth is increasing. Some chapters in this book talk about the ways you can realize the highest possible increases in your wealth through investments. This chapter is not primarily about the highest return on your money. That can (and often will) occur when the world monetary situation has taken a surprise turn and given overseas investments a serendipitous increase. But the primary thought in setting up foreign havens is rarely to make a killing through high interest on deposits. Rather, it is to *protect* the principal and gain a respectable return that is safer or less subject to taxations than U.S. institutions.

The people who have brought the greatest fame to "numbered Swiss accounts" are the Nazi officers who remained alive and well heeled after World War II on money that they had stolen and stashed in secret accounts. There were, however, even more Jewish merchants who were able to use funds they had wisely put away in Switzerland to arrange a new life in a new land when they accurately read the signs of decay in the early days of the Third Reich. In more recent years Mafia bosses have revived the intrigue of the numbered account. While secret numbered accounts really do exist, they do not constitute the strength or even the primary attraction of the Swiss banking system.

*All* accounts in Swiss banks are secret and the Swiss have irritated other governments on many occasions by simply refusing to divulge information about the accounts of foreign depositors. But the fabled *numbered* accounts are even secret from the Swiss bankers themselves—except for one key bank officer! The accounts can be opened without a name, and deposits and withdrawals made by the number and some prearranged code words. It is possible to keep the money completely anonymous, though the Swiss are going to demand to be satisfied about its sources. For the most part, numbered accounts remain the domain of those who have something to hide. There is still the overwhelming majority of holders of Swiss accounts who obey every law and make full disclosure of all interest received. Why then, if there is no secrecy advantage, would anyone go to the trouble of setting up and maintaining a long-distance bank account?

### A Place to Hide

There are several major reasons for you to set up any of a variety of potential foreign havens. First, they can serve as a place to put some of the money that you would like to hide from someone. Second, a haven opens many doors for your expanded business interests and activities or to shelter some of your business income from confiscatory taxes. Finally, it may offer the possibility of a safe haven to hide yourself!

Europeans who survived the financial devastations of World War II almost invariably did so by adhering to an age-old principle of money management: "Never keep all your wealth in the country where you live because *anything* can happen—and usually does." Given enough time, almost any nation is likely to let go of its conservative principles and embark on shortsighted economic programs that end up eroding the financial strength of its citizens. Already in our relatively short national history, the United States has made rich people out of many whose holdings were not dependent on U.S. economic integrity. Do not misunderstand the message of this chapter. It is not that our system is all bad and the Swiss system is without flaw. For many reasons I still choose to live in the United States. My implication is that no matter what economic environment you live in (even in Switzerland itself) you will be wise to make sure you have part of your wealth abiding under one or more other systems.

### A Perspective on the U.S.

The last time I was in the Bahamas, I spent some time with the chief executive officer of a local branch of a major Swiss bank there. He had grown up in Switzerland, but spent a major portion of his banking career in Brazil, where he had lived through some scary inflation experiences. His concern about the future of the United States was a sense of moral bankruptcy in the country, that the national character is greatly flawed so that neither the dollar nor the American commitment is respected abroad. He pointed out our total lack of willingness to bite the bullet when necessary to solve economic problems. He also suggested that, while most of his investments were in hard currency such as gold and silver and primarily in Switzerland, he would never be without enough gold to get him anywhere in the world he might want to go in an emergency. He had one child in Europe and another in Africa and he wanted to be assured that he could get to either of them no matter what set of circumstances might develop.

This cosmopolitan banker argued that it was a mistake to keep the majority of your wealth close at hand. I would agree with this opinion if I lived in the Bahamas, but even though I'm not optimistic about the future of the U.S. economy, I still prefer to remain reasonably close to a significant portion of my assets.

There are some ways to make big money through international buying and selling. However, most of the pros who know the ropes of international commodity costs are not going to be reading this book. They have long since opened their foreign corporations and bank accounts. My assumption is that you are interested in the basics of the question: whether, why, and step-by-step how. You'll find these answers in the next section. If you want more details, I'll suggest additional resources for you in the Bibliography.

# YOUR SECRET BANK ACCOUNT

Throughout this book I've stressed the idea that only you can design the unique combination of financial arrangements that's right for your resources and economic objec-

tives. This is no cop-out but merely a restatement of a
basic truth: I can give you information; only you can
decide which parts of it are truth for you.

### Still a Live Option—Despite Rumors

Regardless of what you've heard, Swiss* bank accounts
have not become historic relics. The recent boom in their
popularity has made Swiss bankers less enthusiastic about
opening small accounts. Still they remain hot and are
likely to remain so because their history and popularity
are based on the integrity of the Swiss banking profession, which had been around for centuries before the
colonies gained their independence. From time to time,
we Americans get the word through news releases that a
potential new treaty will result in the agreement of Swiss
banks to disclose information about funds held in their
accounts. While there continue to be negotiations, developments, and news stories, you can be sure that the
Swiss are not going to give up the confidential nature of
their banking relationships. Not only is the revealing of
bank information against Swiss law, it is the mark of
distinction that gives the reputation of absolute integrity
to the Swiss. When you *do* see headlines about agreements to disclose information, the fine print will reveal
that the agreement applies to cases where a court order
has been negotiated because of overwhelming "probable
cause" that the money was stolen or extorted.

You may also get the word that Swiss banks no longer
welcome deposits from Americans because of the dying
dollar and its tendency to drain the blood out of the
Swiss franc. It is true that the dollar is sick and it is true
that the Swiss would do quite well without every Tom,
Dick, and Harry who want to deposit $1000 against the
steady decline of the dollar. However, the Swiss have
been international bankers since long before the U.S.
dollar. They have appropriate legislation to control the
influx of huge sums to exploit currency changes. There is

---

*While this section deals primarily with Swiss accounts, many of the principles of
secrecy apply to any country with "Swiss" laws concerning bank secrecy.

actually a negative interest charged on some accounts, and words like that can be blown out of context in news stories to convince Americans that all the loopholes of Swiss banking have been closed.

The advantages of a Swiss account do live on and will continue to live. They result from basic philosophical stances of the U.S. government and the Swiss government. They will not be treatied out of existence. Next time you see a story about the end of Swiss bank accounts as worthwhile devices for Americans, keep reading between the lines until you discover who released the story. Nine times out of ten, it will reveal itself to be from a government agency that stands to gain if Americans are convinced that one more loophole has been closed.

About a decade ago the Swiss began to be more serious about discouraging dollar movement into their banking system. And recently, some of the insider trading scandals have helped make what might have been a temporary adjustment into a permanent restriction. You can, however, open or maintain a Swiss franc account of up to SF1000,000 without being subject to the negative interest. You can even earn interest on accounts up to the first SF20,000 (that's about 10,000 U.S. dollars as I write this). You can also buy Swiss francs and put them in a safe deposit box. Investment adviser Harry Schultz recommends buying Swiss domiciled mutual funds, provided that 80 percent of its assets are invested outside of Switzerland. These shares are denominated in Swiss francs so you still accomplish your objective.

In almost every case of imposed obstacles to foreign use of Swiss accounts, there is a way to circumvent the problem. It should be remembered that Swiss bankers want to do banking business and are unlikely to establish restrictions to prohibit their own progress. However, there is one lesson our country needs to learn from the Swiss. Current profits, which are valued, are still not the overriding motive for any and all policies. The Swiss will forgo a profit today if they see that it will weaken their position in the future. That is why the Swiss franc remains backed by gold. This is also why the Swiss have kept their inflation in check and progressively reduced their trade deficit. The Swiss account you open will hold its value because, in spite of the fluctuating values of world currencies and political underpinnings, the Swiss understand the basics of economics.

### The Benefits of a Swiss Connection

There are several advantages for you to consider in a Swiss bank account. To begin with, you will have some money outside your own country where it cannot be confiscated by a new government policy. As I have emphasized before, arrange your money in concentric circles, keeping some in liquid forms for emergencies and other categories in ever-widening circles and in ever-increasing productivity. Some of your overseas money should remain in highly liquid forms as mentioned earlier. Other amounts can be invested at higher interest, less liquidity, but equal safety from government intervention.

A Swiss bank account will allow you to deal in foreign currencies, which has become more than a matter of speculation. It is equally important to anyone who travels or deals internationally. One of the truly innovative items of Swiss banking is the multicurrency checkbook. This allows you to deposit your money in a Swiss checking account and then write checks in any type of currency. Your banks will make payment in the currency you specify on the check and deduct the equivalent amount from your Swiss account. You avoid the headaches and exorbitant charges of transferring from one currency to the next at each border.

If you intend to really take action in arranging your financial affairs to survive and prosper regardless of the crash and coming depression, it is a certainty that you will want to open one or more Swiss (or other international) accounts for a well-rounded personal financial program. Should a miracle occur and the crash be avoided, you will still be in a stronger position for making investments anywhere in the world, utilizing the financial advice of the experts in international finance, and maintaining your fiscal privacy.

Finally, the Swiss banking system does something that young American bank employees would have difficulty even believing—they do not use your money to make money for them. They *will* of course be happy to invest your money if you so request, but they will not loan out your deposit to someone else before you can get out the door. American banks automatically and by policy keep all money working. They could not possibly pay off all their depositors at the same time, but most Swiss banks could. They earn their profits from rendering the services connected with handling your money—not using your money while you're not. No banking system is absolutely sound. The Swiss have some unfortunate chapters in their banking history but overall their banking system is the soundest in the world. Even so, if I lived in Switzerland and carried a Swiss passport, I would still expect to keep some of my wealth in another country.

### The Problems

Just for balance, let me note a few of the factors that many would consider deterrents from opening and utilizing Swiss accounts. To me, none of the objections is of sufficient weight to rule out the Swiss connection, but I do want to give you all the facts.

First, a Swiss bank account is likely to be less convenient because it is in Switzerland instead of a half mile from your house. Even though writers are fond of waxing eloquent about the shrinking nature of our world, your money in a Swiss account is going to be several days away from you. Our modern communications *will* allow you to get your Swiss banker on the phone for about $4.00 for three minutes, but the turnaround time for the transaction and completing of business remains limited by human clerical speed and the turtles who deliver the U.S. mail. Even if you decide to use the direct-dial powers available to you, there are only two or three hours each day when your workday overlaps the 9-to-5 of Swiss time zones. You *can* move the money a little faster by having it wired between your Swiss bank and one of its correspondent American banks, but the cost of the wire is usually fifteen dollars or more, the messages can often be garbled, and your confidentiality goes out the window since a record is kept of every wire. Convenience is an insurmountable factor and the obvious conclusion is that you don't try to use a foreign account as you would a local account. Keep the number of transactions few, simple, and economically self-supporting. Don't put money in Switzerland that has to be home for Christmas—unless its trip home can pay for itself!

There's no FDIC in Switzerland—that is, there is no government agency that exists to insure the safety of bank deposits as our Federal Deposit Insurance Corporation does. The Swiss have less government on every score than we do and their hesitancy to gamble with depositor money makes such a safeguard unnecessary. But as previously stated, we don't really have deposit insurance here in the U.S., as we think we do. Even the director of the FDIC has admitted that his fund could in no way expect to pay back major runs on a large number of banks. So, while Swiss bankers cannot offer you the promise of FDIC security, American bankers may offer you the promise but not the reality.

Swiss bankers are going to pay you lower interest rates than you get in lots of other places. They will require advance notice of withdrawals in many cases. And, as stated before, they will even charge you part of your interest in some cases. These are disadvantages that you can live with if you are committed to the importance of having some of your money beyond the grasp of governmental regulations. Actually, the Swiss withholding tax on interest paid is not overwhelming and can be regained if you are not afraid to lose your anonymity. You see, the tax was instituted to try to discourage secrecy among those unwilling to pay for the privilege. The way it works is that when your money earns interest, 30 percent of it is withheld and mailed to the Swiss government by your Swiss bank—not with your name but in one check along with everyone else's withheld tax. If you want to stay anonymous, you wave goodbye to the 30 percent of your interest and consider it the cost of privacy. If, however, you are reporting all interest earned (as the IRS requires) there is no need for your high-priced anonymity and you can get a large part of your 30 percent back. All you have to do is file a form R82 with the Swiss government, which will remit to you 5/6 of the withheld money. It's your decision: if you value the secrecy, you can forfeit the 30 percent withheld from your interests earned, or, if you figure the IRS always knows everything you do anyway, the forms R82 are available from the Swiss bank where you are doing business.

The negative interest tax was instituted to discourage international speculators from rushing large sums of money (like a million dollars or more) in and out of Swiss francs just to make quick profits as various national currencies fluctuated. But unless your investment is likely to be in excess of $250,000 you are not in much danger of trouble from the negative interest tax. While the Swiss do have a few rather inconsequential taxes on foreign banking transactions, they are unlikely to hinder you as long as you are not making a large number of transactions unnecessarily and are availing yourself of the advice and counsel of the branch manager of the Swiss bank in your own city.

The remaining problems result from human error—yours, the Swiss bank's, or a combination of both. When you are delivering detailed messages over thousands of miles between people who speak different languages, the stage is set for all kinds of misunderstandings and gaps in communication. For starters, the Europeans often use commas where we would use periods and use periods where we would put commas. If you anticipate this reversal, it won't stump you. But if you don't know it's coming it can do amazing things to your deposit or withdrawal. Also, the European dates are written with the number of the day first. In America, December 5, 1983 is written 12/5/83 while the European would write it 5/12/83. Such a change could make a significant difference in checking on your interest computations!

When you correspond with your Swiss bank, a typewriter is your best friend. For some reason we Americans, who have more typewriters than any other nation on earth, will undoubtedly try to handwrite a quick note to our Swiss bankers. It is an invitation to misunderstanding. Always type your communications to Swiss banks and keep them as simple and direct as possible. Whatever you do, avoid explaining things with figures of speech—the Swiss are not dumb, but neither are they educated in U.S. television lingo.

The final area of human error results from the noncomputerized nature of Swiss banking transactions, the rapidly changing values of many currencies, and the time lag inherent in international transactions. If you initiate a transaction today to buy gold with dollars, there are the variables of the cost of gold now and when the instruction is received, the value of the dollars now and when your message is received, and natural time lags. If you make the request on Wednesday and it arrives after the gold transactions close on Friday, it will be handled on Monday or Tuesday—nearly a week after you issued the instruction. The Swiss have tried to computerize their operation, but so far it has not been possible to develop programs that are acceptable. Transactions are still manual and therefore are still subject to the problems of human error. This is complicated by the fact that Switzerland's policy restricting immigration is keeping specialized banking personnel from entering the country freely. The result is a gradual lessening of efficiency and professional care from the transactions of Swiss banks. Even so, the average mistake that you think you find in your statement will eventually prove to be your own failure to take into account some minor fluctuation of values or some incidental change by the bank because of the method you choose to achieve a certain objective.

In spite of these few problems, a Swiss bank account remains a bargain in a time when you cannot be optimistic about American political and economic direction—or the lack of it.

### Types of Accounts

There are a number of kinds of accounts that you may choose from. As you might expect, they offer the ever-present balance between security and interest. If you choose an account that can deliver higher interest, you can expect somewhat reduced safety for the investment and considerable reduction in liquidity.

A *current account* is what the Swiss call a checking account. Unlike your neighborhood American bank, they will not issue a neat little checkbook since the use of your current account will be more select than paying the light bill and the PTA dues. Most often you will send a letter or a wire to inform the bank of deposits and withdrawals from your current account. The name refers to the fact that the balance may be changing at any time. Usually there is no interest paid on such an account, though most holders of current accounts have made significant gains during the recent past by merely having their money stored in Swiss francs while the dollar was being devalued.

A *deposit account* is similar to an American savings account except that there are some restrictions on the amounts that may be withdrawn. Ordinarily you can withdraw up to $3,000 each month with no advance notice, but if you want to withdraw more, you need to give up to three months prior notice. The amounts vary but the basic idea is similar to the Certificates of Deposit available in U.S. banks, except that you make small withdrawals. If your deposit account is kept in Swiss francs, the bank will pay you about 1–3 percent interest, not "compounded semiannually," but paid once a year. You can get higher interest if you ask the bank to keep your account in some currency other than Swiss francs, but, by doing that, you lose one of the primary values of the Swiss account.

What the Swiss call a *savings account* usually pays 3 percent interest but requires six months notice for withdrawal of more than $1,000. Here again is the similarity to the American Certificate of Deposit except for the ability to make withdrawals and the low interest.

The *investment savings account* raises the interest a

little and tightens the liquidity. If you suspect that you are going to have a sudden need for more than $350, you probably should not consider an investment account.

The *fixed deposit account* closes the periodic withdrawal option out completely. You agree to place a fixed amount of money in the account and leave it for three months, six months, or a year at a time. Interest rates vary, with a higher interest going naturally to the money that is committed for the longer periods of time.

A *custodial account* is the place to put your gold bullion or your original Rembrandt. It is quite similar to the American safe deposit box in that *you* pay the bank for the storage service and they give you no interest and lay no hands on your possessions. It is unlike an American safe deposit box in that it will still be available without complications even if American banks have a sudden declared bank holiday as they did in 1930 following the stock market crash. If you can store cash, gold, silver, or art objects in your custodial account, the bank will keep it secure and even if the Swiss bank should fail, your possessions will not be considered part of the bank's holdings. If you are looking for the closest thing in the world to 100 percent financial security, buy gold or Swiss francs and store them in a custodial account in a Swiss bank. More likely, you will want to include this absolute in your *balanced* financial plan, putting your emergency funds there and then launching into the higher-risk ventures with other portions of your money.

*Trust accounts* are another way of using Swiss banking expertise. Like trust funds anywhere, these are arrangements where you *trust* your money to the management of some experienced, professional investor. Though the Swiss are fine bankers and of unquestionable ethics, they are not, on the average, much better investors than any other nationality. My advice is to do your homework and manage your own investments if they total less than one-half million dollars. Above that, you still need to do your homework but your research should be directed to finding the right advisers. If you've made substantial money as a physician, business owner, or farmer, you'll be better off to do what you do best and pay someone else to help manage your investments. You still need to stay on top of your financial management.

Some Swiss cities sell *municipal bonds* just as American cities sell bonds. One major difference is that the cities don't seem as likely to go bankrupt in Switzerland as they do in the States. A second, equally significant difference is that these Swiss bonds are denominated in Swiss francs, which have regularly increased in value relative to the U.S. dollar over recent years. The bad news is that Swiss law prohibits the sale of these bonds to nonresidents. However, your Swiss bank can buy one of these bonds for you if the bank happens to be selling it for another customer. These government bonds are tax-exempt as in the United States and there is no withholding tax on your interest.

*Swiss stocks and mutual funds* are also available to nonresidents with restrictions, but they are really no better or worse than American stocks and mutual funds. If you are going to get into the stock market, do it in one that you can check daily.

*Eurocurrency accounts* are for your use in buying and selling amounts of currency in any country other than its native country. For example, your Swiss banker could establish such an account for you if you wanted to purchase and hold 10,000 Dutch guilders. In such a case you are the one out on the limb since the Swiss bank acts only as a broker for you. You have to be the one to know *why* one currency in another country is likely to be a particularly good buy and just how long you ought to keep it. In any case, don't hold it a full year since the U.S. Interest Equalization Tax applies to contracts of twelve months or more. These are pretty risky for the novice. They certainly do not need to be listed under the safer and more secure aspects of Swiss banking. However, with your security established, they may prove to be a useful and exciting area of investment productivity.

*Certificates of deposit* are used in a way similar to Eurocurrency, with the Swiss bank purchasing for you a specified amount of the currency of a given nation. There is no withholding tax and no negative interest tax. The Swiss bank is not responsible for the outcome of your investment or for the failure of the bank where the investment may be made.

### Types of Banks

The banks of Switzerland fall into three categories: big banks, private banks, and other banks.

Five banks qualify as big banks. They are the Swiss Credit Bank, Union Bank, Swiss Volksbank, Bank Leu, and Swiss Bank Corporation. These are the retail banks, with much larger assets than other banks in the country. Walking into one, an American would feel more at home since they have much the same appearance and services of the American bank. They are the go-getters of Swiss banking and the first three have offices in major U.S. cities. These retail banks are the most likely to give the American novice the kind of understanding service and Swiss philosophy that will accomplish his purposes in opening a Swiss account in the first place.

My personal feeling is that the Bank Leu is probably most responsive to the needs of the small investor (i.e., people with accounts under $100,000). Bank Leu provides a good variety of services and is solid and reputable. I have dealt with Bank Leu and its branches both in Switzerland and in the Bahamas and have found them to be dependable and reliable.

The private banks are rather unlike anything familiar in American banking. They are less like banks as we think of them and more like the private lending capability of one rich individual. The private banks are not incorporated. This relieves the owner of the obligation to publish financial statements and therefore allows the owner to get into many types of lending endeavors that might never even be considered by other banks. However, since the private banks are not incorporated and the liability is therefore not limited, the banker himself must stand behind each loan. His personal fortune is on the line every time he agrees to a deal. The chances of your becoming involved with a private bank on your first

Swiss account are remote. They have to choose their customers carefully because of the potential risk in every decision. While the private banks *do* perform all the same services that the big banks perform, you might do well to think of them as the country clubs of Swiss banking, with participation by invitation only.

There are a number of *other banks* in Switzerland. These are, of course, branches of major American banks as well as branches of banks representing other countries. They tend to be like the private banks in that they cater to specific groups—often the non-Swiss population. Various ones of the other banks have their unique advantages but overall I have not found that their strengths ever compensate for their weaknesses. For example, the Swiss branches of American banks are sometimes subject to American laws concerning availability of information. My feeling is that if you are going to the trouble of having a Swiss bank account, you ought to go all the way and have your account with a *Swiss* Swiss bank.

### Legal Limits

Until recently, the amounts that could legally be taken out of the U.S. were so small that it was scarcely worth the trouble. But the Treasury Department has increased the "small account exemption" on foreign financial accounts to $10,000, and now you can open a foreign bank or brokerage account worth up to $10,000 and not have to report its existence to the U.S. government. In an age of declining financial privacy, this is a real breath of fresh air and a great opportunity.

The increase of the small account exemption has been a gradual process. Basically, the Treasury has taken a common-sense approach to the foreign reporting requirement. The feds don't want to bother with negligible small accounts. Prior to 1982, the small account exemption was only $1,000—hardly worth worrying about. Then it was raised to $5,000, a modest amount. But now that it's $10,000, it's worth serious consideration. This is a truly confidential opportunity the private investor won't want to pass up.

Here's how it works. Instructions on filing the 1040 tax form for 1986 state on page 23 that you can check the "No" box to the question, "Do you have a foreign bank, brokerage or financial account?" if "the combined value of the accounts was $10,000 or less during the whole year." If the foreign accounts exceed $10,000, you are required to file form TD 90-22.1. The form is sent to the Treasury Department in Washington, D.C., where your name, address, Social Security number, and detailed account information are placed on computer. The Treasury form requires you to reveal the name and address of the financial institution, account number, type of account, etc. I firmly believe that private investors should avoid the form if at all possible. Last year the IRS disclosed that checking the "Yes" box increases your chances of being audited. I don't like the idea of being put on a computer list. In case of a national emergency or monetary crisis, the government may impose foreign exchange controls or call in the gold. The Treasury list of foreign account holders may come in handy for selective prosecution or audit.

### Seven Foreign Alternatives to Avoid Government Reporting Requirements

Actually, a $10,000 foreign bank account is not the only offshore investment that avoids Treasury reporting requirements. Here is a full list of potential non-reportable, non-taxable, private investments outside the country de-developed by Dr. Mark Skousen in his newsletter "Forecasts & Strategies."

1. $10,000 foreign bank account
2. Foreign-based credit card, overdraft privileges, line of credit, useful in making sensitive private purchases when traveling abroad
3. Nondividend-paying foreign stocks (if you take possession of stock certificates)
4. Precise metals certificate program, representing ownership of gold or silver outside the United States
5. Safe-deposit box in a foreign land

6. Non-income producing real estate—apartment, flat or condo out of the country for personal or business use
7. Foreign insurance products—annuities, whole life, endowments, etc.

As you can see, it's quite possible to invest substantially more than $10,000 abroad and legally avoid government reporting requirements.

### Opening Your Swiss Account

Anybody who can really afford to open a Swiss bank account can probably afford to make a trip to inspect and talk with a few alternative banks. A person can legally carry out $9,999 without reporting it to the U.S. customs authorities. This doesn't include the cost of your ticket and you can charge most of your expenses on American Express, Master Charge, or Visa.

If you are not concerned about total secrecy, however, forget that $9,999 and take as much as you like in a cashier's check. Obviously, opening your account in person is the best way to do it—and involves an enjoyable vacation to one of the world's most beautiful countries. There is something to be said for the face-to-face contact when it comes to gaining clear understandings and accurate information.

If, however, you are unable or unwilling to make the trip in person, the entire transaction can be handled by mail. Allow yourself plenty of time. Don't rush into opening a Swiss account in order to make some sale or purchase. Dig the well before you need the water, and make sure your Swiss account is running smoothly before you begin using it extensively.

To open an account by mail, drop by the local library. The reference room will have the American Bankers Association's *Directory of Foreign Banks,* and you can jot down the names and addresses of the specific banks you think you might want to deal with. Type a simple one-line letter requesting current information on types of banking services available and current interest rates. Don't give any information beyond that since it cannot help and may serve to confuse the issue.

When the response comes back, you can compare the answers on an equal basis and make your decisions. Write another simple letter to open your account and send it along with a bank money order in U.S. dollars. For example, you might write:

> Gentlemen:
>    Enclosed is a Cashier's Check for U.S. $00,000.00. Please open a Swiss franc deposit account for me in the name of —————————. Please send all correspondence to me in English at the above address.
>    Thank you for your assistance.

When your Swiss bank opens your account, it will temporarily hold the money while it returns several things to you to make it all legal. You should receive (1) a credit slip showing the amount of your initial deposit in Swiss francs; (2) a legal-length paper with statements of Swiss banking policies and procedures (you will probably be asked to read this, sign it, and return it); (3) a signature card on which you should place all signatures you wish to be able to transact business in the account; and (4) an application form with information about ways you want the account handled.

The bank will assign you an account number that you will use on all future transactions. However, this is an additional identification, not the only one, and you do not have one of the infamous numbered Swiss accounts. Once your account is functional, you can make deposits, withdrawals, or transfer transactions by mail. It's similar to banking by mail in your own hometown except for the time lag.

Your money is safe once it's in Switzerland. No matter what happens in this country's economic system, your money will always have a welcome passage back *into* the U.S. and, if things turn out to oppose the exit of money from the U.S., yours is already safely across the border and cannot be forced to return.

*How to Use You Account*

This book can only give you advice and information. It is not my purpose or responsibility to tell you how to use your Swiss account. There are some people who intend to utilize the secrecy of a Swiss account to intentionally *evade* the payment of U.S. income taxes that would normally be paid. There are others whose purpose is to protect their wealth and *avoid* by skillful maneuver all the taxes they can legally avoid. Avoiding is legal—evading is against the law and the IRS is well-known for its never-say-die pursuit of money it suspects may be owed to it. To the IRS, "it's not the money, it's the principle" and they will literally spend $100 to regain $10. Considering that mind-set on the part of the IRS and adding in the myriad sources of information and cross-checking that flow into IRS computers, you need to make your decision carefully and be fully advised of the consequences if you decide to try evasion of U.S. taxes. For my own affairs, I am convinced that the amount I might save through evasion would not be worth the constant anxiety that a fatal flaw might occur in my concealment. That's a personal opinion for me—you will, of course, make the decision for you.

If you are not likely to be a focal point for IRS scrutiny, you are the kind of person whose Swiss account might accidentally never be recorded on Stateside records. If you've never had a Swiss account, it is understandable that you might simply overlook checking the little box on your income tax form. Few accountants ever think to ask about Swiss accounts when they are doing your tax return for you. It is simply an oversight, not a blatant effort to deceive, and the IRS is not likely to be vigorous in pursuing a small-timer unless the source or amount of money tends to attract attention of other government agencies.

U.S. citizens who have bank accounts abroad are now being asked to file a new form 90-21.1, which is sent directly to the Treasury Department rather than the IRS. The significance of this move is that the names of foreign account holders will be centralized at the Treasury Department in Washington. The Treasury has added an important warning; failure to file a report can, "under certain circumstances," result in a fine of up to $500,000 and imprisonment of up to five years. Many experts believe that the purpose of this new regulation is to allow the Treasury Department to collect information and set up criminal prosecution where the IRS cannot obtain enough information to prosecute a tax-evasion case. This clearly means that the United States is beginning to get tough about foreign accounts. An IRS study showed that 60 percent of tax returns failed to check the box on whether or not they had a foreign account. The new form requires the name of the bank and account numbers, as well as the address of the branch if the accounts are valued at more than $10,000. In my opinion, this is an ominous sign that shows that financial privacy in this country is nonexistent. As any government attempts to make foreign holdings less attractive, it is a certain sign that there are some very good reasons to have some foreign holdings. Each individual must assess his or her own situation to decide if the risk of a secret account is justified. If the decision is yes, then it is imperative that you maintain an absolutely low profile. A little paranoia in covering your tracks can be quite helpful. And by all means, be sure that the stakes are worth the risk.

## HAVENS NEARER HOME

Both the Bahamas and the Cayman Islands operate under Swiss banking laws. In other words, the privacy aspect of Swiss banking is also available just off the Florida coast. Some of the Swiss banks have branches in the Bahamas. For large accounts, the Swiss Credit Company is probably the best option and for smaller accounts (under $100,000), stick to the Bank Leu. Interest rates are low or non-existent. Even so, people who have been keeping their accounts in Swiss francs enjoyed considerable appreciation because of the dollar decline.

For people in the United States, the Cayman Islands tend to be the best all-around tax haven. Here we are talking about a person who has business interests arranged so that he can spin off some of the activities to a foreign operation and build up some wealth in it as a means of avoiding taxation—or at least postponing it until the time when he might want to bring the money back into the United States.

Tax havens also represent the basic economic wisdom of never putting all your nest eggs in the same basket. There is just as great a chance that money sheltered in the Bahamas or Caymans will be endangered as that it will be sucked into American economic disaster. However, the chance of the bottom falling out at the same time everywhere is relatively small. The political risk in the Caribbean is obviously greater than in Switzerland, but there are also some tax advantages. So, hedge your bets, spread your money, be prepared, not just for *any*thing—but for *every*thing.

## CHOOSING A TAX HAVEN

If you own and operate a company, you may wish to consider basing that company in one of the small countries of the world that is easily accessible and makes a good deal of its national income by allowing businesses from other nations to do business tax free.

You do not have to *live* in the haven country to have your company incorporated and doing business from there. In fact, there are ways that such an arrangement can be set up for you by mail for a cost of as little as $2,000, which includes the legal fees of attorneys in the shelter country as well as nationals who are paid $100 or so a year to serve as your rubber stamp board of directors. For the details of how to set up a foreign corporation in the Cayman Islands and other places around the world, you should see *How to Do Business Tax Free* by Midas Malone or Robert Kinsman's *Guide to Tax Havens*. A newer reference but not as comprehensive is Mark Skonsen's *The Offshore Loophole*.

As is true of foreign bank accounts, tax havens must be given constant, careful, and cautious attention lest the pennies saved be swallowed up in dollars lost through oversight. *Personal Finance* has provided an excellent check-list of factors that ought to be considered as you try to touch all the bases in evaluating a potential tax haven selection.

1. *Income tax rules* vary from low to no taxes at all. Others have high taxes for income earned outside the haven—which is your most likely situation.
2. *Remittance tax* refers to the country's policy of withholding a percentage of money you are trying to bring home from your haven. Balance these costs with the income tax situation.
3. *Estate taxes* are especially significant if the entire haven corporation is in your name. Some havens have low income tax but really sock it to your estate if you die. If you are in a partnership or a larger-than-you corporation, don't worry too much about estate taxes.
4. *Corporate law* of the haven can make a big difference. For example, can changes be made easily or do they literally require the country's legislature to act? Do all directors' meetings have to be held *in* the country?
5. *Trust laws* will determine how business may be transacted. Make sure your haven uses English laws, as most civil law countries who do that do not recognize the trust.
6. *Treaties* between the haven country and your homeland could nullify all the tax shelters you thought you were creating. Know the implications for you of all treaties between the haven and your homeland.
7. *Secrecy* varies both within the haven itself and between the haven and the IRS's demands for information.
8. *Costs* need to be all listed at the front end. Tax havens make their revenues from establishing enterprises, but you need to be sure you know all initial and continuing fees.

9. *Geographic accessibility* can be important when you do need to visit your company away from your country.

10. *Climate* can be of major interest if you plan to take advantage of your haven's vacation offerings in connection with your regular business trips there.

11. *Residence and immigration* restrictions could be important if you have any anticipation of ever moving to the tax haven. Some countries allow it; others do not.

12. *Communications* are an obvious necessity if you expect to transact business with the haven.

13. *Language.* You are at an obvious disadvantage if you do not speak the language of your haven—either the official language or the language used for commercial dealings.

14. *Political climate* is of great significance when considering some of the Caribbean tax havens. Some small nations are on the brink of chaos, which could well mean nationalization of your holdings. Be sure you check this variable out.

15. *Local counsel* will be needed by your haven corporation sooner or later. Make sure of their skill and willingness to be of assistance to you.

16. *Banking facilities* make an important difference because you are going to be moving funds in and out of the haven.

17. *Currency in use* may be that of other countries or it may be a local free-floating variety. You need some certainty about ranges of monetary value and exchange rates.

18. *Remittance controls* may cancel the other positive features of a tax haven. It won't matter how much your company makes if you can never take it out of the country!

19. *Permissible activities* should be investigated in case your corporation expects to form a bank, insurance company, or real estate development company. Some of these are restricted in some havens.

Tax Havens of the World

| Country | Tax Structure | Most Popular Uses | Legal System | Currency | Language |
|---|---|---|---|---|---|
| BAHAMAS | no corporation or profits tax; no personal income or capital gains tax, and no estate or inheritance tax. But real property tax on value of improved property. | banks and trust companies | based on English common law | Bahamian $ | |
| BERMUDA | no direct taxes on individuals or companies. Annual fee of $650 for companies | banks, trust and insurance companies | based on English common law | Bermudan $ | |
| CAYMAN ISLANDS | no taxes at all on income or capital: "exempt" companies and trusts have freedom from tax guaranteed for 20 to 50 years respectively. Incorporation fees payable | banks; trusts companies | based on English common law | Cayman $ | |
| CHANNEL ISLANDS | personal and corporate income tax at flat rate of 20%: no wealth or gift tax, no capital gains tax and no estate duty; companies not carrying on business there and not controlled from there may be exempt from any tax but £300 annual fee | banks; insurance and trust companies | unique customary law but in commerce and tax, English law followed | £sterling | English and French |

Tax Havens of the World Cont'd.

| Country | Tax Structure | Most Popular Uses | Legal System | Currency | Language |
|---|---|---|---|---|---|
| HONG KONG | standard rate 15%, main forms of direct taxation: property tax, salaries tax, profits tax, interest tax | trading companies and trust | English common law | Hong Kong $ | English and Chinese |
| ISLE OF MAN | standard rate 21-25%; no capital gains, wealth tax or estate duty, no company tax on foreign source income if control outside island | trust and unit trusts | similar to English common law, but with local variations | £sterling | English |
| LIECHTEN-STEIN | corporate net worth 0.2% of capital (0.1% for holding and domiciliary companies who pay no profits tax); coupon tax on dividends 4% | "anstalt" and "stiftung" | Austrian civil code; Swiss property law | Swiss franc | German; English and other languages used |
| LUXEMBOURG | based on German tax laws, rates between 21% and 41%; holding companies exempt except for annual tax of 1% or assessed value of securities | holding companies | civil law; commercial law based on German law | Luxembourg franc-Belgian franc | German and French |
| MONACO | no direct taxes on bona fide resident; no withholding tax on income from funds invested in Monaco paid to non-residents; businesses deriving at least 75% of turnover in Monaco pay no tax | administrative offices and trusts | Monaco law | French franc | French |

Tax Havens of the World Cont'd.

| Country | Tax Structure | Most Popular Uses | Legal System | Currency | Language |
|---|---|---|---|---|---|
| NAURU | no taxes or duties of any sort | trusts | English common law | Australian $ | English |
| NETHERLANDS ANTILLES | basic corporate income tax rates of 27-34% with municipal surcharge of 15% on the tax; special facilities reduce effective rate to 2.4-3% for finance, patent holding, shipping and aircraft companies | investment and holding companies | Dutch law | Neth. Ant. guilder | Dutch, English and Spanish |
| NEW HEBRIDES | no direct taxes, value added tax on land subsidiaries | | English and French law | Australian $ and New Hebrides franc | English and French |
| SWITZERLAND | basic cantonal rates between 25 and 35% plus federal rates, concessions for domiciliary, holding, service and international sales companies | holding and domicillary companies | Swiss civil law | Swiss franc | German, French and Italian |

20. *Available data* is a significant factor. If you find that answers and assurances are impossible to obtain before the fact, imagine what it will be like after your operation is in business.

*Personal Finance* has also provided an excellent chart that places the basic information about the havens of the world in a clear, concise, and usable form for the businessman beginning his investigations. Check the chart, write lots of letters to find out if things have changed, but do not set up a tax haven until you have dug your toes into the sand of the haven's beaches.

## EXODUS MOVEMENTS

A number of people are exploring the alternatives of an exodus from the United States. Some find Australia rather attractive for their specific requirements. Others plan to follow their money into some tax haven. These groups are growing, and various newsletters are published regularly (most of them from addresses outside the United States) that promise to encapsule the latest political and philosophical developments with impact on any person's need to move to protect his wealth. Consultant services are also regularly advertised to assist individuals who need answers to specific questions regarding living conditions and financial climates in the nations contemplated as destinations for modern Exodians.

In the late 1960s an organization called the Phoenix Foundation was created by a group of individuals who believed in the concepts of private enterprise, personal freedom, a strong gold-backed dollar, and limited federal government. Since these values were difficult to find in most existing countries, the foundation decided to exert its efforts to help the creation or support of small countries striving for independence. Members of this group hoped to be able to create a country that would offer a kind of life-style they were seeking.

For individuals who are interested in considering the characteristics of life or business ventures around the world, Doug Casey's book *The International Man* is a valuable resource. While Casey reviews the benefits and dangers associated with foreign business ventures, the key to the book is a detailed analysis of five nations that are identified as "last frontier" countries. An additional forty-five nations are analyzed with a view to financial and personal freedom, taxes, costs of living and other aspects of residence. Even if you, as I do, choose to remain in the United States, it certainly is a worthwhile exercise to consider potential alternatives should circumstances change dramatically.

Although I believe there are psychological and political advantages to maintaining a loyalty to one nation, it is hard not to argue the philosophy advanced by John Milton over three hundred years ago: "Our country is wherever we are well off."

## CHAPTER 9

# HOW TO PROTECT YOUR PERSON AND PROPERTY

You've seen it in the movies, but no one under fifty has any real basis for even imagining the kinds of shortages and value changes that follow major civil conflicts or upheavals. Perhaps if you multiply the public paralysis during the Arab oil embargo by the supply loss of a national transportation strike by the way things were in the worst blizzard or flood you ever saw, then you are approaching an understanding of the kinds of shocks you may experience.

As we consider in this chapter the various aspects of providing for and protecting your family and property, you might recall in your mind's eye scenes from classic movies, like the *Grapes of Wrath* or *Gone With the Wind.* Will you find yourself like Scarlett O'Hara, gnawing on a peppery radish found in the dirt next to the hollow shell that had once been the most stylish home in the region? Will you be clinging to life and trying to work through the shocked disbelief of what is happening? And will you find yourself unbelieving as you pull the trigger to blow away a renegade soldier who will most certainly kill you if he doesn't get what he wants? All things are possible and the probabilities are high enough to warrant preparatory action.

## REASONS TO BE CONCERNED ABOUT PROTECTION

If you recall Chapters 1-4, and if the warnings mentioned there had the ring of truth to you, then the necessity for basic protection of your loved ones and the things you have provided for them is obvious. Even a slight possibility of a period of massive civil disorder, unrest, or lack of food following a natural economic disaster is ample motivation for anyone to give serious thought to the methods of protecting the things that are important to him. Even if *none* of these predictions comes true—and I hope they will not—the rising U.S. crime rate in itself is significant enough to demand that some precautions be taken. The chances of your being exposed to some type of crime in this country are already high. Almost three out of every ten citizens are victims of some type of crime each year.

### Violence in Black and White

There is an unfortunate tendency on the part of most people to overreact to the problem of racial violence today or the prospect during the social trauma that will follow an economic collapse. We made it through the violent summers of the 1960s, and the more naive among us have decided that all the problems of the ghetto have been ironed out (or bought off). This is not true. The central city of all major urban centers is seething with unemployment, hunger, frustration, and impacted anger. The only reason the terrifying "burn, baby, burn" days passed into history is that minorities learned that those actions tended to hurt them more than they hurt anybody else. The frustration remains, however, and while a little of it is being worked out in lobbying and demonstrations for larger and larger pieces of federal largess, the anger is real and dangerous. In fact, the federal giveaway is making the problem worse instead of better. By conditioning a significant number of people into habitual dependency on Uncle Sam, we have locked them into a frustration cycle with high expectations and low realities.

As suggested in Chapter 4, this is hard to accept when viewed in the light of simple numerical realities. Where are the guns in America? Well, the ghetto seems to be replete with Saturday-night specials that are likely to blow your hand off the thirty-ninth time you shoot them. The real firepower in America, for better or worse, is in the suburbs. The middle and upper class can afford more guns and they buy more of the kinds of weapons that can be turned into effective warfare. Hunting rifles, shotguns, and more expensive handguns will outlast the Saturday-night specials and sawed-off shotguns anytime.

However, long before we reach the point of comparing the firepower in the urban arms race, we need to stop and realize how completely unlikely it is that (1) the ghetto troops will make it to the suburbs and (2) that they will do great damage when they get there. If you live between ten and thirty miles from the center of a major metropolitan center, and *all* the looters from your city's center take off in all directions, their numbers are going to quickly diffuse. By the time they are twenty miles from the center city, the percentages have whittled their presence to something like fifteen or twenty raiders to the square miles. Stop and think how many people live within a mile of your house. Then think about the number of high-powered deer rifles in your area. And then picture a bunch of looters riding through your subdivision firing at random with red-hot handguns—a suicide mission at best.

### Preparation Is Better Than Worry

People who have been in combat tell me that while war definitely *is* hell, the anticipation is even more devastating psychologically. Often the nightmares and fears we have are much worse than the actual situation during a crisis. You simply do whatever you must do next rather than agonizing over all the myriad possibilities. If it comes to you and you are prepared, you will do what you can. If it comes to you and you are not prepared, you will still do what you can. The point is to stop picturing the gory details of everything that might possibly happen and prepare for eventualities.

You should neither ignore the probability of riots, looting, and civil chaos, nor overreact and turn your home into a fortress with steel-plated shutters and arsenals. *Preparation* is one thing—ruining every day of the present because of potential dangers of the future is something else again. Be sane as you prepare.

The likelihood that acts of terrorism and vandalism will affect you indirectly is probably more significant to your planning than threats of direct aggression. The possibility of your house being attacked is not as great as some other dangers. The chances of your electric power source being under siege are quite high. Utilities are not prepared to defend against guerrilla warfare, and you can almost count on being without electricity, gas, water, and telephone service while reason and order take a recess. You should also anticipate the absence of some services that you seldom notice today. Sanitation and animal control workers are not likely to continue their thankless job when the chances of their being paid are low and odds of being injured high. Retreat consultants report that police and fire fighters are the most active group (next to Mormons) in making extensive plans to escape the turmoil that seems just over the horizon. More than almost any other segment of society, these individuals have an opportunity to observe how slender the thread is that holds order together in our society. You should be prepared to keep your household warm, well fed, and protected while the rest of the world runs around frantically trying to settle things.

### The Family That Prepares Together . . .

This kind of preparation is going to mean a much greater commitment than the purchase of several cans of food and a checkerboard. You and your family will need to start now practicing the kinds of skills and self-discipline that will be needed. If you have trouble making it through a whole Saturday with the family together, then you need to start systematically working up to the kinds of family understanding, honesty, and togetherness that will enable you to endure a time of crisis. One key question is whether you see your family surviving *because of* the cooperative efforts of all members or *in spite of* nagging and troublesome behavior.

The changes required to get ready for the time of crisis will not be easy changes to make. They will most certainly not be changes that are encouraged or facilitated by the society around you. Your home environment should emphasize quality resources rather than the products of planned obsolescence in our throwaway society. You will have to change the personality and value system that Madison Avenue has given you over the past thirty years. It may sound romantic to think of bucking the tide and being a true individual, but nobody likes to be laughed at. Being seen as an eccentric millionaire is even tougher when you are a long way from having a million dollars.

### Coming out of the Closet

An unusual degree of commitment is required to make private preparation for catastrophe and an even greater challenge comes when you recognize the importance of involving some friends or neighbors in cooperative planning and preparing for traumatic times. At this point you must take a major emotional risk. If you want to get results, don't mention your ideas tentatively and expect other people to reinforce your timid expressions of concern. Many individuals who are deeply worried about the future are afraid to admit this concern. Before putting your own convictions on the line, you need to spend a significant time with yourself. Get to know your own value system and decide whether you are really willing to accept the inevitable slings and arrows of social abuse for physical and emotional security in a time that is not inevitable, only highly probable.

At the same time, you need to be careful about creating antagonism. Many people simply do not wish to hear about your vision of the future. They have too much invested in their status quo. When you first mention your concern, you may anticipate some polite kidding. If you continue your persuasion, the kidding will begin to lose its politeness. Unless you want to alienate some friends and become known as a hopeless paranoid, you should simply state your views once and then let your example serve as a gentle reminder for your friends who may be open.

All of this talk about commitment is not idle conversation. The steps to total preparation are numerous and expensive in energy, time, and money. Unless your value system tells you to take these steps, it is unlikely that you are going to convince other people or carry through to ultimate personal success. Remember, though, that each improvement in your readiness will bring an equal rise in the quality of your family's life today and tomorrow. This, of course, is simply my opinion—until it becomes part of your commitment.

## RX FOR SURVIVAL

Don Stephens started out to be an architect in Los Angeles. But because he was tuned in to what was happening in the world around him, Don became interested in the most effective and systematic way of preparing for the upheaval he saw on the horizon. Eventually Don Stephens' interest in preparedness and retreats for the duration took over as his prime business interest. Today Don is the unquestioned expert in the field of preparing your home—and your retreat—to withstand shortages and hardships. His booklet *Personal Protection Here and Now* is the most concise and readable breakdown of defensive approaches, which range from survival lockers to automatic weapons.

I recommend Don's books. If he is ever in your area to conduct a survival seminar, take advantage of a valuable opportunity. Don has a style that is serious and direct, while maintaining a sense of perspective. With regard to self-defense, he recommends:

1. *Learn to use common sense* in keeping a low financial profile and staying out of places where you are more likely to encounter personal danger.
2. *Forget about depending on others* for your protection. You cannot pay enough taxes to have public protection available whenever and wherever you may need it.
3. *Practice being alert.* Most people need to force themselves to become more alert to the indicators of danger that are quite imminent. You have prob-

ably learned defensive driving. You need to get in the habit of reading your environment continuously as a hunter does as he walks through the woods.

4. *Pre-think the levels of force* you might be willing and obligated to use in a specific situation. Like a defensive driver, be thinking ahead at all times about the best response you would make in situations that potentially could evolve. If you resort to force, you want to use the least possible necessary to neutralize your attackers, but too little could be disastrous.

5. *Weaponless defense* is quite possible for those who choose not to carry weapons. The first and best is to run. The next is negotiation. Others include the use of keys, combs, or aerosol sprays to disable or distract an assailant long enough to gave you a head start at running away.

6. *Arming yourself* opens many possibilities. There are several nonlethal defense tools such as blackjacks, yawara sticks, tear gas, and mace. Knives are not recommended since you have to use them at close range and are likely to be doing so with someone with far more experience at "cutting and pasting" than you. Somebody always loses in a knife fight—and nobody may win!

7. *Handguns* are available for every level of defense. Stephens recommends a light High Standard two-shot .22 Magnum derringer concealed in a wallet for close-range single attackers and a Colt .45 automatic Combat Commander or Lightweight Commander for any other circumstances. His rationale is that no other handgun is so perfectly designed to stop an assailant completely with one hit. Other handguns will wound or slow down, but even lethal hits will often leave the intruder with enough time and energy to do considerable damage. Only the .45 will cause immediate unconsciousness 95 percent of the time, due to general system shock to the brain.

8. *Shotguns and rifles* are more likely to be used in defending your home or retreat. While hunting rifles have plenty of power and impact, the shotgun is more likely to stop an intruder without the misses going through the wall and into the residence next door. One suggestion is to use a shotgun with a flashlight mounted on it in such a way that whatever is in the light is in the sight.

Later we will talk about the variations of defensive weaponry for your home and for your retreat. Of course, a major value of having a working knowledge of guns is the role they can play in providing meat for the table.

### Location, Location, Location

There's an old retailing adage, "There are three important principles for success. They are location, location, and location." The same thing is true in terms of survival. There are some locations in our country where the problems of survival are going to be greatly intensified regardless of preparation.

High-danger areas have been identified previously in the book. However, if you live in a large metropolitan area of 1.5 million or more, your anxiety is well justified. If you must keep a business location in this type of area, planning a separate retreat is even more essential than for more fortunate folks. If you can buy even a small amount of property in an isolated area you should be able to rest easier. Small towns, especially those with an agricultural base, should avoid the worst of the chaos. At the same time, most small towns have less than a two-week supply of food in the grocery stores and warehouses. They too are dependent upon regular shipments of food from major distribution centers. Towns that are dependent upon factory employment will be only slightly better off than large cities, unless you prefer to be robbed by someone you know.

Try to avoid large cities with obvious financial and social problems, where you are likely to be subjected to a paralysis of supply for food, fuel, and services. My personal suggestion is that you go south because of the warmer weather—southeast for agricultural strength, southwest for isolation. Other experts recommend the inland northwest and intermountain areas that they believe will be less populated because of very cold climate. With adequate planning and the use of greenhouses these areas should be able to provide an adequate food supply. Much of your decision will revolve around personal preference and your current location. If you currently live in Baltimore or Atlanta, the Pacific Northwest is not a viable option for your retreat.

If you are extremely mobile, it makes a great deal of sense to find what you believe to be your own optimal location. I know one successful physician who left a $200,000-a-year medical practice in Orange County, California, and moved to a small town in northern California. While his income has dropped dramatically, his living standard has improved immeasurably. Additionally, he has been able to make provision for an uncertain future that would have been impossible in his old practice.

If you do not have the flexibility to find another location, then the development of a pure retreat is an almost essential insurance policy. In this chapter we will talk about things you can do to improve the security of your existing house, develop self-sufficiency in a primary residence, or plan an isolated retreat for your fall-back insurance.

It seems a drastic step to sell out, load up, and move to another location. The decision is yours. If you firmly believe that the bad, bad times are coming, then no charge is too drastic if it helps you prepare. If you are still only marginally concerned, it is unlikely that you will follow through with relocation—just yet.

### Move Up to Less
One other note on location and relocation. When you relocate, avoid the temptation to buy a more expensive home for your family. There's always a tendency to try to move up in status and storage space. You can use the storage, but that extra status is just going to use up

dollars that you'd rather have in gold in downtown Zurich. Keep reminding yourself that this relocation is not like the others. You are not trying to move up the homeowner's ladder. Increasing your monthly mortgage payment is going to make it even harder for you to make preparations. A far better course would be to drop down one or two mortgage notches (which should be easy if you are moving from urban to suburban or rural) and invest the saved dollars in the kinds of future security described throughout this book.

As you choose a new home, force yourself to think in terms of living there in the midst of a chaotic social upheaval. What are the *walking* distances? What storage facilities exist or can easily be added? What about protection of the site? Is there room to farm or put in a garden that is not next to a public highway? Are there alternate methods for obtaining heat, water, and power?

You won't find all the requirements in any home unless you pay too much for it. It is wiser to find a place that you can purchase cheaply and renovate into a self-sufficient sanctuary for the crisis. The first and most important step in this process is finding the right location with regard to the small town, and with regard to your own family's needs.

## PROTECTION OF YOUR HOUSE

Throughout this book, my approach is to help you start where you are and gradually add successive layers of protection. Each layer will be of use in the present as well as in the future. This principle is even more applicable when it comes to protection of your house because so few American homes have taken that number one step—the fire detector.

Even the most skilled burglar is not going to carry off everything you have, but a fire will. Most robbers will avoid homes with people in them, but a fire won't. You and your loved ones can sleep through a burglary and survive, but it doesn't work that way with smoke and fire.

Make sure your family is protected from smoke and fire. Don't fall for expensive smoke and fire alarm systems that are peddled with scare tactics (unless you have extensive wealth in your house and get the smoke and fire component as part of a more elaborate total protection system). There are many serviceable alarms on the market that will do the job for under fifty dollars. Make sure you get one that is approved by Underwriter's Laboratory, or you may just be buying a wall decoration. Install your detector and try it out periodically to be sure it is still sensitive and to be sure all family members know the appropriate reflexes in a fire. These detectors can be powered by your house's regular electrical system or by batteries. That decision is yours. If you are a slow battery replacer you may be better off going with household current. On the other hand, if your fire starts coincidental to (or as a result of) a power outage, you have no more protection. The ideal system works on both systems—household current until it runs out, then rechargeable batteries—but that costs more money. Whichever style you choose, get the fire protector today. You need that protection regardless of what the economy does.

While you are at it, purchase some inexpensive fire extinguishers and position them where fires are likely to start—in the kitchen, next to the fireplace, in the workshop, in the automobile. Make sure each member of the family knows how to operate them and check them periodically to be sure they are charged and that all chemicals remain active.

## PROTECTION FROM OTHERS

Now that your house is safe from *you,* we need to look at some of the things you should do to make it safe from others. Ideally you should hire a burglar to come in and tell you what needs to be done to foil his efforts. Since this procedure might have undesired side effects, try checking with your local police or locksmith. You need a professional, objective eye to point out the things that need doing.

On all doors, get locks that cannot be opened from the outside without a key. Pin tumbler and dead bolt locks offer the best protection for outside doors. Try to avoid locks that require a key on the inside since they can trap your family in case of a house fire. Be sure that your windows cannot be forced. Make provisions for those sliding glass door panels that lift out too easily. Modify the way things are built, always remembering that while you want to keep others out, you don't want to trap your family inside.

Once your home is locked and secure, move out to the yard. Put a fence around it with one or more ferocious-sounding dogs inside the fence. A prowler can say he was just taking a shortcut through your yard, but when he climbs the fence to do so, he appears a bit more committed than a casual neighborhood stroller. You may also wish to run a trip wire along the top of your fence that will sound an alarm when anyone starts over the fence or cuts the wire.

Make your house an unattractive target for anyone considering burglary. Rich Italians today are learning the virtue of looking poor. Theirs is a model for us to consider. Always make your house look like you are inside. Inexpensive twenty-four-hour timers will turn on lights and radios at various times of the day and in different parts of the house so that someone watching your house for a long time still won't be able to be sure you are away. Stop all regular deliveries so that a pile of newspapers or milk bottles doesn't invite an intruder. Have a neighbor mow your grass and pick up your mail—you can return the favor. Keep curtains closed on first-floor rooms—make it hard for the burglar to know what will be encountered inside the house. Vary your routine of coming and going as much as possible. Don't leave notes on the door about how long you'll be away. Don't leave recorded messages that say you are away, just that you will return the call as soon as possible. And should you return home and suspect that you have been burglarized or that someone is still in the house, don't go in, go next door and call the police and wait for them to enter. This is not only safer, it also assures that fingerprints and evidence will be preserved.

## Budgeting and Building a Security System

The experts in electronic warning devices give the following rule of thumb about the appropriate amount to spend. Add up the value of the items in your home that might be resalable and spend about 2 percent of that total figure on electronic warning and/or surveillance systems. The simplest device I know of is a sonar alarm that can be placed anywhere in the house, aimed at any space, and depended upon to sound a terrible alarm if anything moves in that area. These clever devices can be set so that they overlook the movements of pets or a book falling over on a shelf, but go off immediately if any other movement lasts longer than one-half second.

Beginning from this basic unit, you can add on indefinitely to include wired windows and doors, multiple sonar units that report to a master unit, systems that are tamperproof and power-failure-proof, systems that sound alarms, turn on lights, lock windows or doors, and even call the police. A fire and burglar alarm specialist will jump at the chance to explain his wares and provide you with estimates and proposals. Remember to be a careful consumer in this field, especially as there are many ways to get robbed by the experts who make your home burglarproof.

You will need to give consideration to the differences in protecting your regular home and your retreat home if you have one. Things stored in the retreat ought to be well hidden as a first option, locked up securely as a second choice. Remember that anybody who is nosing around your retreat can do it at their leisure since you will probably have chosen a place that is isolated. Plan a retreat that can be locked and secured, but think more of the clever ways to store things in hidden areas.

Should the worst expectations come to pass and you have to defend your family's life and possessions in an attack by lawless groups, there will be a significant differ-

ence in the firepower necessary, assuming you have decided to fight rather than give up the things the attackers
want. For the person who is serious about building up an
arsenal for defense, Mel Tappan's *Survival Guns* is a
comprehensive analysis of the kinds of batteries that
might be appropriate in various circumstances.

If you are attacked at home, there are likely to be only
a few intruders to deal with, a brief time of attack,
unarmed burglars, short-range shooting situations, and
nearby neighbors to be considered. If, however, you are
attacked at your retreat, there is a greater likelihood that
it could be by a larger, organized band of well-armed and
experienced looters. Your shooting will be at longer distances, for longer periods of siege, and with less prospect
of nearby neighbors rushing to help.

None of us likes to think about the need to actually
take another person's life. For my part, a protective
system is preferable to violence. Isolation and camouflage can also reduce the danger of violence. But, regardless of your defenses, there can come a point where the
safety of your family is at stake. Each individual should
evaluate his or her value system in advance to determine
how this confrontation is to be handled.

### Protecting Your Valuables

Assuming that a thief gets into your house and is ready
to load up a pillowcase or two, you should rest easy and
know that you have placed the really valuable things
where he (1) can't find them or (2) can't get at them.

One of the oldest and best security practices is *hiding*
things. Forget about the top shelf of the closet or under
your socks. Think more along the ancient architectural
lines of secret compartments, sliding panels, and floor-
boards that can be lifted up. Use also the places that a
burglar is unlikely to look, like a buried strongbox under
the ground in the back corner of the basement or crawl
space. Try hiding valuables in hard-to-get-to places, like
under the insulation in the narrow eaves of the attic.
Unless the burglar has come with a purpose of finding a
certain thing that he knows to be in your house, your

best bet is to put it where he will never see it and if he does will think that it is something else. David Krotz's book, *How to Hide Almost Anything,* is a valuable resource for the amateur carpenter who wants to know how to build secret compartments and hidey-holes.

If you are storing articles of high value, you may want to investigate the installation of a safe or vault. I say "installation" because if it is something that you personally can carry in and set in the corner, you can be sure that a burglar can carry it out almost as easily. A cheap vault is useless and the thief can probably turn the whole thing over on its impressive front and drill through the back in a matter of minutes. If you decide you need a vault, then go all the way with imbedding in concrete and steel, shearproof bolts, and a recessed head for concealment under a floor or carpet or behind a wall.

My advice, however, is that you depend on your own ingenuity for hiding your household valuables and "chaos money" in a fireproof, burglarproof way, and then put the really heavy stuff in a safe deposit box that is not under the control of a bank. These are available in most cities in the financial district or the companies that provide armored cars. These are more likely to be available should there be an extended bank holiday. They are not as likely to be locked up for an IRS audit in the event of one of the box-holders' death.

## SUPPLIES FOR THE DURATION

Most people can survive for only about three minutes without oxygen. In severe weather you can survive about three hours without protection. Three days without water is usually the limit that the human body can endure. Three weeks without food is a difficult but endurable hardship. Unless there is an unusual medical malady, most people can survive from three months to three years without the services of a physician or most of their pharmaceutical requirements.

While the foregoing approximation of limitations is subject to many individual differences, it does suggest a hierarchy of needs in your planning activity. Clean air, protection from the elements, water, and foods should rank very high on your list of immediate concerns.

## Food for Survival

The Mormon church has encouraged all its members to have two years' supply of food on hand. Regardless of what happens in our nation, this is an excellent recommendation that would stand a family in good stead in the event of natural disasters or loss of employment. Church officials estimate that only 10 percent of Mormons have actually followed through and stored this much food.

*Two* years' worth of food seems extreme, especially for people who have the capability of growing some food. A six-months' supply would be a reasonable length of time to begin your purchases with. There will be a short period when no food is available. Then there will be another time period when food will be available in stores at very high prices and through the black market. There are, however, some excellent reasons for the two-year supply. If it became necessary for you to move to your retreat in early summer, over a year would elapse before you could hope to begin harvesting your own food. This assumes that you would have a supply of seed already on hand, will make no major mistakes in learning, and experience no adverse weather. The pilgrims who first came to this country suffered great hardships because it took three years for them to become self-sufficient. A two-year supply will be a good investment if you can afford it. You are certainly not going to *lose* any money by nailing down any food in a spiraling inflation era.

When you begin storing food, you will need to do it in stages. The first stage is to provide immediately for a survival situation. There are companies in every major city that stock and supply dehydrated and freeze-dried foods packed in cans so they can be stored for long periods of time. While regular canned goods will be some of your larder, you will find that these take up a great deal of space. You are also paying far too much for water and sugar. You can add those later when you are ready to prepare the food. But remember that weight is important since it is possible that you may have to move everything you have set aside. Incidentally, when stored at a temperature of between 50° and 70° Fahrenheit, most canned goods have a shelf life of approximately a year. If storage temperature is 80° or more, the shelf life is cut in half.

The freeze-dried and dehydrated kits are expensive and occasionally too low in nutrition to keep an adult healthy. You may select kits that come packaged and labeled and even organized for your systematic use. Today, one person can plan to survive on a minimum of approximately $600 per year. But you will probably spend considerably more than that just as you do for regular food. You'll also need around fifteen to twenty cubic feet of storage per person. You are never going to have too much food in a society that is uncertain about its monetary system. Food may be the surest barter item for quite some time after the crash.

In buying your food for storage, be sure to compare prices and ingredients. Sometimes a bargain package will be nutritionally inferior to more expensive units. Ask for a list of ingredients before you buy. Many of the more exotic items offered by the storage companies have more chemicals than food. Take the time to examine the complete list of items and order only those that are appropriate for your needs and taste. I have yet to find a single program that I would buy without modification, but the Simpler Life program (Appendix C) comes close.

## GOOD HABITS FOR TODAY AND TOMORROW

Don't make the mistake of buying a big cupboard of freeze-dried survival food and then ignoring the rest of your food storage habits. Build some common-sense positive habits of food usage. Buy in bulk when possible, even for daily use. Rotate cans and packages to use the oldest first. If you are going to eat a case of something this year and you can make the room, buy the whole case in January instead of one can at a time. You might as well transfer some of the nation's food supply to your house now—it won't be there for the transferring when the panic hits. Start from the assumption that all the stores *are* going to close and you will have to feed your family anyway. Once that basic assumption is made, the other procedures follow naturally.

Get your family out of the junk food habit. You don't have to become a health-food addict to realize that half of our food today has as much nutrition in the wrappers as in the food itself. Become sensitive to the useless dollars in your grocery budget and the wasted calories consumed by your family without equivalent nourishment. Wean your family from the American sugar diet and reeducate them to the solid taste and nutrition of real food. There's a lot of similarity between junk food and dollars as they relate to solid food and gold. The hollow commodities keep us feeling full but give no substance. When the showdown comes, whole, healthy foods will be even more important than they are today.

Long before the crisis, transfer your family over to the habits of eating that will be useful when all of us are forced back to basics. You'll be able to reduce your medical bills, too.

Rotate your stored food by having regular "survival meals" to get your family used to the program. Otherwise, you could all end up with adjustment problems that could cancel all the advantages you had worked to assure.

Try to eliminate sugar and fried foods. Emphasize farm fare—vegetables and fruits. You'll need some animal fat for stamina, but think more in terms of tuna protein and bean protein. With your emergency store in the closet or basement, be sure the cupboards are crammed full of things you can use repeatedly, then fill the freezer with meats and fish and other things. When the crunch comes, eat your way from one to the other. Empty the freezer first, because the power may go off. In that case, a small smoker unit can give thawed food three or four additional months of shelf life. When the freezer food is gone, move to the kitchen cabinets and eat from them.

Save your light, portable survival food until last because you may need to make a move or may even see the crisis ease before you get down to a regular diet of dehydrated food.

### Be Sure to Add Water

If you decide to make the dehydrated or freeze-dried foods a major part of your security program, remember to store plenty of water. If you have a water purifier ready, you may be able to prepare enough water from local creeks and rivers, but they are, at best, an undependable source. You should have an emergency quantity of water stored—at least twenty gallons for each family member. And next time you run across a rain barrel at an auction sale, think about it—your roof and gutter system is a ready-made water reclamation device. Dehydrated food goes better with plenty of water! Either make provision for chemical water purifiers, charcoal drip purifiers, or the fuel to boil the germs away. The use of 32 milligrams of iodine per gallon is one of the best antibacterial agents you can use. Of course, running the water through a charcoal silver ion water purifier before storage will be even more reliable. To eliminate the flat taste of storage water, you should shake it occasionally and pour it back and forth between containers before using. A convenient means of storing water is in a quality water bed. A king-sized water bed will hold more than 300 gallons and be functional as well. But remember that this much water will weigh about 2,500 pounds. Be sure that your floor construction will handle this load.

At home and at the retreat, you will need to consider the fuel required to keep generators and farming equipment running. If you are about to purchase a car, give some extra thought to a diesel engine. Diesels are not as peppy as your old internal combustion, but they will go a lot farther on a gallon and don't require expensive tune-ups. More important, diesel fuel can be stored for relatively long periods of time while ordinary gasoline requires special additives at periodic storage intervals. At the very least, make sure you have provided sufficient fuel to get your car from the house to the retreat.

Don't forget adequate medical and first-aid supplies. If any member of your family is dependent upon a specific medication, you should make necessary arrangements to have adequate (and rotating) supplies of these drugs. Try to decide which medications are really necessary. If you are like most Americans, there are one or more drugs you ought to kick—most likely a nasal spray, pain reliever, or laxative. Does anybody in the family seem blind without his glasses? Better find the money for that backup pair that won't be available in a crisis.

Everyone in the family should learn first aid. The Red Cross has regular, inexpensive, and highly effective classes for all ages. Even your youngest may be able to save a life—and may have to.

Stockpile items that are essential to your family's unique needs. Special soaps, detergents, and hygiene products may need to be bulk purchased—they'll never be any cheaper. Remember paper supplies, matches, batteries. Have enough of these to last six months.

### Practice Personal Adjustments

One of the adjustments that will hit us hardest will be the necessity of staying in one place. Few of us can stand to stay home for a whole weekend without running down to the shopping center for something. It's not always something we need—we just want to be with people, to be where the action is. You and your family probably need to recognize your urge-to-go habits. It's a habit you can break and one that you should break, no matter what the future holds. Practice. Spend some intentional time at home together. Plan your shopping trips more carefully. Stay in the house, out of each other's way, and productively occupied. Don't count on television. You must build today the kind of family strength, stability, and communication that will allow you to survive the disease that will be rampant even among the prepared—cabin fever.

As mentioned previously, you will want to have some

real money for trading throughout the crisis. Bags of pre-1965 silver coins will be ideal for this purpose. Think of this as your bread and fuel money. You'll want to have some gold coins available for larger purchases. When you see the economy falling rapidly, try to dispose of your greenbacks as quickly as possible.

If you own several firearms, remember that your guns become useless as soon as you fire your last bullet. Don't count on the sporting goods store still being open for business. Stockpile a six-month supply of ammunitions unless you foresee a time coming when your ammunition may be an accepted trading commodity.

Don't overlook the importance of storing fuel for heating. Wood can be stored easily, inexpensively, and systematically. With the right wood stove or fireplace arrangement, you can be prepared for warmth and cooking power as long as necessary at limited cost. National forests usually have wood you may cut and haul simply by asking. Many farmers and landowners are happy to have you remove timber. And one of the best urban sources is a residential building site just as the framing is completed. Be sure to ask permission. Otherwise you risk arrest and eliminate the wood-gathering opportunity. This treated lumber burns faster and hotter than logs, but when it is free and there is an unlimited supply, the burning rate is inconsequential. It stacks neatly and squarely and ages well. If you must purchase wood, turn time to your advantage by buying several winters in advance, thus enabling yourself to purchase cheaper, greener wood that will age until you are ready for it.

Once the essentials for food, shelter, and warmth are taken care of, you should look to the supplies that will enable you to make your siege more comfortable and productive. Stock up on lanterns, candles, batteries (batteries last longer if stored in the freezer), kerosene, wicks, lamp oil, alternate sources of cooking and heating, and additional clothing and blankets. Remember that unused material will be valuable when you want to make something for a purpose you have failed to think about. This suggests the need for needles, thread, patches, zippers, and buttons. Tools for all types of repairs will be at a premium when old things have to do because all the new things and replacement parts have disappeared. Make sure there is a way to lock up your tools and other repair equipment.

Traditional sources of energy are not totally dependable today. In planning for the future, you should consider alternative power sources or learn to do without electricity. If your property contains a stream that flows across hilly terrain, you may be able to utilize a relatively inexpensive form of hydroelectric power. You will be amazed at how little power is actually necessary if you do proper planning.

Think of radios as information giving, not diversion producing. There will be nothing to listen to but bad news and propaganda for a while, and you may be able to tell more about what is actually happening by monitoring police, fire, Coast Guard, or military channels. It will also add immeasurably to your communication capability if you learn the skills and equipment of Ham or CB radio operation. However, don't depend on electricity to run your radios. Either have battery capability or provide an electric generator and sufficient fuel. Radios with solar batteries can be purchased. Finally, be sure that you have built your library with the crisis in mind. Not only will you want to stock up on books that will be enjoyable to read in the long hours without television, but you will also need to build up a bank of skill manuals and how-to books about topics you'll need to master. These may range from *How to Fix Plumbing* to *How to Make Candles at Home* to *Recognizing Wild Plants That You Can Eat Safely*. Don't overlook reference books and books for solving human relations problems.

## SUMMARY

I believe that hard times are inevitable. The extent of suffering is impossible to forecast. Even so, I am equally sure that the kinds of preparations suggested in this chapter can do nothing but strengthen your body, personality, and family whether we face feast or famine. Get ready for the worst, and you will do well at handling the best.

First, make the necessary preparations to supply your family with food, shelter, warmth, and water for six months. Subsequently, make provisions to hold out longer, to protect your necessities from those who would steal them from you, and to turn a period of devastation into a time of strength, enjoyment, and growth.

I am convinced that storing food and other supplies is the easiest part of your challenge. The greater challenge is to build a family structure that can cope with the social and emotional stresses of the future well enough to survive, prosper, and even enjoy the material provisions that you have made.

## CHAPTER 10

# BUILD YOUR OWN DREAM HOUSE FOR NIGHTMARES

Our review of the calamities that cloud the horizons of the coming decade seem inevitably to stimulate a strong urge to run away. Even a wise general knows when it is time to retreat. Fortunately, proper planning can give us the ability to retreat to something that is positive rather than merely running away from negatives.

When the subject of retreating arises, the mind's eye immediately begins to picture a castle and a moat and an inexhaustible supply of everything. While it might be nice for you and your family to enjoy all the luxuries of this type of home while the world outside is looting and starving, only a few of my readers will find it practical to plan toward this end. Such a step would probably require you to spend more time defending your wealth than enjoying it.

## WHY RETREATING?

Although the idea of a retreat constitutes many different things to different people, the need for some method of getting your family out of the line of fire is obvious. Providing shelter, supplies, and safety will require some planning and practicing in the present to make sure that all systems will function effectively in the time of crisis when there will be a scarcity of electricity, gas, food, and water.

Your resources and personal assessment of the forthcoming social upheaval will determine the extent of the retreat preparations you are willing to make. If you have come to foresee a mild—mostly economic—realignment of our nation's imbalances, with some minor shutdowns and shortages, then your retreat may indeed be a matter of some supplies in a foot locker and a heightened awareness of the ways daily routines may be temporarily altered. On the other end of the spectrum, your scenario of the cataclysm may include total social collapse and a period of up to two years before control is regained. If so, your retreat plans will obviously be more elaborate.

Provisons for retreating are a natural result of the thought sequence that anticipates and tries to prepare for the future. The degree to which you prepare is not merely a matter of finding out the state of the art in retreating and ordering one of each. As you read this chapter, your basic task is to compare each of the alternative descriptions to your concept of the future. Compare your expectations with the preparations necessary to meet that kind of future.

If you have read the previous chapters of this book and any three of this week's newspapers, you don't have to be sold on the inevitability of major social and economic problems ahead. You know that there's no way we are going to get out of this mess without some national suffering. Now, let's look around for the best ways to prepare your physical settings for survival and success.

If you begin to plan your own retreat and you want more information, there are several excellent resources. As I mentioned in the last chapter, Don Stephens is the leading expert on retreating. Don and his wife, Barbie, started early in the 1960s investigating the various ways of escaping and retreating. They lived through the planning stages and early ventures of some of the theoretical utopian plans and were ahead of the back-to-nature fads that grew in popularity in the 1970s. Don was the person who originally put Harry Browne in touch with retreating as an approach in planning for potential monetary crisis. He has been most helpful to me in preparing this section of my book. Through Don's training in architecture, an enduring interest in an area with mushrooming data sources, and some good old creativity and ingenuity, this couple has come out knowing more than anybody else about retreating.

As you plan your retreat, just remember that it is a matter of your priorities. You may want to make minor provisions, the kind that can dovetail nicely with your vacation and recreation needs. Or your expectations may entail the ultimate in seclusion properties and independence equipping. The extent and nature of your preparations remain a personal matter. Whether or not you will need a retreat is, in my opinion, less subject to debate.

## THE PROCESS

Once you have finished this chapter and done your initial thinking about the extent of retreat preparation you believe necessary, sit down and spend some serious time committing your plans and timetables to paper. As usual, you will find your activities will become more realistic once they evolve from the nebulous back of your mind to the concrete reality of a timetable and budget.

Your first decision concerns the amount of time you are willing to take to be as ready as you want to be. It would usually prove wasteful—even if you have the money—to rush out and buy everything you expect to need for the emergency. Most people don't have that kind of extra money and so they eventually settle (either by trial-and-error or by thoughtful planning) for a sort of concentric circle plan. This means that they set specific time deadlines to accomplish a limited survival program, then set a subsequent time period for carrying all aspects of the total plan a little further.

The alternative to this coordinated planning approach is to make one major decision and build every other consideration around that. A common shortsighted approach is to purchase the perfect piece of real estate at a cost that weighs the planner down with high payments that nearly prohibit the continued development of a plan. Not only are the payments burdensome and contributing to the nation's inflationary spiral, but when the economic collapse comes, the retreater will not own the retreat. It won't matter how perfect the retreat is if you haven't planned well enough to protect it from foreclosure.

Your inner circle of planning may be a matter of accumulating the necessary food and supplies to be as ready as possible if the collapse occurs sooner than I anticipate. The one-year plan that follows may include buying a small piece of property and stocking an old house or other dwelling on it while you begin gardening and planning for a permanent retreat. During the next year you may begin to actually build this retreat while you continue to purchase other items that will be useful in your survival strategy.

Of course, all this timing is going to hinge on your personal projection about how long the country can hold out before it blows out. If you are convinced that things can't last for more than a year, then you might forget the gradual build-up idea and sell what you have and sink the proceeds into immediate preparation. My assessment is that the general crisis is probably two to four years in the future, with a 50 percent probability for the end of 1994 and an 80 percent probability by 1996.

A concise summary of some excellent common-sense suggestions for things you should consider for inclusion in your early planning stages was suggested to me by Don Stephens. They are things that need to be done right away regardless of crises, but may require the motivation of impending disaster to make you do them. For example, you need to force yourself to go ahead and get all necessary dental work done. Get your eyes checked and new glasses ordered. Keep the old pairs in good enough repair to serve as backups. *Think survival*—and take a class or a vacation that toughens you up and teaches you how to get by when the soft living stops. Do some hunting and fishing—not just to buy up a bunch of expensive and fancy equipment, but to be sure you can feed yourself if you need to. Try some *preservation* methods on meat and vegetables and fruits—methods that don't depend on freezers or microwave ovens. *Plant a garden* and learn how to grow enough of things you will eat; go to the grocery only half as often. Raise some *animals* like chickens, ducks, or rabbits, and learn how to prepare and cook them. Become a *repair* person, gathering the necessary tools and materials and experience to fix things when they can't be replaced. Be sure you make a distinction between the person who *repairs* and one who only *replaces* parts. Talk to your doctor and make provisons for the *medical* and *pharmaceutical* needs of survival should the drug stores be closed or looted. Learn some *first-aid* procedures and how to splint, lower a fever, or deliver a baby.

Get your *finances* arranged by removing money from banks and putting it into gold, silver, and other commodities that grow with inflation. Get your investments into places that are highly and quickly liquid. Determine what happens to your home when the mortgage is called in. Reinvest in depression-proof places and store these investments out of reach of governmental snooping and illegal grabbing.

Store essential equipment, like firearms, ammo, spare parts, seeds, old clothing and new fabric, a sewing machine, used furniture and bedding, tools to do things you need to do, and books to tell you how to do them. The specifics of your preparation will follow naturally once you have worked out the timetable by which you feel compelled to accomplish preparedness.

The key to success in making your preparations is to plan and proceed in a way so that you are always ready no matter when the warning buzzer sounds. Once this readiness has been established, you will have the feeling of security from which you can calmly continue to get more ready.

### You and Your Ark

Some retreat writers suggest the use of recreational boats as getaway and survival vehicles. My opinion is that boats might *limit* rather than enhance your flexibility and ability to escape and survive. There are a few people who have the kinds of equipment and skills to retreat by water, but to me the problems of securing fresh water and food if you are on salt water—or of navigation to

safety if you are on a lake or river—cancel the few
advantages. The one exception would be a houseboat
that might be used as a retreat cabin. Even here, if it
remains in the same location, it becomes more a cabin
than a boat, and if it moves around, it consumes extremely wasteful amounts of fuel, which is likely to be
scarce. Mobility *is* a desirable option in your retreat
planning, but my opinion is that true flexibility is harder
to accomplish on the water than on land. If you are
interested in sea mobility, because you are an expert
sailor and you live close to some major body of water,
you may want to investigate this subject in greater
detail. If you choose this method, you will want to
make sure you make regular trial runs and even arrange
strategic stashes of food, water, and fuel in places where
you are sure it will be safe and you have easy access
to it.

## LOOKING FOR LAND

Far too many people make the largest single purchase of
their lives on the basis of luck or chance. Whether you
are buying a home or a retreat location, don't let yourself
be forced into taking less than you had hoped for simply
because an easy-to-buy property happens to come available at the time you are eager to buy.

Perhaps the first rule in buying a place is to get yourself in a position of not needing the things you are going
to buy. This sounds contradictory but it *is* true that you
can be most methodical and careful about the land you
are inspecting if you are not needing it as a place to
unload your truck! The same principle holds true with
houses and retreat properties—let your six-month plan
provide temporary comfort and security that allows you
some leisure to consider several alternatives.

Purchasing a site for a retreat is tricky. Although your
retreat may offer you many happy hours of vacation
relaxation, you should avoid some of the qualifications
one usually seeks in a traditional vacation home. Remember that your retreat has to afford a self-sustaining

environment and should not depend on the station-wagon-load of supplies you customarily bring in for a weekend.

Be systematic in the choice of land. Start by deciding where you want to live. As we have suggested previously, you may need to approach the impending crisis by a well-planned move to a more temperate climate. If that is needed, do it before you begin to look for your retreat. It will be dangerous for you to have five hundred miles of chaos and marauding bands between you and your well-stocked retreat.

Get your home where you want to be during the crisis. For some, a new residence may also serve as a retreat haven. If you can arrange your work or profession in such a way that this is possible, you are most fortunate. If you must still maintain a base of operations in a large metropolitan center, begin to look around at the possibilities for a safe retreat site. Don't rush. Make your list and check it twice. In making that checklist, be sure to include the following items:

1. *Climate.* All the beauty in the world can be canceled if the climate is too harsh. Why would you want to provide twice as much firewood and insulation when you could avoid these by starting in a warmer location?

2. *Cost.* You are caught between the need to ignore cost and concentrate on getting what you need and the need to maintain your financial independence. Don't consider cost first, but don't buy until you have explored every possible alternative within your allocated budget. For example, you may be able to make the land pay for itself by making a small down payment and selling the timber to pay the mortgage.

3. *Community.* Do you plan to create your retreat as a single-family locale or are you thinking in terms of a place where several families may work together? This could make a huge difference in what you buy (i.e., how much space, the cost, the ways of paying for it, and the possibilities of dividing the tasks required for survival and maintenance).

4. *Commitment.* Signing on the dotted line is quick and easy compared to the hard part that comes when you start digging stumps and building fences. Spend some time working on a farm before you buy your retreat. It can make an enjoyable and enlightening vacation and can help you to be more realistic as you decide how many blisters and backaches you are willing to endure. There is always a trade-off between dollars and sweat—you can spend more of one if you are unwilling or unable to spend the other.

5. *Choice.* Once you are in the area that you have found through careful research, be sure to choose a piece of property according to *your* interests and not by the opinions of real estate agents, chambers of commerce, previous owners, or community consensus. Other people may be able to give you valuable input, but they cannot see things from your viewpoint.

6. *Isolation.* Avoid the charming country places that are frequent weekend haunts for city people. These are the first places they will go when they have to get out of town. Stay away from main highways and out of view from any public roads. Stay away from residential developments and never buy land downriver from a dam or nuclear power facility that could become the target for sabotage in a national emergency.

7. *Neighbors.* Get a good idea of the kind of neighbors you will have. It is more important to picture them in the event of a national crisis than just seeing how they act when you make a social visit. Do they seem like the kind of secure people who will remain self-supporting and calm in such a calamity—or might they become your nearest enemy?

8. *Environment.* Don't buy land just because you like the view. There are many more important things to consider. Some are: soil conditions, flood plains, extremes of climate, thunderstorms, salty air, and

insects and plants that may be hazardous to your health.

9. *Topography.* Mountain cabins are colorful but they are hard to get to, exposed to the elements, and invariably uphill from the water supply. Choose land that can grow food *naturally,* perhaps without the aid of a gasoline tractor. You need some level land with enough slope for effective drainage without erosive runoff.

10. *Water.* No other element is quite so important. You have to have it, probably without the county water works or dependence on electric or gasoline pumps. Is there running water? Where does it come from? Is there a water table that will facilitate digging a well? How does the drilling rig get in and out? Are there adequate slope and stony soil to facilitate sanitary disposal of sewage and waste? How does the waste-disposal path relate to the supply of fresh water? Is there sufficient natural water to irrigate your crops? How much money or sweat is required to accomplish the irrigation?

11. *Natural Shelter.* Warm air rises to hilltops and ridges. Cold air sinks to valleys and canyons. You will want to know exactly where your house will go before you buy the land, and you ought to see the sun come up and go down on that spot and have a good idea which direction the wind blows most of the time.

12. *Fire.* Fire travels fastest uphill through brush. If you build on a hilltop, clear the brush and make sure you have an escape route. Keep a fifty-foot section of ground plowed as a firebreak around your property. Fire-retardant shingles on your house may keep your house from burning when your neighbor's property is burning and filling the wind with sparks. Lightning is a potential cause of fire. A lightning rod costs little and provides a lot of protection.

13. *Vegetation.* The trees and shrubs already on the land can tell you what other crops are likely to

grow there. Beech, sugar maple, hickory, black walnut, and white oak trees indicate rich land. White pine, scrub oak, and scrawny trees are typical of poor land. Willows, poplars, and elder bushes may suggest too much water and the need for drainage. Weeds are even more indication than trees and bushes because they follow cultivation, whereas trees usually precede it. It's not really important to know the types of weeds. What does count is what they look like. Dark green, lush, leafy growths mean those plants are well fed and there's plenty of nitrogen in the soil. If the growth is sickly, scrawny, or pale, and apparently eking out a miserable existence, then it's likely that your crops are going to have to do the same.

Speaking from experience in buying land, my feeling is that you get more good buys from knowing people who may be thinking of putting a piece of property up for sale than reading some aggressive real estate agent's listing in the newspaper. I have been successful in placing ads requesting land for sale in a weekly smalltown newspaper near the area I was seeking. You should be willing to spend a little more for an ad that will be noticed. Here's an ad that helped me find the land I was seeking:

SELL YOUR PROPERTY AND STILL FARM IT.
City man wants to bring his family back to the country. Would like 40 to 100 acres of land with woods, crops, pasture, and water. You can live on the land as long as you wish. Send details to Box————.

It is not terribly difficult to find an older farm couple whose children have left the nest and who would like to get their money out of the land without saying good-bye to the farm. If you can make an arrangement like this, you should be able to negotiate a better price and have somebody to teach you some of the things that you may not know about farming.

The old adage "Your terms, my money or my terms, your money" simply means you can offer somebody a great deal more money if they are willing to spread it out over a long period of time. If you pay more than 29 percent of the total price as a down payment, the seller will probably encounter some tax problems. In negotiating this kind of transaction, it's important to remember the advice mentioned earlier about not pledging your other assets in buying real estate and involving a good attorney in drawing up the details of the agreement.

When you buy a farm or a retreat property, it is important to try to buy one with a creek or spring on it. If that's not possible, be sure that water is available by digging a well.

## YOUR HOUSE

One of the greatest challenges in designing and building a structure for retreat survival and comfort will be shaking loose from the kind of decision reflexes society has given you about housing. It's easy to worry too much about factors of status, style, and appearance more than the factors that will really make a difference in how you live.

You may have the option of renovating an existing farmhouse. This can be a good intermediate step, but should not be allowed to color your evaluations of available properties. Don't value a farm more highly because it has an existing structure. You may end up paying more to weatherize and remodel it than you would spend to build from scratch a retreat home perfectly matching your specifications. The farmhouse may prove valuable as a place to live while finishing your retreat home, but it is not likely to be designed for the kind of services you will want it to supply.

### Buy, Build, or Contract

The best place to save money on a retreat home is by doing much of the work yourself. If you fear that your amateur carpentry and plumbing will cost more in the long run, you have two options: either get the tools and necessary practice to do better work or resign yourself to the necessity of paying the price for tradesmen to do it for you. If you do decide to serve as the contractor on the job (and almost everybody has to subcontract some part of the job), you will need larger doses of patience and persistence. Experience will soon teach you that you get more value from small companies and individual craftsmen who are likely to be doing the work themselves rather than delegating it to a passing laborer or a major construction firm.

Bargain carefully and ask every question twice before the project begins. Be on the lookout for hidden costs and overruns. If you have the time but not the expertise, try to be on the job most of the time. Even if you are not looking over the workman's shoulder, your presence will have a positive influence on the quality and pace of the work.

If you find yourself having to subcontract the majority of the work, you may need to give a little thought to whether or not you have the self-reliance and drive that will be essential for surviving in that retreat when it is finished. You need to discover the satisfaction that comes from the attitude that "if anybody can do it—I can learn, too!"

Your new skills may begin at the beginning with the excavations and ground-moving stages. Why hire a bulldozer driver when you can rent a small dozer and learn to drive it yourself. You may even want to consider purchasing a small, used, $3,000 to $5,000 bulldozer, as it will never lose its value to you as long as you work the land. Some jobs are too big to learn on, but you should not just consider cost if a skill is involved that you need to learn for survival. Better to take a little longer and become a more skilled person. Besides, if you put in the septic tank and drain fields yourself, you are going to be the one who knows most about repairing them.

When you design your house, don't fight the land or the weather. The house you see frequently in an area may present a clue to the type of structure for the local weather and temperature extremes. Give thoughtful consideration to the traditional styles and building materials, but don't accept anything without asking why and coming to your own design decisions. In some instances, early settlers gave up the use of energy efficient natural materials as soon as they could afford to build the kind of houses associated with modern civilization. Consider stone where stone is plentiful, adobe in the desert, and unfinished wood in the forest and in the shelter of trees where cooling is a major challenge.

### The Modern Cave Dweller

The underground house is an idea that has become more and more popular as costs of energy and maintenance have risen. Such a house can now be designed and constructed for about the same initial cost as a house of similar size above the ground. The advantages are tremendous, ranging from no maintenance (except mowing the roof) to low heating costs ($1.29 for a winter in one case I am familiar with). Since the earth's temperature does not fluctuate as much as the outside air, an underground house need only be warmed a little to be comfortable year-round. Once the temperature is right, an underground house has perfect insulation all around. At a depth of eight feet the winter earth temperature will approximate the average yearly air temperature of the area. Architect Malcolm Wells, one of the pioneers of underground housing, reports that his underground office is a comfortable 67° in the summer when the air outside is 95°.

Many designs are available with specifications that solve problems of dampness, mildew, and other concerns of the uninitiated. Such homes not only are cool in the summer and warm in the winter, but they are tornado and hurricane protected, extremely quiet, and can be designed with large windows in some parts and skylights in every room to reduce any claustrophobic problems. Rather than needing maintenance, they can only get better with age since the concrete gets harder and harder with passing time. There is little to burn so insurance rates are low. The underground house may be the perfect retreat home for you, but don't expect a local builder to figure it out for you. If you see the values and get the underground bug, send off for the plans described in the bibliography and get the detailed plans and the benefit of someone else's trial and error. Then, settle in for a gradual step-by-step evolution of your own cave. You can utilize the services of local subcontractors, but you need to be ready for them to make light of such an unorthodox approach to home design. However, the indications are that the underground dwelling is likely to become more and more common since the utility companies seem intent on driving their customers out of traditional structures.

Whatever design you choose—above or below the ground—you should make sure that you allow sufficient storage space. If you are building from scratch, you may find it efficient to first construct your storage barns, and tool sheds. This will allow you to proceed in a more orderly fashion on the house and give you more opportunities to learn about the terrain and character of the setting.

When you build your retreat home, make it small. If you have extra money to put into it, let it go into quality materials instead of into extra space or luxury appliances. Do you really need a separate dining room or both a den and living room? Insulate the house, over, under, and all around, including double panes in the windows and doors. Overinsulation is a better mistake than underinsulation, especially in view of the coming ice age.

By all means, have a place to burn wood, but do not let that place be a beautiful but inefficient masonry fireplace. An open-front masonry fireplace pulls more heat out of your house than its fire can put in. Either add glass-front fireplace doors, or better still, add a freestanding iron stove or metal fireplace to the house. If the stovepipe has to be exposed all the way to the ceiling of the house, it will produce even more heat.

Make maximum use of the sun's warmth in the design of your house. And remember the principle that warm air rises when ventilating for summer coolness. When you are designing for function rather than appearance, you can do some desirable things, like connecting buildings so that you can go from one to another without stepping out into the snow, grow food in your solar-heated greenhouse year-round, or bring in the dry firewood without changing to your boots.

Your retreat home becomes a unique extension of your own personality. Your design will naturally amplify the aspects that you value most and leave off some things that others might consider to be necessities. It becomes in that sense a self-actualizing project as well as one that can provide safety and comfort for your loved ones in case of a disaster, or in case of a regular vacation.

## YOUR FOOD

The last thing on your list of wishes may be to become a farmer. A few years ago, our society discouraged us from growing food unless we were willing to commit fully to a farming career. Already rising food prices have prompted almost a third of all U.S. families to start victory gardens to help them survive the war against inflation. During the times of uncertainty, there will be plenty of motivation to plant and grow food for survival. Whoever can produce food will become richer than almost anyone else.

Surprisingly enough, the survival motivation to learn how to grow your own food quickly gives way to the excitement and satisfaction that comes from eating food that tastes better, costs less, and is demonstrably more nourishing. You may look with condescension on those wild-eyed organic food nuts you meet more and more often these days, but don't be too critical until you have compared doctor bills. You don't have to become a hippie to get your first taste of self-sufficiency satisfaction. Even the simple experience of growing tomatoes in your window box may hook you with the joy of growing your own food.

As you are looking for your retreat property, you should give special attention to the lay of the land and its appropriateness for becoming a self-perpetuating ecological food factory. In our plastic society we quite naturally begin to absorb the idea that man plants in spite of the dirt, that the main service of the soil is to prop up the plants so that the farmer can dump on the fertilizer and insecticides. This is an unnatural approach and only leads to the plants making greater and greater demands for the petroleum-based fertilizers, which are becoming more and more expensive.

Keep the same plant in the same soil year after year and you will have to do all the work. Learn to rotate your demands on the soil and you can soon sit back and let the soil do most of the work. Moreover, the soil will do the work gladly if you will set up your food production facility in a way that you help the soil live and let live.

One of the most admirable traits of the old farmer is his patience and harmony with nature. It only takes time and a little attention to the basic laws of agriculture. Remember, the basic laws of farming were in action long before man invented tractors or fertilizers. You can use steps that will reinstate natural cycles that allow the soil to feed the animals, the animals to feed the soil, the human beings to enjoy the overproduction of both by understanding and facilitating these natural processes.

### The Lowdown on High Farming

The Europeans of the last century practiced what they called "high farming," in which they established some principles of sequence and rotation that allowed them to turn tiny land areas into no-waste ecological wonders. For years our nation has had land to spare and we have foolishly wasted, exploited, and even fought the principles of natural farming, trying to force the land to yield things it did not want to grow. Yet the principles of high farming remain valid and are perhaps even more valuable as we begin to cross the threshold of a time when your family will survive by growing its own food.

Even if our world were not in economic trouble, it would still be facing a resource shortage and an insecticide proliferation that could drive us all to self-sufficiency anyway. The fact that our society is being gradually buried under its own garbage is a further reminder of the wisdom of the old natural ways when there was no such thing as garbage, only fuel for the continuation of the growing-feeding-nourishing chain.

High farming is a systematic, natural approach to the use of small farms by dividing the available land into four sequential categories that are alternated by season. By this method, the soil is not drained or depleted by unnatural demands. In high farming the land that has grown a demanding crop is given a subsequent season of growing a crop that builds up the soil's nutrients. During the next season it can lie fallow or serve as grazing pasture for animals who fertilize the soil with their manure. Even the grazing sequences can be arranged in a way that the life cycles of the animal parasites are interrupted, and the land is grazed from pasture status down to an almost-plowed condition by the time the pigs have had their turn.

The excitement and order of a self-sufficient system can become a great hobby for you as you purchase the land for your retreat and initiate the growing processes. Even if you have to put off beginning construction until later, you can begin cooperating with the land immediately. Plant your slow-maturing crops immediately. Fruit trees and vineyards should also receive your immediate attention. It is better to have a tent home on a self-sustaining farm than a beautiful house on retreat property that has not yet cut the cords of dependence on the food and service that will be unavailable when the crisis begins.

### The Small Retreat

Although a significant degree of self-sufficiency can be acquired on very small amounts of land, unless you are a vegetarian, total self-sufficiency will require enough space to grow hay and grains that you need for livestock. You'll also need wheat to make bread. At the outset you will have to accept the fact that some of the things you need will have to be bought outside the microcosm of your retreat.

Your supply of silver coins will be helpful to you in making necessary purchases. You may decide to store some of the necessities you require in advance. Be careful in using gold coins. Because of their high value, gold may attract more attention than you want. In the initial days of the crisis, barter will be your best medium of exchange. Through arrangements with friends and neighbors you should be able to trade skills or possessions that you have in abundance for items that you require.

If you are able to live on your retreat property, I strongly urge you to stock a few animals. Since they require daily care, you are gong to have to live on the property, have someone there who can help with these chores, or "board" your animals with a neighbor. When the time comes for the retreat to be your home all day long every day, the chores of keeping the farm will provide diversion as well as food.

The pioneers who have studied the concept of self-sustaining farming almost unanimously recommend the keeping of one or more cows. No other single farm item will so completely supply the good health and natural pacing as that of a cow's machinery. The cow's body is a natural processing plant that eats food that is inexpensive, produces food that is healthful and expensive (milk, cheese, butter, yogurt, and cottage cheese), and leaves behind that which is absolutely essential to farming on limited amounts of land (rich manure for fertilizer). If you have a small piece of property and are quite isolated, you should consider goats or sheep as alternatives to a single cow. Cows require regular "freshening" if they are to produce milk. A couple of goats or milk sheep may be easier to keep on a small retreat. In addition to milk, they can provide the self-sufficient retreater with meat, wool, and leather.

Get a cow (or a goat or two), a couple of pigs, a few hens with a rooster, and a couple of rabbits. Set yourself up to confine them in movable pens that will allow you to control the fertilizer supply for any section of your land at any time. Remember also that you are wasting effort any time you harvest and transport feed to the animals when you can move the animals to the food and leave them to harvest it as they graze.

With only an acre or two, you will probably only be able to graze your animals during the summer and will need to plan to bring in feed for the winter months. (Obviously, the extra preparations for cold weather provide further reinforcement for the earlier advice that you move toward the Sun Belt for your retreat home.) You will need to provide a small barn or shelter for your cow (and perhaps some other animals) during the winter months. If you keep a steady supply of good, clean straw underfoot, your cow will mix it with rich manure that will make better fertilizer than money can buy.

Caring for these animals is a simple matter for those who know how, but it can be puzzling if you are doing it page-by-page from a manual. For this reason, you will want to begin now arranging opportunities to familiarize yourself and your family farmhands with the sights, sounds, smells, and pleasures of animals and their care. While you will certainly want your retreat library to include books that can guide you as you develop your farm, you will also want to begin establishing friendship with your neighbors who may have years of experience in working with animals and crops in the exact climate and setting you are taking on.

It is likely that your desire to spend time at your retreat will increase steadily as you become more and more captivated by the natural symmetry of life in ecological balance. Even while you remain in your city home, you can begin enjoying the delicious fruits of your weekend and vacation labors at your retreat. This growing ability to avoid the spiral of food costs can also enable you to have additional funds to prepare for the time when goods and services halt. In short, your small retreat farm offers you cheaper, more wholesome food and a chance for your youngsters to establish contact with food that grows on plants instead of in plastic containers.

If you only have an acre, begin by dividing it in half. Put half in garden and half in rough pasture. These two halves can be alternated every four years, or you can leave the grass half in pasture and transport its supplies of manure to the garden half as it is needed. If you are going to keep pasture, it is wise to further divide the grass half of your land into four parts so that you always have some freshly sown pasture, some two-year-old pasture, some three-year-old pasture, and some four-year-old pasture. The farm will be more productive if you rotate it this way.

Sow a grass, clover, and herb mixture and alternate your grazing animals on it. You may wish to graze them on tethers or along strips inside a run created with an electric fence that can be moved easily. Jersey cows are well adapted to tether grazing since they were bred for this purpose in the Jersey Islands of Britain.

On the other half acre you will want to do your best possible intensive gardening. If you made good use of space and of the natural fertilizers produced by the grass half acre, then you should be able to feed your family well on a half acre and have some produce to store, sell, or use for barter.

Divide the garden into four plots. If you are rotating the full acre each year, turn one quarter of your grass land into garden land and one quarter of the garden land into grass land. The first year after grass, put in potatoes. The next year, after potatoes, put in cabbages and cabbage-type vegetables. After the cabbages comes the year of root plants. These are the ones whose roots are the part you ordinarily eat. The year after the land grows roots, it should grow peas and beans and then return to grass land for four more years of strengthening. If this rotation seems too troublesome to you, mulch gardening may present a simple solution. Be sure to check Ruth Stout's books in the bibliography.

If at all possible, a garden should be or become a part of the place where you live. Even if your space is limited, you can become accustomed to growing times, space required, varieties preferred, seeding procedures, and the relationships of one set of plants to another. If you have restrictions that will keep you from purchasing retreat land immediately, you should still be able to arrange to begin your self-education in farming through swapping some farm labor time for experience, by growing a garden in your yard or a friend's yard, or even planting a remote garden plot on a bit of unused public land somewhere. Time is the essence of successful farming. Farming takes time, but so does the learning process. You should begin your learning immediately and, if possible, short-circuit some of that learning time by cultivating some farm friends who have already been through several cycles of seasons.

I didn't believe that almost total self-sufficiency could be obtained on only one acre of land until I became acquainted with Raymond Murphy of Chatham, Massachusetts. Murphy has fashioned his house lot into a beautiful and productive acre that includes his own greenhouse, an astonishing array of livestock, seventy-four hives of bees, five kinds of fruit trees, four kinds of nut trees, strawberries, raspberries, grapes, and a quarter-acre vegetable garden. Discharged from the Marines in 1948, Murphy migrated to Chatham, bought his acre in 1958 for $1,300, and has since paid for everything as he added it. There's no mortgage on the house and the Murphys need only about $3,000 a year for living expenses not supplied by their acre. This amount is easily gained by sales of things grown on the farm—honey, pheasants, and peacocks. Raymond Murphy's acre doesn't have to be an exception. It can be emulated easily on your retreat land with time, sweat, and careful planning.

### Five Acres or More

There are, of course, advantages to having all the extra property you can afford. If nothing else, it can afford you extra privacy and allow a place for hunting. If you have five acres, you can support your family and leave plenty of quality produce to sell to folks who don't grow their own.

With five acres you will do things by the same principles and rotations as on your one acre, but in larger chunks. Assuming that one acre is set aside for house and buildings, orchard, and garden, the rest can be involved in a high-farming-type rotation of animals and crops except for four halfacre plots for rotation and two acres for the grass and grain growth to support the rest of the farm and its animals.

The productivity of four acres of carefully cultivated and naturally cycled land can easily support your family and supply an inexpensive but lucrative roadside vegetable and fruit stand where your children can learn about private enterprise. They will learn that good products are always in demand. Their customers will find that the food is better since it is not picked green to provide time to travel through a long marketing channel. Because your naturally grown products will be better and tastier, repeat business will be common. This applies also to eggs, honey, and other surpluses.

## A RETREAT WITHIN A RETREAT

When I am convinced that the depression has reached a critical stage (see Chapter 12), I plan to move immediately to my own retreat, which I have been working on since 1976. This property consists of forty-eight acres with a small stream that has been dammed up to provide a lake where we are able to water our stock and stock the water with fish. Although there are a couple of acres that are intensely cultivated, there are also wooded acres that can be used for hunting and for fuel supply. In addition to a small, well-planned house that has been built according to the principles discussed earlier, we are also developing a retreat within a retreat.

The ultimate retreat is an office (it could be a studio for an artist or a guest room for someone else) that is relatively close to the main house but built underground with a single large room and a couple of small compartments. It could be used in the case of a major calamity. It is furnished for my purposes as an office but with two couches that make into beds. It has a kitchenette and a compact bathroom. There is ample storage space for our food supply that is safe from spoilage because of the temperature control. It is a combination retreat, food and wine cellar, storm shelter, and office. Because of the way it has been built, all the construction costs have been capitalized as a business expense. Since it is (1) totally separate from the house, and (2) not used for any other purpose, it meets the stringent IRS regulations concerning a home office. Though technically it isn't used for any other purpose at the present, it will be an attractive ultimate retreat in case the worst of all possible worlds should evolve.

## SUMMARY

For those interested in developing self-sufficiency, the *Mother Earth News* is an intriguing publication. John Shuttleworth put together the first issue of the magazine on his kitchen table in Hendersonville, North Carolina, in 1969. Since then it has grown to a point where it has been described as the "most powerful medium for change in the whole alternative life style movement." It includes articles on alternative energy, organic food growing, and stories of people who have exchanged city life for remote farms and attempts at self-sufficiency. *Mother* has everything from articles on goat keeping and jam making to new construction techniques. During the rapid growth and early success of this periodical, some of the staff was relatively inexperienced. Consequently it was necessary to check the accuracy of some technical information contained in this exciting publication. But as it has gained maturity, the quality of material is returning to its former levels.

Another magazine which may interest you is called *Organic Gardening and Farming*. It can stimulate your thinking on aspects of food production you are currently interested in. Technically, I have found it to be excellent.

Your retreat plan should be one that allows for a positive, healthy productive orientation. Even if we somehow avoid the major depression that appears inevitable, your retreat can open the doors to a positive, healthy life-style as you use it on weekends and whenever you have an opportunity. At the same time it is a good investment, providing for peace of mind, family togetherness, and an ark in the event of a flood of troubles.

# CHAPTER 11

# SETTING UP
# SURVIVAL TEAMS

When Benjamin Franklin was attempting to stir his fellow revolutionaries to united action against the oppressive government controls and confiscatory taxes of Britain, he summarized the situation in the immortal phrase, "We must all hang together, or else we hang separately." About the same time Patrick Henry was proclaiming the policy, "No taxation without representation." Two hundred years later, we are finding that taxation *with* representation is not so hot, either. Today, the quiet revolutionary who seeks relief from confiscatory taxes and oppressive government control frequently finds fundamental wisdom in another of the colonists' mottos, "In union, there is strength."

## WHY GROUP RETREATING?

In the preceding chapter we looked at some of the pleasant, practical ways of achieving comfortable, independent living. While independence as a goal is to be fervently sought, few individuals or families possess such a complete arsenal of survival skills that they can make it entirely on their own. As John Donne, the English poet, suggested, "No man is an island apart unto himself." Most of us must confess that there are certain areas where we need the assistance of others. Although this need not be the kind of helpless dependence that offers nothing in return, it is psychologically and emotionally comforting to feel that there are other people who can be counted upon in times of crisis. Many retreaters are finding numerous, practical reasons for pooling some of their resources and sharing their survival concerns and skills.

## Combined Strength

Probably the most significant reason for forming survival teams is to gain the combined strength that comes from working together. To illustrate the importance of group unity, Chairman Mao once presented his strongest associate with a bundle of slender bamboo reeds that were tied together by a single cord. He then challenged his robust young disciple to break the sticks. After the assistant admitted his inability to accomplish this objective, the Chairman untied the cord and gave each of his older associates a single reed. When the challenge was repeated, it was an easy task for each of his assistants, even the weakest, to break each slender bamboo shoot.

## Financial Resources

By pooling financial resources, a group of survival-minded families can accomplish objectives that no one of them could do independently. In Chapter 6, I suggested that about $15,000 was a reasonable amount to allocate for food and retreating if an individual has $100,000 in an investment portfolio. Usually $15,000 will not provide a great deal in the way of property or protection, although people who are very skilled have been able to get by for less. How much easier it would be if five families of comparable resources put together $75,000 to purchase a significant piece of property, perhaps with a large farmhouse. By sharing the availability of this property and work assignments, you could have an attractive weekend retreat and a working farm to provide support when the real crisis comes. Even if you have $50,000 to devote to retreating, think how much more complete your surroundings would be if you were able to create a compound with five other individuals so that your total investment would equal $250,000. Another financial benefit that accrues to an individual searching for retreat property comes from the economies of scale. Since one individual can afford fewer acres than several people working together, the group can purchase larger amounts at a smaller price per acre. Land in less than twenty-acre parcels may sell for four times as much per acre as a tract of five hundred acres or more.

### Diverse Talents

Unless you are a unique person who is able to do everything well, there are some challenges associated with retreating (or survival) that will be almost impossible for you. Certainly it would be comfortable to depend on someone whose special expertise could supplement those areas where you feel less competent. As mentioned earlier, I am currently trying to develop as many survival skills as possible. At the present time I enjoy creating a retreat that my family can enjoy on weekends and holidays. This individual approach has proved educational and stimulating. You may remember, however, that I had purchased a total of forty-eight acres for this family retreat. Within the next two years I will add three or four other families to my survival group. My goal is to have a complete survival team assembled by the beginning of 1989. In the event that you may have parallel interests, I will outline the characteristics that I believe are associated with an ideal group for retreating.

1. *Farm management skills.* Several of the most essential skills are those that have to do with growing food, the care of domestic animals, and the management and use of timber resources. In earlier days, these were pretty well associated with the typical farm family. I was fortunate to find an elderly couple who wanted to sell part of their farm while retaining possession of the other portion. In addition to gaining an option to buy additional property in the event this couple should decide to sell their remaining acres, I gained an immeasurable amount of information through the accumulated wisdom and knowledge that they have gained in their fifty years in a farm setting. Neither of these indi-

viduals have ever taken a course at an agricultural college, but they know more about the practical aspects of allowing the earth to work for them than any professor of agricultural science that I have ever known. You may be able to find an individual who has other practical skills but remembers lessons learned while growing up on a farm. Some people are even able to gain an adequate working knowledge of these concepts through written resources. However these skills are acquired, they are actually essential for an optimal retreat setting.

2. *Construction and Repairs.* Even if you buy property with an existing house, substantial construction skills will be required in order to renovate to meet your survival needs. There will be shelters and pens that need to be constructed. If your roof begins to leak during the siege, you will not be able to call a neighborhood repairman. Consequently, the more of these types of skills you can have in your group, the more pleasant your retreat will be. The ideal background for this individual is architectural or construction/civil engineering. Hopefully, this person will have some practical experience in the construction business. An associate of mine with no technical skills feels very fortunate in being able to work out an arrangement with a retired Navy man who had spent many years in the Sea-Bees. Don't overlook the need for the ability to repair engines, rig water pumps, or unclog drains. Generally, a person who is good in one of these technical areas will be able to extend this expertise to perform similar duties.

3. *The Healing Arts.* When you are in an isolated location for any period of time, basic medical skills are vitally important. You can learn to deal with some emergencies through the Red Cross training mentioned in Chapter 7. Your group will be immeasurably strengthened, however, if you are able to bring a practicing physician into it. While an M.D. with a specialty in general practice or internal medi-

cine is preferable to a dermatologist or plastic surgeon, anyone who has gone through medical school has been exposed to the basic concepts of medicine. I particularly feel that physicians of the Seventh Day Adventists faith are uniquely qualified because they typically have a better background in nutrition and preventive medicine than many of their colleagues. Of course, an experienced nurse would have 90 percent of the medical skills required for survival in a retreat setting. The ability to prescribe or to perform open heart surgery is not likely to be as critical as the ability to treat simple infection or accidents.

4. *The Ability to Teach.* If your group can have one individual who is a knowledgeable and inspirational teacher, this ability will prove a valuable asset for your children as well as for the entire group. Youngsters who may be growing up or spending some extended period of time in a rather isolated environment need to learn basic academic and study skills that will enable them to become productive members of society when it is time to move forward from the retreat. Adult members of your clan will also benefit by the presence of an individual who can draw practical and inspirational lessons from a knowledge of the past and the experiences of the present. This need not be a Ph.D. or a university professor. Frequently, we tend to become too specialized or esoteric in our approach. A person with a wide range of basic knowledge is more valuable than the world's leading scholar on the mating habits of the South American bumblebee.

5. *Legal Liaison.* Although legal training may be relatively useless during the height of a crisis, a good attorney can provide invaluable assistance in the preparation period and when order begins to be restored. Tax angles, incorporation procedures, and continuing evolution of government regulations are but a few of the matters that can require legal knowledge. If your group does not include an attor-

ney, be prepared to spend substantial amounts of money in legal fees in order to gain the optimal organization and financial advantage for your team. Legal training will also be of assistance in anticipating the evolution of the new form of order that will prevail following the clashes. Tax and corporate attorneys are preferable to criminal and international specialists.

6. *Combat Training.* In a recent conversation Don Stephens recommended that I should suggest the talents of a veteran with combat training and battle experience. This individual could serve as a war chief for the group in the event that they should have to deal with intruders or a group of hostile marauders. While I can see that some defensive skills would be helpful, I have not yet decided that preparation for armed combat should be one of my major priorities.

7. *Charismatic Leadership.* While the dangers of a heavy ego trip are inherent in the presence of a dominant leader, any group retreat will require some leadership skills. I would prefer a situation where no individual is totally dominant. The Romans recognized the desirability of having one person who was their political leader and another individual they could ask to provide leadership in time of war. The same thing has turned up in many primitive cultures. Many of the American Indian tribes would have a war chief, a medicine man, and a food chief. This kind of division of authority seems preferable to allowing one individual to become a dictator. A leader who is able to coordinate activities and to establish consensus by drawing people out would be preferable to an authoritative approach. When a number of families are living in reasonably close proximity, it would be important to have a person with the ability to draw out minority opinions and resolve conflicts. These skills should be present in one of the previously mentioned roles rather than an individual recruited specifically for his or her leadership abilities.

*Security*

If you believe there is a high probability of armed conflict at your retreat, obviously several people will have a better chance at survival than a single couple attempting to protect themselves against a group of enemies. My personal feeling is that a retreat setting can help eliminate the greatest danger of armed attack. Many experts disagree and believe that during the height of an economic crisis there may be several months when retreats may be happened upon at any time by wandering bands of vagabond looters. They urge retreaters to be prepared to maintain an around-the-clock watch to prevent being overcome by a surprise attack. In this instance a group of responsible adults who can take turns at watching would reduce the hardship imposed on each. Certainly this scenario would put an overwhelming demand on the strength of two parents in a typical family. Of course, if an attack does come, the presence of several individuals who are able to help in the mutual defense of a retreat would be a powerful discouragement to looters. In such instances, strength in numbers would be a very valuable asset of the group approach to retreating.

There are other advantages of having the combined strength of several people working together. Many tasks are simply too difficult for one or two adults to handle by themselves. There can certainly be advantages to sharing some of the demanding work at planting and harvesting time.

Whether your security concerns focus on armed terrorists or stealthy burglars, people working together can provide better protection at less cost to each family. Fencing, electronic alarms, lookouts, and camouflage are all easier when the requirements are shared.

Building a simple barbed-wire fence is almost an impossible task if you are working alone. If four or five people work together, a much more elaborate fortress can be erected in an almost enjoyable setting. You'll also find that people working together will come up with much more ingenious ideas than a loner thinking in isolation.

### Religious Unity

Many of the group retreats that are already organized have been formed along religious lines. In Utah, the Pacific Northwest, and the Canadian Wilderness there are several groups of Mormons who have banded together in this manner. Several conservative religious groups who expect communism to play a major role in the coming crises have also planned for survival in a similar manner. There are also sects that might be described as Christian communists (not communists in the Soviet sense) who have adopted an intense emphasis on the Golden Rule in their retreat planning.

For people who are committed to their religious beliefs and organizations, the religiously oriented retreat can provide an added catalyst for cohesion. People of similar beliefs tend to work together more effectively than those who share diverse points of view. While not essential, a sense of religious unity among the group is an important consideration.

### Pleasant Association

As I suggested in the section on religion, association with people you enjoy is practically an essential for life in any type of setting. Freedom of association is guaranteed by the U.S. Constitution. You should anticipate that attempts will be made to restrict this freedom within the next decade. The loneliness of isolation will be a major challenge for many people during the period of retreating. Most of us have been conditioned for togetherness through the collective nature of our society. At this point I still enjoy the opportunity to work alone on my retreat. But as I have indicated previously, a limited degree of interdependence will be a valuable asset within the next three to five years.

The importance of associating with people you like may be especially important for people who are part of large, close families. As we will see in a few pages, there are many advantages for people of several generations within the same family working together because they share a common commitment to their mutual survival.

### Division of Labor

More than simply shared effort, the division of labor creates an opportunity for each person to specialize in what he or she does best. In 1776 the father of classical economics, Adam Smith, described the economies of specialization in pin manufacturing. By dividing work into three specialized functions, a unit of three workers could produce almost twice as much as when the same three workers each had responsibility for manufacturing the entire pin. The marvels of mass manufacturing and the high-speed assembly line are testimony to the technical advantages of specialization.

Although our society may have carried this specialization too far, division of labor would suggest that a single individual would not be expected to be an expert in each of the important survival skills that have been talked about in this book.

### Tax Advantages

Several group retreats have been set up as religious organizations. For many years, established religious bodies have their well-planned retreats where members can go for seminars, meditation, or simple relaxation.

Several survival groups have decided to set up their retreats as nondenominational religious organizations in order to secure tax advantages. In this manner, the property is not taxed and contributions to the retreat by the various members are usually tax-deductible. The nondenominational approach is less likely to be challenged by the IRS than those that are associated with an unusual religious viewpoint. As I write this, there is a case pending that involves the Liberation Church of California. They are being refused IRS recognition as a church and appear to have been chosen as a target to challenge nonconventional religious groups that have controversial tenets. With nondenominational groups the government is left in a more tenuous position. There are at least 100 of these nondenominational retreats throughout the country. Challenges to nondenominational groups or established religious orders are risky for the government because it raises the specter of separation between church and state.

There are three unique approaches that I have seen work very effectively. The first is where the entire property is developed as part of a religious retreat. The second is where individual members own their own residences and dedicate or contribute a part of the property to the church. This facility can be developed into a group meeting house, guest house, or office for members who want to work at the retreat. Members have access to this and share maintenance equipment or even recreational facilities. In some instances the money to purchase or construct these items has been contributed by members and deducted as a charitable contribution. In other instances members have contributed property or equipment and have received a sizeable tax deduction. Finally, some large group retreats have found additional tax advantages from incorporating as a city. This approach will be discussed in greater detail in another portion of this chapter.

### Time Savings

Many concerned individuals find it difficult to make the necessary retreat preparations because they are too involved with their business or professional life to do the planning, find a suitable site, direct the construction, purchase equipment and supplies, and perform the other tasks that are necessary for a desirable retreat. Few skilled professionals feel that they can justify taking off the necessary time to become their own carpenter, plumber, or realtor. At the same time a group may be able to attract individuals with the specialized knowledge required to perform these tasks. Another alternative is for them to hire a specialist and share the cost. It is considerably less expensive for a builder to come in and erect five structures on one site then to build one house at an isolated location. On an individual basis, it is less expensive to excavate for three hundred feet of underground water pipe on one site than to do excavation for sixty feet of piping on each of five locations.

### Other Shared Economies

As previously indicated, land purchases can be made much more advantageously with the power of group purchases. The same is true in quantity purchase of dehydrated food, electrical equipment, ammunition, or almost anything else you will need in quantity. Prices will almost always decline with volume. When there is a backlog of orders, large purchases receive factory priority. A few years ago Sears was able to obtain Michelin's new tubeless, steel, radial tire before they were available to Michelin's own dealers because of the tremendous power of their volume purchases.

Additionally, a well equipped retreat will need many relatively expensive items such as chain saws, farm equipment, canning supplies, and perhaps even hydroelectric generators or power equipment. If some of these items can be shared by a number of families, this will be much less expensive than if each couple has to attempt to provide a full range of equipment by themselves.

# APPROACHES TO GROUP RETREATING

### Group Retreating on Wheels

One novel approach to the group retreat is illustrated by the experience of a California-based group called Liber-Vans, which is a mobile group retreat. This is a collection of families who are equipped to function like a modernized gypsy colony. Each family owns its own recreational vehicle. Collectively the group owns property in two or three sections of the country. At the present time they enjoy alternating visits to the various retreat properties that they own. In the event of a crisis they would congregate at the most convenient location. They could set up to remain at this location on a sustained basis, but at the same time maintain the flexibility to move to whatever other location they felt might be more appropriate. The Liber-Vans group has also built in the option to live abroad or set up on unused property that they do not own if this should be necessary.

Another similar group has purchased property on the Canadian border of the United States so they can cross in one direction or the other without having to worry about checkpoints and existing bureaucracy. They do not use this ability at the present time because it is illegal and unnecessary. Yet they have created the capacity to deal with a potential problem that might be tied to their survival under a particular scenario.

This type of mobility is especially important for people who expect communism to be a part of the ultimate crisis. There are other groups who fear that some totalitarian form of government may prevent them from practicing their religion. Consequently, they are concerned about their ability to get out of the United States and into the Canadian wilderness.

Obviously, the mobile group retreat, regardless of its equipment or design, has the tremendous advantage of flexibility and mobility. On the other hand, the cost of owning multiple recreational vehicles may be prohibitive for some groups. Others will want more protection for the investment required. Another important consideration is the energy dependency of most recreational vehicles.

### The Extended Family

Margaret Mead once suggested that one of the major failings of contemporary life is the diminishing dimensions of family life. The current emphasis on the nuclear family with parents and young children eliminated some important dimensions that were previously associated with family living. A generation or so ago it was not uncommon for a child to grow up in a living environment where grandparents, an unmarried uncle or aunt, parents, brothers and sisters, and perhaps a married older sibling with children lived together in the same house or at least on the same farm. While we tend to think of the lack of privacy and limited space, there are some important advantages that a child gains from this type of environment. Older relatives are able to provide wisdom from the past as well as a tie with the history and traditions of the family. Young nephews and nieces provide an opportunity to learn some of the skills of child rearing. The presence of several adults of working age furnished much needed manpower in managing the demands of life in a heartier era. At the same time the presence of older members of this extended family offered a means of teaching and supervising children who were not old enough to assume their place in the fields.

This type of arrangement was often necessary in the farm-based society a few years ago. Today, variations on such an arrangement have several advantages for survival. Some of the family retreats that I know about today grew out of a concern that an older couple has developed. Because of their years of experience, they may be more concerned about the economic trends of the nation. In many instances their married sons and daughters are caught up in the excitement of getting ahead and rearing their own families. Since the children have known nothing but prosperity, they may lack the perspective to perceive the need for retreating. In these instances the older parents who have had more time to accumulate capital resources can build the family retreat with provisions for each of their grown children and their families. This facility may be a retirement home or simply a vacation home. The supposition is that the children are not willing to join in the survival efforts now, but will see the wisdom of their parents' decision when the cities are burning and there is looting in the streets.

Older parents who wish to move in this direction need to be aware of the danger of overselling relatives. Pushing too hard can easily raise suspicion of paranoia. Parents who are able to indicate that this is a matter of importance to them and are willing to share their convictions are more likely to experience a responsive reception that those who are ardent evangelists.

Most middle-class Americans are aware of family compounds that more wealthy citizens enjoy. During the Kennedy administration the family home at Hyannisport was an exciting model for many families to envy. This type of arrangement could easily double as a vacation and survival retreat. The major danger is that an ideal vacation resort may not be the optimal place for depression survival. If survival retreating is one of your major concerns, you may be more reticent about sharing your facility or its location with vacationers and acquaintances.

In summary, the family compound is especially appropriate when parents are successful and wish to help or be close to their children. At the same time there is an unusual degree of potential for disappointment if children display no interest or sympathy with their parents' beliefs. The chance for unequal effort (especially among in-laws) has the potential for conflict.

### The Two-Family Compound

The union of two families who are willing to share a site, equipment, and other expensive facilities in a survival situation can afford some benefits if the families are compatible. As I have stressed previously, the desirability of sharing expense is an important advantage. If you decide to investigate this approach, I would strongly advise that your arrangements be kept on a businesslike basis to avoid potential conflicts. Be sure to plan a system for resolving conflicts before your first disagreement arises. Generally, shared living quarters are undesirable except in emergency conditions because they impose a tremendous strain on normal family relationships.

### The Survival Commune

In every generation communal living has attracted a number of followers. In theory the idea has much to support it. Unfortunately, I know of few instances where this type of arrangement has had long-term success.

In my opinion, communal living has been successful only with families. Most everyone is willing to share their resources with their own children. Often that generosity will extend to brothers, sisters, or parents. When it comes to acquaintances or strangers, trust and generosity tend to be somewhat restrained.

For some people, especially the young, communal living has been an exciting experiment—at least for short periods of time. I must confess to a personal bias against the premise, "From each according to his abilities, to each according to his needs." My personal value system is based on the premise that each individual should be rewarded in direct proportion to his or her contribution. In my experience, this has proved to be fairer and more productive than any other arrangement. In conducting a research project for the Sloan Foundation, a university colleague of mine had the opportunity to visit the last truly communistic village in the Soviet Union. As he visited the agricultural community, the signs of its ultimate demise as a communistic experiment were already obvious. Cold Siberian mornings produced an unbelievable number of illnesses. People who dreaded facing the demands of the collective farming effort knew that their needs would be met from the community till. Unfortunately, this unproductiveness became so epidemic that there was insufficient food to go around at harvest time.

The same type of experience had something to do with the foundation of our historical Thanksgiving feast. Originally, the colonists had attempted a community farming effort. The harvest was so slim and the winter so cold that many of the original settlers died. The following year it was decided that each family should have its own plot to cultivate. The result was a harvest so bountiful that the pilgrims were able to invite the local Indians to share in their feast of thanksgiving. While they were appropriately thankful to divine providence, which had sustained them in their efforts, there was also reason to be thankful for a better incentive system that allowed their individual efforts to be rewarded in accordance with their own productivity.

For a short period of time during an intense crisis, the communal approach to sharing responsibilities and resources might be a viable alternative. If this is your interest, I encourage you to read elsewhere. The bias of this book is too much toward the individualistic ethic to have answers to the questions you will raise.

### Voluntary Survival Compounds

Having already explored the idea of an extended family gathering for extended survival, it is only natural that people who lack the family unity of interests could develop the same idea among individuals who share common interest values or religious beliefs. The basic idea is for a group of families to share a portion of their resources in the purchase of a particular piece of property. Depending on their own interest, they can erect a major structure that will provide housing for the entire group or they can erect individual residences while sharing a common security system, farm equipment, or a barn.

My first acquaintance with this concept came several years ago when I met with a group of six young professional families near Atlanta. These individuals were able to purchase about twenty-three acres of property immediately adjacent to a state park. With the aid of one of the members who is an architect, they designed the entire facility along a common theme. Each family had its own house and small garden plot. The more affluent members of the group were able to build larger and more expensive homes. Collectively they shared an orchard, a barn, a tractor, two small lakes, and a church building that doubles as a recreational building, part-time office, and guest house for the entire group. Individuals who used the facility most frequently for an office were expected to make larger contributions to their church. Since all of the individuals were members of a conservative, congregational religious group (Church of Christ) they experienced no difficulty in obtaining official recognition of their tax-exempt status. Since their particular religious group does not require seminary degrees or formal ordination, each family alternated serving in an official ministerial role. This meant that each year a different family was entitled to receive a $300-per-month tax-free housing allowance.

When I first visited this facility, I was impressed with the aesthetic advantages of this cooperative effort. The entire property was landscaped along the lines of an old Southern community. From the road facing this property only one of the smaller houses could be seen. Upon reaching the top of a small hill where this house was located, you could see a narrow roadway leading down into a large stand of tall pine trees. Along the roadway were numerous pecan and fruit trees, their whitewashed trunks guarding the approach to the compound. As I passed through the pine grove, I saw the remaining five houses built around two small lakes. The roadway led between the two lakes, over a damn where a replica of an old-fashioned covered bridge had been erected. The church building, which resembled no other church structure I have ever seen, was built on a small peninsula that extended into the larger of the two lakes. It commanded an imposing view of both lakes that were rimmed with weeping willow and dogwood trees. The roadway ended with a group of houses, but a pathway led over the hill into another valley where a community barn housed six cows and four horses. Only after I had gained the trust of this ingenious group did they share some of their protective planning with me. By combining resources they had been able to erect a much more extensive fence than any individual family could have afforded. Two of the peaceful-appearing collies who roamed the property were trained to attack any uninvited visitors who penetrated the area. An almost completely concealed cave had been dug in the rear hill of the property. While this commanded a view of all the houses, it also contained an extensive food supply and a sizable collection of weapons.

In this instance, the compound served as the major residence for each of the families. Six individuals held full-time jobs in Atlanta, approximately thirty miles away. Carpooling was used to conserve energy in the daily trips to work and taking the children to school.

A group of individuals with greater financial resources could use the same concept to develop a retreat apart from their primary residence.

### Commercial Survival Compound

Unless you are fortunate enough to have four to eight close friends who share concerns and interests, you will find it difficult to develop a voluntary survival compound like I have just described. In this case your best alternative may be a commercial survival development. To illustrate this idea, I will share the experience of a psychologist in the Midwest who decided to combine the best tenets of retreat planning and private enterprise in his own commercial development.

After examining various pieces of property for over a year, this psychologist was able to find an eighty-acre farm being offered for $52,000. After negotiating with the owner, he was able to secure the property for $38,000 plus an agreement that allowed the owner a life tenancy on the family farm. Through conversations with the Department of Agriculture, this individual was able to secure federal assistance in building a five-acre lake by damming up a small stream that ran through the center of the property. His own expenditure for this lake was slightly less than $5,500. By spending an additional $4,500 he was able to run a road past the old farmhouse to the lake. He then proceeded to sell six eight-acre plots with lake frontage for $15,000 each. Next he made a charitable contribution of eight acres to a nondenominational church, which he had helped to incorporate. The value of the adjoining property had already been established, so he was able to claim a $15,000 contribution. Since he was in a 40 percent tax bracket, this translated to another $6,000 in income for him. In other words, he had spent a total of $48,000 on the retreat. His income from sales and tax savings amounted to $98,000. Through some simple planning and judgment, he found himself with a clear title to twenty-four acres of property and with over $50,000 to spend for his own retreat. Ultimately he persuaded the other residents of the compound to help him erect a common facility that served as the church and recreational area. As the "minister" of this church, he received a tax-free housing allowance. Later he was able to rent the facility at a nominal price for seminars and group sessions at the retreat. While an optimal arrangement as far as cash flow, he lost much of the secrecy that is typically associated with a retreat setting. Your approach to a commercial survival compound can be as varied as your imagination and particular situation demands.

### Commercial Survival Community

Anyone who has read Ayn Rand's monumental *Atlas Shrugged* has doubtless daydreamed about the desirability of living in a community like Hidden Valley. This, as you may recall, was the community that the producers of society finally retreated to when they became tired of supporting an unproductive majority in their cities and towns. Although Rand fails to describe the financial arrangements surrounding Hidden Valley, I am confident that this was organized as a profit-making project according to the best tenets of private enterprise.

At the time I was preparing this chapter, Don Stephens and some co-developers were putting together a commercial survival community in the Pacific Northwest. They plan to accommodate sixty families. "Mountain Haven" is envisioned as a complete survival city. The total property will be broken down into five clusters of eight to twelve families that would live around a common square or circle. Each family within the group will be capable of self-sufficiency in terms of food and other essentials. They also have the potential of trading for things that they choose not to produce for themselves or that someone else could produce better.

Stephens described the basic design of these clusters as a natural doughnut. While each family has access to five to ten acres, this will not be evenly spaced out over the entire property. Central areas will be developed into homesites and there will be surrounding areas of natural timber and foliage that isolate the entire community from the outside world. If an outsider wandered onto the property for two hundred or three hundred feet, there would be no indication of developments.

In addition to the obvious advantages of combined strength and proximity to individuals with common interests and values, the concept of a survival city has many additional advantages. First, if a group incorporates as a city, they are able to eliminate a level of taxation. By providing a school, firefighting facilities, and police department, they are not obligated to pay for the same services that may be provided by the county. This obviously is more practical when the group is planning to reside in the retreat area on a permanent basis rather than waiting to move there as a last resort. The possibility of establishing an independent police department has additional advantages for people who are extremely concerned about security. A police department, no matter how small, has access to fully automatic weapons and other firearms that are not available to the general public. Legally all members of the community can be deputized so that they can carry concealed weapons. The idea of a whole town composed of deputies may be frightening to some, but other individuals have found this reassuring.

If the idea of a survival community appeals to you, you can start from scratch and build your small community and then apply for incorporation. Another approach is to buy a city. Occasionally a real estate agent will offer an entire town for sale. Typically, these consist of nothing more than a grocery store and perhaps a small motel with three or four cabins. There may be a post office and a couple of other houses. In my opinion, the difficulty of locating a town for sale plus the likelihood that the location will not be ideally suited to security make this an interesting but not very practical alternative. There are, however, at least two group retreats that have utilized this approach.

One of the most original approaches to a retreat community is represented by the person who read that the General Accounting Office of the U.S. Government was offering an obsolete missile site for sale. This individual arranged to purchase this site for less than 10 percent of its original value. To the government it was simply an obsolete silo with little tax value. The developer decided to maintain the government character of the entire installation. He maintained the original "No Trespass" government signs and attempted to maintain the facility so that it looks like a real government installation. The group even maintains a guard in khakis to discourage intruders. Since much of the installation is below ground, the group has almost an optimal degree of protection.

## YOUR STRATEGIC RETREAT

In the military, when one person runs for cover, it looks like cowardice, but when a squadron or group of people move back together we view it as a strategic retreat. By using the principles developed in the previous two chapters, you can make your retreat a strategic move that will provide for survival and strength. The biggest battle of the future will be survival. Begin now to develop your strategy, practice maneuvers, and prepare to defend your personal, physical, psychological, and financial resources. The world's oldest form of defense is not kung fu or karate. It is the time-honored tradition of running from a situation that is overpowering. I remember hearing of a pragmatic Confederate recruit who refused a cavalry appointment because, "When I get ready to retreat, I don't want no horse slowing me down." Retreating may be contrary to the tradition of the Alamo, yet "he who turns and runs away, lives to fight another day."

# HOW TO FACE
# THE FUTURE
# WITHOUT FEAR

## CHAPTER 12

# COUNTDOWN
# TO ARMAGEDDON

To students of biblical prophecy, Armageddon refers to the scene of the final battle between the forces of good and evil as prophesied in Revelation 16 to occur at the end of the world. More generally, the word refers to any decisive battle in which there is great destruction. Certainly, we are entering into a period where there will be a decisive battle between the positive and negative forces in our society. There will be many casualties in this conflict, and the destruction of a way of life.

The purpose of this chapter is to identify a series of steps that will enable you to avoid being one of these casualties. In many ways this chapter is a summary of everything that has gone before. Recommendations that are made throughout the book will be briefly mentioned here without the support and documentation contained in previous chapters. Several steps are outlined that you need to take immediately. Others can wait for as long as six months. Several signs are suggested that will indicate that the curtain is about to go up on the greatest economic depression of your lifetime. Finally, I will suggest some things you could do to survive this depression and to help you move through it to a new era of prosperity.

## TAKE TIME FOR AN IMMEDIATE CHECKUP

In business management, any description of the planning process begins with an assessment of the current situation. Knowing where you are is just as important as knowing where you want to go. This assessment or checkup should include every area of your life that is important to you.

1. *Your health.* If you have not had a complete physical checkup in the past year, make an appointment immediately. Make this examination complete enough that you know that it is safe for you to begin a program of vigorous physical activity. This activity will be required for you to get in top physical condition and do the variety of jobs that may be associated with other parts of your planning. Critically assess your physical condition and the habits that relate to your health. This will enable you to do a better job of planning for the various supplies that you may need for survival.

2. *Your food and water supply.* How would you survive if your regular food and water supply were cut off? Decide how much and what kinds of food you want to stock. Compare prices and quality of competing approaches and sources. Begin to develop a stockpile immediately. Keep some at your primary residence and a larger amount at a retreat location. After developing your alternative water supply, be sure that you have a means of purification.

3. *Review your physical security.* Contact a member of your police department or a security consultant to evaluate your current residence. Call a locksmith and ask him to make some changes that make your home safer and more secure. At the same time, begin to consider where you want to be during the forthcoming depression. This may involve some basic thinking about moving your principal residence or developing a survival retreat.

4. *Intellectual inventory.* Based on a consideration of the kinds of knowledge you would need to survive an economic catastrophe, what courses should you take as part of your personal preparations? Review the books recommended in the bibliography that follows the next chapter. Decide which of these resources are most important for your well-being.

5. *A psychological review.* Subject your own mental health to the same type of assessment that you give your physical surroundings. You may need to de-

vote special attention to some key relationships. Perhaps some psychological counseling would be helpful for you as an individual or your family. Don't forget about the contribution of a meaningful religious conviction.

In working with business clients, I recommend that the chief executive officer spend a weekend at some isolated setting once each year to review the current status of the organization and to develop plans for the immediate and long-range future. The same type of advice is appropriate for individuals and families. In either case, if you fail to plan, you are planning to fail. I urge you to make a commitment to develop a detailed plan for your family's future within one month of reading this material. If you are unable to spend eight to ten hours on the important activity within thirty days, the chances are very good that you will not get around to taking the steps that could insure your safety and survival. Each of the actions recommended in the following paragraph should be a part of your short-range plans. Ideally you should resolve to initiate each of the recommended actions within six months of the present time.

## PHASE I: DO IT NOW

*Fitness*
1. Improve your eating habits. As suggested in Chapter 7, begin to develop good nutritional habits that will enable you to feel better and perform more effectively whether we experience feast or famine in the future. Remember the two-sentence summary of good nutrition, "Avoid foods with chemical additives or refined sugar and flour. Eat as many natural foods (especially fruit, vegetables, and nuts) as you can and two tablespoons of miller's bran each day."
2. Start a regular exercise program. If the physical examination recommended above indicates that you can safely begin an exercise program, you have no

excuse for being physically unfit. Remember, the best exercise you can do is the one that you will do. Choose a program that will provide for good muscle tone as well as cardiovascular conditioning.

*Finance*
1. Buy one bag of pre-1965 coins immediately. Plan to make additional purchases of silver coins (up to one bag per family member) as soon as possible.
2. Watch for additional buy signs. No matter what the price of silver coins when you read this book, you should make arrangements for at least one bag. Add additional silver and a few gold coins as your resources allow and whenever the prevailing price drops below 90 percent of the last year's high.
3. Set up a foreign account. Begin immediately to explore your preferences for a foreign account. You may want your account to be maintained in Swiss francs or Japanese yen. Decide if you want your account in the Bahamas, Switzerland, or some other haven. Then take the necessary actions to open the account even if it has to be a very small one at the beginning.
4. Evaluate investment gemstones. If your resources are sufficient, review the principles of gem selection as suggested in Chapter 6. Explore avenues for purchase that seem most convenient and reasonable for you. Arrange for purchase and storage of your gems.

*Your Survival Retreat*
1. Start a victory garden. As soon as possible, start to develop some experience in growing some portion of your own food. It may merely involve putting a tomato plant in a window box outside your high-rise apartment. Expand this experience as soon as possible. Consider the advantages of organic gardening in your plans.
2. Check out retreat property. If your previous analysis causes you to conclude that you do need to plan

a retreat, start shopping for desirable property immediately. Even if you lack sufficient financial resources at the moment, the experience you gain in learning to evaluate property and prices will be extremely valuable. Having access to a retreat property will be an important foundation when you begin some of the other activities that follow.

3. Buy at least a six-month supply of food. Regardless of whether you decide to utilize a wholesale grocer and purchase cans of conventional food or the preferable route of storing dehydrated foods, secure your basic six-month supply immediately. As your resources and facilities permit, expand this supply to whatever level you feel will be most appropriate for your needs.

4. Stockpile other basic supplies. Make a list of the other items that you feel will be necessary during the duration. Be sure that you have adequate water (and means to purify it), medical supplies, batteries, and eye glasses. Carry a small notebook with you and jot down items that you think of at stop lights or in the middle of the night.

5. Purchase weapons for hunting and protection. Unlike some survival experts, I do not recommend an extensive arsenal for protection. If possible, however, you should have personal access to a 12-gauge shotgun, a rifle, and a handgun (preferably a .45 caliber automatic).

6. Develop provisons for communications. Purchase or adapt your CB or Ham radio equipment for battery capability. Start monitoring police, fire, coast guard, or military channels. In addition to providing good experience, this can substantially broaden your knowledge of what is really going on in society.

### Intellectual and Psychological Preparation

1. Purchase a basic survival library. After reviewing the basic bibliography contained at the end of this book, purchase the references that you feel would be most helpful for you. Items marked with an

asterisk have my priority recommendation for your basic library. Having these books on your shelves will not help at all unless you actually take time to read them. Books on many of the specialized topics discussed in this manuscript will provide more details than a comprehensive book like this one can do.

2. Start a positive meditation program. Using the principles suggested in Chapter 7, begin a practice of meditation and affirmation. Meditation will provide relief from stress that accompanies modern life and the affirmation program will help program your subconscious for a more positive approach to living.

3. Monitor key relationships. Guard against the tendency to become so caught up in professional pursuits or preparations for an economic depression that you undermine some of the most important relationships in life. Proper retreat preparations should enhance your family relationships. Yet undue obsession with any aspect of your preparation can alienate family members.

4. Mention your concern to three or four of your best friends. Don't become so evangelical that you alienate those associates. Mention your personal plans and perhaps give them a copy of this or some similar book as a birthday or Christmas present. This is about as much as you can safely do without endangering the relationships that are important in the present.

5. Enroll in helpful courses. Through the continuing education program of a local college or other community organization, you should be able to identify numerous evening courses that can provide much needed information. To help cope with headaches created by concern about the future, take one or two courses every six months. This will make you a better informed and more competent individual.

6. Practice your escape plan. If you plan to survive the depression in some retreat setting, don't assume that you will be able to drive to that location on

major highways. Get a detailed map of your surroundings and identify secondary roads that will lead to your destination. Earthquakes may make some roads impassable, and civil disorder will almost certainly create obstacles to your usual mobility.

7. Test your plans. At least once a year, I suggest that you and your family plan to live for a week off the supplies that you have provided. This will enable you to test the completeness and palatability of your provisions. Avoid the temptation to prepare for this exercise by extra stocking of the refrigerator. If you plan to retreat with a group of individuals, you should practice this temporary exercise together and compare results. You may even want to try bartering for the items you have overlooked in your planning.

8. Practice your survival skills. Camping is a good exercise to provide practice in self-sufficiency. In addition to being a wholesome family activity, it provides you with a chance to practice surviving without electricity and modern conveniences. Your children may even gain an appreciation of bathtubs and running water after a few days of hauling water from a stream. After you have developed the skills of camping and foraging, you might attempt a survival trek where you survive on the resources you are able to find in a wilderness setting.

## HOW TO KNOW
## WHEN IT'S TIME TO MOVE

Have you ever sat in the audience of a musical production waiting for the curtain to rise? You wait expectantly for an indication that the main event is about to begin. The overture to this depression has been an extended one. Astute observers have long recognized that an economic and societal breakdown was likely. I believe that the ultimate depression will not happen until we have lived through another apparent economic recovery and an additional siege of very high inflation. There are several key events that may provide a warning signal that the collapse is coming. While I anticipate that this will be between 1993 and 1995, the presence of any three of the following factors in any six-month period will be a warning to me that I should begin to move aggressively to a defensive position.

1. Double-digit inflation for a period in excess of one year.
2. The Dow Jones average drops below 600.
3. Three major cities are unable to meet their bond issues, and Congress is unable or unwilling to bail them out.
4. Three major banks fold, using up all the reserves of the Federal Deposit Insurance Corporation.
5. Major crop failures reduce the nation's food stockpile below the 1974 level of a twenty-three-day supply.
6. Two U.S. cities are hit by major earthquakes.
7. Rioting and major guerrilla activity break out in three U.S. cities.
8. Unemployment rises above 10 percent of the work force.
9. The government outlaws foreign bank accounts or ownership of gold for private citizens.
10. An extended nationwide strike of teamsters, police, firemen, or longshoremen.
11. Winter storms immobilize three or more major cities during a power failure.

In my opinion, the presence of any one of these events increases the probability of a major economic breakdown by 10 percent. Two or more of these events occurring within a six-month period would raise the probability of a depression by 25 percent. Whenever three of these warning signals exist simultaneously, I believe that the chance for an imminent depression rises by 50 percent. Whenever this happens, I plan to move immediately to put my contingency preparations into operation.

## AFTER THE CRASH

When the signs mentioned above and your own judgment convince you that the crash has begun, you will need to begin your last-minute preparations with a genuine sense of urgency. Unless you are in the center of an urban ghetto, there will probably be a few days where you can take care of some last-minute details.

1. Eliminate existing financial risk. Despite warnings of the precarious economic circumstances that prevail, most people will still have a significant number of their assets in paper dollars. Additionally, there will be debts that may have some contingent liability. Once the signal for a retreat has been sounded, move quickly to gain as much liquidity as possible to clear up your debt obligations.

2. Move more fully into hard currencies. At this late date the prices for gold and silver coins will be exorbitant. Nevertheless, when you see that the last obstacles to a full-scale depression have been removed, you should begin trading in your dollars, even if you have to swap a wheelbarrow full of them for a few pieces of survival currency. At this point I would not be interested in contracts or receipts for silver or gold in some distant location. I will want to take immediate possession of items I have previously trusted someone else to hold. Some people who have made extensive preparations for a depression by purchasing through a trusted financial organization in a distant city may be left with receipts that are as worthless as their paper dollars.

3. Finalize your food supply. Make whatever last-minute adjustments you can. Expect supermarket prices to be at their highest as other people are beginning to realize what you have been anticipating for some time.

4. Begin your retreat. The decision to leave for your retreat will be one of the most difficult you have

ever made. Many individuals will wait just a little too long as they try to earn a few more dollars to see them through the crisis. In some ways, people who lose their jobs early in the crisis or experience a business failure will be fortunate because this will provide them with the incentive to move to their contingency plans. When your city begins to be affected by rioting, looting, and massive civil disobedience, it is a good time to take whatever vacation you may have coming. If you own your own business, close it down for a few days or delegate authority for security and operations to a subordinate. Promise this subordinate a major promotion if the operation is successfully managed during the crisis. If he or she succeeds, they will have earned the promotion and gained some valuable experience. More important, you will be out of the line of danger during a critical period.

5. Prepare to protect your resources. While you will want to delegate authority for protecting resources in critically dangerous locations, you will need to make provisions for other resources as well. Hide the majority of your precious metals and gems where an intruder will not find them. You should keep a few coins handy for your own use and to convince an intruder who may penetrate your other defenses that he has found your reserves. Regardless, whatever defense method you have decided to use, this will be the time to put them into operation. Extreme diligence will be required during the first few days of the crisis. Gradually the violence will become more sporadic.

6. Keep a low profile. In the first chaotic weeks you should avoid showing any signs of your comfort or preparedness. It will be far better to look poor while living rich. Ostentatious living will not merely create enmity among the less fortunate, it will move your name to the head of the list for potential robbery or looting victims.

7. Look for co-survivalists. As the initial tensions subside, a new order of life will be established. If you have not made plans for a group retreat, you will want to identify individuals with common interests. You and these other individuals may be able to swap resources, join in mutual assistance, and provide the basis for restoring order.

8. Look for opportunities. As the new order begins to emerge, there will be countless opportunities for building personal wealth. As has always been true, individuals with good survival skills and a keen eye for opportunity will see many exciting prospects for success. There is no reason to feel guilty about your ability to profit from an unpleasant situation. Society will need producers and doers much more than guilt-stricken penitents. Your opportunities will provide a means of helping individuals. This assistance will not be in the form of giving your resources to the less fortunate. Instead, you should plan to exchange some of your resources for the assistance that other people can offer you. This will be the basis on which the new order of society will emerge.

9. Exercise leadership. Crisis has always brought out the best in exceptional people. The ability to survive and prosper during the coming depression will sharpen the leadership skills that you already possess. Plan to use these skills in a positive, productive manner to help rebuild a civilization out of the economic ruins of our past mistakes.

10. Be thankful. Those individuals who come through the trials of the coming depression will have many reasons to be thankful. You should be thankful for the good sense to have prepared for a crisis and appreciative of the physical and intellectual capabilities that enabled you to prepare for these problems. Be thankful, too, to have been spared the unavoidable catastrophes that will strike some well prepared people. Some individuals will be thankful to God for providing their deliverance. Others will

be grateful for their own initiative and insight. Another group will recognize that their survival and prosperity came from their diligent efforts to utilize and expand their God-given abilities and talents.

# CHAPTER 13

# INVENT YOUR OWN FUTURE

In our journey through this book you and I have come a long way together. Most of the scenery on our trip has been rather unpleasant. If you are feeling a little pessimistic, I can't blame you. And yet I hope you do not view pessimism as the pervading theme of the book.

Let's be honest with each other. There is no way any book can shatter the placid complacency of a truly contented person. You wouldn't have picked this book unless you, too, were concerned about the economic future of western civilization. Now that you have faced up to your anxiety and discovered that there are valid reasons for concern, I hope that you are left with a determination to use your newly acquired knowledge to make a potentially unpleasant situation as positive as possible.

The kind of pessimism I advocate is actually optimistic realism that recognizes the complexities of our world, but moves on to survival and prosperity.

Richard Lovelace once wrote, "Stone walls do not a prison make, nor iron bars a cage." In a similar way a declining dollar need not create a personal depression. In the coming crisis I am more interested in helping you avoid personal depression than economic depression. By this time I hope you have accepted my premise that a severe economic adjustment is essential.

There is an immutable law that both individuals and nations must reap what they sow. This country has sown the wind of financial irresponsibility; it must reap the whirlwind of economic catastrophe. In the United States we have been intoxicated with the abundance of our vineyards, but the days of wine and roses have ended.

There's got to be a morning after when we awaken to a Herculean hangover with economic headaches for nations, cities, and families.

Do you remember the fable about the ant and the grasshopper? During the warmth of the spring and summer the grasshopper had a glorious time, while the ant was busy making preparations for the cold, barren days of a winter that he believed was inevitable. This ant must have appeared rather paranoid. While the ant seemed quite happy with his disciplined approach to preparation, the grasshopper was on a perpetual high. With the advance of autumn the ant's vision seemed more reasonable. But the grasshopper kept arguing that the weather was a temporary aberration. "We had a cool spell last May," he recalled, "but things got warm again. There is really nothing serious to worry about."

That's how it is today. It is no longer summer. Fall is in the air. You can continue to ignore the warning signs or you can begin, even at this late date, to make preparation. Whether you prepare or not, the winter will be cold. No amount of personal preparation will postpone the killing frost, but preparation can make survival possible and perhaps even pleasant.

I believe that the winter will be severe, and I am planning accordingly. If it turns out to be milder than anticipated, so much the better: my retreat will still be a pleasant place to spend weekends. The vegetables I grow will be tastier and healthier than anything I can buy in a store. Investments in gold, silver, and diamonds will have held their value and appreciated, and my supply of food will save many a trip to the grocery store to purchase supplies that are certain to cost even more in the future.

## THE FUTURE OF THE FUTURE

John McHale has suggested that, "The future of the future is in the present." Individuals have greater flexibility than large organizations, such as governments. Consequently, we can make adaptations much more quickly.

This nation's stage is already set for the next act. As an individual you can still make some adjustments.

There is a Chinese proverb that says, "All the flowers of all the tomorrows lie in the seeds of today." A unique characteristic of man is that we can make the future what we would like it to become. Perhaps not totally, but we do invent our own futures.

Let's pause a moment for a bit of perspective. A noted public figure has said, "Politicians have strained their ingenuity to discover new sources of revenue. They have broadened perilously the field of income and property tax. When I was a boy, wealth was regarded as secure and admirable, but now a man has to defend himself for being rich as if it were a crime." The speaker was not a right-wing businessman. It was Socrates, who lived about four hundred years before Christ, speaking as he surveyed the scene in ancient Greece.

Professor Nathan Adler, a prominent psychologist at the University of California, Berkeley, and an expert on youthful dissent, rebellion, and anarchy has described a particular youth group:

> They were long-haired and young, wore wild, bright-colored clothing, sometimes they frolicked nude in the streets, chanting obscenities at their elders—and consumed generous amounts of dope. Reared during an age of doomsday-oriented crises, they were protesting the growing materialism of their parents' generation.

The description is familiar, but he was not describing college campuses of two decades ago. He was simply discussing the Bouzingos, a French youth movement in the 1830s. Dr. Adler comments:

> At the decline and fall of Rome, during the Renaissance and the Reformation, during the French Revolution and the Napoleonic Wars—during each of these periods, we find a social movement and a personality style that emphasizes intuition, immediacy, and self-actualization, and transcendences.

A review of history often causes the observer to conclude that people have always been pessimistic about the future. There is a natural temptation to say that since the world has survived other critical periods, why should we worry about the crisis that confronts us today? During each of the periods where there was the kind of breakdown in order such as Dr. Adler has described, we find that it signaled the end of an era. Life goes on. People continue to survive, but the world is not the same.

This book was written to help you understand why things are going wrong and how the ultimate collapse will occur. More important, it can serve as a blueprint for an ark that can provide safe passage for you, your family, and your possessions during the flood of imminent calamities. Unlike any other book on the market, it gives guidelines and suggestions in a variety of key areas: personal investment and finance, family protection, health and nutrition, retreat planning, and survival skills. With this outline you can begin to build your own personalized defense system, you can and must be the master of your fate, the captain of your soul.

If I can convince you that you don't have to be dependent on anyone else to solve your problems, a major purpose in writing this book will be satisfied. Our society has taught us a variety of subtle forms of dependency. We depend on other people to teach our children, cook an increasing number of our meals, perform a multitude of minor services for us, guarantee our finances, and even pass judgment on whether or not our life-style is satisfactory. No one has forced this dependency on us. We have freely and voluntarily given up our birthright of individuality and self-sufficiency.

There is nothing wrong in letting other people do things for us. The danger is that we may lose the ability to care for ourselves and thus become dependent upon an undependable source of support. The millions who are dependent upon the government for one form of aid or another are a dramatic illustration of this problem. Although many people fail to recognize the symptoms, a very similar problem is the majority of citizens who are dependent upon other people for approval and acceptance. David Riseman calls these the "other directed" people. When you think about it, it is rather absurd to realize how much we worry if other people are going to approve or legitimize our dress, our behavior, our lifestyles. How far this is removed from nature. Animals seem to accept their stripes or characteristics with no apparent concern. They are what they are. Therefore, they must be what they are supposed to be. No one ever worries that a cat's coloration is definitely lower middle-class, or that a dog is only a mediocre barker. Yet we apply those judgments to ourselves and to others on a regular basis.

Self-sufficiency and independence can be the keys to a happy tomorrow regardless of how the scenario of the 1990s unfolds. You will find happiness and contentment only if you feel fully capable of standing on your own two feet. That's really what maturity is all about. No person is a mature adult as long as he or she depends on other people to solve problems and give approval or credence.

For years I devoted my energies to building a professional reputation as a business educator and consultant. Why should I take time to care for my yard, reasoned I, when my hourly consulting fees were thirty times what the yard man charged. By devoting every waking hour to my professional activity, I developed an outstanding professional reputation and a bland one-dimensional life. At some point (I don't even remember the catalyst) I decided that if the world I had come to know were to change significantly, I would be unable to function. I was counting too much on a professional reputation that would have little value if my worth were measured for the number of practical things I was capable of doing. As I began to take time to do some things for myself, a remarkable transformation began to take place. First I found that my happiness was no longer dependent upon the approval of other people. I began to practice making decisions that I thought were truly best instead of doing what I thought other people would approve. My worry and anxiety declined and my zest for life grew dramatically.

Make no mistake, this can be a frightful transition. Some of the people that you think are your best friends may choose to reject you. Even if you held leadership positions in your church, you may find that your involvement is approved only as long as you are so dependent upon the group that you are willing to accept its decisions without questioning. You may find that your parents, spouse, and children prefer a person who can be manipulated in predictable ways. You may find that out of a multitude of acquaintances, you have only a few friends who are worthy of the name. But those friends are the ones with whom you can build a life that matters.

A search for self-sufficiency cost me dearly. A marriage of sixteen years collapsed and with it the financial accumulation of a very successful career. My former wife and children moved halfway across the country, and I started over from scratch in a new town. Despite the initial loneliness and pain, it was invigorating to find that I could establish relationships with people who knew nothing of my professional accomplishments. Moreover, new relationships that were formed on this basis were almost immediately deeper than the so-called friendships developed over the past decade or two.

A key turning point came when I met a woman who had gone through the same type of experience. At our first meeting we talked for hours about our mutual concerns and dreams. Each of us admitted wanting to retreat where we could provide a degree of independence against potential calamities while enjoying a life-style that this would provide. As days went by, an important relationship began to emerge, but I wasn't content with the progress we were making. Casually, one evening, I gave her a copy of two of the best books I had written. She accepted them graciously and put them away. I was a little bit disappointed, but fully expected a report during the next day or two on how superb they were. A couple of weeks later, when I had heard nothing, my curiosity forced me to ask. It was devastating to learn that she hadn't even begun to read them. Evidently my look of hurt disbelief prompted an explanation. "Look," she said, "I want to be impressed with you as a person, not with your balloons."

I didn't know what she meant by the phrase *balloons,* so she explained, "Most people try to get by on their balloons. It may be money, good looks, or achievements. These are really nice to have, but it is dangerous to fall in love with the balloons rather than the real person. The balloons are nice for a while, but they won't support a real relationship."

A lot of things fell into place with that explanation. Balloons look pretty on festive occasions, but when problems arise, balloons don't contribute much to the solution. Only by being independent can you have something of value to offer when you give yourself. Otherwise, you merely offer a pale imitation of the real thing. It may be smoother and prettier, but it doesn't have the substance or potential of the genuine article.

## THE MANAGEMENT OF TOMORROW

Several years ago I was reading the magazine published by the World Future Society and noticed a reference to a graduate-level business course entitled, "The Management of Tomorrow." I contacted the professor who developed the course at Georgia State University and found that his students were exposed to projections about the future of management practice as well as techniques for managing the future. This latter objective is what I want to provide for you. You cannot change the world, but you can have a tremendous impact on your portion of it. With informed judgment and common sense you can manage the future rather than being ruled by it.

Take a look at that word, "Management." I had taught the subject and practiced it for years before I ever saw the richness that is contained within the word itself. You remember the little game the children used to play in seeing how many more words they could find in a larger one. The most important concepts of management are contained within the word itself.

The first three letters suggest the importance of the individual. Great business organizations have been described as the lengthened shadow of a single individual.

Certainly, this book has stressed the importance that you as an individual will have in inventing your future and assuming responsibility for the kind of life you seek. It is impossible for me to stress too much the importance of depending upon that individual that looks back at you from the mirror each morning. Ralph Waldo Emerson summed up his essays on self-reliance by saying, "Trust thyself, every heart vibrates to that iron string. Accept the place that divine providence has found for you; the society of your contemporaries, the connection of events."

Five hundred years before Christ, Buddha said, "Whosoever shall be a lamp unto themselves and a refuge unto themselves . . . shall reach the very topmost height." Neither of these two great thinkers was suggesting that success would come easily. Your intelligence, planning, and effort must be combined with self-trust to make the difference. I agree with Cervantes: "No man is more than another unless he does more than another." This is your challenge: to do more than your contemporaries in anticipating the problems that lie ahead and, by doing this, to provide protection for those who are important to you and thus to be an example for others to emulate.

If you look toward the end of the word manage*ment* you'll notice that successful management involves others. Independence and self-sufficiency doesn't have to mean total isolation. You gain tremendous strength when you know that your success and survival are not dependent upon other people. Yet life is much more pleasant when it is shared by strong, independent and caring friends. It is also a great deal easier to share work and responsibilities with other people. Chapter 11 stressed the importance of cooperation and team play in survival planning. True cooperation can take place only between equals, neither of whom has abrogated personal initiative to the other. These relationships are not common, but there is no other type that is fit for the human being. I refuse to accept the fact that there can be a good master or a good slave.

The original concept of private enterprise provides an ideal example of the kind of cooperation I am describing. The butcher, baker, and candlestick maker each handles an individual talent, activity, know-how, and goal. Their hours and operations may be very different, but each is free to pursue an interest in a way that preference or personality suggests. Each is clearly responsible for the quality of his product and is entitled to whatever degree of success or failure is generated by these efforts. While this may seem to describe a great deal of independence, each is cooperating with the other since eventually each must exchange goods and services with the other in order to improve his standard of living.

Exchanging ideas, efforts, time, or talent with another person because it is a desirable choice for both of you is a far cry from depending upon someone for charity or feeling responsible for an individual who is unable or refuses to care for himself. There is not room or time in your life for you to truly share the essence of life with many people. Jess Lair described the vast improvement in his life now that he has five or six friends instead of boasting of having five hundred people on his Christmas card list. In his popular book, *I Ain't Well, But I Sure Am Better,* Lair proposes that the ideal arrangement for a human being is to have five or six human beings that are so important that a good job offer in a distant state would not even be a temptation to move away from them.

The first four letters of the word *mana*gement form a Polynesian word used by the Swiss psychologist Carl Jung to describe the aura projected by people who are in touch with themselves and the world around them. I would translate the term *mana* as "the charisma of excellence." Doubtless, you have known people who exuded this quality. Regardless of the situation, they seem to be sufficiently confident of their own abilities that they have provided a rallying point for others.

Charisma is a quality that cannot be bottled, sold, or taught. Yet the assurance that comes with awareness and preparation provides much of the confidence and competence that is associated with this attribute. Once you have taken the steps outlined in this book, I can assure you that you will observe the darkening clouds of economic and social disorder with a kind of serene confidence that conveys to everyone that you are managing your own tomorrow.

Peter Drucker has said that we live in the age of management. Professional managers run most of the large organizations in our society. Few individuals know the names of the chief executives who run giant corporations such as IBM, General Motors, and Exxon. While outstandingly competent individuals, none of them is known in the same way that the dynamic entrepreneurs who founded these organizations were.

As a leading writer in the field of management, Drucker has suggested that the time of talking about management has ended. It is now time to practice it. That is certainly true in the area of business and governmental organizations, and even more imperative when applied to your personal predicament. This book cannot be described as a Distant Early Warning system. As I prepare the manuscript, I fear that our economic problems may accelerate even faster than I have anticipated, causing this book to appear too late to give you a chance to act on my recommendations. Whenever you read these words, I assure you it is time for action rather than an age of contemplation.

Perhaps the most significant message contained in the word *management* is in the first eight letters of the word. An almost plaintive plea implores manage me! The French novelist Francois Rabelais expressed this sentiment in the sixteenth century:

"How shall I be able to rule over others if I have not full power and command myself?"

An inscription on the ancient temple at Delphi said, "Know thyself." The Grecian guide to self-knowledge is deceptively simple. The great Spanish novelist Cervantes recognized its complexity and added a key phrase. He said, "To know thyself is the most difficult lesson of life." You obviously know more facts about yourself than anyone else. Yet the truth of knowledge can elude those who know all the facts. The key to understanding the people in the world around you is to start with yourself.

The maxim "Know thyself" looks good on paper. But if you have tried it, you know that one of the greatest hurdles is being able to see yourself objectively. We all have built-in biases about who and what we are. These biases can color our self-images until we really cannot accurately weigh our own abilities. It is very difficult to see ourselves as others see us. In the same way, we often cannot be objective about our emotional selves because we have built up defenses that hinder accurate self-evaluations.

Our insight about ourselves usually contains a number of convenient blind spots. The individual who can see, much less speak freely and honestly, on his faults and abilities is rare.

Several years ago, Frankie Szymanski, a star center on Notre Dame's football team gained a reputation for humility. Although he was outstanding on both defense and offense and had been named to most of the All-American teams, he was never heard to brag or speak highly of his own abilities in football. One day Frankie appeared in court as a witness. The attorney asked if he was on Notre Dame's football team, and Frankie replied that he was. Next the attorney asked the young man what position he played. "Center," answered Frankie without looking up.

"How good a center are you?" demanded the attorney. The shy young man squirmed a little, but answered confidently, "Sir, I am the best center in the history of Notre Dame."

Coach Frank Leahy, who was in the courtroom, was shocked by such a statement from the usually modest boy. Afterward the coach asked Frankie why he had spoken as he did.

Szymanski blushed and responded, "I hated to do it, Coach, but after all, I was under oath!"

The Notre Dame star center knew his ability and had tested it on the field. While physical abilities are often easy to test, elusive inner strengths are difficult to probe. Each of us must discover who we really are, and we must learn to like what we find. But how can we overcome both the natural and the social barriers to self-objectivity?

Nena and George O'Neill in *Shifting Gears,* an important book about coping with changes, stress the importance of clarifying life stances to find ourselves in what we believe and stand for. They identify seven keys to creative self-management that can help any individual develop a firm benchmark for coping with life.

| | |
|---|---|
| 1. Don't ask permission | Do it |
| 2. Don't report | Check things out with yourself not others |
| 3. Don't apologize unnecessarily | This is telling others you are a self-diminisher |
| 4. Don't recriminate yourself | The missed-opportunity syndrome keeps you from moving forward |
| 5. Don't say "I should" or "I shouldn't" | Ask "Why?" or "Why not?" |
| 6. Don't be afraid to say no or yes | Act on what you think and feel |
| 7. Don't put yourself completely in the hands of another | Be a self-determiner |

When you take charge of your life, you no longer need to ask permission of other people or society at large. If other people will be affected by what you do, you should tell them of your plans and ask for feedback. Listening to feedback and taking this into consideration is important but it is not the same thing as asking permission. When you ask permission, you give someone else veto power over your life. This is not a noble thing to do. You will always wind up resenting that person and will never achieve your true potential.

### The Functions of Management
Every student and practitioner of management is intimately familiar with the basic functions of planning, organization, and control. Managers have many kinds of

activities, but their ultimate responsibilities in management revolve around these duties.

Chapter 12 has provided the essence of a plan for you to follow in getting ready for the greatest challenge this country has faced since the early 1940s. Regardless of your resources, you will need to organize your purchases and preparations with the most essential items to be taken care of most quickly. Other desirable but less essential items can be saved in the event there is time to take care of these as well. Whether it be food storage or investment strategy, you should practice regular and careful control. At least once every six months, sit down and review your achievements during the past six months. Identify the specific goals which you plan to achieve during the next half year. Keep your list of goals constantly before you so that you are not diverted by temporary improvements in the economic picture.

## WHAT IS THE FUTURE YOU SEEK?

The first step in inventing your future is to decide what kind of future you seek. I firmly believe in the motto, "Whatever the human mind can conceive, the human spirit can achieve." If you really believe this is a doomsday book, you haven't been reading closely enough. At this late date I do not believe that it is possible to avoid an economic depression. Yet I feel this coming depression can be a great opportunity for individuals and the nation. Good planning will not eliminate tornadoes, but planning can enable you to sit comfortable in your storm shelter while the winds howl around you.

Given some bleak economic prospects for the immediate future, what is your personal goal? Do you wish to pursue the dream of total self-sufficiency? Can you and your family live as the Swiss Family Robinson in an isolated setting? Do you prefer sharing hardships with a group of like-minded friends who form an extended family or survival community? What about the possibility of living in a small town that is less likely to experience the severe dislocations experienced in major cities? Any one of these alternatives has several sub-objectives that need to be considered.

The most important thing about goals is having one. The Roman philosopher Seneca observed, "If a man knows not what harbor he seeks, any wind is the right wind." To put it in a more contemporary idiom, "If a person doesn't know where he is going, any road will take him there." As one of the characters in *South Pacific* suggested, "If you don't have a dream, how are you going to make a dream come true?" If you have not formulated your life's goal or your objectives for the coming decade, sit down with several sheets of paper and jot down some ideas. Then brainstorm these ideas with other members of your family or close friends. Remember, however, responsibility for your goals must remain with you.

Be sure that your goals are worthy of you. Nothing is more frustrating than spending your life in the pursuit of a dream only to discover that the dream is a nightmare. Former advertising executive Jess Lair tells how an almost fatal heart attack gave him a sense of real perspective in determining his life goals. While in his thirties, Lair was president of his own advertising agency. He lived in one of the most expensive suburbs in the United States, sent his children to exclusive private schools, owned two expensive cars, and was clearly a young man on the go. One day he had lunch with his financial advisor and evolved a plan whereby he would work twice as hard at a job he despised in order to secure enough financial resources to retire at age fifty. On his way back to the office, Lair recalls how his "Norwegian heart said, 'You can go that way if you want to, but I'm not going with you.'" He suffered a massive heart attack and had to give up his thriving business.

The Lair family moved out of their upper-middle-class ghetto and rented a rundown house on ten acres outside of Minneapolis. Jess enrolled in a graduate psychology program while the family income dwindled to about one-tenth of what it had been before. Strangely enough, the family found they enjoyed their reduced circumstances more than the frantic race to stay ahead of everyone else.

The irony of life was brought home to them when their landlord, a successful Twin City attorney, would come out to his property about once a month and walk across his investment. He would look longingly at the children riding horses and at the fresh vegetables growing in a garden. Then he would return to the city and work harder than ever in order to make sufficient money to some day move to the farm and live like the Lairs. Today, Jess and his family live in Bozeman, Montana, where he teaches an occasional class at the University of Montana, conducts a few seminars, does some writing, and spends most of his time hunting and fishing with friends who are so important that nothing could lure him away. The heart attack taught him that riches could not be obtained by money alone. In a similar way, poverty cannot be eliminated by money.

One of my purposes in writing this book is to help you gain or hold on to all your riches. I want to help you to have sufficient money to see you through the depression of the 1990s, but this will not guarantee your prosperity. Money has no brain, but a dollar in one person's hand is very different than it is in another's.

A long time ago I saw a play in which the main character said to her child "Be careful what you set your heart upon, for it will surely come to you." Don't wait to begin your survival program until you have accumulated enough money. If you feel poor now, the feeling of poverty is probably bottomless. You cannot quench this thirst through the accumulation of possessions or awards. It is like a shipwrecked sailor who tries to quench his thirst by drinking seawater.

Make the financial provisons that I have suggested, but always remember that prosperity depends more on wanting what you have than having what you want.

## THE JOURNEY ENDS—AND BEGINS

In our journey together we have documented the decline and fall of the American dream. We have explored the reasons behind these problems and assessed a variety of projections about the immediate future. I have described my vision of how we are moving toward an inescapable monetary and economic collapse within the next few years.

Despite this gloomy background I have attempted to paint a cheerful picture of how planning and discipline can provide for genuine prosperity for you while for the majority survival will be the issue. We have explored investment strategy, ranging from positive thinking to diamond selection. Proven techniques for timing and choice have been identified for your evaluation. We have also looked at a variety of techniques that can be used to protect your person, property, family, and health.

One of the major rewards that I have experienced from writing this book is that it has helped me crystalize a blue-print of how I plan to cope with the challenges that confront me. If my plan is not totally suitable to you, there are numerous sources that can provide additional direction and assistance.

Success is a journey, not a destination. I hope that the portion of the journey we have shared together has been successful for you. The ultimate measure of your success will be the degree to which you are able to spend your life in your own way.

I hope you will be concerned about the problems of our future, but not so concerned that you fail to enjoy the pleasures of today. I want you to begin immediately to make preparations for economic depression, but not with such anxiety that you suffer personal depression. Don't procrastinate beginning your survival program, but don't proceed with such desperation that you fail to savor the good that still survives in our society.

> If one advances confidently in the direction of his dreams and endeavors to lead the life which he has imagined, he will meet with success unexpected.
>
> —Henry David Thoreau

# APPENDIXES

# APPENDIX A

# Bibliography of Key Sources

This bibliography attempts to accomplish two major objectives. First, I want to provide credit for the distinguished authors who have helped shape and influence my thinking. In working with my publisher, we agreed that extensive footnotes would make the book appear too scholarly. While most of my readers will not be interested in reviewing my references, I do want you to be able to identify some of the sources I have read in preparing the manuscript. Second, I want to share the books that I have found to be most valuable in planning for the future. The best are marked with an asterisk.

An even more extensive listing of appropriate references is contained in Don and Barbie Stephens' book *The Survivor's Primer and Updated Retreaters' Bibliography* (Spokane, Wash.; Stephens Press, 1976). Harry Browne calls this the most useful retreat volume available by the most knowledgeable professionals in this field. It discusses possible reasons for concern, potential hazards, choices for course of actions, plus over 950 annotated listings providing the details about responsible crisis-proofing through advance preparation.

## Chapter 1

This chapter was put together after an extensive reading of newspapers, periodicals, government reports, and foundation studies. The references suggested below are useful for an overview of the entire subject matter discussed in this book.

Harry Browne, *New Profits from the Monetary Crisis* (New York: Warner Books, 1979). As a follow-up to his previous works, Browne describes an emerging "third investment era" and outlines a recommended investment approach that analyzes such investment media as the stock market (especially warrants), real estate, gold, silver, foreign currencies, fixed interest, commodities, and collectibles.

Harry Browne, *Why the Best Investment Plans Usually Go Wrong* (New York: William Morrow, 1987).

Susan E. Foster, *Preventing Teenage Pregnancy: A Public Policy Guide* (Washington: Council of State Policy & Planning Agencies, 1986).

James P. Grant, *The State of the World's Children, 1987*, (New York: Oxford University Press, 1987).

Frances Moore Lappe and Joseph Collins, *World Hunger: Twelve Myths* (New York: Grove Press, 1986).

Joseph R. Peden and Fred R. Glahe, eds., *The American Family and the State* (San Francisco: Pacific Research Institute for Public Policy, 1986).

*Howard J. Ruff, *How to Prosper During the Coming Bad Years* (New York: Times Books, 1979), 325 pages, $8.95. Describes Ruff's view of the future on how to provide for a breakdown in the delivery of goods and services. A summary of the ideas, recommendations, and philosophy contained in his newsletter.

E. F. Schumacher, *Small is Beautiful: Economics As If People Mattered* (New York: Harper and Row). In an important break with traditional growth economics, Schumacher describes his view of emerging hazards and presents ideas on possible solutions to them.

William Simon, *A Time For Action* (New York: Berkeley, 1980).

Ruth Leger Sivard, *World Military and Social Expenditures, 1986* (Washington: World Priorities, 1986).

Chapter 2

*History*

Crane Brinton, *The Anatomy of Revolution* (New York: Vintage Books, 1965).

*R. E. McMaster, Jr., *Cycles of War: The Next Six Years* (Kalispell, Montana: War Cycles Institute, 1977). A former instructor at the U.S. Air Force Academy and commodity trading advisor for Hornblower and Weeks, McMaster reports that he has spent the last thirteen years in researching this book. It documents the large number of business, weather, and other cycles that point to an extremely high probability of war, national revolutions, rioting, and other conflicts in the very near future.

Arnold Toynbee, *A Study of History* (abridged by D. C. Summerwell) (London: Oxford University Press, 1947).

*Futurists*

Ravi Batra, *The Great Depression of 1990* (New York: Simon & Schuster, 1987).

Lester R. Bown et al, *State of the World 1987: A Worldwatch Institute Report on Progress Toward a Sustainable Society* (New York: W. W. Norton, 1987).

Lester B. Lave and Arthur C. Upton, eds., *Toxic Chemicals, Health, and the Environment* (Baltimore: The Johns Hopkins Univ. Press, 1987).

Dennis Meadows et al, *The Limits to Growth* (New York: Signet, 1974).

*Alvin Toffler, *The Eco-Spasm Report* (New York: Bantam, 1975), 117 pages, $1.50.

*Robert Vacca, *The Coming Dark Age* (New York: Doubleday & Company, 1974), 221 pages, $2.50.

State Department, *Global 2000* (Washington: Government Publishing Office, 1980).

*Economists*

Robert L. Heilbroner, *Business Civilization in Decline* (New York: W.W. Norton & Company, Inc., 1977). An expansion of Heilbroner's previous work that focuses on the deterioration of a market system in the world of the future. While I agree with Heilbroner's assessment of emerging problems, I disagree with his assessment of the way to cope with these problems through collective planning.

*Robert Heilbroner, *An Inquiry into the Human Prospect* (New York: W.W. Norton & Co., Inc., 1974).

John A. Pugsley, *The Alpha Strategy* (Corona del Mar, Cal.: Common Sense, 1980).

### Earthquakes

Jeffrey Goodman, *We Are the Earthquake Generation* (New York: Berkeley, 1983). Dr. Goodman has used his background in archeology and engineering to develop an interesting description of the potential impact of earthquakes affecting the world in the period between 1980 and 2000. His research centers on the predictions of psychics concerning the changes to be affected but supplements this data with scientific sources.

### Astrology

Geoffery Dean and Arthur Mather, *Recent Advances in Natal Astrology—A Critical Review 1900-1976* (Isle of Wight, England: Para Research, Inc., 1977), 608 pages, $17.00.

### Climatology

H. H. Lame, *Climate: Present, Past and Future* (London: Methuen, 1972), $55.00.

### Religion

Hal Lindsey (with C. C. Carlson), *The Late Great Planet Earth* (New York: Bantam 1973).

### Other Problem Areas

Gene Antonio, *The AIDS Cover-Up? The Real and Alarming Facts about AIDS* (San Francisco: Ignatius Press, 1987).

Ruth Leger Sivard, *World Military and Social Expenditures 1986* (Washington: World Priorities, 1986).

Victor Gong and Norman Rudnick, eds., *AIDS: Facts and Issues* (New Brunswick, N.J.: Rutgers Univ. Press, 1986).

## Chapter 3

*Henry Hazlitt, *The Inflation Crisis, and How to Resolve It* (Lanham, Md.: University Press of America, 1983). In an updated version of a 1968 classic, Hazlitt covers, in very clear and understandable terms, the nature of the problems we now face, ways we could solve them, the policies that we will probably actually use to make them worse, and ways that individuals can try to protect themselves.

## Chapter 4

The best scenarios of how an economic collapse might occur or the challenges of survival under any form of serious catastrophe are typically presented in fictional form. Some of the sources identified below help explain how a collapse may occur. Others suggests some of the ways that people will approach the challenges of survival.

John Brunner, *The Sheep Look Up* (New York: Ballantine Books, 1981). The author assumes that humans are killing the planet with chemicals, drugs, indifference, stupidity, and greed. A frightening description of how people are forced to come to terms with their impacted environment.

Paul E. Erdman, *The Crash of '79* (New York: Pocket Books, 1976). Written by a former Swiss banker, this book describes a worldwide collapse brought on by a nuclear misunderstanding in the Middle East. A frightening picture of the power of petro-politics.

Ayn Rand, *Atlas Shrugged* (New York: New American Library, 1970). This monumental work of objectivism describes a breakdown in society brought on by a revolt of the producers against having to bear the burden of the lazy majority. Many of Rand's predictions have already taken place.

## Chapter 6

The Browne book referenced in previous chapers has helpful material about depressionproof investments.

Daniel Cohen, *Gold: The Fascinating Story of the Noble Metal Through the Ages* (New York: M. Evans, 1976).

## Chapter 7

Herbert Benson and Miriam Z. Klipper, *The Relaxation Response* (New York: Avon Books, 1976).

Harry Browne, *How I Found Freedom in an Unfree World* (New York: Avon Books, 1973).

*Linda Clark, *Get Well Naturally* (New York: Arco Publishing, 1965).

*Kenneth H. Cooper, *Aerobics* (New York: Bantam Books, 1972).

*John Henderson, *Emergency Medical Guide* (Third Edition) (New York: McGraw Hill Book Company, 1973). The author recently retired as corporate director of medical affairs for Johnson & Johnson. This book provides an excellent, thorough, yet easy to understand description of how to deal with a wide variety of medical emergencies from infectious disease to burns and accidents.

Beatrice P. Hunter, *Food Additives and Your Health* (Morovia, Cal.: National Health Federation, 1978).

D. C. Jarvis, *Folk Medicines* (Greenwich, Conn.: Fawcett Publications, Inc., 1958).

Ari Kiev, M.D., *A Strategy for Success* (New York: MacMillan Co., Inc.), 136 pages, $6.95.

*Jane Kinderlehrer, *Confessions of a Sneaky Organic Cook* (Emmaus, PA.: Rodale Press, Inc., 1971), 206 pages, $1.50.

## Chapter 8

*Douglas R. Casey, *The International Man* (Alexandria, Va.: Kephart Communications, Inc., 1978), 113 pages, $14.95. Described as the complete guidebook to the world's last frontiers for freedom seekers, investors,

adventurers, speculators, and expatriates, this book analyzes the opportunities, costs and risks of doing business
in fifty-three countries around the world.

*Robert Kinsman *Guide to Tax Havens* (Homeland,
Ill.: Dow-Jones-Irwin, 1977), 283 pages, $17.50.

Midas Malone, *How to Do Business Tax Free* (Wil-
mington, Del.: Enterprise Publishing Co., 1976), 158
pages, $14.95.

Mark Skousen, *The Offshore Loophole: Techniques
for Investing Abroad with Safety and Privacy* (1986; available from Mark Skousen, P.O. Box 2488, Winter Park,
FL 32790).

## Chapter 9

David Krotz, *How to Hide Almost Anything* (New
York: William Morrow & Co., 1975), 175 pages, $5.95.

Ira A. Lipman, *How to Protect Yourself Against Crime*
(New York: Avon, 1982).

*Don Stephens, *Personal Protection Here and Now*
(Stephens Printing Company, P.O. Drawer 1441, Spokane, Washington, 99210, 1975).

*Survival Guns* (The Jenus Press, Inc., P.O. Drawer
75455, Los Angeles, Calif. 90075, 1977), 458 pages, $7.95.

## Chapter 10

Bradford Angier, *Survival with Style* (New York: Vintage Books, 1970).

Jethro Kloss, *Back to Eden* (Greenwich, Conn.: Lust,
1981). An updated version of the original classic by Jethro
Kloss presents his recommendations based on forty years
of experience with American herbs for health and healing. Natural nutrition with detailed recipes and instructions for living off the land.

Patrick Rivers, *The Survivalists* (London: Eyre Muthuen,
1975), 224 pages, $4.95.

Ruth Stout, *How to Have a Green Thumb Without an
Aching Back* (Birmingham, AL: Cornerstone, 1974), 195
pages, $1.95.

Ruth Stout and Richard Clemence, *The Ruth Stout No Work Garden Book* (Emmaus, PA.: Rodale Press, Inc., 1971). Based on articles originally appearing in *Organic Gardening and Farming,* this summarizes Ruth Stout's many years of experience with mulch gardening.

Underground Housing

*Alternatives in Energy Conservation: the Use of Earth-Covered Buildings* (Washington, D.C.: Superintendent of Documents, 1975), 353 pages, $3.25. This is a copy of the proceedings held in Forth Worth, Texas, sponsored by the National Science Foundation. Stock number on this valuable booklet is 038-000-00286-4.

Malcolm Wells, P.O. Box 1149, Brewster, ME. 02631.

In-Earth Designs, P.O. Drawer 1441, Spokane, Washington 99210.

Davis Caves, Inc., Armington, ILL. 61721.

## Chapter 11

Spencer MacCallum, *The Art of Community* (Menlo Park, CA.: Institute of Human Studies, 1980).

Melford Spiro, *Kibbutz: Venture in Utopia* (Cambridge, Mass.: Harvard Univ. Press, 1975).

*Don Stephens, *Greenpapers #4* (Reprints of 4 articles, Spokane, Wash.: Stephens Press, 1976).

## Chapter 12

Since this chapter summarized much of the information contained throughout the book into a series of action steps, no specific references are recommended. One rather detailed checklist of supplies is suggested, however.

*Don and Barbie Stephens, *The Survivor's Primer and Updated Retreater's Bibliography* (Spokane, Wash.: Stephens Press, 1976).

## Chapter 13

*Jess Lair, *I Ain't Well, But I Sure Am Better: Mutual Need Therapy* (New York: Fawcett, 1981).

*Nena and George O'Neill, *Shifting Gears* (New York: Avon Books, 1974), 281 pages, $1.95.

Henry Thoreau, *Walden and Civil Disobedience* (New York: New American Library, 1973).

# APPENDIX B

## KEY SURVIVAL RESOURCES

*Newsletters*
Personal Finance (biweekly) $118*
Box 1462
Alexandria, VA 22313

Forecasts & Strategies (monthly) $135*
7811 Montrose Road
Potomac, MD 20854

Offshore Banking News (monthly) $90*
301 Plymouth Drive NE
Dalton, GA 30720
404/259-6035

*Gold and Silver Merchants*
Deak & Company
1800 K Street N.W.
Washington, D.C. 20006
800/424-1186

LaSalle National Bank
135 So. LaSalle Street
Chicago, IL 60603
312/443-2102

*Regular rate. Most newsletters will offer promotional rates (less than half price) to new subscribers. Most also sell your name and address to scores of other newsletter publishers.

*Precious Stones*
Mr. Charles D. Knechtel
Brazilian Gemstones USA, Inc.
Rockefeller Center Box 2403
New York, New York 10185
212/459-9022

*Diamonds*
Mr. Chuck Ferrill
The Sidiam
Suite 1216
2670 Union Avenue Ext.
Memphis, Tennessee 38112
901/452-0188

*Food*
Simpler Life Food
4660 Jett Road N.W.
Atlanta, Georgia 30323
404/255-3262

# INDEX

## Balancing the Books